Aloha Dreams

MINDY FORD

PUBLISHED BY FIDELI PUBLISHING, INC.

ISBN: 978-1-948638-49-4

Translation: Elvira Kraja

Consultants: Cynthia Wallace and Rachel Workman

Editors: Jennifer Dolly, Karen Ford, and KJ A. Lewis

*This is a work of fiction. Names, places, characters, and incidents
are either the product of the author's imagination or are used
fictitiously, and any resemblance to actual persons, living or dead,
events, or locales is entirely coincidental.*

For information, please contact
Fideli Publishing, Inc.:
robin.surface@fidelipublishing.com
www.FideliPublishing.com

In Memory of Marcia White, my 10th Grade English teacher and High School Newspaper Advisor. Year after year, I spent countless lunches, study halls and time after school in Room 205. Within the walls of her room, many of my creations came to life, while she devoted not only her time, but also her advice and encouragement.

As long as I live, I will forever remember her radiant, proud smile when I told her that I had published my first novel. She has touched so many lives throughout her career. I can only speak for myself, but I know that what I say could be uttered by so many people whose lives she molded and influenced—Thank you Mrs. White. Thank you for always believing in me. You were a great mentor, but more importantly, you were a wonderful person. You will be forever and greatly missed.

Marcia Cooke White
1949–2019

For Sara Jo Butler—
a true believer in Kale and Devan.

Acknowledgements

Thank you to Jen Dolly, Karen Ford and Cynthia Wallace for your countless hours editing and reading. I couldn't have done this book without you and the patience of all of your families and friends who allowed me to consume large amounts of your time.

So much appreciation and thanks goes to Robin Surface, who patiently answered all my questions, no matter how silly and repetitive they were.

Special thanks to Elvira Kraja, who has been correcting my Italian and teaching me a thing or two about the beautiful language.

Please know that each and everyone one of you holds a special place in my heart for your part in helping me on my way to making my *Dreams come True!*

Prologue

As she walked over to the bed, he sat up straight and tried desperately to keep his eyes on the television. She fluffed up the pillows and lied down, then let out another long sigh.

He daringly looked over at her and asked, "Can I get you something?"

She looked at him with "come hither" eyes. He inhaled deeply. *What's happening? We just had a discussion — a painful discussion — about doing whatever it takes to just be friends.* He bit his lip trying to prevent an erection. He was unsuccessful.

"If you don't need anything, I'm going to go ahead and leave so you can get some sleep." He stood up and walked over to the door.

"No! Don't leave," she pleaded.

"Monty, you need to rest."

He went over to the bed and bent down to kiss her forehead. She grabbed the front of his shirt. "I said, *don't* leave."

He could see the hunger in her eyes and didn't know if he had the strength to deny her. *Her plump lips just demand to be kissed. No, this behavior is not acceptable.*

"Devan," his voice was stern and hard, but she didn't loosen her grip on his shirt. His eyes shot daggers at her, and he demanded, "Let me go!"

"I'll *never* let you go!" With her free hand she grabbed the back of his head and pulled his lips down to hers. Before he knew what was happening, his shirt was on the floor, her hands were in his hair and their tongues were intertwined.

She pulled him on top of her and reached for his belt buckle. He moved to give her room to complete the maneuver. She pushed him off her and onto his back, then unfastened the belt and pulled it off.

Instead of setting it to the side, she looped it around his wrists and jerked it tight. She then lifted his hands above his head and looped the belt over the headboard, pulling it even tighter.

When he was rendered completely helpless, Devan had full control. She yanked his shorts and boxers off, leaving him completely naked and subject to her deepest desires. She climbed on top of him, and he groaned. She slowly pulled off her slip, revealing her perfectly shaped breasts.

He was trying not to breathe so heavily, but he couldn't help it. She looked him dead in the eyes and licked her lips very slowly.

"Do you have any idea what you do to me?" he asked.

A wicked grin spread across her face, and she answered him with her own question. "Do you have any idea what I'm about to do to you?"

Just then, the hotel door flew open, and Justin was standing in the doorway…

Chapter 1

September 2011

Kale pulled in to the driveway. "Here we are!" He got out, grabbed the crutches, then helped Devan out of the car and walked her to the front door. She glanced down at her ankle. Just one more week and she'd be done with the supporting devices.

"Would you like to come in?" she asked, fumbling with her keys.

Kale hesitated. He knew he shouldn't. Things had been a little insane since they'd come back from Hawaii. Justin had taken off to who knows where, and Jeane had threatened to take his kids just like Devan had warned him she would. For right now, the children were safe at his parents' house. Getting caught was not something either of them had planned. The lawyer they'd spoken with advised them to keep their distance until everything calmed down. That would be difficult for sure. This evening would be the last time Devan and Kale would see each other for quite a while.

"Just for a few minutes? I won't bite."

"Okay."

She unlocked the door. As they went in, Kale took off his shoes in the foyer. When he was done, he helped Devan take hers off. She looked down at the curly hair that was resting on his shoulders. She couldn't help but think, *He's such a gentleman. Justin would never have done that for me.*

He stood up and his six-foot-five frame towered over her. "Here, let's get you situated." He led her into the living room and had her sit down on the couch. Since there were no lights on, Devan couldn't see anything other than the kitchen and the couch where she was sitting.

"Do you want me to turn on the light?" he asked.

"No, just come and sit for a minute."

Kale sat in the loveseat directly across from the couch, remembering the lawyer's warning: *As long as I keep my hands and my lips to myself, everything will be okay.*

"Thank you for taking me to the doctor today and for driving to the lawyer's tonight." Devan could only see his silhouette against the loveseat.

"Sure, no problem."

She got up and hobbled over to where he was sitting and plopped down next to him. He took a deep breath. *I just want to grab her and kiss her. She smells so good.*

"Well, we're home and hopefully the worst is over." She took ahold of his hand. "We'll do everything we can to make sure this goes smoothly. Robert has been a family friend for years and he's the best in town," she said, referring to the lawyer.

Even though the room was dark, the intensity of her eyes hypnotized Kale. He belonged to her, heart, body and soul, and he always would. He leaned down, touched his lips to hers, and she returned his kiss. "I'm sorry. I shouldn't have done that." He jumped up from the loveseat.

She took his hand pulling him down. He knelt on the floor in front of her and placed her hands in his. "I am so sorry about the mess I got us into."

"If I remember correctly, I was on top and *you* were tied to the bed. I'm the one who should be apologizing," she paused, "but I won't." She slid her hands from his and pulled his chin close to hers. "I won't apologize for loving you, and I won't apologize for this." Devan slanted her lips over his, kissed him deeply and moved her hands behind Kale's head as his hands found their way around her waist. She leaned back, pulling him up on the loveseat. They fell back in a tight embrace, him on top of her. There was more passion in their kiss than she'd ever experienced before. *I'm his forever.* As she reached for his belt buckle, a light came on in the corner of the room.

"You couldn't wait, could you?" They looked at the newly lit part of the room and saw Devan's husband sitting in the recliner glaring at them.

Devan woke up gasping. She flipped on the light that was sitting on her bedside table and yanked the sheet and blankets off her feet. Her ankle was still wrapped. She felt a hand on her thigh and very slowly turned over to see Justin asleep. It was another dream! Devan glanced at the clock which read 2:58 a.m. Grabbing her robe, she went downstairs, got a bottle of water, switched on the living room light, sat down on the couch and stared at the empty loveseat in front of her. What would have happened next if Justin hadn't ruined her dream? Devan stared a few minutes longer then stood up. She was intent on starting her day instead of trying to go back to sleep.

Later that day, Devan's cell phone rang.

"Hello?" she answered reluctantly, not recognizing the phone number.

"Hey, it's Roni, I wanted to call you with my new number. I have about ten minutes left of my lunch. Can you chat?"

"Yes, I needed to talk to you anyway. I had another dream last night," Devan said.

"Oh? Was it as juicy as the one in Hawaii where you had Kale tied to the bed?"

Devan silently wished it had been that good. "No, but it was getting good until Justin spoiled it! Again!"

"Damn him. Let me guess. He caught you in the middle of making mad, passionate love?"

"Roni, I said it wasn't that juicy. This time it started off where the other one ended. We were back here, had just met with the lawyer and he walked me in to my house. The house was dark, and I convinced him to stay. One thing led to another and we were kissing. While he was on top of me on the loveseat, I reached for his buckle and all of a sudden a light went on. Justin was sitting there." Devan sighed revisiting everything that she had seen in her dream. "Do you have any idea how disappointing it is waking up to Justin after being with Kale in my dreams?"

"I can only imagine. Ugh! Why must he destroy your happiness, even in your dreams." Veronica paused, "Oh, hello, Callie. Sure, I will help you."

Veronica whispered to Devan, "Callie just showed up and wants me to help her with her art project. We will catch up later."

"Wait! Are you up for some wine and snacks at my house this coming Saturday with Maggie and Kristy?" Devan asked. "My parents are taking the kids to a movie and want them to spend the night. Justin is out of town again supposedly with his dad for work."

"Yeah, sounds good."

❧ ❧ ❧

Devan set down three wine bottles and four glasses on the deck table and lit the citronella candle. Kristy came out with the meat, cheese and cracker tray. She placed it on the table then sat down in a chair.

"This is exciting, our first girls' night in forever!"

Devan laughed and sat down.

"It will be nice for the four of us to hang out like we did back in the day. Only now we have alcohol," Devan opened one of the bottles.

Veronica came out carrying another two bottles of wine. "Dee, a citronella candle in the middle of September, really?"

"I was getting eaten up this week waiting for the bus with Callie. I think it was because we had such a late rainy season with all that flooding."

Veronica sat down. "I think you are delusional. We are wearing sweatshirts for Christ's sake."

"Roni!"

Veronica sarcastically apologized. "I'm sorry, Kristy. I forgot you recently found God."

Kristy smacked her arm. "You are a *biotch*." Veronica had been teasing her ever since she found out Kristy had been going to a new church that she absolutely loved and would not stop talking about. She was constantly trying to convert Veronica, so she would be able to see her heathen ways.

Veronica nodded. "Sure am, but you missed me." She got up and gave her a hug.

"I did," Kristy smiled. "Where in the hell is Maggie?" she asked.

"Kristy! Language!" Veronica mocked her.

"Right here bitches." She was carrying another bottle of wine and what appeared to be a box of chocolates.

"Well, I think we have enough wine for the entire neighborhood," Devan giggled pouring wine in all the glasses.

Four out of the six bottles were gone. The women were lit and having a blast talking about old times.

"Hey, remember the day Roni showed up with black lipstick?" Kristy mentioned.

"How about when Devan showed up with black hair? I assumed she was joining me on the *dark side,*" Veronica laughed. "I never thought you would keep it."

"It's crazy when you look at how close we all were in grade school and then in high school we split into two's," Devan said.

"Yeah, do you have any idea how hard it was to stay best friends with a cheerleader?" Veronica complained.

"Oh please, I got made fun of so bad for being *Death's* best friend," Maggie retorted.

"And look at us all now. Kristy married her high school sweetheart, Maggie's husband had an affair with a man from Craigslist, mine had an affair with that slut Desiree, and Devan is…"

"Hold on—Maggie, can you please explain that?" Kristy questioned. Maggie put her glass down and rolled her eyes.

"Honestly, it is embarrassing," she sighed. "I caught him lip locked with some guy in the parking lot of the gym we went to. I took a picture with my phone and left. I didn't dare stay for my workout. When I got home I decided to do some investigating. He was such a moron. He left his computer up, so I hit history." She shook her head in disgust. "Oh, my dear friends, I cannot even begin to tell you the things that I saw. I wasn't as shocked as I should have been though. As I was looking over things that he had searched, a message popped up. I clicked on it and it was from some guy on Craigslist replying to an ad. An ad that my, I believed, straight husband had placed. I will spare you all the details. Trust me, if you knew half of the shit that I know now, you'd wish I'd never told you."

"So, what happened next?" Devan asked though she knew she probably shouldn't have.

"I dry heaved. The history went back a few months. Here was the man I vowed to love in sickness and in health, and he cheated on me. It was bad enough he cheated, but the thought that he did it with a man nauseated me. I am not homophobic or anything. I believe that you should be able to love who you love. This was *my* husband, with whom I still had sex." Maggie shivered creating a ripple effect through the girls. No one could fathom what she had gone through.

"So, he came home, caught me on the computer and started screaming and yelling at me saying horrible things, such as, I was a horrible wife, and that's why he strayed. If I could have learned to cook better and not burn anything, I might have been worth something..."

Veronica interrupted her. "Mags, I have had your cooking. You're like Betty fucking Crocker herself!"

"I may or may not have taken a few classes after I left. Regardless, whether it was correct or not, it didn't matter. After a few years of therapy, I finally accepted it wasn't my fault. He did what he wanted to, and I sure as hell didn't make him gay. He was probably using me for a cover up. That, I learned from my gay bud, Stefan. So, I packed up my shit and moved back home with mom and dad. A few months later we got a dissolution. End of story."

It was silent. No one knew what to say. They all had their own issues over the years but nothing that even came close to that. Veronica broke the silence with the answer to the one question Devan and Kristy were both wondering in their head.

"Don't worry, she got tested and all is good, not even one STD!" The two girls seemed to breathe a sigh of relief.

Maggie chuckled. "It's okay, guys. This was about five years ago. I am over it. I promise I'm okay. That being said, I ask that you guys keep this to yourselves. I think being known as a woman who was once married to a gay man may actually ruin my chances of ever having a real relationship again."

"Yeah, not exactly dating profile material," Kristy put her hand on Maggie's shoulder. "I am so very sorry though."

"I'm glad you got help. To live with something like that is unimaginable!" Devan gave her a hug which was disrupted by a loud buzzing on the table. "Hold on." She peeked at her phone and smiled.

"But our dear sweet Devan here has the love of her life messaging her every day," Kristy disclosed. Devan immediately turned five shades of red.

"Oh yes, the great Kale Iakona," Veronica commented.

Maggie spit out her wine. "What?"

Devan looked at Veronica, "You never told her?"

"Dude, no, your secrets are yours and yours alone. It's not my place to be telling your shit."

Devan was surprised. As close as Maggie and Veronica were, she thought she would have definitely shared that with her.

"Thank you. I just assumed that you would have told her, or that you could read each other's minds. That means a lot to me," Devan said appreciatively.

"Oh, I am extremely thankful I can't read what is going on in that," Maggie pointed to Veronica's head.

"You hush! I have a beautiful mind with pictures of—"

"Zombies, demons, and Satan!" Maggie interjected.

"Really, Mags?" Veronica gave her a dirty look.

"Okay, so since I am here and know something, can I have all of the details? I can't believe you never told me!" Maggie acted like she was hurt, but she really wasn't. She and Devan weren't as close as Devan and Veronica had become over the past year. Devan opened another bottle and lifted it off the table to start pouring glasses when she stopped and set it back down.

"Roni, I keep forgetting to ask. Why did you have your number changed?"

"Ugh…" Veronica groaned. "I keep getting bill collectors calling for my asshole ex. I shouldn't be surprised! He was too lazy to pay the bills when we were married, but it's shitty he gave them all *my* number. Don't defer to me, Dee, tell Mags your story."

Devan picked the bottle back up and began pouring her glass first. "Okay ladies, let's fill these glasses, because this next story is a doozy." Devan told Maggie most of what had happened. There was laughter and tears.

"Did you message Kale back yet?" Maggie questioned.

"No."

"Let's do a group selfie," she suggested. It took twenty minutes to take one picture with which everyone was happy.

Meanwhile, across the country, Kale and Jeane were out to dinner waiting for a potential client to arrive when Kale's phone vibrated. He looked down and slid his finger across the screen. It was from Devan. It was a group picture with the caption 'Wish you were here!' He responded, "*Not as much as I do!*"

"What are you smiling at?" Jeane snapped.

"Oh, Pete sent me something funny."

"Well, I need you to pay attention, and put your phone away. Signing Mr. Carter could mean great things for our company and a great deal of money in our pockets."

Kale put his phone in his pocket and thought to himself, *Put money in our pockets. Money! That's all she cares about. If only she cared half that much about our children.*

A short round man came up to the table. He was dressed in a tan jacket, a black cowboy hat, a gold horseshoe and black bolo tie, dark Calvin Klein denim pants, and black alligator boots.

"Evening folks," he paused for effect. "I'm Kevin Miles Carter of Carter Petroleum."

Kale and Jeane both stood up, extended their hands and introduced themselves.

The dinner meeting went well. Mr. Carter was a delightful southern man who appeared to really like Kale.

When Jeane excused herself to use the restroom, Mr. Carter pulled his chair closer to the table and leaned in toward Kale. "Son, I like you. If I decide to start this new chapter in my life with your company, will I get to work exclusively with you, or will I have to work with *that* woman?" He pointed in the direction of the restroom.

Kale was shocked. "I can tell by the look on your face you think I don't like dealing with women in business." He glanced in the direction of the restroom, as if he was checking to see if she was on her way back. "There is just something about her I don't like. I just don't trust her."

"Well Mr. Carter—"

"Call me Kev. Mr. Carter is my daddy."

"Okay, Kev," Kale hesitated, wondering how he was going to explain without losing Kevin's interest in the company. "I do the architecture for the buildings. I am really not involved in the business end at all."

The man furrowed his brow. "Hmmm, well, tell you what, I will gladly do business with *you*! Not—"

Jeane showed up and interrupted his thought. "You will? Oh, that is wonderful! I will have my office give you a call—"

"No, I want Kale, here, to be my right-hand man," Mr. Carter insisted.

"Well, Kale is just the architect."

"I know, that's what he told me, so if you want my business, you will find a way that Kale can be my man." He picked up his hat that was under his chair and shook Jeane's hand and then Kale's. "I'm going to Belize for a bit. I'll give you a call, sir, when I get back. It should give you enough time to figure out how this will work." He put on his hat, touched the brim, and nodded to the two of them. "Miss Jeane, Kale," he said then pivoted around and made his way toward the exit.

Jeane scowled at Kale as Mr. Carter walked out the door. "What the hell did you say to him?"

Kale stood and raised an eyebrow as he pushed in his chair. Then Jeane stood and did the same. "I didn't say anything. The man said he wanted to do business with me. I tried explaining that I don't do that part of the job." They started slowly toward the door.

"Clearly you didn't try hard enough! I'll discuss it with my Uncle, and maybe we can have him *think* that he's working with you for a little bit." Jeane was thinking hard as they made their way toward the car across the parking lot. "And you'd better go along with it and not screw this up!" Kale didn't say anything. He unlocked the doors to the car and got in. He wasn't worried about it and wasn't about to pull the wool over this man's eyes. Kale would be honest even if it meant not getting his business. As he was getting ready to put the vehicle in drive, Jeane reached over and grabbed his chin.

"I'm *dead* serious Kale! If you do anything to screw this up…I will destroy you! I will leave you with nothing! No job, no kids, no life!" Kale had heard this threat more than once, but that is all it was to him, an *empty threat*. Jeane, however, was serious. She would destroy Kale Iakona and all that he had ever built.

Back in Ohio the girls were still enjoying their night.

"Hey, are any of you going to alumni night in October?" Maggie poured another glass of wine.

"I am," Kristy said.

"You have to because your husband is a football coach, and I have to because I am a coach. What about you two?" Maggie asked Veronica and Devan.

"I don't like that kind of stuff," Veronica replied.

"Yes, anything positive or fun, Veronica can't do." Kristy sassed.

Veronica just glared at her.

"But you are single. What if one of the guys we went to school with got all hot and sexy?" Devan challenged.

"You don't have to go to the game since everyone is meeting at Urban Myth afterwards. Remember Jasper Reynolds?" Maggie asked with excitement.

"Maggie! Seriously? Ew!" Veronica grimaced.

"But…you liked him," Maggie frowned.

"Yes, *liked* past tense of like. I presently do not like him. I was seventeen then. I'm about to be thirty-three."

"His band is playing that night," Maggie muttered.

"Then I am definitely out," Veronica stated.

Devan slammed her hand down on the table. "Okay, if Roni goes I will," Devan smirked at her.

"Sorry, I have a hot date with Netflix that night," she smiled at Devan.

"Come on. What if Nate shows up?" Devan was hopeful.

"Nate? As in Nathaniel Cavendar of Cavendar Funeral Home?" Kristy questioned with huge eyes.

Veronica blushed, and it didn't go unnoticed.

"Whaaat?" Maggie's jaw dropped. Devan was sure Maggie would know about her best friend's crush.

"Dammit, Devan, I kept your secret."

"I'm sorry, I thought for sure if anyone knew it would be Mags," Devan declared.

"Okay, yes, Nate Cavendar. I had a big crush on him in school, but I didn't say anything to anyone, especially you, Maggie, he wasn't considered *cool* according to our entire school. I got chastised enough as it was. Besides he probably wouldn't have had anything to do with me anyway."

"First of all, Nate was *very* cool. No one even tried to get to know him. If our classmates had, they would have seen how intelligent and sweet he truly was. Second, that's bullshit! You never said anything because you were afraid of rejection. And finally, I'd bet a million dollars he would have totally given you the time of day! He was so nice. I don't know why everyone had to make his life a living hell." Devan defended.

"Well, he was cute," Kristy commented.

"Yeah, really cute," Veronica reflected and stared off into the dark sky for a moment then turned back to face the girls. "Okay, if he goes, I'll go."

Chapter 2

The next morning Devan received an invitation for brunch from Veronica.

"Last night was fun," Veronica stated while adding a lot of cream to her coffee.

"Do you want some coffee with that cream?" Devan asked before taking a sip from her cup.

"Don't knock it till you try it, Dee!"

"Nah, I'll stick with my tea, but I agree last night *was* fun." Devan said. "It's been a while since I have been able to let loose like that." There was a sparkle in Veronica's eyes that Devan had never seen before which made her want to know about the guys Veronica had dated since her ex-husband. She wanted to ask about it last night when they were all together, then decided not to. It might be a sensitive subject that she wouldn't appreciate being brought up in front of everyone. Devan knew they had been divorced for a few years and yet, she never heard Veronica talk about dating *anyone* and wondered how best to approach the subject when Veronica interrupted her thoughts.

"Dee, I feel the wheels in your head turning so fast, I can almost smell the smoke coming out of your ears. What is it?"

Devan was quiet for a minute. Veronica's eyes looked as though they were trying to pierce through her soul. "Why don't you date?" Devan finally spit out. "You were all excited when we talked about Nate last night."

"Yeah, I can't quit thinking about him," Veronica shared.

"Have you even dated at all since your ex?"

"Not really,"

"So why don't you date?"

"Why don't I date? Well, it's pointless really."

"Don't you want to find your lobster?"

Veronica giggled. "If you are referring to the saying 'lobsters mate for life,' I am sorry to burst your bubble. Look it up. They have flings."

Devan gave her a scowl, however, she pulled out her phone and Googled it. After she read a short article about lobsters she glanced up with a disappointed face.

"Told ya," Veronica said.

"Okay fine, still don't you want to know what is out there?"

"Nope. I have no interest in even going on a date. I gave up on love a long ass time ago. Not all of us get to meet our 'Prince Charming' when we are sixteen years old."

"Yeah, and you see how well that has played out. Have you ever considered looking Nate up?" she suggested not ready to give up.

Veronica took a sip of her coffee, "It's just not worth it. I don't want to ruin the fantasy I have of him."

"That's ridiculous." Devan felt irritation bubbling inside of her. She knew there was a better future for Veronica, and that she wasn't destined to be alone forever. Devan also knew that one day she would have her forever with Kale, she just didn't know when.

"Is it? Think about it. I have in my head the perfect man. Sure, it's Nate on the outside, but on the inside, he's *sooo* much more. I can't even begin to tell you what I want. Just know that my dream man probably does not exist, and I refuse to accept anything other than him. I'd rather live with the fantasy and the regret of not knowing than the regret of finding out he's horrible like all the other men I ever dated. Who's to say he would even give me a chance?" Veronica took a long sip of her coffee before releasing a sigh.

"My poor friend, I am so sad that you really think that all hope has been lost. What if he is your true love?"

"Listen, I totally believe that true love exists. Take you and Kale for example."

Devan blushed. "As for most of us in the world—NO! True love does not exist. There is no soul mate out there for me. I am pretty sure I have never even been in love."

"Roni, how can you say that? Weren't you in love with your ex-husband in the beginning?"

Veronica snickered. "Well, looking back on it now, I settled. Sure, he was sexy and charming at first. It was exciting in the beginning as most honeymoon stages are, but…it was as if everything wore off and we did what we assumed the next step was. Instead of finding people more suitable for us we just decided it was easier to stay with one another. Then he got bored and forgot to send me the memo that he moved on and that I should too."

"You settled? You don't seem like the type to just settle for anything."

"No, not now because I learned my lesson! Guess he preferred nasty whores instead of me."

"You know you are a thousand times better than Desiree, right?"

"I'm not a complete moron, of course I do." Veronica snorted at that. "He completely downgraded. Anyway, now I just have my fantasy dream man that does not exist, and I am content knowing he will never be in my reality."

"Come on, describe your perfect man." Devan egged her on.

"Okay, I'll play your game, Dee. I want a giant with dark curly hair. It doesn't have to be long, maybe past his ears. I don't care about the color of his eyes or if he has facial hair. Wait, I take that back. No Freddie Mercury pornstache. God rest his soul. And nice clean teeth—all of them. He needs to be nice, compassionate, funny, sweet, and have a dark, sexy side."

"What the hell does that mean?"

"You know, dark like—"

"Like you?" Devan laughed.

"Well, yeah, a little. I'm a bit on the odd side, not every man likes that. He needs to get my strange sense of humor and be able to deal with strolls in the cemetery, watching abandoned places and Victorian era documentaries. You know…weird shit on YouTube. I don't want a man that looks at my oddity collection and runs home screaming to mommy!"

"Your oddity collection?"

"I have some *strange* things. You wouldn't be interested." Veronica crinkled her nose and shook her head as though Devan would not approve of her treasures.

"Oh, but I am. I don't have to be anywhere until 4 p.m. Please show me your collection."

Later, at Veronica's house Devan was excited to see the *collection.*

"I bet that something in here will freak you out." Veronica said opening a door to a dark painted room.

"This is my office, and over here," she pointed to her bookshelf, "is my collection of antique books."

Devan stepped over closer to it. "Okay, I'll take your bet. What are we wagering?"

"If you aren't completely freaked out, I will go to the bar on Alumni night, and you have to be my date!"

Devan grabbed her hand and shook it. "Deal!" Devan knew she had this in the bag. She dropped Veronica's hand and looked up at the shelves and read the titles.

1824 Journal of Medicine, Hill on Insanity, Medical and Surgical Electricity,1924 The Household Physician, A Complete Housewife's Guide, The Virginia Housewife, Tuberculosis Medical Book-Pulmonary Consumption. The Art and Practice of Embalming, Sanitary Science for the Undertaker.

"Wow, nothing surprises me aside from the housewife books."

"Oh, those are a riot. The things that were expected from women are unreal. The top two shelves range from 1798 to the 1930s. I haven't read all of them, but what I have read is fascinating. The world then compared to the world now is so different, even in areas that you think wouldn't change much."

"Okay so that's not really disturbing. What else do you have?"

Veronica pointed to the top of the book shelf where there were a bunch of bottles. There was *Cholera serum, pink embalming fluid, cough syrup, morphine,* and the list went on. "They used morphine for all kinds of things including coughing and rubbing on gums of teething babies. Heroine tablets were used to help asthma, opium for diarrhea, arsenic and mercury to treat syphilis. It's insane."

"Very interesting, still not creeped out though."

Veronica sneered at Devan. She was harder to crack than Veronica had given her credit for. She pulled a red velvet box out that was about eight inches on all four sides. "Open it." she demanded and handed it to Devan.

Devan gasped when she complied. There were about a dozen glass eyes. "These are medical grade and supposedly have been worn pre-WWII."

"Nope, still not shocked."

"Okay, here," Veronica picked up a black satin pouch that was tied and sitting on the shelf next to where the prosthetic eyes were.

"Hold open your hand." She poured the contents into Devan's hand.

"These are civil war bullets and mini-balls. Most have been fired and could have killed someone. Maybe they went right through their hearts, and you are holding them in your hand!"

"It's cool but still not at my stopping point." Devan replied moving the balls around in her hand.

Damn! Veronica wasn't giving up though. She continued to show her friend some other oddities.

Devan didn't even wince until she noticed something on the desk. "Um…what is that?" she gestured to an aquarium, "and that?" she indicated another one with a sour face.

"Oh, that is my terrarium."

"Yes, I can see that, but what is moving in it?" Devan questioned.

"Those would be Paul and Gene. They are large Russian snails and are often used for escargot."

"Ew, now that is gross! Are you planning on eating them?"

"No! What the hell? They are my pets."

"Wait, Paul and Gene as in Paul Stanley and Gene Simmons from KISS?"

"Very good!" Veronica was impressed. "Sadly, Peter and Ace didn't make it through last winter."

"So, what is in the other container then?" Devan asked.

"Oh, that's Freddie. He's a Pacman frog."

Devan recoiled, "Okay, now I have seen enough."

"Says the girl who released over one hundred frogs from biology class. Oh, wait. I know what will make you weak in the knees. My ex hated her. Hold on." Veronica left the room and came back holding a rose hair tarantula.

"Ugh….no thank you. Just for the record, the snails are much more disgusting than a big hairy arachnid."

"I give up!" Veronica bowed her head in defeat.

"So, you will go to Alumni night at the Urban Myth?"

"Yes, I will go! I lost the bet."

A grin spread across Devan's face. She knew just what she was going to do, to prove her friend wrong. Even Veronica had a soul mate, and Devan was going to find him.

The next day Devan drove up to the Cavendar funeral home. It was obvious that she hadn't been to that side of town for quite some time. Grass and weeds had grown up to her waist. Devan knocked on the door. Needless to say there was no answer. A shutter fell when she knocked making her jump. She peeked in the window. It was so dark inside nothing could be seen. Devan had heard he was still in the business. She pulled out her phone and searched for Cavendar Funeral Home 2011 but found nothing, so she typed in Cavendar, Nathaniel. An article popped up:

> Cavendar Funeral Home Closes Its Doors After 140 Years of Service.

Poor Nate, she thought. She read more,

> On March 17, 2001 an important piece of Erie Township's history closed its doors. Nathaniel Cavendar, son of the late Charles Cavendar, former owner of the funeral home, confirmed that the building was officially closed.

Devan sat on the porch reading the article when an elderly woman approached her.

"Hello? May I help you, dear?"

"I'm looking for Nate Cavendar."

"He's my nephew. How do you know him?"

"We went to school together."

"Oh, that's nice, dear. I am sure he will be pleased to see you. He is working as a mortician for the Payne Family's Crematorium and Funeral home. You can probably catch him now." The woman paused, "He doesn't get many visitors, especially pretty ones like yourself."

Devan thanked her and hopped into her car then drove to the next town. She knew right where it was because it was near Mayfield Diner, the place where she had worked in high school.

Devan walked in the building and was greeted by a short stout man who she assumed to be in his 50s.

"Ma'am, I'm George Payne. Are you here to set up arrangements?" the man asked with a slight southern accent.

"Hello, Mr. Payne. I'm sorry to bother you. I'm looking for Nathaniel Cavendar. I was told I could find him here."

"Oh sure. He's about ready to go on his lunch break. Let me fetch him for you. Won't you please have a seat?"

She sat down in a plush navy chair that was comfortable and noticed her surroundings. The décor was in navy, cream and grey. The woodwork was a brilliant cherry wood.

"Hello, I am Nate Cavendar," a very deep voice said. Devan stood up and smiled. Nate's hair had darkened from a deep brown to a raven black. It was to the nape of his neck with some strands tucked behind his ears. He was incredibly tall, maybe even taller than Kale. Nate was a little more slender than Kale, but not by much. His white button-down dress shirt sleeves were rolled up to his elbows, allowing her to see definition in his forearms. He took off his dark thick rimmed glasses exposing his chestnut brown eyes showing long eyelashes. Nate looked just a little rough around the edges with a dense goatee and an overgrown five o'clock shadow on his tan Native American skin. Nathaniel Cavendar was GORGEOUS!

"Hello Nate."

He stared at her for a moment with curiosity then he realized who she was.

"Devan! Devan Montgomery!" His surprise shifted to worry. "Oh no, what happened?"

"Nothing, nothing at all."

"Okay, then to what do I owe the pleasure of this visit?" he asked with his gravelly voice.

"I came to see *you*, Nate. Mr. Payne said you were going to lunch soon."

"Yes, I was just going to run to the Mayfield Diner."

"Uh, how about if I take you to Applebee's instead?" Devan wanted to avoid the diner due to the rumors that her lecherous former boss was still working there.

Nate rubbed his jaw, "*You* want to take…*me*…to lunch?"

"Yes,"

He seemed a little leery. "What's going on? Are you sure everything is okay? I haven't seen you since high school." He was puzzled.

She understood how he had to be feeling and admitted, "I know it's a little awkward, but we were friends in middle school and kind of in high school, right?"

"Yeah, you were all right," he joked as he smoothed back his shiny black hair.

"So how about lunch with an old friend? My treat."

"Okay," he grabbed his leather jacket that was hanging in the coat room. "Let's go."

When they sat down at the table, Devan told Nate what had transpired in her life after school ended.

"Oh Devan, I am so sorry. I was sure you and Hawaii—"

"I know." She brought her glass to her mouth. "Shit happens. So, what about you?" Devan couldn't keep the intrigue from her voice. She was dying to know if he was single.

He set his sandwich down. "No kids and never been married. After my Dad died, I couldn't keep up with the State's demands for the funeral home, and my dad had taken on so many charity cases there was hardly any money left. I was forced to close up shop. My mom moved to Virginia to take care of my grandpa and left me the house." He paused and appeared lost in thought for a minute, and then he went back to talking about the funeral home.

"I'd love to get it going again, but I need manpower. I also can't afford to do all the renovations to get it back up to the State's standards. It's been sitting there vacant for ten years." Devan opened her mouth to say something, however, he blurted out a question that she hadn't expected. "How did you find me anyway?"

"I saw your aunt."

"My aunt?" He raised an eyebrow.

"Yeah, she came up to me outside of your funeral home."

"Are you sure?"

"Yes, Nate. She asked me how I knew her 'nephew'. Then she told me how to find you."

"You must have had a dream," he laughed. "I only have one aunt, and she died about twenty years ago."

"Nate, I swear to God, she said she was your aunt and—" Devan was beginning to question herself and was a little creeped out. Maybe she *was* going crazy and had a dream. Deciding to push it out of her mind, she quickly gathered herself remembering why she was there. "You know what, it doesn't matter. I found you, and that is what is important. Wait, what did you say right before you asked me how I found you?"

"I want to do a renovation on the funeral home." He spoke slower so she could catch every word.

Renovation, renovation, renovation. Devan repeated that word, thinking hard. *Didn't she know someone who did that kind of work?* The word kept repeating in her mind. *Renovation, renovation, RENOVATION! Of course, Vinnie!* She had an idea. "Well, Veronica VonStross's brother, Vincent, does renovations. I bet he'd give you a good price."

"Ver...on...i...ca Von...Stross." Nate had a smile on his face as he enunciated all the syllables.

"Yeah, you know her?" Devan knew he did just by that smile.

He took a drink of his water. "Oh, yes, the pretty Goth girl."

Devan grinned, "Yes, that's her."

"The two of you were the most appealing girls in school."

Devan's face turned a light shade of red. "What?"

"Oh, like you didn't know. I got to know you when I helped you with that history project, and you helped me let the frogs loose. I just thought you were the real deal. I was jealous of Kale, but he was a really good guy."

"Well listen, I looked you up today to see if you would come hang out with us after the Alumni Football game in a few weeks. Maybe you could talk to Veronica about the renovations or maybe ask her out on a date." *Oops, that was a bit forward.*

"Isn't she married?"

"Not anymore—"

"What makes you think she'd even be interested?" He peered over the rim of his glasses at her.

Devan, hesitated then responded with, "Look, you are single, and she is single. She likes tall guys and you are what six-foot-fiveish?"

"Last time I checked, about six-foot-seven or so." *Damn he is taller than Kale!*

"Okay so you are extremely tall, that's perfect." Devan waited for him to say something, but he didn't. "Listen, she is just as pretty as she was in high school if not prettier. Worst case scenario you can at least make a new friend that can help make your dream become a reality with the renovation."

Nate didn't wait any longer. "Okay, name the time and place."

Devan was quite pleased with herself. This chance meeting couldn't have gone any better.

"So, who all will be there?" he asked.

"Veronica, Maggie Frasier, Kristy McDaniels—I mean Kristy and Pete Monahan, and me."

"Oh yeah, I saw they got married. I liked Pete. He was a really nice guy."

"He still is." Devan asserted.

"Okay sounds good."

They talked some more, and he explained how he wanted to restore the funeral home back to its original state. Devan was amazed at the way his mind worked. Nate had it all figured out.

⁙

"Hey, I am going to be in town the weekend of the nineteenth. Don't tell Devan yet, I want to surprise her." Kale talked into the phone to his best friend as he fumbled with his hair.

"Dude, that's perfect. That's the alumni game. We are all meeting up at Urban Myth after. Why don't you just show up?"

Kale pulled his hair back and put it in a man bun so it would be out of his face.

"I don't know Pete..."

"It would be perfect! I can see Devan's face now."

Kale pictured her beautiful smile and gorgeous blue eyes looking back at him.

"All right." He hadn't seen anyone since Hawaii. This would be a fun time with old friends. Right then Kale's phone signaled call waiting. He pulled the phone away from his ear to see who was calling. "Sorry, Pete, I have a business call coming in that I have to take, I'll catch you later."

Kale switched over to the call. "Mr. Carter, how are you?"

"Boy, I told you to call me Kev because Mr. Carter is my daddy."

"I'm sorry Kev. It's a nasty habit trying to show respect," Kale replied.

Kevin chuckled. "I like you kid. Listen, I am actually calling to apologize."

Kale was confused. "Apologize? For what?"

"Well you see, son, I wasn't so nice about your business associate. I did not know she was your wife as well. I would never be disrespectful like that, and I am terribly sorry."

"Kev, it's quite all right. Jeane is an abrasive woman. I don't expect anyone else to enjoy being around her when I can't even stand her myself." It was clear Kevin didn't know what to say to that. Kale continued, "I'm sorry! I shouldn't have said that. Sometimes I get so frustrated, my mouth has a mind of its own. Kev, does your wife work with you in your business?"

"No, she surely doesn't."

"Believe me, it's probably a good thing. Twenty-four hours together on some days is twenty-three and a half hours too long." He heard Kevin chuckle.

Kale and Jeane had done nothing but argue about how he was going to work with Mr. Carter. Kale decided that he would do what he needed to do for him even if it meant stepping out of his normal role. He really liked this man and to hell with what Jeane thought.

"I have a lot going on the rest of the year, I won't lie to ya. How about I give you a holler after the holidays?" Kevin told him.

"That sounds just fine, I will look forward to your call then." Kale agreed.

Chapter 3

October 2011

Devan pushed open the large heavy door and entered into the dark veiled ambiance of what was known as Urban Myth. It had been a while since she had been there. The main lighting was still the blue and purple neon lights that she remembered. A glance around the room proved that nothing had changed, as there was still a black light in every corner. It was dark giving it a sense of mystery, nevertheless, Devan got a type of satisfaction from it that she could not explain.

Maybe it was the fact that *here* she was just Devan. She wasn't someone's wife nor someone's mom. She felt as though she were in her early twenties again, and it brought a sense of familiarity that she cherished. It was almost as if Devan was back in the life of simplicity where responsibilities were minimal and chances for fun were in every corner. She could feel the freedom her twenties had given her, and at that instant she felt amazing. Devan was determined to enjoy her night at Urban Myth.

She spotted Veronica at the bar. "Whatcha drinkin'?" Devan asked.

"Oh, you know, plain old water with lime. I still can't believe I let you talk me in to this!" Veronica groaned.

Devan pulled out the stool next to her. "Stop your whining. It's not like you had anything to do tonight, besides you're going to have a good time."

"Oh, and you know this because—"

"You never know who might come through those doors," Devan smirked. She was sure that Veronica wouldn't be able to guess what she'd done.

"Whatever, Dee. I just lost a bet," she scoffed, "I'm not here searching for my next husband!"

"That's right, you did lose! Hey, you never know—John Cusack could walk right in here tonight holding a boom box over his head that is playing 'Your Eyes' by Peter Gabriel."

"Right. Then, we can go in a room where we can sit on the table where a birthday cake sits in between us and we can have our first kiss!"

"Um, wrong '80s movie. I was talking about *Say Anything*. You are talking about *Sixteen Candles* with Molly Ringwald and Michael Schoeffling."

"Whatever! Are you going to have me to do an '80s movie montage next?" Veronica rolled her eyes.

"I might!"

"Do I look like the type to watch those yuppy teen romances? Besides, I am more of an 'Edgar Allan Poe' John Cusack not a 'Lloyd Dobler' John Cusack kind of girl."

"Well you evidently watched enough to know his character's name," Devan pointed out. "Excuse me," she tried to get the bartender's attention. "Can we get four shots of tequila?"

"Uh oh! And please make mine Jager," Veronica told the bartender.

"Not a tequila lover?" Devan was surprised.

"No, that shit is nasty." Veronica's nose crinkled, and frown lines formed on her face.

"I could have sworn you liked Margaritas."

Before she could tell Devan *no*, someone sat down next to her on the other side of her stool and tapped her on the shoulder.

"Keep your hands to yourself, asshole." Veronica removed his hand from her shoulder.

"Roni, it's me, Jasper." Veronica whipped her head around and just glared at him, a mixture of disgust and disappointment on her face as she took in his appearance.

"Here," he handed her what seemed to be a headshot. Devan just watched in amusement biting her lip, so she wouldn't laugh.

"Yes, I remember who you are. I don't need a picture."

His stringy bleached blonde hair was all in his face, and it looked as if he hadn't washed it in over a year. "I have dreamed about you so many times throughout the years. I wondered where you were, how you were, what you were doing and what could have been."

Veronica was too distracted to hear a single word he had said. He had gauge holes in his ears that were humongous. She got closer to see them better.

"I can see that man's face through your ear lobe. Wow!"

There was no holding back that one. Devan was feisty in school but not as bad as Veronica. She knew when to shut up, most of the time—though often let her opinion come out whether you wanted to hear it or not. Veronica was quite different. She had no filter, and she simply didn't care.

"Pretty cool, huh? Hey, I got these done too." He lifted his shirt to show her his nipple rings.

Veronica was not impressed and decided to try to get a rise out of him. "Does this hurt?" She tugged on one of the rings.

"Uh, yeah…," he winced.

"That's what I thought," she sneered and scanned the rest of the bar.

He kept talking, however, Veronica was so rude that she even quit pretending to listen. Instead she was checking out the rest of the scenery when something *big* caught her eye.

"So, don't you think we should? I'm kind of famous now and…"

Veronica shoved the headshot Jasper had given her into his chest. "Are your songs being played on the radio?"

"Well, no, not yet."

"Do you have a manager?"

"No."

"Do you even have a Facebook page or a website?"

"Not yet."

"I have never heard of your band until tonight. I've never even seen a flyer. So, I would say you are not even a smidge on the famous side there, slick. Not saying it couldn't happen, I hope it does for you, but right now, dude, you are not famous. Fame doesn't matter to me anyway. I'm just not interested," she said slowly, then got up and walked away. Devan tilted her head in the direction that Veronica was going, and her mouth fell to the floor.

There he was, Nathaniel Cavendar, in the flesh. All six-feet-seven of him. Devan couldn't bite back a sharp response to Jasper before joining Veronica. "Better luck next time, slick. I did hear American Idol will be having auditions in Cleveland next month. You should put that on your calendar," Devan sarcastically suggested to Jasper turning her head as she followed her friend.

"Nate Cavendar! Well, isn't this a nice surprise!" Pete gave the man a slap on the back.

"Hey Pete, Congrats on head coach and the wife." Nate winked at Kristy.

"Hi Nate, I'm so glad you could make it," Devan said. "You remember Veronica VonStross?" Veronica pushed her way forward.

"How could I ever forget her? Hello, Veronica," Nate purred before grabbing her hand, kissing it and then hugging her tightly.

Damn, he is smooth! Veronica glanced back with a huge grin that transformed into an open jaw gawk.

"Hey, Hawaii! It's been a long time. I didn't think I would see you here. Heard you were in the Evergreen state with the cold and the rain. How does an islander such as yourself even survive there?" Nate extended his hand.

"Not well, my friend, not well. I can't wait to be back permanently," Kale admitted.

Devan whirled around to see her knight in shining armor. It took everything she had to not run and jump in to his arms. She knew other people would see making it not the best idea.

Devan swallowed hard. Given the dreams she had been having about him and her intake of alcohol, she wondered how she could keep her hands to herself. She took several deep breaths to contain her excitement and closed her eyes tight. *Just friends, just friends, just friends* she chanted to herself. *He is not that gorgeous. I do not want him. I can't want him.* Devan tried to convince herself. Opening her eyes and looking at him was a mistake. To Devan, Kale was irresistible. He was wearing his weathered black leather jacket over a plain white tee. His hair was pulled back and he had a thin goatee. Kale flashed a smile at her and she had to look down, only then noticing the vintage pair of black Doc Martins he was wearing. She wiped her mouth with the back of her hand to make sure she wasn't drooling.

Loud music began to play so they seated themselves in an open booth. Devan felt Kale's hand slip next to hers on the seat just like old times. She glanced at him, and he gave her that lopsided grin of his that always indicated he was up to something. Her heart thumped painfully as he slyly slipped his large fingers between hers.

She glanced over at Veronica for support, but her friend was resting her face on her hand with her eyes fixated on the back of Nate's head. She was enchanted.

When the set was over, the girls got up to use the restroom, and the guys went to order more drinks. While Devan was washing her hands, she looked in the mirror and smiled. "So—"

"Dee, don't even—" Veronica put the lipstick back in her purse. "Just because my longtime crush walked in to the bar tonight does not mean he's my long-lost love." Veronica was clearly trying to control her composure. Her calm exterior didn't last long. "Oh my God, he smells so good. I could feel his muscles tighten when he hugged me!" she blurted out.

Devan was giggling, she knew exactly how Veronica was feeling right now. She experienced the same thing every time Kale embraced her.

Jasper was waiting for Veronica right outside the bathroom door hovering like a stalker. "Hey, so what did you think?"

Veronica brushed past him rather quickly. "I didn't know you could sing. Maybe there is hope for you yet," Veronica replied while trying to escape him. She went over to Nate who handed her a drink that she instantly downed. He put an arm around her and rested his hand on her hip.

He looks pretty cozy there, Devan beamed knowing that her friend was basking in the moment.

"You guys are pretty good." Nate complimented Jasper.

"Yeah? That's it? Just pretty good? And excuse me, uh, Roni is with me tonight."

Nate dropped his hand from Veronica's hip and apologized. "I'm sorry. I wasn't trying to offend you. I think you are talented, but I believe Miss Von-Stross is here with her friends."

Kale handed Devan another shot of liquid courage which didn't last more than a second. She set the glass on the bar and headed back over to Veronica.

Jasper stepped up closer to Nate and stared him down. "I remember you…the mortician punk. Ah yes, the necrophiliac…Lurch is it?"

Are we really back in high school? What the hell is the asshole's problem? Devan was beginning to get angry. She balled her hands up in to a fist. That was low, even for Jasper.

"It's Nate, though *you* can call me Mr. Cavendar, and I believe that Miss VonStross is here with her friends," Nate repeated.

"She is obviously *not* here with you. No way would she be seen with a creepy corpse lover as yourself." Jasper moved closer to him. Nate had a good half foot on him. It appeared as though a stick was about to get in a fight with a tree trunk.

This guy is stupid! Devan could not believe what she was about to witness.

Veronica pushed Jasper away from Nate. "Actually, I am here with him," she told Jasper.

"Yeah, right. You are just trying to be nice. Well, he doesn't deserve someone being nice to him. He's a fucked-up undertaker. Look at him— what a loser. He's a bean pole for Christ's sake." Jasper retorted.

"Really? A bean pole? Did you not see him?" Veronica asked then faced Nate. She scanned him from top to bottom practically salivating. "I like what I see!" Veronica took another shot that was sitting on the bar and downed it. Her hands went to the back of his head and she pulled his face down to hers and kissed him. Being Veronica, she couldn't give him just a peck. She had to go into a full make out secession. Nate was stunned at first but then reciprocated her passion quickly cupping his hands around her cheeks. After a few seconds, their kiss was interrupted with someone pulling roughly on her arm.

"Bitch! If Jasper says you are with him then why are you kissing on—ew is that the Grim Reaper?"

Devan recognized that unpleasant voice, Desiree. Devan walked closer and was spotted. "Oh, it's—"

Desiree didn't get to finish her sentence. Veronica seized a handful of her hair and pulled her back. "Listen, you useless homewrecking whore..."

Desiree screeched and started swinging towards her. "I didn't wreck your home. Can't wreck a home that is already fucked up."

That pissed Veronica off even more. Veronica's entire body shook with rage. Her eyes narrowed to slits.

"I didn't take him away," Desiree flipped her hair. "He was running away from you."

Apparently, Jasper decided it was a good time to attack Nate, so he punched him square in the jaw. Nate hardly flinched.

"Oh shit! You are going to regret that," Pete commented trying to pull Kristy out of harm's way. Kale came up behind them, snatched Jasper's hands, put them behind his back and held them there.

"Come on, you pussy, hit me! Hit me you, morbid bastard! Come on, you sick fuck!" Jasper screamed.

"LANGUAGE!" Kristy's voice rose above the clatter of the fight.

"I'm not going to stoop to your high school mentality. Grow up man!" Nate clenched his teeth.

"Oh, *I* will." Devan shoved Nate out of the way then punched Jasper in the stomach. "That was for Nate." When he bent over in pain, she grabbed his hair which had a disgusting wax-like texture then kneed him in the groin. "That was for Veronica." Then she slapped him as hard and she could. "And that is because you are an asshole." Devan let go of his hair and inspected her hands. *Oh my god I will need Dawn dish soap after this. That is absolutely disgusting.* She desperately wanted to wash her hands.

"You fucking bitch," he grimaced in pain trying to escape Kale's clutch.

Kale squeezed Jasper's hands tighter. "I'd watch my mouth if I were you," he growled.

Some of the band members joined in the fight. Two of them jumped Kale, which made him let go of Jasper who then went straight after Nate.

Before anyone knew it, the cops were there, and half of the bar patrons were beating on each other.

Maggie was fashionably late and had missed all the entertainment. When she arrived, she saw the tables on their sides and chairs thrown everywhere. "What did I miss?" she questioned surveying the disaster that was once the bar.

"Oh, nothing, just some *losers* causing trouble by trying to pick a fight with people who are out of their class." Veronica explained to Maggie, her voice growing louder and louder as she projected it toward Desiree who was across the bar in handcuffs.

"Oh my! Guess I wasn't too late," Maggie voiced as she checked out the officer who was behind Desiree and had his back to her. "Look. At. That. Ass!" Maggie was delighted as it was her turn to take in the scenery.

Veronica stepped away from the bar where she had just done another shot with Devan to see who Maggie was complimenting, only to find that it was her brother who had Desiree in handcuffs. She punched Maggie's shoulder and gave her a scornful expression.

"Excuse me, Officer—" Maggie started, and Vincent spun around. "Oh my god." Maggie muffled under her breath completely flustered.

"Maggie? Maggie Fraiser? It's Vinnie."

Vincent VonStross, local cop, freelance construction worker specializing in renovations and Maggie's childhood crush. Veronica and Vincent didn't resemble one another at all. He was two years older than Veronica, six-foot-one, had light brown hair and hazel eyes. Veronica was five-foot-five, naturally blonde, though she dyed her hair dark, and had bright blue eyes. The only physical feature they had in common was their pouty lips. Veronica took after their father and Vincent after their mother. Both were naturally attractive.

Vincent took out his wallet and handed Maggie a business card. "I have a few more statements to take and a few of these assholes to book. Give me a call tomorrow. We can catch up." As he walked away, she stared after him in complete shock. "See ya, sis," he hollered to Veronica.

"Hey thanks for taking care of my light work," she yelled back.

"So, what did happen?" Maggie asked Veronica getting back to reality.

"Well to make a long story short, Jasper, Nate, that slut Desiree, Kale, Devan, and a bunch of other people ended up in a fight. Desiree, being the stupid ass she is, had drugs on her as did a few other people—including Jasper."

"Huh!" Maggie was astounded. "Wait—Nate?"

"You see that sexy stud over there in the black sitting with Kale?"

"Yes. Are you serious? That's him? Oh my," Maggie smiled.

"Yup, and just wait until I tell you the rest."

The seven of them stayed and cleaned up. It was last call by the time they were done. It was obvious Veronica and Devan were experiencing the effects of the booze. The girls did one last shot together that was not needed.

"I think that we should not drive." Devan giggled.

"You think?" Veronica slapped the table and laughed.

Kristy and Pete were getting ready to leave when Kristy went up to the cackling girls.

"Hey guys, get your coats. We are going to take you home."

"Wait, if you do that then I can't…shhh! Come closer—" Veronica said.

Kristy bent down.

"If you take me home, I can't ask Nate out on a date. Oh my GOD! That's soooo funny! Nate and date rhyme," she howled with amusement.

"YES! It does" Devan chimed in and began giggling hysterically.

"Guess what Kristy?" Devan asked.

"What?"

"Roni made out with a GIANT!"

"Yes, a sexy giant! Dude. I kissed a GIANT, and I liked it!!" Veronica buckled under her laughter.

"You sure did. I am a very proud friend this lovely evening," Devan stated.

Kristy was annoyed. She never saw Devan this way, and it was irritating.

Kale walked up. "Hey guys, go ahead and go. We will take care of these two," he patted Pete on the back. Maggie left the same time they did.

"Come on, girls, let's get you home," Kale helped Devan up.

Nate assisted Veronica with her coat. "Where do you live?"

"Why? Are you going to take me to my bed?" Veronica winked.

"I just want to get you home safely." Nate said with a kind smile.

"Are you going to drive my car?" Veronica wanted to know.

"If you would be more comfortable with that, I can." He peered down into her glossy blue eyes.

"Did you drive a hearse here?"

"No, I drove my truck."

"What kind is it?"

"F250."

"That'll do I guess, I just really want to ride in the hearse one day BEFORE I'm dead."

"I promise I will take you in it one day soon."

That made Veronica happy. "You are a gentleman, NOT a necrophiliac."

Nate chuckled. "Well, thank you."

Devan snickered at her friend. "Call me tomorrow." she shouted to Veronica.

Kale supported Devan's weight as he unlocked his truck and helped her in.

"For the record, Kale, you are a gentleman too and not a necrophiliac either," she burst out laughing.

Kale was amused. He had never really seen her like this. The only time that she even came close was when she was hyped up on pain meds in Hawaii when she hurt her ankle. He would never tell her exactly how wild she was that day. Devan would be mortified, and Kale would never forget how close he came to breaking his promise to her.

"Are you hungry?" he asked.

Devan was too busy struggling with her seatbelt to answer him. He leaned over and fastened it for her. When Devan reached for his hand, he looked at her. She didn't say anything and locked on his eyes as though she was searching for something. It lasted well over half a minute, then she finally responded. "What would you make me?"

"I figured we would run through a drive thru."

Devan still had a tight grip on his hand. "No, I want a grilled cheese sandwich with Muenster cheese and basil tomato soup."

That was specific. "Okay, I will drive you home and make that for you."

She let go of his hand. When they got to her house, he helped her out of his truck. She wrapped her arms around him. "Thank you."

"You're welcome." Devan reached up, tugged on his beard to bring his chin down, and gazed in to his green eyes. He felt paralyzed. He couldn't turn away. She stood on tiptoe and kissed him ever so lightly. Her lips were warm and soft just like he remembered. Devan opened her mouth and kissed him more passionately. He kissed her back with just as much exuberance then pulled away from her. Kale was ashamed that he just let that happen.

"Devan, I'm sorry. We can't do this."

"Why?"

Kale stared into her eyes. It was as if they were pleading with his soul. "I made you a promise to respect you and to never let something like this happen again."

Devan sheepishly turned away and apologized. He hated having to deny her knowing that he could get away with kissing her all night. Kale hated to do the right thing at that moment more than anything.

Devan twisted back around and grabbed ahold of his hand. "Are you upset with me?"

"Oh, God, no, Monty! I won't lie. I am upset with this situation, but I am not upset with you for doing something that I so desperately wanted."

She hugged him again and looked up at his face. "Why can't we indulge just a little? You are here. Jeane is across the country. Justin is gone. The kids are at my parents, and I am right in front of you willing and ready." Devan shook her jacket off and let it fall into a heap on the cement.

Kale knew no good would come of this, still there was a hunger in him that was excruciating. He picked her up, her lips collided with his. Devan wrapped her legs around his waist. He walked into the house with her while not missing a single stroke of her tongue. Then took her to her bedroom and laid her on the bed. Kale took off his shirt exposing his perfectly sculpted chest. He heard his phone ringing from his pants. Pulling the phone out of his pocket, Kale tried to answer it, however, it wouldn't open and kept vibrating and ringing loudly. When he was finally able to answer Jeane was screaming obscenities at him, accusing him of cheating. Somehow, the phone was still ringing. Between the screaming and the loud ring tone, he was getting a migraine. Kale dropped the phone and slumped down to the floor, passing out from the stabbing pain in his head and neck.

Kale opened his eyes and reached for the ringing phone. It finally stopped ringing when he opened it. The alarm was going off. He noticed that he missed a text from Devan.

> Thank you for the ride home. I hope I wasn't too much of a burden.

Kale quickly responded:

> It was my pleasure. Let me know when you want to get your car.

She told him:

> Dad already took me to get it, thank you though. Let me know if you need anything or help with the house.

He remembered thinking that the grass could use one last cut for the year.

> Can I borrow the riding mower?

> Sure. I need to run a few errands. The garage will be unlocked.

Kale was glad it had been a dream. Well most of it was a dream. The rest was a complete nightmare. He was glad that she wouldn't be home when he got the mower. Seeing her after a hot dream like that could result in actions that would have serious consequences.

Chapter 4

Kale was out mowing the grass when a petite woman with dark curly hair came up to him with a basket. He shut off the mower as she spoke. "Welcome to the neighborhood. I'm Alison Jenkins."

"Thank you, ma'am. I'm not officially here yet, just trying to get stuff ready for the big move. I am Kale Iakona." He took the basket from her and extended his hand.

"No kidding." She acted like she knew him. "Miss Jenkins from Erie Central High. You are the *exchange student from Hawaii*." Kale almost dropped the basket. "I *did* know Hawaii was a state by the way."

Devan spun around and punched Kale right in the mouth. Her hands flew to her mouth in shock. "Oh, my god, Kale! Are you okay?"

She handed him the compact mirror from her bag so he could check out the damage.

"So, that wasn't intended for me?" he asked as he looked in the mirror.

"I am so sorry! I thought you were James. He keeps messing with..."

"Miss Montgomery! That is unacceptable behavior and you both need to come with me," a short curly haired teacher said and grabbed Devan's arm.

"Ma'am it was an accident, she didn't..." Kale tried to explain.

"I don't know who you are mister... Mister?"

"Iakona, Kale Iakona," he said extending his hand.

"Ah, yes, the exchange student from Hawaii."

Kale snickered. "Um, ma'am, you do know Hawaii became part of the United States back in 1959, right?"

"So, you think you're smart, huh? That's fine. Both of you can sit in detention.

The teacher took them to her classroom and wrote out the detention slips. "I'll be seeing you both after school."

"Yes, ma'am," they said in unison and walked out of her classroom.

He gave her a big bear hug. "Wow, this is amazing! I have got to tell Devan."

"Aww, still together after all these years?"

Kale looked at the woman, "Sadly, no, but we are close friends." His eyes dropped.

"I'm sorry to hear that."

He could see the sadness in her eyes. "Actually, Miss Jenkins, she lives just down the road."

"Are you kidding me?"

"No ma'am."

"Well, I live on the other side of your neighbor there," she pointed to her house. "Please bring Devan over one day this week for coffee. I would love to catch up with you kids. I know I gave you a hard time in school. I *was* rooting for you two though. You would bring back memories from my youth ever so often."

He thought for a moment then replied with, "I am going back to Seattle next weekend. What day is good for you?"

"Any day after four o'clock in the afternoon."

Kale smiled, "Good, I'll see you sometime this week."

Devan called Veronica later that moring, in hopes that she would be awake. She was dying to know exactly how her night ended with Nate.

"Do you remember what happened last night?" Devan asked Veronica.

"Are you talking about the bar fight, Jasper being creepy or me making an ass out of myself and kissing the hell out of Nate...then when he took me home, I basically tried to jump him?"

"Damn. You too?"

"Me too? Are you saying you hit on my dream man last night also and may have sexually harassed him?" There was a tinge of sarcasm in Veronica's voice.

"Oh, god, no!" She paused realizing how awful that sounded. "I mean he is definitely one fine specimen, I will say that. What I'm trying to say is…I kissed Kale last night and pretty much tried to get him to have sex with me, I think."

"You did what?" It was hard to tell if the tone in Veronica's voice was more of a shock or judgment.

"Oh, come on you did the same thing." Devan tried justifying her actions, even though she knew it wouldn't work.

"Yes, then again, I'm not married, and neither is Nate."

"I know, I know." Devan was embarrassed and disappointed in herself.

"So, what happened?"

"Kale was great. He didn't give in to me, which was a good thing…I guess."

"Yeah, but it would have been a GREAT thing if he had, right?"

"Oh, if you only knew." Devan took a deep breath, "He's so passionate and gentle, yet rough when he needs to be. The way he caresses my whole body, hell I can't even describe it. And his lips, when they are on my neck and then he slowly bites it's so…"

"Hot?" Veronica filled in for her. "Yeah, don't get yourself too worked up there, missy. You guys made a pact that he is clearly insistent on keeping. I'd be willing to bet it was for your benefit and not his."

Devan heard some shuffling outside her window and caught a glimpse of Kale's dark hair. "Shit! Speaking of the devil, he's outside right now returning my mower. I have to go."

"All right, I'll talk to you later."

"Wait, I almost forgot!" Devan said into the phone. "Kristy called, and she and Pete are having a cookout. You are invited. I'll text you the time and address. Bye." She hung up before Veronica could even say a word and walked outside to meet Kale.

When Devan met up with Kale, he told her all about Miss Jenkins. "Oh, how cool is that?"

"Right? So, when is good for you?"

"Let's shoot for Wednesday. Oh, and I am to tell you Pete and Kristy are having their last cookout of the season at one o'clock this afternoon, and you have been nominated to do the grilling. They said they have everything, but no one can cook a steak as good as you can." Which was true. Kale was very talented with the grill.

True to form, Kristy and Pete had a wide variety of food set out, and, as he promised, Kale, was at the grill with the meat. They were having a great time. Kristy and Pete were trying to touch base with all the people who were there.

Justin went to the cookout for a short time, and when the kids got rowdy, he was nice enough to leave with them and let Devan enjoy the rest of the evening with her friends. She was grabbing another water from the cooler when Nate came up to her.

"Hey, I wanted to thank you for finding me. It's nice to hang out with the living sometimes." he joked.

"Yeah, we aren't all that bad." she replied.

"Can we have a private chat for a minute?"

"Sure, what's on your mind?" She was somewhat concerned.

"I don't want to come off as really strange…even though it is something I cannot deny being. Um, I don't really have any friends."

Devan interrupted him right there. "Yes, you do, Nate. Look around you…there is not one person here who doesn't like you," she grinned.

He smiled back. "Thank you. I like these people too, but I know you better than anyone else here. I'm getting to know everyone again, I just have known you the longest…" He was almost stuttering.

"Where are you going with this Nate?" Devan couldn't take him stumbling over his words. He was always well spoken and very well mannered.

He exhaled slowly then answered. "I need some…um…dating advice, and I know I can trust you. I want to ask Veronica out on a date."

Devan giggled. "So, do it."

"It's not that easy. What if she says no?" He gave her a wide-eyed look. Anyone who had ever met Veronica knew how she was. She was blunt, had no filter, and could out-curse the worst cursing sailor. "You see I have really only dated two girls in my entire life. The death business isn't that sexy, I guess," he confessed.

Devan peered in to his chestnut brown eyes. "First of all, Veronica won't say no. Second of all, you *can* trust me, I won't say anything. And third, just put a stripper pole in when you renovate." she sarcastically suggested. "That will spice up the place."

"That *would* give a whole new meaning to Wake," Nate chuckled. "Are you sure she won't say no?"

Devan cleared her throat. "Okay, did I or did I not see her kissing you last night?"

His tan face reddened. "Well, she was just trying to get rid of Jasper, and she was under the influence."

"Haven't you ever heard that drunk people can't lie? I think the alcohol gave her the courage to do something she may have wanted to do since high school," she slipped in.

"You really think so?"

"I know so."

"Okay that makes it a little easier to ask her out. That *was* a pretty amazing kiss," he reminisced.

"Hey, I was thinking about the renovation thing," Devan said. "I think you should speak to Kale. He might have some ideas for you, too. He's been an architect for a little while now. I'm sure he could at least help you with the structure and redesign." Devan was convinced that Kale would be able to help Nate. "Kale," she yelled for him.

Kale jogged over and sat down next to Devan. "What's up?" he asked then took a bite of the rib he was holding. He reminded Devan of a caveman and she tried not to giggle.

"Nate wants to start renovating his family's funeral home. He wants to restore it back to its original state."

"Really? Like old fashioned?" Kale's excitement didn't go unnoticed.

"Yes. Well, for the most part. I obviously want to keep the running water and flushing toilets," Nate laughed.

"Oh dude, that's awesome!" Kale was interested. "Do you have the original blueprints?"

"I haven't found them yet, but they should be there somewhere. However, I do have some pictures we could use as a reference."

"I can work with pictures too," Kale commented then finished off the meat. He was chewing loud enough for Veronica to hear when she sat down beside him.

"Ew! You know you are supposed to close your mouth when eating, right?" Kale purposely chomped his jaws as loud as he could toward her ear.

"Ignore these two," Devan swatted at Kale and Veronica. "Continue please."

"Oh, I was just going to say I have yet to get in the attic. That's probably where the blue prints are," Nate sighed.

"Well, like I said, I can try to work without them. We won't be finished moving here until mid to late November, but after that I should be in the clear." Kale told him. "Don't worry, I'll make the time to work with you."

Nate's eyes lit up.

"Wait, what are we talking about?" Veronica hadn't caught on.

"Nate wants to fix up the funeral home and make it look like what it did when it was first opened," Devan explained to her.

"So, you want to replicate it from 1861?" Veronica questioned.

Nate was pleasantly surprised to hear she knew the year his family began the funeral home.

"Do you have a contractor yet?" she pressed on.

"No, I don't. It was really just an idea. It's something I have been thinking about for a few years."

"Well, if you are serious, my brother, Vinnie, does renovations on the side. This would be right up his alley. I can set up a meeting, if you want," Veronica offered.

Nate smiled down at her blue eyes looking up in to his. "Do you work with him?" he raised an eyebrow at her.

"I can," she said with a twinkle in her eye and a smile on her face.

Oh, this is going to be perfect. Devan was happy with herself. Her match-making skills seemed to be better than she imagined.

Kale glanced over at Devan and had a strong feeling he knew what that devious grin on her face meant. The flirting was unbearable to Kale as he continued to watch Veronica and Nate interact. He set his plate down. "So," he intervened, "I was thinking about doing something later. Would you guys be interested in coming with me?" he asked the three of them.

"Like what?" Devan was curious as to what he was up to.

"I don't know, bowling? A haunted house?" Kale shrugged his shoulders.

"Hey, I heard they are having ghost tours this month at Lakeland Estates. What about that?" Veronica piped up.

"I forgot about that. Yes, there is a haunted tour and dinner where they have you dress up in the 1800s attire similar to those photos you can do at fairs and amusement parks. I think you need to make reservations though." Nate commented.

"That sounds awesome. Let me make sure Justin is okay with it." Devan pulled out her phone and sent him a text. A few minutes later she received one back. "Okay, he's fine with it."

"Let me call them and see if they have any openings." Veronica took her phone, that was sitting on the table, and got up. She came back two minutes later. "We are in luck. They just received a cancellation and the six of us are penciled in. The tour starts at five o'clock. Dinner is at seven o'clock."

Chapter 5

ale, Devan, Veronica and Nate arrived and were outside Lakeland Manor waiting for the doors to open. Pete and Kristy had other plans and had been unable to go.

After a few minutes someone stepped outside and held the door open for the four of them to walk in. "Welcome to Lakeland Manor. I am Chadwick, and I will be your host for the evening. Do step inside."

The man was dressed in a Victorian tuxedo much like a butler or footman. "Gentlemen to the right and ladies to the left. In those rooms you will be fitted with the proper attire."

The girls were greeted by a woman dressed in a simple Victorian black dress. "Good evening. My name is Sarah, and I will be assisting you tonight with your garments."

"Your look is amazing." Veronica marveled at the black silk taffeta material. The skirting met the piped waist with cartridge pleating. The front closure was trimmed in velvet covered buttons. The collar around the neckline was in hand embroidered cotton batiste. The sleeves were full and puffy at the shoulder and were trimmed in three bands of flat velvet piping. Piped seams ran fully down the arm ending at a finished edge on the cuff trimmed with black lace.

"Are you wearing a mourning dress by chance?" Veronica asked.

"Why yes, yes I am. Black was worn for the deepest of mourning. The color of cloth lightened as the mourning went on. The length of mourning depended on the relationship with the deceased." Sarah went over to a large closet, started pulling out clothing and hung it up on an empty clothes rack while continuing to educate the girls. "For an example, widows were expected to wear the full mourning attire for two whole years. To mourn parents or children, it was worn for one year. To mourn grandparents and siblings it was worn about six months. Sometimes the griever would wear it until his or her own demise. Now normally, you would put on your clock stockings and shoes or boots, but we are not going to do that. Tonight, we are going to begin by putting on the bloomers and then the chemise." She handed them the articles of clothing, and they put them on.

"Next, I will help you with your corsets." Sarah slipped behind them. "You will close the front of it while I pull the ribbon that is laced up the back and tie it. I will be tying it more loosely than how it was worn during Victorian times. While it was the norm back then, it was later found that it often caused health issues if they were pulled too tight."

After she tightened both women's corsets, she walked over to a closet and pulled out two items that looked like skirts. "These are petticoats. I'm going to drop them over your head and then tie them in the back." After that, she went over and grabbed the strange large objects that resembled a bird cage with no bottom. "These are your crinoline cages. They are what give the full bottom," she explained as she helped Devan into the object.

"Wait don't the petticoats go under?" Veronica asked as Sarah finished up helping Devan and then moved over to help Veronica.

"In most dresses yes—this one is different. Petticoats can be used as either."

After they were completely dressed, they met the men in the hallway. Both Nate and Kale were mesmerized by the women. Veronica was in a pale blue taffeta ballroom gown that complimented her hair, and Devan was dressed in a black evening gown made of silk brocade and wool.

Chadwick cleared his throat to get the distracted couples' attention. When he saw they were finally all looking at him, he gestured toward Nate. "This gentleman is dressed in the traditional regency attire. The Regency era's peak was from the 1800s to the 1820s but lasted well into the Romantic era that began in the 1830s and ended in the 1850s." Nate had an elaborate top hat on his head. "You will notice, he has the signature top hat, typical dress shirt with removable jabot." Chadwick stopped when he noticed a couple of raised eyebrows among the group. "It's the fluffy piece that looks somewhat like a dickie." Chadwick pointed up at Nate's chest. There was a nod of acknowledgement. "He is wearing a cavalier vest and a Valencia Brocade Tailcoat."

He pointed to Kale next. "This gentleman is dressed in Victorian era clothing, which overlapped with the Romantic era as well. He has a stable brushed cotton frock coat and vest, a coachman hat, a traditional white dress shirt and four-in-hand tie." He turned up his nose as he gestured to both men's legs. "As you may notice, they are wearing the pants and shoes they came in with, and the coats are on the short side for the way they would have been during the eras that this attire is from. That is because these men are above the average height of men then, which was around five feet five inches. Well, they still exceed the average height of today, however, that is a different matter entirely." Chadwick peered down the hall, "Where is the rest of your group?"

"I'm sorry, we had originally made reservations for six, but the other couple had a change in plans," Devan answered.

Chadwick couldn't hide his disgust, "Follow me, if you will."

They followed him down a long hallway that had grey walls, marble floors, and real candle sconces on the walls for lighting.

"The Lakeland Estate was built in 1837. It is a Gothic revival mansion that has twenty-six rooms. We are currently standing in the large entrance hall." It was easy enough to get lost in the details, but he kept adding more to it. "There is a drawing room through that first door on the right, next to that is the dining room. Of course, a library which we will see, is to the left. There is the smoking room where the gentlemen would withdraw after dinner. Adjacent to that is the famous ballroom, where the governor's ball, cotillion and other extravagant parties were held.

This is the second oldest house left in our quaint town. The oldest house is located behind the former Cavendar Funeral home. It belonged to Nathaniel and Elizabeth Cavendar. The Cavendars were one of the first families to come here in 1809 when George Christensen founded Erie Valley, which is now called Erie Township."

Everyone looked at Nate. "Why are you looking at me like that? I thought you guys knew all of this. Our town history was taught to us in fifth grade."

"Excuse me, sir," Devan spoke up.

"Yes, madam?"

"We have a Cavendar descendent with us." She motioned to Nate.

"I apologize for not having recognized you, Mr. Cavendar. Due to your height, you certainly aren't forgettable," he stated as he perused him from the top of his head down to his feet as though he had the altitude and stance to be able to do that.

"Since there is a descendant of the Cavendars with us, *he* can tell you about his *dark* family history with the Lakelands—that is, *if* he knows it." The snark in Chadwick's tone was enough to grate on Devan's nerves.

Nate sighed, "Nathaniel Bryant Josiah Cavendar was my great-great-great-great-great-grandfather. He and his wife, Elizabeth, came here from England in 1809 after his parents died in a fire. He brought his younger brother, Oswald, whom he had rescued from the fire, with him. He built a furniture shop shortly after he built his Georgian colonial in 1810. The remains of the house are still there. Oswald went into business with Joseph Lakeland in 1817. Some time passed and in 1843 Joseph accused Oswald of having an affair with his wife, Jonetta, when she became pregnant after years of trying to conceive. When the baby was born, he had black hair like Oswald and resembled him. Joseph went mad and rode over to Oswald's house on Walnut Street, which is no longer there, and shot him. He never took into consideration that Oswald was related to Jonetta."

"What an ass!" Veronica shook her head.

"He was not a very good shot, but the seventh shot went straight into his heart finishing him off. There is a rumor that the bullets are in a jar somewhere in the old Cavendar house. A *rumor* is all it is." Nate said blatantly.

"Oh my god! Who knew we had such a gruesome town history?" Veronica couldn't suppress her shock.

"Well, it was swept under the rug amongst a lot of other things that have been in this town," Nate glared at Chadwick. Devan didn't miss the glare and wondered what else was swept under the rug that she didn't know about.

"Um, yes…well we must continue the tour." There seemed to be something that Nate wasn't saying that dealt with both he and Chadwick, who was suddenly eager to continue the tour which struck Devan as odd.

"What I didn't mention is Jonetta was Nathaniel's and Oswald's second cousin from their mother's side, who had come to America a few years after the Cavendars had. While in those days it was perfectly acceptable to marry your cousin, Jonetta had no interest in either of the brothers. She swore until the day she died that her son, Marcus, was, in fact, Joseph's son. I'm sure there is still a picture around here where you can see the close similarity of Marcus and Joseph." Nate took a deep breath and continued, "Now, Nathaniel was also a coffin maker, as a lot of furniture stores made coffins back then. He decided to start performing the services that were needed and did what he could at that time to prepare the body for viewing. He was the only one within one hundred miles that could provide that service. So ol' Nate picked up his brother's remains, cleaned up the mess and went home to prepare the body for viewing."

"Wow! Could you imagine having to embalm your own brother?" Kale asked.

"They didn't embalm here in the states until a man by the name of Dr. Thomas Holmes performed the first one in May of 1861 during the civil war. It was done so the soldiers' bodies could be shipped back home. However, it was only done if they or their families could afford it."

"Wait! So, they had formaldehyde back then?" Veronica asked intrigued.

"No, Dr. Holmes made a mixture of arsenic, zinc, mercuric chlorides, turpentine, and alcohol. Unfortunately, it wasn't very good. A lot of the soldiers that had been embalmed still had a fair amount of decay when they arrived home. Nevertheless, it was a lot better than receiving the bodies in full decomposition. Formaldehyde was used after the war ended. Embalming actually died out for a while because most people died closer to home. It didn't return until the 1890s." Veronica was enamored with Nate's knowledge.

"So, when Oswald died, Nathaniel had to take care of a rapidly decomposing body? Ugh! I'm grossed out and feeling a bit of empathy for the man," Kale said.

"That's just what they did in that time period, but don't worry, he handled it quickly," Nate replied. "As someone in the field, I can assure you that a lot of us would rather take care of our own than let someone else do it. My grandfather took care of his father, my father took care of him and I took care of my father. I'm not saying that someone wouldn't do a better job, it's just that we know what kind of care we take and respect we show the dead that we feel a responsibility and consider it an honor, I guess you could say."

When Nate finished with his family and funeral service speech, they continued following Chadwick for the tour.

Later during the tour, the girls needed to use the restroom. It became a big ordeal. Sarah, who had helped them get dressed, had to come and explain to them how to use the restroom due to the layers they had on.

After Veronica washed her hands, she went into the restroom sitting area. She observed the room and went over to something that caught her eye. She picked it up and as she examined it, she realized it was a music box. She saw a key and turned it. Music started playing and as she listened, she began looking at the pictures on the wall.

"That one is Nate," she heard Devan say. "The taller man with the blackened hair is Nathaniel, and next to him is his brother Oswald—very, very nice gentlemen."

"How would you know?" Veronica twisted around expecting to see Devan. "Hey, where did you go?"

Devan came out of the bathroom drying her hands. "I was just using the restroom."

"No, you just told me that Nathaniel and Oswald were nice."

Devan threw the paper towel in the trash and looked at Veronica with wide eyes. "No, I didn't. How would I even know that?"

"But—but," Veronica stammered.

"Ladies, may we return to the others now? There is one more place I want to take you before you sit down to your elegant dinner," Chadwick stated impatiently. Veronica decided to keep her mouth shut.

"This is the servants' quarters. It is said to be haunted by a footman named Jonathon Reyes, who was my great-great-great-great-uncle. Jonathon was a very unhappy soul who was rumored to be a disgruntled employee. There are several stories that led to that assumption but only a few that I know. Some say he was a killer on the run who found employment here at Lakeland. Others say he was addicted to morphine."

"Maybe he just had a hard life," Kale commented.

"Whatever the case," Chadwick shrugged, "they found him lying here in a pool of his own blood with a gun in his hand. Suicide is what was documented. We will never know the real story of why poor Jonathon Reyes took his own life, *if,* indeed, he did."

Veronica was still trying to wrap her mind around what happened when she was holding the music box. She considered asking Devan, but she didn't want to appear weirder than usual. Despite not giving a shit if people thought she was quirky, she did care if they thought she was outright crazy.

After a moment's pause, Chadwick announced it was time to head to the dining room for dinner. Devan glanced in the room again before she followed the others out. An eerie feeling encompassed her as someone came up behind her.

"That's not right. It *was* murder," Nate said to Devan in her ear.

"What was murder?" she asked him and waited for a response. She spun to face him, but no one was there. A cold shiver went down her spine. She hurried to catch up with the others.

They walked into the dining room where dinner was waiting for them. A young woman dressed as a maid and a man dressed as a servant stood on opposite sides of the long rectangular table which was stylishly set according to the time period.

"Wine?"

"Yes, please," Veronica answered.

The woman poured red wine into everyone's glass. "This wine is a cabernet from California, but many years ago Joseph and Oswald made a Catawba wine from the vineyard that used to be in the back, past the gardens. In the Edwardian Era the rich would often have seven course meals, however, tonight there will be six. The first course will be half a grapefruit. The second is Chicken a la Reine soup. The third would normally be a type of fish, but the third will be the main course tonight. That is Chicken Florentine, rice pilaf, buttered green beans, sliced tomatoes, and applesauce. The fourth will be iceberg lettuce with oil and vinegar and will be served with saltines and sharp cheddar cheese. The fifth will be peach crisp with hard sauce,"

"What is hard sauce? It doesn't sound appealing." Veronica commented.

"It's more or less an icing," Nate said in her ear.

"Your sixth course will be served in the drawing and smoking rooms. You will be served coffee or tea with a dish of chocolate and nuts."

When they were finished eating, the men were taken to the smoking room, and the women were taken into the drawing room and served tea.

"This is amazing, isn't it?" Devan asked before taking a sip of her tea.

"It truly is, but what I really want to do is get inside the old Cavendar house." Veronica was intrigued.

"Nate said the remains were there so I'm thinking there isn't much left to it." Devan mused.

Veronica took a sip of tea and set it down. "It's been a few years, but it is quite intact from what I can remember." Devan looked at her with curiosity in her eyes. Veronica elaborated, "Back when we were kids, Vinnie dared me to go in to the cemetery on Cemetery Road. Naturally, I did. No one is allowed in it after dusk, so we were trespassing. There was a spooky old house on the hill that fascinated me. Vinnie was trying to get my attention, but I was too busy looking at the house. It was dark, but I could see a faint light in the window. I just kept staring at it in a complete trance. Meanwhile poor Vinnie had to come in there and drag me out. A cop had pulled in and caught us. Mom had apparently called them when she couldn't find us herself. That was my first ride in a cop car."

First ride? Devan was afraid to ask how many times Veronica had been in a cop car. "Are you sure it was the Cavendar house?"

"Yeah, because the cemetery is catty-cornered to it on Main Street next to Waldings Food market, and then the funeral home is on Mulberry Lane. It has to be the house. Cemetery Lane and Mulberry both dead end in to Main Street. There are no other cemeteries on that side of town."

"We should go check it out. Let's go talk to Nate about it." Devan said getting up from the table.

Meanwhile Kale and Nate were talking in the Smoking Room.

"Any chance you are free tomorrow, so you can show me the funeral home?" Kale asked.

"Yes, I can do that," Nate answered thoughtfully.

"Great! I want to take some pictures. Do you know where those pictures are that show its original state?"

"I do, and since we will be there, I can see if the blue prints are hidden somewhere there as well."

"Why don't you invite Veronica?" Kale suggested.

"Oh, I don't think she would enjoy that."

"Oh puh-lease! Do you not know her? The little Goth girl *not* interested in an old funeral home? Come on, Nate. Get with the program!" Nate chuckled, and Kale went on, "I think she would be interested in anything you said or did. She's clearly into you."

Nate turned red. "Oh I don't know about that—"

Kale laughed, "Really dude? You can't be that dense."

"Okay. I do want to ask her out you know, but I just haven't found the right thing to say."

"It's simple…just say, *Veronica would you like to go to dinner?*"

"I'm certain it has always been effortless for you. It's not as easy for someone like me."

"Here you try—"

"I can't."

"Dude, yes you can. She's not going to say no," Kale tried to assure him.

"That's what Devan said."

"Well there you go. Now repeat after me. Veronica would you like to go to dinner sometime?" Kale coached.

"Veronica, would you like to go to dinner sometime?" Nate repeated.

"Yes! I would love to," a voice said from the doorway.

Both men stood up and turned around to see Devan and Veronica eavesdropping.

"She said *yes.*" Kale whispered.

Nate smiled, "She did, didn't she?"

"Go talk to her." Kale grinned as he gave Nate a small push.

After they took off their costumes and put on their regular clothes, they met up in the foyer. While Nate met with Veronica, Kale approached Devan. "Come on Monty, let's take you home." He walked her to his truck and helped her in.

"Kale, the night is so clear, let's find an open space so we can look at the stars," Devan proposed.

Kale searched for the spot that would give them the best view and pulled in. They watched the stars in the bed of the truck without speaking.

"Kale. Look! A shooting star. Make a wish!" Devan pointed up.

They both closed their eyes and imagined how wonderfully enriched their lives would be if they could just be together. Devan pictured all five of their children running in tall grasses in Hawaii, while she and Kale rocked in a porch swing holding hands watching them.

Kale on the other hand saw Devan pregnant with his child. Even though he knew she didn't want to have anymore children after she had reached the age of thirty, he couldn't help but always want that baby that was half Iakona and half Montgomery. However, he would be very happy adopting her kids as his own. He loved them very much. *One day they will all be mine!* "Do you ever wonder what our kid would look like if we had one?" Kale asked.

Devan opened her eyes and tilted her head towards his. "I think *she* would have your hair, your skin, my nose—"

Kale stopped her, "And what is wrong with *my* nose?"

Devan laughed, "Nothing is wrong with your nose. You asked if I ever thought about what our kid would look like so I'm telling you what I pictured."

"All right, then carry on. As long as you don't hate my nose I think I'll be okay."

Devan rolled her eyes and continued, "She would have my eye shape but your green color. She would have your smile—"

"Okay I think you are wrong."

"Enlighten me, Iakona, what do you think she would look like?"

Kale tugged on his beard. "First, *she* would be a *he*. He would have skin a color in between yours and mine. Looking at my kids, he would probably look more like me feature wise. He would be tall, and handsome."

"Oh, obviously, we'd make a beautiful child," Devan added.

"Exactly! He'd have your blonde hair though, and I think he'd have your blue eyes."

"Really? Why is that?" Devan asked.

"Blue eyes are predominant in your family and my mom's. Mom's side is only half Hawaiian. Her mom was mostly German and had blue eyes. My dad and I are the only ones with green eyes that I know of."

Devan's phone signaled that a text had come in and interrupted their quaint dreamy visions in their heads. Justin needed to leave so he asked Devan to come home. That ended their stargazing. *Of course, Justin had to leave, that's why he was being so nice earlier.* Something didn't sit right with Devan. She'd had the feeling all day that he was up to something.

In the meantime, Nate took Veronica home. When they reached her house, she asked him to come in. She brought him a drink, and they talked for the longest time about the funeral home and the renovations Nate wanted to make. They also discussed Nate's ancestors, and he went into further detail than what he had said on their tour. Veronica was absolutely enthralled. Finally, Nate decided he needed to leave and did just that. As he was driving home, he replayed the evening in his mind. Maybe, just maybe his dreams could come true.

Chapter 6

Kale scanned the ballroom until his eyes had found what they had been searching for his whole life. There she was. Miss Montgomery! Her hair was pulled up in a perfect bun with only a few ringlets hanging elegantly around her *beautiful* face. Her eyes lit up like two stars in the midnight sky when she saw Kale. Miss Montgomery blushed and looked away quickly but not without flashing a bright smile first. His friend, Nate, nudged his elbow.

"That is Miss Montgomery. Her family moved here just last year. She is *my* Veronica's southern cousin," he stated proudly.

"I recommend you introduce yourself. She is quite fair, and her family comes from good stock." Nate disclosed.

A second beautiful young woman with dark hair headed toward them, all but dragging Miss Montgomery behind her.

Kale saw the women approaching the two of them. His hands were getting clammy and sweat started to pool near his brow.

"Good evening, Mr. Iakona and Mr. Cavendar. What a lovely turnout we have," the young woman said. "I am very pleased you both could honor us with your presence. I'd like to introduce my cousin, Miss Devan Marie Montgomery." She shoved the girl forward.

Kale took a step back and admired her beauty. The orchestra played the opening riff of the next song. "I quite enjoy this melody. Would you, Miss

Montgomery, accompany me in a dance?" Kale bowed and held out his hand for her to take. She graciously accepted then he led her out to the floor. He put his free hand on the small of her back, and they began to waltz. They danced round the room, unaware of their surroundings as though a spell had been bestowed upon them. Their eyes never wandered away from each other. When the music came to a halt, Devan curtsied to him. He gave a bow and was about to leave when she grabbed his hand again.

"Follow me," Devan mouthed. They ran out of the ballroom into the long hallway. She looked back and gave him a sly grin.

"Where are we going?" he asked. She let a giggle escape her lips and continued running. Their shoes were loud as they met the marble flooring in the long corridor When they reached the door, Kale realized it wasn't the way he had come in. She flung the door open, and they ran down the stairs. "I ask you again, madam, where are we going?"

"To heaven." Devan ran with him until they found themselves in the middle of the vineyard. She let go of his hand and caressed his cheek. "You sure are a handsome fellow." He stood looking down at her. Devan grabbed ahold of the lapels on the jacket he was wearing and pulled herself close to him. "Miss Montgomery, I hardly think that a woman of your class should be out here alone in the dark with a man she has never met."

"I have known you for a very long time, Mr. Iakona."

"This was the first time we have ever met so how is it possible that you have known me for a very long time?"

"We have met many times over the centuries, my love." She put her hands behind his neck pulling his head close to hers.

Her lips were almost touching his when he said, "You must be mistaken and have me confused with someone else."

Devan pulled him tight kissing him hard and deep. He didn't refuse, nonetheless, he kept his hands to himself for fear they might be seen.

"I must insist, Miss Montgomery. This is highly inappropriate," Kale insisted as he finally pushed her away gently.

She laughed. "I thought my kiss would refresh your memory, sir. It appears I must try harder." Devan took his hands and put them on her waist. She placed her hands on both sides of his face and kissed him again this time with more of a gentle manner, parting his lips gently with hers and whispered, "Do you remember now?" Her hands moved from his face down to his chest, and she rested her head there comfortably. He closed his eyes and put his chin on her head. There was something recognizable about it. "Don't you remember when we got married?"

Kale opened his eyes and investigated his surroundings. He was on the beach and the warm water was washing over his feet. His proper ballroom attire was replaced with a tuxedo, white shirt and a lei. Devan was dressed in a beautiful white wedding gown with peach accents. Glancing around, Kale saw everyone he had ever met sitting, watching the ceremony. "We never got married," he replied dropping his arms. Kale stepped back and the scenery changed again. They were in a high school gymnasium. This was familiar.

Devan placed one hand on his shoulder and the other on his hip. She looked different but the same—younger. As the music played, they danced. He was comfortable with this. "Do you remember now Kale Kai?" Her blue eyes stared up in to his. He held on to her tighter and rested his chin on her head again and closed his eyes. When the song was over, he opened his them. His back was against a large tree. It was green everywhere with grass and trees. Kale saw a tendril out of the corner of his eye. It was the willow tree. Devan moved her head off his chest and gazed up at him. "Kiss me like you have never kissed me before." Kale obliged. When the kiss was over, he opened his eyes. He was in the same place, his arms still embracing Devan, except it was no longer bright outside. The sky was dark and angry. Lightning flashed across the sky and the sound of thunder exploded around them. Kale knew this, and he didn't like it one bit. "Why would you bring me back here to relive this nightmare?"

The downpour drenched them. Devan looked up at him. "I release you Kale Kai Iakona. I release you from my heart and soul." She slowly retreated backwards. The rain froze right where it was. Everything was suspended in time except for them. Devan kept walking backwards.

"Stop, stop this! I don't want to be here," he yelled chasing after her. Kale kept running and the grass grew taller. The trees transformed into mountains, and he could see the waterfall in the distance at his uncle's and aunt's place. Devan dropped to the ground. When he reached her, she held her hand up for him then pulled him down. They faced one another. "Why do you keep running away from me?"

She smiled innocently. "I haven't been running from you, Kale, I have been leading you—leading you to right here where our future lies."

He looked out to see all their kids laughing and playing in the water. He smiled then, but it disappeared. "I know this is just a dream," Kale said sadly as he stood up.

Devan put her hand out and he helped her to her feet. "Maybe it is, on the other hand, don't you want it to be your reality?"

"Devan, you know more than anyone that I have wanted this my whole life."

"What if I told you that you could have everything you desire?"

"I would ask what the catch is."

"There is no catch, just dance with me. Every chance you get, dance with me, and I will always bring you back here." She lifted his hands and they began to waltz again.

Their clothes changed one last time back to what they were originally wearing. The grasses and clear sky turned into the bold beautiful ballroom where they first met. When their eyes locked, they both were taken aback and quit dancing. Devan dropped his hand and grabbed the bottom of her skirt. "I'm sorry, sir, you'll have to excuse me." She ran out of the room, and he followed. This time the hallway didn't end. He ran after her until she vanished into thin air.

Kale bolted upright and checked his phone, "Shit, I'm late."

When he arrived at the café, Nate was there sitting at a table. "I'm sorry, man, I just woke up."

Nate smiled. "You're not late," he said pointing to the clock on the wall. "It's nine fifty-nine."

"Yeah, I'm fifty-nine minutes late."

"No, Kale, you are one minute early. We were supposed to meet at ten o'clock, not nine o'clock. You seem a bit flustered. Are you all right?" Nate appeared genuinely concerned.

"Yeah, sorry. I didn't sleep well. I had a really strange dream."

"Do you remember it?" Nate inquired.

"Yes, I almost always remember my dreams especially when they are about *her!*" Kale let out a huge sigh.

"Devan?" Nate asked even though he already knew the answer.

"Yeah. It's not something I should be admitting to anyone," Kale stated.

Nate thought Kale looked strange. *Perhaps it's a combination of stress, longing and frustration.* Nate could only imagine how he would feel if he were in Kale's shoes. He decided to just be honest with Kale and wanted him to know that he could be trusted. "Kale, it's safe to talk to me. Devan explained a little of how you got to where you guys are now. She didn't go into too much detail, but I can sense that what the two of you have together runs deep."

"What did she tell you?"

Nate told him what Devan had said, and Kale was relieved she didn't tell him *everything*.

"I'd like to hear your side of it though."

"Some other time. It's too damn upsetting," Kale replied, letting out a breath he didn't know he was holding.

"Fair enough, but may I ask one question?"

"Shoot," Kale said then took a drink of his coffee.

"Was it love at first sight?"

"Oh, god no! I don't remember when we met when we were babies, or much about the second time. The third, however," Kale laughed, "was a mutual thing. Let's just say the animosity was very real. Then when we met again, well, after we realized who the other one was, I was a little pissed off at first. I didn't want to like her at all. From what I had remembered she was this snobby little brat with big glasses. She had changed, she was beautiful."

"She still is."

"Oh, she's the most beautiful woman in the world," Kale agreed. "I still swear to this day I fell in love with her that week. I just remember looking deep into those gorgeous blue eyes and wanting never to leave her side. It was weird thinking crazy shit like that when you're just a teenager. Now when I think about it, I bet it was when I rescued her from the water. I just remember it was that moment I felt the need to always protect her."

"How do you feel now?"

Kale started to feel like he was in therapy, all that was missing was Nate holding a note pad and pen and Kale resting on a couch.

"Nate, my man, you are killing me here. I feel the exact same way as I did then. No—that's not true." Kale closed his eyes for a minute, gathering his thoughts then opened them and took a deep breath. "As time goes on and as we get older, I swear I love her more each day. When I look at her, I see the twelve-year old brat that I couldn't stand, the gorgeous blonde teenager, who I fell in love with, and the dark-haired beauty I can't get out of my head and heart no matter how hard I try. I see a wonderful mother, best friend and lover. I see my past, what is, and what could have been." Kale's demeanor changed slightly. "She's that fucking itch that you are only an inch away from reaching, and you know damn well once you get it you will be completely satisfied."

"Do you really think if you could have her your life would be perfect?"

"It would be pretty damn close, my friend," Kale said. He hesitated, undecided if he wanted to say what was on his mind.

Nate was watching him. "What is it, Kale?"

As painful as the memories were, he decided he could tell Nate. "Those three years without her were unbearable. Right now, I'm just so happy that she is within walking distance."

"From the sound of it, that's a perfect analogy." Nate lifted his cup to his lips, his phone signaled that he had a message.

"Veronica?" Kale asked.

Nate checked and nodded with a smile.

"So, how was it to see her after all these years?"

"It's interesting to say the least. Here, one of the girls I had a crush on in high school just kisses me out of the blue. I can't say I never thought about it before. However, I don't consider that our first kiss." Kale gave him an odd look. "As I mentioned before…she was inebriated that night. She probably doesn't even remember it."

"Oh, she's remembers it. I saw that whole thing play out. Listen, if she pretends she doesn't remember, you should just go a long with it. If she's anything like she was in high school, and I have a feeling she is, she is going to keep you on your toes, Mr. Cavendar," a grin spread across Kale's face. He was in a much better mood. Talking to Nate was the right decision.

"That's what I'm hoping for," Nate replied.

⚜

"Hold on guys—I grabbed the wrong keys. I'll be right back." Nate walked down the road to his house while Devan, Veronica and Kale waited patiently. He came back with the keys in one hand and a crow bar in the other. He pried off two boards that were nailed on the door before unlocking it. Nate warned them before opening the door, "I haven't been in here since I was…I honestly don't know…it's been more years than I care to say, and it wasn't in the best shape when I closed it up. Please be very careful and watch where you step."

He tried the doorknob, but the door didn't budge. "Everyone brought a flashlight, right?" he asked as he tried the door again. There was a collective nod, although it wouldn't matter if the door wouldn't move. Nate gave the door a kick and it swung forward. "Home sweet home," he said quietly as they all stepped inside.

The door led to a large room where there were settees, sofas and end tables that were covered over with dusty sheets. Underfoot was a threadbare carpet whose original color could not be discerned under the heavy layer of dirt. Each of the walls was decorated with floral wallpaper that was faded and peeling. There were many rooms branching off the main room.

The old funeral home didn't look as bad as he had led them to believe. It was clear it could use a deep cleaning and a couple of improvements such as new carpet and wallpaper, still it wasn't as bad as it could have been. The most ominous feature of the room was a closed casket, pushed up against the wall farthest from them.

Nate pulled the sheet off a couch and told them to take a seat while he tried to get the lights on. He went to the fuse box and flipped a switch. Only half of the lights switched on, creating an eerie glow. "Well, I suppose we will still need our flashlights." Nate gestured to the flickering bulbs and to the ones that weren't lit at all.

Next, Nate beckoned them to follow him down a dark hallway which led to the basement. The stairs creaked under their weight as they each descended.

"Spooky," Veronica said in a creepy voice behind Kale.

"Yeah, a little more than I like," Kale griped.

Veronica scoffed, "Aw, is the big bad man afraid of the dark?"

"No, I just don't appreciate anything that is death related. You are lucky I like *you*, my little morbid friend," he teased.

Nate turned around and asked, "Considering death is my specialty, are you sure you want to associate with me?"

Nate flipped on a light that lit half of the room in which they were standing. Nothing appeared out of the ordinary. He went to a door and they followed. "This is our storage room." When he opened the door, there was a strong odor of moth balls and a faint scent of gasoline and turpentine mixed together.

"Ugh what is that?" Kale groaned.

"The moth balls or the formaldehyde?" Nate asked.

"I know the moth ball smell. So, I'm guessing the other smell is the formaldehyde," Kale turned up his nose in disgust.

"Yeah, it's not exactly pleasant, and you only had a hint of some old stuff. I will gladly open a new container for you. It will clear your sinuses in two seconds flat!"

"Oh, I'm good, thanks for the offer though. Ugh, how do you work with that stuff?"

"You get used to it after a while," Nate chuckled.

They walked in the pathway which led to another door that had a padlock on it. Nate pulled the keys out of his pocket and unlocked the lock. When he opened the door, Kale and the girls gasped. Caskets lined the walls. "Relax guys it's just another storage room. I assure you, there are no corpses in this building other than maybe a small rodent or two."

Nate led the way to the back of the room where there was another door with a padlock. He forced the door after getting the padlock off. Thick cobwebs lined the doorway and a musty, stale cigar smell overwhelmed them. "I have only been in here once, many years ago, when Dad was searching for something. I may have been about four years old. So, I am unsure of what we will see."

He went over to a window and tugged on the boards with the crowbar. "Kale, would you mind giving me a hand?" Together they pried off the pieces of wood to let light in.

"It looks better with more light in here," Kale remarked as he cast the last one to the floor by the window.

"At one point the whole building needed new electricity. My grandfather decided to only replace the wires on the other side. Then he closed this side off completely since it hadn't been used in many years, and he didn't feel it was needed at the time."

Devan looked at Nate with curiosity in her eyes. "Wait. I could have sworn when we worked on that 8th grade report together, that he had lived on this side of the building."

"No. That was my great-great-granddad. He stopped living there in 1910, when he built the house that I live in. However, he would still use the office until about 1915."

"So, no one has lived here since then?" Kale asked.

"My grandfather made an apartment, for a time, upstairs on the side where we just were. I lived there for a few years before my dad died. After he passed, I moved back in with my mom. I didn't want her to be alone." A brief look of sadness crossed his face.

There was a bookshelf filled with old dusty books. In the corner of the room was an 1870s colonial rolltop desk open with papers scattered across it. Nate went over to it and searched through a few drawers for the blue prints. "Feel free to take a glimpse around if you want," Nate suggested. "Just be cautious." He reminded them as an afterthought.

Devan decided to sit down on a couch-like chair and take in her surroundings before going anywhere else. As she sat, the dust that covered the piece of furniture quickly turned into a cloud right above her head, causing her to cough. Devan had seen the couch-like piece of furniture before but had no idea what it was named.

"Nate, what is this called?"

Nate glanced over to where she was. "Oh, that is a Victorian Lady's fainting chaise."

"Seriously? Why in the world would someone give a horrible name like that to such an exquisite piece of furniture?" she wondered.

"People would have pieces of furniture available just in case someone would faint. Some people even had fainting rooms. It was a very different time."

"Why would they faint?" Kale questioned.

"My guess is it was the heat or their corsets. Corsets would be pulled considerably tight which would result in limited blood flow."

"Oh, that must have been what the lady, who helped us get dressed, was referring to yesterday when she said it could cause health problems."

"Yes. If the corset was laced too tight it would have reduced lung capacity, possibly change the shape of your ribs, weaken the back and chest muscles and reduce pelvic size. That would be a bad thing because cesareans were not much of a choice when it came to giving birth. There were multiple digestive and other reproductive issues, including miscarriage, according to my great-great-great-great-uncle's documentations. They had maternity corsets and corsets for men as well."

"You're kidding!" Devan was shocked.

"No, it was as absurd as it sounds. Even pregnant the woman wanted to have the appearance of a very trim waist."

Devan shuddered at the thought and then wondered about the men. "What about the guys though?"

"They wanted smooth silhouettes like the women. It was all part of the fashion. From my understanding, though, not many men wore them."

Devan had more questions but decided to save them for another time. Though Nate was happy to answer her, she could tell he was focused on finding what he needed, and she didn't want to distract him more.

Kale was across the room near a small table. "What's this thing?" He picked up a type of stainless-steel instrument.

"That is a mouth closer. It does exactly what its name suggests. Morticians used it to close the deceased person's mouth."

As soon as Kale heard 'deceased' he set it back on the desk and wiped his hands on his pants while grimacing.

Nate laughed and went over and picked it up. "See, these two prongs were placed into the nostrils and the sliding adjustment piece was slid under the jaw. The mortician would then screw the device closed shutting the person's mouth. It was left there until the body's tissue became firm enough for the mouth to remain closed while the embalming was completed. I promise, it has been sterilized."

Veronica came running in from another room. "Look! Just look at what I found! 'Titanic, Giant White Star Liner, Sinks After Collision with Iceberg on Her Maiden Voyage.' 1800 lives are reported lost in the world's greatest marine disaster. This is dated Tuesday, April 16, 1912."

"Oh my god, that has to be an original!" Devan exclaimed snatching it out of her hands.

"I'm sure it is," Nate replied with certainty.

"Dude, that's at least worth $400," Kale commented.

"There are probably a lot of things in here that I'm sure are worth a pretty penny these days," Nate said while shuffling papers.

"You can have it if you'd like," he told Veronica.

"I could never take it, but I do want to look at it. Kale is right you could sell it to help pay for the renovations. I have only been in two of these rooms, and I think you could make several thousand dollars with the antiques I have seen." Veronica stopped and looked around at the different artifacts before going on. "Personally, I don't think I could part with most of it if I was in your shoes."

"I think you have a great idea there. It is something we could discuss over that dinner. Are you available Wednesday at six o'clock? That's my early day."

"Yes," Veronica responded immediately.

Nate remembered Kale and Devan were there and dipped his head. "I'm terribly sorry. Where are my manners?" he chastised himself. "Devan and Kale, would you want to join us that evening?"

"Oh no, thank you. We already have plans with an old friend that afternoon." Kale said.

"Well, all right." Nate conceded after making sure that Kale wasn't trying to pull the wool over his eyes because he felt like they would be intruding. Not to say it would have been bad even if he had been lying about it, either way, he would have Veronica all to himself. "Veronica, you're more than welcome to the paper, my dear. I think you would enjoy it more than anyone I could sell it to." He smiled warmly at her.

She sat down next to Devan with a huge grin on her face.

"He called you dear," Devan whispered.

"I know."

Devan giggled. It was so cute to see Veronica in love, and Devan didn't even question if it was infatuation.

"Kale, when are you going back home?" Veronica wondered.

"Friday, unless they change the date on the orders for my deliveries."

"Well, why don't you tell Jeane they changed the orders, and then you stay until Sunday?"

He turned around. "Why, what is so special about this weekend?"

"It's her birthday weekend." Devan told him.

"It's your birthday?" Nate asked.

"Well, not until Monday, but I saw a flyer for a Halloween party at the Urban Myth for Saturday. I would like to go out and celebrate, and I would love it if the three of you, Maggie, Pete and Kristy would come too."

Nate got up and walked over to Veronica. "Your birthday is on Samhain?"

"For the last 32 years," she smiled.

"What is Samhain?" Kale asked.

"It is the pagan holiday that marks the end of the harvest season," Nate answered.

To Kale it sounded like a foreign language, and Devan could see it all over his face.

"It is also known as Halloween," Devan piped up.

"My birthday is March 20th," Nate mentioned to Veronica.

"Ostara!" She exclaimed.

"That's right. Also known as the Spring Equinox," he said for Kale's benefit.

Kale still had no clue as to what they were talking about.

"It's another Pagan holiday," Devan noted in a hushed tone.

Kale stood up. "This is very interesting and all and I don't want to be rude, but I'm starving. Would you guys want to go grab some grub when we are done in here?"

"Why don't you guys come back to my house? Mom will be dropping off the kids soon, and I have a full fridge," Devan suggested.

At Devan's house while they were preparing lunch, Devan spoke quietly to Veronica, "You are so in love with him."

"Oh stop. I just really like him," she paused, "a lot!"

"Yeah—you like him so much. You are in love, just admit it."

Veronica swung her chair around. "Okay, maybe—no it's not possible." Love has never really existed for me—"

"Yes, Roni, it is possible."

"I haven't even gone out on a date with him yet."

"Maybe not, still you should see the way you look at him. The spark in your eyes when he is around is amazing. He's compassionate, and yesterday he exhibited his intelligence. He is sweet, and you could consider the fact that he is a mortician is a little on the dark side. I'd be willing to bet he'd take a stroll with you in a cemetery anytime you asked. Aren't those on your perfect man list?" Devan pointed out, repeating all the qualities Veronica had mentioned to Devan while describing her "dream man". Veronica couldn't do anything but smile. Everything Devan was saying was true.

"Uncle Kale!" The kids were home. Kale walked in the kitchen with one kid hanging on his arm and the other tagging behind.

"Your children have arrived, madam," Kale commented as if she didn't hear them.

"I see that," The kids didn't even say hello to her. They were both so very excited that Kale was there.

"I think I know what you are talking about," Veronica said to Devan. "I bet it's the same thing I see with you and Kale."

"Oh, you hush."

After lunch Cyrus begged Kale to play with him outside, while Callie decided to stay indoors. She was fascinated by Nate.

"You are taller than my Uncle Kale, and I've never met anyone taller than him—ever! What is your full name Mr. Nate?"

"Nathaniel Cavendar, what's yours?"

"Calista Jameson. What's your favorite color?"

"I don't really have one, I like them all. What is your favorite color?"

Calista had to think then bellowed, "Pink, purple, blue, green—I guess I like them all too. What do you do at work?"

Devan walked in. "Callie, give the man some space, please. You are practically sitting on him."

"He doesn't care," she shrugged and squeezed in closer than she was before, if that was even possible. Veronica was getting a kick out of it.

"It's fine, Devan, I don't mind at all. I'm enjoying her inquisitive mind."

"Anyway, before I was rudely interrupted," Calista sneered at her mother, "I asked, what do you do at work?"

Nate looked at Devan with a raised eyebrow as if to ask permission to tell her daughter what his profession was. Devan smiled and nodded. She sat down and eagerly awaited her daughter's reaction.

"I am a mortician also known as an undertaker."

"What do you take under?"

"Well, Miss Calista, when a person dies, they go to a place where they are cleaned up and prepared for viewing. The people who work there make them look nice for their friends and family. It helps the loved ones of that person to say goodbye to them for their everlasting rest."

"So, you help dead people, and you help their family and friends."

Nate smiled at her. "That is a lovely way to think of it."

Veronica and Devan took a seat in the living room and continued to listen to Callie ask Nate all sorts of questions. Both women were impressed at how well he handled children. One more thing Veronica could add to her list.

Chapter 7

On Tuesday, Veronica invited Devan over after she got off work. Veronica had three crates sitting outside her door. Devan did a double take. "Um, Roni. What exactly are we doing today?" She gestured to the crate that said embalming fluid on it in faded, chipped black letters.

"Ha, don't get your panties in a bunch." Veronica aimed the shovel at the packaging that was sticking out with the plastic showing tulips on it and she explained, "It's full of tulip bulbs. All the crates are, with the exception of that one." She pointed at the crate near Devan's feet. "That beauty is special, it has daffodil bulbs. I ordered it from eBay from a funeral home in Chicago that was closing." Veronica picked up a crate and carried it over to the flowerbed.

"*Of course,* you did. Was this a purchase before or after Nate came back in to your life?"

"Truthfully, I've had it over a year," Veronica confessed shooting her a look.

"Listen, I don't even need you to help me plant. I just wanted someone to talk to while I did this and *maybe* wanted some advice about my date tomorrow."

Devan's face gave away her doubt. She did not believe Veronica one bit. "You need advice about a date?"

"Yes. I haven't been on one in ages, and I want to make a good impression. I mean—I'm really nervous. There I said it," Veronica admitted as she pulled out several bulbs.

"Okay, it's pretty easy. All you need to do is be yourself. He's going to like you for who you are."

"But being myself often scares people away—"

Devan interrupted her, "Oh please, Roni, you aren't as scary as you think you are."

"I disagree. I have scared away every guy that I have ever been out with."

Devan rolled her eyes at Veronica's statement and noted, "I think you are giving yourself way too much credit. You have just had terrible luck in that department. From the sounds of it your ex was a real winner, after all he slept with that slut, Desiree." Veronica nodded in agreement. Devan continued, "Dare I say the name Jasper?"

"No, no, I see what you are getting at." Veronica's phone vibrated. "Oh damn, Urban Myth is closed until further notice. A pipe broke and flooded the bar. Guess my birthday is canceled."

"Okay so let's figure out what else we can do," Devan proposed. She knew Veronica was looking forward to enjoying her birthday with her friends.

"Well, Saturday, my Grandma VonStross is coming in and we are having a big family dinner. She does this every year for Vinnie and me. Maybe this year, we will just need to get an extra table."

"I don't think we should impose on your family plans. We can do something another day." Devan remembered the way Veronica had talked about the woman when they were young. She was afraid of her. "Besides, isn't she the woman you hated and were scared to death of as a kid?"

Veronica chuckled. "I never hated her. I was a little afraid of her, then that all subsided when my parents made me go stay at her huge house when we were in middle school. We bonded then. She is a spitfire of a woman, but her heart isn't as dead as she wants everyone to believe it is. However, I'm pretty sure my scariness was inherited from her. After all she's been widowed five times. I'm convinced she frightened them all to death."

"And you want your friends to be near her?" Devan folded her arms over her chest and stared at the eerie crate.

Veronica peered up at her, hands covered in the black dirt from the flower bed. "No, it's decided. You are coming. I will call her and let her know that there will be extras." Veronica gestured towards the second crate. "Will you please throw me some bulbs?"

Devan bent down, opened the embalming crate, tossed a few tulip bulbs her way and hissed, "Okay, although it may end up being your funeral not your birthday."

Veronica took one look at her and laughed, "Well it's a good thing I'm inviting Nate then."

That Wednesday Kale and Devan went to pay Miss Jenkins, their former high school teacher, a visit. They knocked on the door as Devan held a basket with an assortment of muffins. Miss Jenkins answered the door with open arms. She invited them in and they sat down to an antique walnut table. Alison asked them what they were up to and what had happened in their lives until now. They told her without all the depressing details.

"Who is that?" Devan pointed at a picture of a young woman on the wall.

"Oh, that's Billie, my daughter. Her name is actually Wilamena. She's almost done with college, nevertheless I'm not ready for her to leave," Alison sighed.

Kale kept staring at the picture. The girl seemed familiar, but he just couldn't put his finger on why.

"I didn't know you had a daughter," Devan replied, her surprise evident.

"Well, I'm a single mom. It's not something teachers wish their students to know. Plus, the school board would most likely frown on it."

"Why? Being a single parent is heroic," Devan quipped.

"It sets a bad example because I was a young unmarried parent."

"That's crap," Kale mumbled still trying to figure out the picture.

"Billie is my everything; the very breath of my life. You kids will meet her soon. She should be coming home from school in a few minutes. Tell me more about your kids."

They talked about their children until Billie walked in. "Hello, I'm Wilamena," she introduced herself.

Kale stood up and shook her hand. He leaned down and stared in her eyes. He knew these eyes. He did. Kale couldn't quit looking at her. Devan could tell the poor girl was getting uncomfortable. She nudged him and whispered. "Stop staring. You are freaking her out."

"I'm sorry. You just really look like someone I know," he told Billie.

"Well, she resembles me when I was her age, except she has her father's eyes."

Kale glanced at the picture and then back at Wilamena, then at Miss Jenkins.

"Did you ever marry?" he inquired knowing it was none of his business. Kale had a hunch, and he was determined to find out whether or not he was right.

"No, I didn't. Billie, will you go get the mail?" She left the room and Miss Jenkins began to talk. "Her dad wanted nothing to do with us when he found out I was pregnant. He lives in another state. I went off to college after the summer when I saw him last, and I found out I was pregnant. I wrote him a letter. We didn't have cell phones or email back in that day," she reflected. "I never heard back from him, but I kept sending him letters and pictures of her until I graduated college and got a job and my own place. Then I gave up."

"I am so sorry," Devan said.

"Me too. I loved him with all my heart."

Kale jumped up. "Oh my god! Will you excuse us for a minute?" He pulled Devan out of the room. "I know why her daughter looks familiar."

"Okay."

"Monty, check out the picture on the wall."

"Okay," she agreed as she directed her attention to the portrait.

"Imagine her with poofy dark hair."

Devan squinted at Kale. "Okay, but I'm not sure what you are getting at."

"I don't want to spell it out..."

She looked again for what seemed like an eternity to Kale.

"Remember the locket? The dude, Will, at the marina—he's her dad."

"Come on Kale, that's really farfetched. You must not have gotten enough sleep last night."

"No, it is her. I can feel it in my blood." He walked back in the room. "Miss Jenkins?"

Devan grabbed his arm, "Don't do this," she begged under her breath. "Please call me Alison."

"Alison, what's her dad's name?" he demanded.

"William," Alison forced out.

"And he goes by Will?" Kale's eyes got huge.

"Yes."

"Did he work at a marina?"

"Yes. What is this? You are scaring me," Alison stammered.

Oh my god he's right, Devan thought to herself.

"He never received your letters," he said putting his hand softly on her shoulder.

She almost dropped her coffee cup. "How would you know that?"

"I know him. Did you have a locket with a picture of the two of you, a long time ago?" he went on.

"This is too intense. I don't know if I can handle this."

"Yes or no?" Kale asked sternly.

"Y…Yes," she stuttered.

"We found the locket at the lake a few years ago. He never got your letters and apparently you never got his."

Kale sat and explained everything to Alison. By the time he was done she was sobbing. "I'm sorry, I wasn't trying to hurt you."

"Kale, you didn't hurt me. You gave me something I haven't felt in a long time…hope!"

"Do you want me to call him? Please let me call him."

"Yes, but don't let him know I'm here. And don't mention Billie."

He took his phone and called the marina. He asked if Will was still working there, and the person on the phone must have said it was him.

"Hey, man, it's Kale from a few years ago. You called me Stretch."

"Kale, that means the man and not the vegetable, right?" Will questioned.

"Yeah, that's the one."

"Are you calling to make reservations? We'd love to have you guys back."

"Not yet. I'm calling for a different reason. That story you told me about Alison, was her last name Jenkins?"

The phone was silent for a moment until he heard Will's quivering voice on the line.

"Yes."

"I need to tell you something," Kale stepped outside. "Dude, she never got your letters, and she never got married."

"How..."

"I just became her neighbor, and I put two and two together." Kale was too excited.

"This is not a funny joke, Kale."

"No, Will, it isn't. I would never joke about something like this," Kale spoke in a serious manner.

"Is she there? Can I talk to her?"

Kale walked back in the house and handed the phone to Alison. "I can't," she mouthed.

"Please, Alison, he deserves to hear your story as you do his." Kale begged.

She took the phone reluctantly and a tiny 'hello' escaped her lips while tears streamed down her face.

Kale grabbed Devan's hand and took her outside.

"What just happened?" she uttered completely dumbfounded.

"Remember before you hated me on our trip to the lake in 2008?"

Devan sighed, "I never hated you Kale."

"Well, you know that guy, Will, who is at the marina? I gave him the locket we found, and the next morning he told me this sad story about his first love. They had something really special for a few summers. Then one year he wrote her and called her, and he never heard back from her. He stayed single all these years, and he never knew what happened to her—until now."

Devan knew the story. Will had told her himself while trying to make a point about her and Kale, but Kale didn't need to know that.

That Friday, Devan met Kale at the car rental place to pick him up. "Are you sure you can drop me off at the airport tomorrow?" Kale asked struggling to get in the car.

"Yes, I wouldn't have offered if I couldn't. And I'm sorry, Justin took the SUV before I had a chance to tell him to take his own car. I know how you hate anything smaller than a truck with a lift kit." Devan tried not to giggle at him though she was quite amused.

"It doesn't have to be that big, it just can't be this small. Listen, you try being six-foot-five and squeezing into a Miata. Not fun." Kale grumbled, then he realized how ungrateful he sounded. "But, I do appreciate the ride and the extra time I get to spend with you."

Devan blushed because she enjoyed the extra time with him too, even though she knew she shouldn't. Devan turned to smile at him then remembered something.

"Oh, I need to give you fair warning about Roni's grandmother."

"Warning?"

"She's a bit abrasive." Devan tried to sound more informative than rude.

Kale laughed, "Like my grandpa?"

"Kale, I said abrasive, not amusing."

"Oh, she can't be that bad. If she's anything similar to Roni, I can handle her." Neither one of them had any idea what was waiting for them when they arrived at Veronica's party.

Mrs. VonStross had rented out the banquet hall in the fanciest Italian restaurant in town. Devan walked in first and Kale was behind her with his hand on her back. Veronica had them sit down and continued greeting a few more people. An average height woman who was well dressed sat down next to Devan. Her hair was a light auburn color. It was undeniable that she knew how to accentuate her own natural beauty, complimenting her fair complexion with make-up.

"Hello, I'm Antoinette, Veronica's grandmother." She extended her hand to Devan who was trying not show her nervousness.

"Pleased to meet you ma'am. I'm Devan and this is Kale." He reached across to shake her hand.

"So, the infamous Devan. It's nice to finally put a face with a name. I have heard about you since you were a small girl. It's a pleasure to meet you and your husband— and please don't call me ma'am."

"Oh, we aren't married. I mean, we aren't married to each other. We are—close friends. Our spouses are together. They are always together. Well, they are partners." Devan shook her head with disbelief at her own words. Kale sat back and enjoyed her explanation with a wide grin on his face. Devan's nervousness was showing by way of her explanation about hers and Kale's complicated relationships with their spouses.

"We were both invited and decided to come together, ma'am" Kale spoke for her.

"Pish posh, you are trying to pull the wool over this old woman's eyes. Close friends my ass—and don't call me ma'am."

"I'm sorry ma—Mrs. VonStross," Kale apologized. Devan wondered if Veronica had mentioned anything to her about their relationship. She didn't think she would have. Veronica had been known to keep her mouth shut.

Veronica came over to introduce her friends to her grandmother.

"You are too late, my dear. I already introduced myself," Antoinette huffed.

"I'm sorry, Grandmother." Veronica fixated her eyes on her feet, expecting her grandmother to be ashamed of her for not remembering her manners.

"It's fine as long as you are being a good host. I taught you the proper rules of etiquette long ago, and I trust that you use them." She patted Veronica's hand twice and directed her eyes towards Devan. "Now, while your friends are polite, I don't appreciate being lied to."

"What?" Veronica was confused.

"Kale and Devan here, claim to be nothing more than friends, and you know personally that I can spot a lie a mile away," Antoinette said with her nose curled up as though something foul had passed beneath it.

Veronica rolled her eyes. "Grandmother, their relationship is their business and not yours. Please be respectful to my friends." She gave Devan and Kale an apologetic look.

"My granddaughter is correct, and I apologize for being rude." Her gaze on them hardened. "I was merely stating the *obvious*. However, if you insist on lying to others and lying to yourselves, you might want to change your actions." Antoinette paused then pointed at Kale. "You, sir, stare at her too long, and you, miss," she turned towards Devan, "lean in too close to him.

Don't put your hand on the small of her back when walking in to the room. It completely gives the impression that there is clearly something more than the platonic facade you are trying to display."

"*Grandma*, stop!" Veronica gritted her teeth to keep the other words from coming out that were begging to be spoken. "Grandma, please!"

Antoinette put her hands on her hips. "If you insist on addressing me in a less formal tone then call me Antoinette. Hell, even call me Toni. Do not insult me with that horrendous word. You make me sound like a plump, petite woman who does nothing but bake sweets all day and then gorges herself on them," she snapped.

"Like my mom's mom right?"

"Oh god, there is another one?" Kale fretted to Devan in as low a voice as he could.

"Don't worry, that one is more people friendly," Devan whispered back.

Antoinette glanced over at Devan and Kale as though they were being disruptive children before turning back to Veronica. "Now, I never said Gianna was anything like that, but she was a wonderful cook with a very pleasant personality. That woman could make baklava as if it came from the heavens above."

Veronica was angry, she leaned in close to Antoinette and her voice sounded close to a hiss to Devan. "You know she is alive, right? I suggest you not speak of her in a past tense—she will be here shortly. *She* is the one who made my birthday cake." Veronica pulled away and stepped back from Antoinette. "Just an FYI baklava is not Italian. She learned to make that just for *you* because you told her your mom use to make it all the time."

A short round olive-skinned woman arrived seconds after Veronica had jumped down Antoinette's throat. Her thick black hair was cut short. She had rosy cheeks and dark eyes that smiled. It was Gianna Biasella, Veronica's maternal grandmother.

Her arms were full of boxes. She set the boxes down on the table and opened each one. Devan went over and peeked inside. There were cannoli, biscotti, tiramisu, and other delightful Italian pastries that made her mouth water. "Vincent, would you please get the cake from my car?" Gianna asked her grandson in her broken English accent. She then walked straight over to Veronica and wrapped her arms around her.

"Happy birthday my *ragazza dolce*."

When Gianna released her arms from her, Veronica turned to Devan and Kale.

"*Ragazza dolce* means sweet girl," Veronica explained to them. She knew her friends were not familiar with the Italian language. "*Nonna*, these are my friends, Devan and Kale. Devan, Kale, this is my *Nonna*, Gianna."

Gianna took Kale's one hand, and Devan's one hand and squeezed them between hers. "Call me Nonna Ginny."

Gianna went to Antoinette and grabbed her hand next. "*Ciao*, Antoinette. You look *belissimo* as always." Antoinette's previous attitude seemed to lessen. "I brought two jars of my special salsa for you, and a box of baklava."

Antoinette smiled for the first time that day. Devan couldn't help but wonder if it was the only time that sour woman had ever smiled in her life.

"Oh, Ginny, you have always been so good to me. Thank you very much."

Mrs. VonStross can be nice!

"I thought she was Italian, not Mexican," Kale muttered to Veronica.

"Sause in Italian is *salsa*," Veronica assured.

"I didn't know you could speak Italian," Devan was surprised.

"I can't. I only know a few phrases and words."

Appetizers were being served when Nate came in carrying five bouquets. He handed one bouquet of mixed flowers to Devan, and the second to Maggie. They were rich harvest colors with red roses, orange lilies and yellow poms. The three remaining bouquets were made up of white roses, pink tiger lilies, and white daisies.

He handed one to Giulia, Veronica's mom. "It is nice to see you again, Mrs. VonStross." He took her hand and gave it a kiss like a gentleman of old.

"Why, thank you, Nathaniel," Giulia gushed, surprised.

He walked over to Gianna towering over her by at least two feet. "*Sono molto lieto di incontrarti, signora Biasella. Mi chiamo*, Nathaniel Cavendar," he stated as he handed a bouquet to her. She looked over at Veronica with big eyes and a smile to match.

"*Alto scuro e bello!*" Gianna exclaimed.

"*Nonna*, I know *bello* is handsome but what else did you say?"

Gianna put her hand on Nate's chest, that was as far as she could reach.

"*Alto*—tall, *scuro*—dark," she motioned for Nate to bend down and he did.

Gianna put her hands on each side of his face, "*Bello*—handsome." She kissed each of his cheeks. "*Amore* eh?"

"*Nonna*, stop embarrassing me."

"*Sì!*" Gianna chuckled and let Nate go.

He then handed the last bouquet to Antoinette. "I am very pleased to meet you, Mrs. VonStross. My name is Nathaniel Cavendar."

"Why, thank you. What did you say to Gianna, and where did you learn to speak Italian? Speaking another language is commendable. You must be quite intelligent," Antoinette commented.

"I have picked up a few things over the years due to work. I said that I was very pleased to meet her and that my name is Nathaniel Cavendar, the same as I said to you."

"Might I ask, son, what is your occupation?"

"I am a mortician, ma'am."

The room was silent as everyone watched for Antoinette's response. She smiled at him, "That is a noble profession, Nathaniel, but if you call me ma'am again, we are going to have some words. Do you understand?"

"Yes madame." Nate replied.

"Oh, for Christ's sake, son, call me Antoinette, please." She almost laughed which surprised all who were there.

"If you will please excuse me I have to go back out to my car. I will return momentarily." He walked out and came back in with a stunning large arrangement of sunflowers that were all shapes and sizes with an occasional red rose peeking out between the brown and yellow. Nate handed them to Veronica and kissed her cheek. "Happy early birthday, Veronica."

Veronica set the flowers down on the table in front of her and hugged him tight and reached up and placed her lips lightly on his cheek. A heartfelt smile reached across his face. "They are gorgeous, thank you so much. Major brownie points for the flowers to all the ladies," she said in his ear.

"Well he makes quite an entrance, doesn't he?" Antoinette said to Vinnie.

"He sure does." Maggie answered for him.

"I wonder if those flowers are left over from a funeral?" Vinnie joked.

Antoinette smacked his arm with her purse and Devan couldn't help giggling. Antoinette shot a disapproving look towards her.

"I'm so sorry, Mrs. VonStross. Nate would never do anything like that at all. It was tastelessly funny though, and I bet you yourself are trying not to laugh."

She turned to Devan, "I suppose you are right." The ends of Antoinette's mouth turned upwards creating a beautiful smile.

Chapter 8

Kale handed his ticket to the lady across the desk. Devan joined him at his side.

"You are at gate five, Mr. Iakona," the lady at the counter called out from behind them.

"Do you remember the last time you brought me to the airport?" His eyes were gleaming.

"It was the day after Prom, Spring of 1997. Your parents let me tag along so I could say goodbye before you went back to college," she recalled.

"An—d?" He prompted, causing her to think back farther.

At the airport he said goodbye to his parents and asked Devan to walk him to the gate. "I'll see you in a few short weeks," he said, swooping her into his arms. She wrapped herself around him and they shared a long, intimate kiss that made the stewardess walking by, blush.

"We'll finish this later," he promised.

As he walked away, she whispered, "I love you."

"Well, do you remember?" he questioned, draping his arms around her. They held each other for longer than they should have. Then she gave him an ornery grin. "Yeah, that's not going to happen." He pulled away from her, though his hands grasped her upper arms and his eyes met hers. She saw the twinkle in his eyes that always made her blush and a smile crept across his face. "Are you sure that can't happen now?" Kale inquired.

She wanted it to. She wanted it badly. If only they could go back in time to that exact moment over a decade ago, Devan might not have ever let him go. Knowing how everything transpired, no she wouldn't let him go. Devan would have declared her love right then and there. The whole damn airport would have known that Devan Montgomery was madly, truly, deeply in love with Kale Iakona. She could feel the butterflies in her stomach now just remembering how that kiss felt. She raised up on her toes. Her lips were a mere few inches away from his. They looked good. Hell, they always looked good. Devan veered her head and her lips landed on his cheek. Kale was disappointed, yet he wasn't about to let it show. He had a plan of his own. He let her go and picked up his bag.

"All right, Monty, I'll see you soon. Thank you again for the ride." He walked to security check point and waved. She hated seeing him go but was so glad that he was coming back in a few weeks.

No sooner had she turned to leave when someone grabbed her hand. "I forgot something," Kale pulled her to him and kissed her on the lips. "I know what I promised in Hawaii, but I also made a promise to myself that I would never again leave the state that you were in without you, or at least without giving you a peck. Guess the peck will have to do this time around." He let go of her and ran back to get in line. "Love you, Monty!"

"Love you, too!" she said back though he could no longer hear. Devan was confident, though, that he knew she loved him too.

November 2011

Two weeks later, someone knocked on Devan's door. When she opened it, she saw Alison Jenkins standing there with a conflicted look.

"What's wrong?"

"May I come in?" Alison asked. Devan stepped aside and allowed her to enter.

"What's up?"

"Will wants to come up and see me *soon*. Please say you and Kale will be there when he does. Please, Devan?"

Devan breathed a sigh of relief. She was worried something awful had happened, but the plea had shocked her somewhat.

"Shouldn't Wilemina be there instead of us?" Devan proposed.

"I didn't tell him about her yet. I thought it would be best to do that in person."

"I would be more than happy to support you by being there. I can't speak for Kale because he is out of town and won't be back for another week or so," she informed Alison.

"Well if he isn't available that's okay as long as you will be there."

"Of course!" Devan gave her a hug.

Alison had tears in her eyes. "You have no idea what you two have done for this former teacher of yours."

"What did your parents say about all this?" Devan was too curious for her own good.

Alison's face sank. "Well, I figured they would be happy for me. I mean, they seemed morose for me all those years ago, but—they weren't."

Devan's face gave way to her embarrassment. "Oh. I am sorry, I shouldn't have asked." she mumbled.

Alison shook her head and took Devan's hand. "I was surprised too. Then, I found out about the calls he had made. They were mostly intercepted by my mother. I'm assuming the same happened with the letters."

"What!" Devan couldn't hold in her anger, "How could she have done that to you?"

"I don't know, yet she managed to get my dad to support her efforts as well. So, instead of asking why, how, or when, I just left. I don't even think I want to know their answers because, at this point, the damage is done." Alison's eyes locked on Devan's. "What I know is I was deceived and hurt by my own flesh and blood. I could have had Will in my life, all this time." There, she stopped and sniffled.

"My cold dead heart could have been alive and beating for the true love I mourned for all these years. However, that was taken from me by the appalling people I have called my parents." Tears rolled down her cheeks.

Devan grabbed her a box of tissues and knelt down in front of Alison and clasped her hand. "I am so very sorry." Devan choked on her words, the emotions getting the best of her. She swallowed hard. "I have faith though, that it will all work out for you guys."

Alison tried to smile, but it came off as halfhearted. Devan let go of her hand and sat down next to her on the couch again. "Did you tell Billie anything?"

"Yes, I told her as soon as you guys left the other day. She finally got the whole story, and she cannot wait to meet him. I just hope that he will be as excited when he meets her." Worry lines set into Alison's face.

"Oh, I have met this man of yours, and I can promise you, he will be over the moon."

That evening Devan pulled up the story she had started writing in Hawaii and went straight to the chapter where they had met Will officially. She sat back and stared at the screen remembering everything that occurred that summer. The good, the bad, the ugly and the almost. Devan scrolled up to the first chapter and stayed up reading most of the night. All the old feelings and memories struck her just as hard as they had the night she wrote it. She wished she could be totally happy for Will and Alison, still, part of her was jealous about it, wishing it were hers and Kale's happily ever after.

⁂

The move went smoothly for Kale. In another week Jeane and the kids would be there. Almost everything was ready for them thanks to the Montgomerys, Kale's parents, and his friends who all lent a hand. He had made it back in time and was able to pick up Devan and Alison. They drove to the designated meeting place, walked into the diner and waited for Will to show. When Will came in he spotted Kale right away. Kale got up and let him in the booth.

Will studied Alison and put his hand to his mouth. "You are just as beautiful if not even more than what I remember." He took her hand and placed something in it.

She looked down and saw the locket. Her eyes teared up.

"I lost this—over twenty years ago."

"These two found it the summer of 2008," he said.

"How is that even possible? You know they were my students, right?"

"No—"

"Sorry, man, I didn't have time to go into all that," Kale confessed.

"I had a feeling about Kale and Devan the day I gave them a detention. There was just something special about these two, but never in a million years would I have thought they would lead me back to you."

Devan could see the happiness mixed with anguish on Alison's face.

"Um—I have something I need to tell you that I didn't say on the phone. I have a daughter," Alison blurted out.

"Super! I would love to meet her," he exclaimed.

"That's not all," Alison babbled. Explaining everything to Will so was important to her. She had to do it now while Devan and Kale were still there for support. Alison took a deep breath, "A few months after we got home from the lake that last year, I found out I was pregnant," she paused and took a deep breath.

His eyes began to water. "You mean—are you saying I have a child?"

"Well, she turned twenty-two a few months ago. Her name is Wilamena. I call her Billie," Alison gushed.

"You used to call me Billy," Will almost whispered. He looked at Kale with tears in the corners of his eyes. "I'm a father..."

Kale put his hand on Will's shoulder. "Congratulations!"

"Does she know about me?" he asked.

"I told her about you when I found out the whole story. She can't wait to meet you."

"She knows I'm not a bad guy, right? She knows that I didn't know any-thing about her?" Alison nodded. "Oh my god, it doesn't get better than this. I reunite with my one true love, *and* I'm a father?" His shock and excitement at the news filled the air around them.

Kale got up abruptly, and Devan did as well. Alison and Will got out of the booth and hugged and kissed and cried. They held each other for a long time. Devan and Kale sat down on the same side of the booth, so Alison and Will could sit together. They just stared at one another, afraid to look away.

"I have never been this happy in all my life," Will finally confessed as he grabbed Kale's hand. "Thank you." Kale shook his hand and nodded.

"And thank you," Alison clutched Devan's hand with tears streaming down her face again. "I'm so sorry. I can't contain these emotions, and I'm not even a crier. It's just been so long since I have felt anything like this."

Devan put her other hand over Alison's as her own eyes stung with tears. "I am so happy for you both."

After they were done eating, Kale asked if Will had a place to stay.

"Yes, he does," Alison vowed taking Will's hand. He kissed her.

"Well, I'm going to go pay the bill and you can show this gentleman how to get there," Kale smiled.

"Let me get the check," Will insisted. "You have done more than enough. I owe you my life."

Kale bent down and quietly said in his ear, "Looks like one of us will be getting a happy ending." He stood up, "Seeing the two of you happy is more than enough payment. Come on Monty let's leave these two lovebirds alone."

The ride home was quiet aside from the air blowing through the open windows. When he pulled in her driveway, she got out of the truck and turned to look at Kale before shutting the truck door. "Are you happy?"

"Get back in the truck." Kale shut off the ignition.

"No, just answer me, please." She went over to the driver's side of the vehicle.

Kale dropped his head and stared at the steering wheel and exhaled heavily. "Yes."

She knew he was lying. "Seriously, Kale."

He eyed her scrutinizing face and forced a smile. He continued, "I *am happy*. I am *happy* that I am back in Ohio. I am *happy* that our families can be close again. I am *happy* that I can be close to my parents again. I am very *happy* for Alison and Will—and I am *happy* that I can feel your presence near me." He opened his door and got out of the truck.

"What are you doing?" she demanded backing up.

"I'm proving my happiness." Kale slowly stepped towards her. "I am *happy* that I can pick up the phone and your voice might now be on the other line. I am *happy* that I can just walk right over to your house—" He was chest to face with her. Kale lifted her chin and looked her dead in the eyes. Devan swallowed hard. "and I am *happy* I get see your beautiful face in person." He wanted more than anything to kiss her, however, he was going to do his best to keep that *damn* promise he made to her. "I am *elated* that I am here right now, looking in your gorgeous blue eyes, knowing that you want me to kiss you as much as I want to kiss you." His face got a little closer to hers. She held her breath. There was no way Devan would be able to back down if he put those precious lips on hers again. She knew a simple peck would never be enough. It wasn't at the airport, yet even that measly touch of lips on hers sent a chill down her spine. Her knees started to buckle under her and she had to fight to keep on her feet. "I am *happy* that I can walk away without breaking our promise." He dropped her chin and perambulated backwards to his truck.

"But…"

He cut her off before she could utter another word. "Goodnight, Devan." Kale got in his truck and left leaving her standing with the most bewildered face he had ever seen. After backing out of the driveway, he glanced in the rearview mirror. Devan was still standing there trying to figure out what in the hell had just happened. He laughed.

When Devan walked into the house, Justin was cleaning up the mess from dinner. "You have a good time Dee?" She just stared at him. "You look really confused."

Devan sat down at the kitchen table. "Yes. Are you okay?"

"Why do you ask?" Justin raised his eyebrow.

"Well, you are cleaning—"

"Yeah, I made spaghetti for the kids. We made a mess. You are acting as if I have never cleaned before." He was a little on the defensive side.

"Well, you don't—ever!"

"Can't you just say thank you?" If he hadn't stomped away sulking like a child, she might have started an argument with him about it.

"Thank you!" she yelled.

"The kids are in bed. I'm going to my study for a bit. Cassandra brought over a pie. We saved you some, it's in the fridge."

"Okay." Devan got up from the table and went to the refrigerator and got a piece for herself. "Mmmmm." It was rhubarb, her favorite. She took the pie to her office and opened her laptop.

The day had been bittersweet. Being there to experience Alison's and Will's connection was extrordinary. They were two people who never fell out of love even after almost twenty-two years. It was an amazing love story that needed to be told. For once she could write something with genuine feeling that had a beginning, a middle, and perfect end. Once again, she began to type.

Kale had just sat down after washing down the walls and wiping down the cupboards and floor. He was exhausted but wide awake. He didn't even take off the plastic that was covering the sofa. No sooner had he sat down than the doorbell rang. Kale grinned. *I should have figured.* He was expecting to see Devan, only instead, he saw a much lengthier figure standing on the porch. He opened the door to find Nate with a large antique hat box and a few cigar boxes.

"Hey, I couldn't find your number. I just found these photos and wanted to drop them off before I forgot about them." Kale took the boxes and opened the door wider, "Come on in."

"Oh no, that's okay. I don't want to keep you up. I know how hard you have been working in here."

"You aren't keeping me up. Quite frankly, I'm really not that tired, and I have no TV. Please, be my entertainment. Thank you, by the way, for all your help. It's not easy moving all the heavy stuff by yourself, and I really didn't want to ask my dad or Devan's dad at their ages."

"It's really no problem. I am glad I could be of service. I am surprised you don't have an entertainment system set up yet. It being football season and all." Nate chuckled.

"Jeane is bringing that and the bedroom set with her. She didn't trust the moving guys with something that expensive. I say 'whatever'. It's not like I need it right now anyway. As for football I go to my parents.'"

"I have an extra bedroom with a bed at my house if you want some quality sleep," Nate suggested.

"Damn, I was hoping you'd let me try out one of those coffins you just have lying around your place." They both laughed.

"It's cool. I have the couch, loveseat, and the kids' beds."

"Your feet will hang off their beds," Nate stated.

"Dude, my feet hang off my bed."

"Good point, mine too." Nate laughed then asked, "Did you eat?"

"Yeah about three hours ago. To be honest, I could go for a pizza. How does that sound to you?"

Thirty minutes later the guys were sitting on the kitchen floor eating pizza and carrying on a conversation.

"Are you serious? Miss Jenkins? From high school? I had no idea she was a parent." Nate admitted grabbing another slice from the box.

"Yeah, it's crazy," Kale muttered with a full mouth.

"You did that, you know. You brought them together. They say true love has an interesting way of going back to where it belongs. Reminds me a bit of you and Devan."

Kale set down the pizza that he had in his hand and looked at Nate. "Be honest man, what would you do if you were in my shoes?"

Nate thought hard and then gave him a half smile. "I don't know. I hope that I am never in your shoes. Knowing both sides of the story isn't always a pleasant thing. I see two terrific people, I respect, who are damaged and scarred by something that should be so beautiful. You are in a tangled web, my friend."

"You don't know just how tangled, Nate. I'm pretty sure Jeane and Justin are having an affair, but I have no proof. Jeane is very vindictive, and Devan is convinced she will take the kids away from me if I file for divorce. I think Jeane lied about Joey being mine, yet I don't want to do a DNA test. I was drinking that night and don't remember what happened. I'm almost certain that nothing did happen," Kale paused, "It doesn't matter anyway. I love him and couldn't bear the thought of losing him if the truth comes out that I am not his biological father. Now, do you see how tangled it is?" He took a deep breath. It felt good to finally get all of that off his chest. "Wow!" exclaimed Nate. "It's worse than I could ever imagine. I am so sorry."

Kale got up. "Yeah well, it is what it is. Enough of this sad horseshit talk. What do you have in here?" he inquired, going over to the boxes that Nate had brought in. He picked up the cigar box and opened it. Inside were old photos of the funeral home.

"Nate, these are incredible." He kept sifting through the photos. "Um— no, I spoke too soon." Kale cringed.

"Oh yeah, sorry. There are a few post-mortem photographs in there. They showed such detail of the room though, I really wanted you to see them." Nate knew exactly what Kale saw.

Post mortem, why does that sound familiar? "Oh yeah, Devan told me about a school project she did when you helped her. She explained to me what post mortem photos were."

"Yes, the 8th grade local history project. I felt bad for her. I wish the teacher would have just let me do it."

"I think she enjoyed it, Nate."

"I highly doubt that."

"No, I'm serious, man."

"Thank you for sharing that with me. That's really cool," Nate said.

Kale opened the hat box and pulled an object out that had teal and black feathers dangling from it. It was beautiful. The hoop had white string criss-crossing in every direction to form a web and there were teal beads placed strategically across the white string. The string had been crossed in such a way that in the very center was another, much smaller circle. It had a smaller hoop attached to the top so the owner could hang it up. The soft and silky teal feathers that hung from the bottom could move at the slightest breeze.

"What is this?" Kale asked.

"It's a dream catcher."

"Oh yeah, I think my grandmother had one."

"According to legend, the good dreams are supposed to pass through the center hole. The bad dreams are trapped in the web and disappear in the light of the morning."

"Oh, that's cool," he raved, running his fingers through the feathers.

"After hearing about your dreams, I made that for you. I thought it might help."

"Damn man, you are a really thoughtful guy. Thank you so much."

"They say to hang it above your bed but mine fell behind my pillow and I have kept there ever since. Seems to work fine for me."

Devan's eyelids were getting heavy. She didn't want to stop and continued to fight the sleep her body so desperately wanted. After dozing off a few times, she finally decided it was time to go upstairs. As Devan climbed the stairs, she could hear giggling coming from the study and Justin talking slyly. She crept past the room to the other side of the door where he couldn't see her, but *she* could see *him*. He was face timing someone on the computer. Devan couldn't tell who it was.

Regardless it sounded pretty intimate.

"Mmmm I can't wait to see you again. It's been too long," the woman moaned.

"I know—I need those sexy long legs wrapped around my waist," Justin replied.

"What are you wearing under those yoga pants?" she asked.

"Sweetheart, men don't wear yoga pants. These are lounge pants and the answer is nothing!"

"Mmmm I like that. Why don't you show me?"

"Oh honey, I think you should show me those luscious, double Ds you are teasing me with. Oh baby, let me tell you something—you are so beautiful."

Blech! Devan felt sick from what her husband was saying. That was the reason he had cleaned up after the kids. *I wonder how long this one has been going on. It didn't sound like Jeane.* Even though Devan had never actually caught Jeane and Justin, she knew there was something going on there. If nothing else, she suspected they were friends with extra benefits seeing how touchy-feely they were with each other. Still, Devan didn't have the proof to back the claim. Even more she and Kale had to worry about their kids being affected by everything.

Bitterness welled up inside of her. She couldn't even remember the last time he had called her beautiful. Outside of him cleaning up after the kids tonight, she couldn't remember the last time he had offered to help or complimented her in general.

Big deal, he had let her go out with her friends in October, and then he watched the kids one other night, for her to go with Alison. That had been the only two things he had done for her, and he acted as though he should be praised for it when he was just kissing ass, so he could play with his whore.

Devan did everything for Justin—from getting the oil changed in the cars, to making sure he had clean shirts to wear every day. She made sure the cars were gassed up, and his cigarettes bought, even though she didn't smoke. The only thing she didn't do was buy his booze.

She decided she had listened to enough. Devan headed for her room when she heard something. That hideous laugh she hated. Her ears felt as though they had been set on fire when that laugh pierced them. It *was* Jeane. Devan could have listened longer and part of her wanted to, just to find out more, but at the same time she couldn't bear to hear anymore. Devan went to her bed and curled up in it. Her mind ran with the suspicions she and Kale had talked about. Hell, everyone had had suspicions about Justin and Jeane for quite some time. Yet, without proof it would have been nothing, and by the time she had thought of recording it, the filthy conversation had probably ended. One part of her had wanted to barge in and say *Ha! I have you now, you worthless piece of shit,* but it would have cost Kale a great deal. Without a boatload of proof, Jeane would try to take the kids from him. Devan knew that would kill him. Justin might even try something similar if he thought he could get away with it just to make Devan's life miserable. Neither Jeane nor Justin really cared for their kids. They both often acted as though the kids were a nuisance or an inconvenience. She shuddered to think of how poorly the kids would be treated in either home if the other parent had them. She shook her head *no.*

Devan woke up with her head on her desk and looked at the clock. 3:03 a.m. Another dream. *Are you kidding me?* Then she glanced at the screen and read the last thing she wrote.

Alison and Will held on to one another so tightly. They were together again, twenty-two years later. It might have seemed like forever since they felt that love they so longed for—but the truth was—it never went away. Their love had stood the test of time. Finally, they had their happily ever after.

Devan smiled as a tear trickled down her face. What she witnessed earlier truly *was* beautiful. She wasn't going to give up on her own perfect ending with Kale. Devan knew they both deserved it. A love like theirs was meant to last. She loved him as much as the day she fell in love with him, maybe even more. It could be months or even years, nevertheless they would be together again in the way they were supposed to be.

Chapter 9

The Sunday before Thanksgiving, Devan's family, Kale's and Devan's families and the Montgomerys were all over at the Iakona's for Sunday Family dinner. It had been decided a few weeks prior that Thanksgiving would be held at the Iakona's house this year. It would be the first holiday in three years that they would all be together.

"What would you like us to bring next Thursday?" Elaine, Devan's mom asked washing the dishes that were left over from dinner.

"Well, I was thinking about that, and I was hoping you would make your famous creamy potatoes and apple pie. Devan, are you planning to make your pumpkin pie?" Cassandra questioned. She rinsed off a dish that Elaine had just washed and placed it in the dish drainer.

"Yes," Devan nodded.

"Okay and I will make your favorite rhubarb pie, so everyone will have their pick," Cassandra said wiping her hands on a towel that was sitting on the counter.

"Who is everyone?" Kale walked in and set a dish down on the counter.

Cassandra rolled her eyes at him. "Where was this ten minutes ago when I asked everybody to bring in their dishes?"

"Sorry, I was still eating," he stated and picked up the dish before his mom could and started washing it so she would stop complaining.

"I don't know how you eat as much as you do and not gain an ounce. I mean seriously, dude, you eat *a lot* of food," Devan chimed in shaking her head.

"Anyway, Mother, who is everyone?" he asked again after giving the evil eye to Devan.

"Everyone here, and I thought you would like to invite Pete and Kristy."

"Ma, your house is not big enough."

"Yes, it is—we will have it in the rec room downstairs," his mother countered.

"Well, in that case why don't we invite Nate and Veronica too?"

"You have gotten pretty chummy with him, haven't you, son?" Nahoa came in from the dining room.

"You could say that Dad." Kale snatched a biscuit that was left over from dinner. He took a bite of it and chewed with his mouth open looking Devan right in the face across the table. She scrunched her face and shook her head with disapproval.

"His father was so nice. He was wonderful with Chris's mom when his dad died." Elaine smiled and pulled the chair out next to Devan and sat down.

"Well, Nate is even nicer. You will really enjoy him. And Veronica, well, she is a riot!" Devan laughed.

Kale's phone vibrated. He saw a message from Will. "Hey, can we invite two more people?" he asked. "Will said he will be in town to visit Alison, and he wants to meet up".

"Absolutely. Your grandfather will be pleasantly surprised. I don't think he's had a real Thanksgiving since mom was alive." Cassandra sat down at the kitchen table next to Kale.

"Wait! Your grandpa, Carl, is coming? Kale, you didn't tell me," Devan frowned.

"How could I tell you, Monty, if I didn't know?"

"Oh sorry, son, Grandpa will be at Thanksgiving. Do you want to go with your dad to pick him up as you haven't seen him since we went there for Christmas in '08."

"I didn't know you went there..." Devan said quietly with a pout on her face.

She thought Kale would have told her for sure. She loved Carl, the grandpa she never had. Carl Kahalewai was Kale's maternal grandfather. He was a very sweet and endearing man, and by far the funniest man she had ever met.

"Yeah, well, we weren't exactly speaking at the time," he whispered.

"Oh." There was an awkward silence between the two. Devan couldn't help but be sad. There was no need for what had happened, and there was nothing either of them could do now other than to make up for lost time. She looked up at him and mouthed, "Sorry".

Devan hated even thinking about the fallout of Summer 2008 when emotions escalated almost to the point of no return. She had decided the best thing for both the families was for her to take a hiatus from Kale altogether. That decision did have consequences—for example not having any contact with him for three years. However, neither family was destroyed, and ultimately it didn't ruin Kale's and Devan's relationship. She would still argue, as much as it hurt, it was the best thing at that time. Kale, obviously, would disagree.

He abruptly grabbed her arm and led her to his old room and shut the door. "Um…when we moved to Seattle, the kids had such a hard time getting adjusted. Joey was having behavior problems at school and at home." Kale ran a hand through his hair. "Do you have any idea what it is like for your child to tell you every day he hates you and hates his life? It was terrible. And Sage would act out at her mother every time she was around, which wasn't much, of course." He sat down on the bed.

"Oh, Kale, I had no idea." Devan wasn't sure what to say. She sat down next to him.

"I guess you could say I became depressed. I mean the kids were miserable, I was miserable, hell the weather was miserable, and once again…I had lost you. You have no idea what that did to me," he said with great sorrow.

Devan had tears in her eyes, "You will never lose me again. I am so sorry, Kale."

"I better not!" He wrapped his arms around her.

"But you are completely wrong," she squeaked as she tried to escape from his powerful arms.

"About what?"

"I do know what it's like to lose you."

He hugged her tight, and she returned his embrace. "Promise me, Devan, promise me that no matter what happens we will always find a way to make it work between us. I can't bear the thought of…"

Before Kale could finish his sentence, Cassandra barged in. "Oh!" she exclaimed with surprise. Yet she was delighted to see them in an embrace.

Devan and Kale both dropped their arms from one another. "It's nothing, Ma. We were having a heartfelt talk."

"Okay, well, I'll leave you two alone then. You *need* some heart-to-heart talks."

"Lock the door," he said after her.

"Sure, mm hmm, I believe you," Cassandra smirked, "but the lock doesn't work anymore."

"Ma, it's not what you think. We are trying to have a serious conversation, and we don't want the kids barging in. For the millionth time…we are just friends."

"My sweeties, you will never be *just* friends. Once you realize that…your lives will truly get exciting." She walked out and quietly closed the door.

Kale shook his head. "Sorry about my mom."

Devan continued their conversation before the interruption. "I promise!" She kissed him on the cheek and abruptly left the room.

⚜

Two days before the holiday Veronica had picked up her grandmother from the airport. Before they left the parking lot, her mom called and asked if she could pick up a few things from the store on her way back.

"I can't believe you brought me to this place," Antoinette began to complain as they walked in the store. "Will you please hurry so we can go eat?

I can feel my blood sugar dropping every second we are wasting, and I am afraid I will catch some disease in this cesspool."

Veronica laughed, "Well, Grandmother, not everyone is as sophisticated as you."

"Clearly," she said gawking at a woman in nude leggings that were three sizes too small. "My lord, do you see that? She looks as though she is wearing only a shirt because I can see every dimple of her cellulite and every crease she has. I should offer to buy her a dark pair of pants that won't cut off her circulation or even better a tunic that will cover it, so no one has to see her ass crack through them."

Veronica was too lost in her laughter to notice that Antoinette took off after the woman. When she caught up to them, Antoinette was in midsentence.

"It is forty degrees outside. Shouldn't your baby have something covering her feet?" Veronica forcefully pulled her away from the woman.

"I'm sorry, ma'am, she's on leave from the home."

"You should teach her to mind her own damn business," the woman said and kept pushing her cart forward muttering under her breath about *some crazy bitch.*

"Why did you say that?" Antoinette was furious.

"Grandmother, you have no idea if that lady is carrying a gun or a knife. You have no idea if she would attack you," Veronica tried to reason with her.

"That's terrible. Why would you bring me to such a place?"

"It's a Superstore, not the convenient store next to the whorehouse in the bad part of town."

"Oh, you are just crude," Antoinette scoffed at Veronica's answer as she started to walk away.

"Yes, I know, I'm an Antoinette clone," she mumbled as she went down Aisle Four following her grandmother.

Something caught Antoinette's eye and she stopped abruptly, which caused Veronica to stop in her tracks so she wouldn't run her over. She looked ahead and saw an attractive older man with salt and pepper hair wearing a vibrant Hawaiian shirt.

"Go talk to him, Toni." Veronica giggled.

"What nonsense are you talking about?"

"I see you making googly eyes at the guy down there."

"No…" she was brought up short when a familiar tall young man approached the older man.

Veronica recognized him and waved him down. Kale and the man came up to the women.

"Hello, Mrs. VonStross and Veronica. This is my grandpa, Carl. He's in town for a few days. Grandpa, this is my friend, Veronica and her grandmother, Mrs. VonStross."

"Antoinette," she corrected him.

"Well, it's not every day you run in to beautiful women at the store. I'm very pleased to meet you." He kissed both of their hands. Poor Kale couldn't hide his discomfort.

Veronica smiled as she watched her grandmother blush.

"You are in town, from where?" Antoinette asked.

Carl, who could not keep his eyes off Antoinette, spoke in a slightly deeper voice. "Hawaii. Say, would you grab my arm so I can tell my friends I have been touched by an angel?" he crooked his arm for her to take.

She ignored his pickup line, "You have beautiful islands. I went to Maui on my second honeymoon and Kauai for my third."

"Well, we will have to go there for your fourth then." Carl gave a suggestive wag of his eyebrow.

"I went to Hong Kong for my fourth." Antoinette pursed her lips. She was not amused by his antics.

"How many times have you been married, sweetheart?" Carl's shock registered and he inquired with both eyebrows raised.

"Five. Not that it's any of your business, and I am not your sweetheart." Antoinette narrowed her eyes at him.

"Don't worry, you will be." He winked at her. "But wow, five times! Did you divorce them all and take all their money?"

"Grandpa!" Kale scolded Carl. He wished he'd have had a chance to explain Antoinette's personality to his grandfather before running into her. It might have at least saved him some embarrassment.

"No, they all died," Veronica divulged with a smirk awaiting a smart remark from Carl, but he didn't give her one.

"Are you taken, Antoinette?" questioned Carl.

"Am I taken? If you are asking if I am currently in a relationship, the answer is no, nevertheless, you aren't my type."

"I only want to know you. Besides, what's my blood type got to do with it? I say let's do lunch right now, all four of us," Carl eagerly proposed.

"I have plans." Antoinette tilted her head in a way that made Veronica think she was almost trying to flip her hair.

"With whom Grandmother? You just complained that you were hungry."

"That does it then! Where are we going?" Carl asked taking charge.

They checked out and headed to the Bistro in town.

Antoinette continued to be cold towards Carl during the meal while Veronica and Kale ate their food with minimal talk. They enjoyed the banter between their grandparents. It was quite comical to her while Kale was more worried about Antoinette putting a hex on him for his grandfather's behavior.

"You are quite a woman." Carl stated as he smoothed back his thick hair.

"Is that meant to be a compliment?" she sneered.

"My dear, I have given you only compliments." He placed his hands over hers.

"You told me my auburn hair was fitting for my fiery personality. I don't consider that complimentary." She retracted her hands quickly.

"Oh, but it is. Everything about you is so appealing. Your hair brings out the brightness in your blue eyes. Your skin looks so soft, it is begging to be touched. My bet is you are like a fine wine, you get better with age. Your voice is smooth and sweet as honey."

"I'm surprised you could hear it over that loud shirt you are wearing."

As he began to unbutton the first button, he asked if she wanted him to take it off as he raised his eyebrows a couple of times.

"You are starting to bore me," she said and then sneezed.

"I'd say God Bless you, but it seems as though he already has." Carl offered her his handkerchief, but she shooed it away.

"I'm probably allergic to the terrible lines you have been throwing at me," she snickered while she took out a tissue from her purse.

"Did the sun just come out, or did you smile at me?"

"You must be drunk."

"It would definitely take more than one glass of wine to get me drunk, honey. I'm just intoxicated by your beauty."

The server put the bill on the table and scooted away before she laughed.

"Grandpa, give it a rest." Kale grabbed the bill off the table thankful that this torture was coming to an end.

Veronica let a giggle escape her lips.

"Well, *they* think I'm funny." Carl glared at Kale.

"No, I think you are downright hilarious," Veronica said as she tried to take the bill from Kale. He stuck his arm out away from her. Carl then took the bill out of his hand, and before he knew it Antoinette stole it from under his nose, abruptly got up and handed the server the bill and her credit card.

"A thought crossed my mind…" Carl started to say when she returned.

Antoinette interrupted saying, "It must have had a long and lonely journey."

Carl ignored her comment, "I actually invited *you* to lunch so I should pay."

Antoinette came back with, "Why don't you save your money for a new wardrobe?"

Thanksgiving Day

The Montgomerys and the Jamesons were the first to arrive at Kale's parents' home. Devan went straight into the kitchen and asked Cassandra how she could help with the finishing touches for the feast. Cyrus came up to her and asked her something when she heard Carl's voice. It somehow had slipped her mind that he was going to be there.

"And who is this young fellow here?" Carl scooped up the child and hugged him.

"This is Cyrus, my son," Devan stated proudly.

"What are you doing, girl? How long have you been here?" he asked Devan putting Cyrus down.

"Um...about three minutes."

"Get your tush over here and give me a big hug. Three minutes...humph can't even come to see an old man."

She wrapped her arms around the elderly man. "It's good to see you, Mr. Kahalwai."

"Dear God, child! Are you ever going to call me Grandpa? Let me get a good gander at you." The man eyed her up and down and shook his head, "I didn't know it was possible for the prettiest girl in the world to get even prettier."

His words made Devan's face turn a bright pink.

Kale marched up behind her. "Stop flirting, Grandpa. She's married."

Carl frowned, "Yeah, to the wrong man. I'll tell you that. And you, my favorite grandson, just let this gorgeous creature get away and married a wretched woman."

"Grandpa!"

"Well, it's not like she is here to hear me. Is she?" He looked about the room. *Oh, he is a spunky old man.* Devan thought to herself.

"She will be here in a few minutes, and you'd better behave yourself. Devan's husband is here as well."

Carl whispered in Devan's ear. "She is awful, and he knows it too." Devan giggled. "Don't you laugh, girl!" Carl shook his finger at her, "She's already made a fool out of *both* of you." *Well, he isn't wrong there.* "My grandmother would say she is *pilau.* Which translates to she is something bad or did something bad, and I say in her case it's both."

"Carl, are you harassing our sweet girl?" Nahoa asked as he walked into the kitchen.

"Nope, just stating the facts to your 'should be daughter-in-law.'"

"Well, Dad, you are correct on that. She should be our daughter-in-law."

Cassandra walked by, "She will be...one day. Mark my words."

"MOM!" Kale threw his hands up in defeat.

"Don't talk to your mom that way Kale Kai," Carl chided his grandson.

"Now get out of here and let me visit in peace with my future grand-daughter." With that Kale scoffed and sauntered away.

"Mr. Ka…I mean Grandpa, my husband is here so please, keep that in mind." Devan wanted today to be wonderful and not stressful but could only imagine what would come out of Justin's mouth if he overheard anything Carl said. Then again, he'd have to be paying attention to something other than Jeane.

"Eh, I hear he is just as bad as…" Carl cut himself off. It was as though he and Devan could both sense the cold presence that thickened the air they were breathing. They slowly rotated their heads at the same time to see Jeane coming in with a large covered tray.

"Hello, Grandpa."

"Just call me Carl," he faked a smile. Devan stepped back as Jeane set the tray down and stepped toward Carl with her arms out.

"Carl, it's so good to see you." She hugged the old man with her back toward Devan. Carl scrunched up his face. Devan felt sympathy for the poor man. She knew he didn't care much for Jeane, then again, she didn't know many people who did.

Then it was Devan's turn. "Devan…a pleasure as always." Jeane hugged her and she could feel her face making the same disgusted expression that Carl had made. Just the sound of Jeane's voice made Devan's skin crawl. The doorbell rang, and she firmly pushed Jeane away and called, "I'll get it."

Carl beat her to the door. "Hey beautiful! You didn't bring that sex kitten you call Grandma?" He peeked behind Veronica and saw only a lanky figure behind her.

"I'm sorry I did not. She is visiting my aunt, her sister."

"Wait, when did you meet Veronica?" Devan was curious. Kale came up behind her and put his massive hand on her shoulder.

"Just a few days ago. We ran into each other at the store and decided to have lunch. Just imagine it Devan —Veronica, Antoinette, Grandpa and me sitting at the same table."

The look on Kale's face was enough to make her not want to imagine it.

"Oh puh…lease. It was not that bad, Kale," Veronica commented walking in. Devan saw Nate, who had a huge basket in his hands. "What is that?" she questioned.

"Rolls, biscuits and croissants," Veronica answered.

"Mmmm, croissants. I'll take those down to the rec room." She took the basket from him and pulled Veronica with her. "Okay, Roni, spill. What happened at lunch with the four of you?"

As Veronica and Devan went to the rec room, Kale introduced Carl and Nate then excused himself when his father called him to the garage to bring in more chairs.

When Devan and Veronica came back upstairs, Carl was marveling at Nate's height.

"Do you wash windows?" he asked Nate.

"No, sir."

"Hmm. Okay. Do you play basketball?" Carl pretended to shoot a basket.

"No, sir."

"What is going on?" Kale walked back into the room.

"Carl is trying to guess what Nate does for a living," Veronica giggled. Kale sat down next to her on the tan couch and rested his elbow on her shoulder. Devan smiled trying not to chuckle at how tiny Veronica seemed sitting between Kale and Nate.

"Oh, I know, you stock all the high shelves at the grocery store." Carl stood on tip toe reaching up as if he was stocking a high shelf.

"Nope."

"Roofer?" Carl was not going to give up.

"Grandpa! You are harrassing my guest." Kale put his hands to his head.

"Okay, last one because I'm apparently annoying my grandson," Carl said as he waved his hand at Kale. "Painter?" he guessed again as he pantomimed a painter.

"I am a mortician," Nate smiled. Everyone within the area who was listening to their banter began to laugh.

"Well, that's quite an interesting profession to get into." Carl stepped across the room to where Nate was and shook his hand. Nate stood up making Carl's six-foot frame look small. Carl was completely astonished with Nate's height.

"My god son, you are ginormous. I'm sorry. I'm not making fun of you. I just don't think I have ever met someone taller than my grandson."

"I didn't take offense to anything you have said, sir." Nate put his hand on Carl's shoulder.

"An undertaker huh? You know—I'm not too happy with you guys." Carl furrowed his brow then continued. "I got a birthday card from the funeral home in my town trying to get my business. I'm not impressed. They only want me for my body." Kale sat there shaking his head in disbelief while Carl went on. "But seriously…you are a last responder, huh? I would have never guessed that in a million years. I bet everyone is just *dying* to come see you."

Nate was in stitches. "I like this guy," he told Kale.

"Last responder?" Veronica was puzzled.

"You know what a first responder is right?" Devan asked.

"Duh, my brother is a cop."

"Think about it."

Veronica thought for a few seconds longer than she should have. "Last… Oh…I get it!" There was a roar of laughter throughout the room.

A few minutes later the doorbell rang again. Devan jumped up to answer the door and greeted Alison and Will with open arms.

"Thank you so much for inviting us." Will said as he handed a covered dish over to Devan.

"Where is Billie?" Kale came up behind Devan.

"She went to my parents' home." Alison looked down at the floor.

"I take it you still aren't talking to them." Devan stated.

"It's not that I am not talking to them, I just can't be around them at all!" she explained.

"I can understand that. Just remember they are your parents and even though what they did was terrible, it was a very long time ago." Devan handed the dish to Kale and gave Alison a big hug.

"I know. I'm just not ready to face them," Alison squeezed Devan back. When Alison and Will were teenagers, they had written letters which Alison's parents had withheld from both of them. This caused Alison and Will to believe the other didn't care to maintain a relationship.

"I understand," Devan repeated. "Well, come in, and let me introduce you to people you don't know, and you can catch up with those people you *do* know."

Devan went through the house and introduced each guest.

"Kristy and Pete will be stopping by later," Kale reminded Devan and told Alison. She knew Kristy and Pete as she taught them in high school as well as Devan, Kale, Nate and Veronica.

Cassandra, Kale's mom, announced that dinner was ready and requested that everyone head downstairs. There were excited footsteps, lots of laughter and comments about the good smells.

When all were seated, Cassandra spoke in a loud, clear voice, "I'd like to make a suggestion for a new tradition. Let's go around the table and have each of us tell one thing that we are thankful for this year." They all thought it was a great idea, so they went around the table with each one saying what he or she was thankful for.

When it got to Nate, he stood up. "I'm thankful to have met some wonderful people today and to have my former school mates in my life again. It is so nice to have some real 'live' friends." Everyone chuckled at his joke.

Carl was sitting next to him and stood up when Nate sat down. "I am thankful to be with my family. It's been too long…that includes my extended family here," he smiled at Devan and her parents. "I am also thankful to spend this holiday with my new adopted family. You can all call me Grandpa."

"Here, here, Grandpa," Jeane toasted.

"You can still call me Carl," he told her. Jeane cackled thinking he was just joking with her. He wasn't.

"And finally, I am so thankful to have an adopted grandson that is a mortician. I will put my trust and body in his hands. Make me look beautiful, kid! Oh! And don't forget my future granddaughter."

"Future granddaughter?" Jeane asked taking a sip from her glass before setting it back on the table.

Kale jumped up, "Okay, Joey," he nudged his son, "it's your turn." Then Kale pulled Carl back down to his seat, so he would stop talking.

"Great Grandpa, you crack me up," Joey grinned at Carl. "I'm thankful that I get to be back home with my grandparents and my other family. I have missed you guys so much." He looked right at Devan. "Oh, and that Great Grandpa is here making us laugh our butts off." Everyone chuckled.

Devan had to fight back the tears. *What an amazing kid!*

Kale, who was sitting by Joey, stated how he was thankful to be back in Ohio with his family and friends and was so happy his grandpa had been able to join them as well.

When it was Justin's turn he simply said, "Uh, I'm glad business has gone so well." The others gave him a disgusted look.

Then it was Jeane's turn. She said with a giggle, "I agree with Justin. Business is everything. Hey, where did that bottle of Scotch go?" She got up from the table and headed upstairs to look for it. Justin followed like the sheep he was. *Everywhere that Jeane went Justin was sure to go!*

A half hour had gone by and Jeane and Justin still had not returned. Devan took it upon herself to go upstairs to start bringing down the pies. When she got to the top step she could hear giggling from Jeane. *Ugh!* It was that hideous flirtatious laugh that she so hated.

"Oh, hey, Dee. I was gonna head out to get more Scotch, or whiskey or…" She stopped Justin. "Seriously? Do you really think that is a good idea since it is clear you have already been drinking?" Jeane excused herself and went back downstairs.

"I am only going to the place down the road. It's not a big deal," he slid his coat on.

"Okay, and if that one is closed? After all, it *is* a holiday." Devan folded her arms across her chest.

"Yeah it's a holiday. What do people do on holidays? They fucking drink, Devan. Jesus." He headed to the door.

Devan decided to keep her mouth shut until he egged her on. He turned back around.

"Just because your lame ass is a prude, doesn't mean that other people don't like to enjoy themselves." He reached for the keys that were on the windowsill next to the front door. She was faster than he was and snatched the keys.

"Not everyone needs to drink to have a good time, asshole. That's just you!" She raised her voice at him.

"Jeane does. Why do you have to be such a buzz kill?" He couldn't even stand straight. He wobbled and leaned his back against the door.

"Why do you constantly have to *have* a buzz to kill? I swear to God, you drink more than a fucking alcoholic!" *Oh shit! Maybe that is his problem. No, no, I have seen him go weeks before without anything.*

"Alcoholics can't stop drinking. I can quit anytime I want, but I don't want to. Give me the fucking keys!" He straightened himself up and tried slapping the keys out of her hand.

"Don't you treat her that way!" Carl shouted from behind Devan. She had no idea he was there. "She is trying to save your life or someone else's life by not letting you drive drunk, you fool." He walked past Devan and stood nose to nose with Justin.

"Stay out of this old man!"

"I absolutely will not! I saw how much you had to drink. You have no business being on the road, Mr. Jameson." He poked Justin in the chest.

Justin stepped back, "Fine, fine. How about I just go home?" He stuck his hand out expecting Devan to hand over the keys.

"You aren't getting the keys, Justin!" Devan spat.

"Okay, I'll play this game. I will walk home." He opened the door and walked out while leaving it wide open.

"Don't let the door hit you in the ass on your way out!" Carl yelled after him while slamming the door.

"You didn't have to do that. I was handling it but thank you." She hugged him.

"I know you were, but I'm Grandpa and will not stand for some punk ass drunk talking to my granddaughter that way." He hugged her back. Carl suddenly exclaimed. "Damn it!"

"What?" Devan asked releasing her hold on him.

"He forgot to take that red headed bitch with him." Carl shook his head and Devan just laughed.

Chapter 10

December 2011

Kale received a phone call from Carl asking him to run to the Bistro when it opened. Carl was sure he had left his credit card there. He went to use it and found it wasn't in his wallet then remembered the last time he had it was in Ohio. Kale thought it was weird that he just noticed that the card was missing then remembered his grandfather preferred using cash. When Kale arrived at the restaurant, there was a woman following him in. He held the door open for her like the gentleman he was.

"Thanks," she said and slipped through the next door, opened it and motioned for him to go ahead of her.

His mind was a million miles away, so he wasn't really paying attention to her, but her voice sounded familiar, so he carefully looked at her. "Veronica?"

Hearing his voice, she tilted her head up. "Oh hey, Kale! What are you doing here?" She was shocked to see him.

"My Grandpa called me and told he left his—"

"Credit card here?" Veronica interrupted Kale and the smile left her face.

"Yeah, how did you know?"

"Well it just so happens that my *lovely* grandmother left her card as well," she paused and peered around the seemingly empty room until she saw an occupied table in the corner. She clutched Kale's arm and dragged him over to the table.

"Hmmph, and what do we have here?" Veronica put her hands on her hips.

"What the hell, Grandpa?" Kale questioned him.

Carl stood up and greeted his grandson with a warm hug. "I'm so glad you made it. I was afraid we'd be sitting here all day."

"I am impressed that both of our grandchildren arrived on time," Antoinette stood up to shake Kale's hand. "So nice to see you again, Kale."

"Okay so you wanted us both to come? I think it's weird that you are here together, and I think Kale and I have a right to know why *you* aren't in Boston and *you* aren't in Hawaii." Veronica pointed to Antoinette and then Carl.

"Well, I would think you would just be happy to see us," Antoinette responded.

"We are, Mrs. VonStross, but seriously, what the hell?" Kale sat down.

"Sit down, my dear. I ordered you a nice glass of Rosé," she motioned to a glass near Veronica. Kale reached over and pulled the remaining chair out for her. She sat down instantly grabbing the glass of wine and taking a sip.

"We wanted to surprise you kids," Carl had a huge smile on his face.

"You did a great job. We are both surprised," Kale reached for his water.

"Does dad know you are here?" Veronica questioned.

"No one knows other than you two," Carl stated.

"I find that a bit peculiar. What makes us so special?" Veronica said before taking another sip.

"Well—"

Carl cut Antoinette off. He simply could not contain his excitement any longer. "We got married!"

Veronica spit out her wine.

"Please, enough with the dramatics, Veronica. It's not that big of a deal," Antoinette was stern.

"Um, it is, and way to go on insulting your new husband. Pretty sure it is a big deal to him," she pointed to a frown on Carl's face.

"I simply meant there is no need for your ridiculous theatrics. Yes, we eloped. He asked, and I said yes."

"You what?"

"We eloped," Antoinette answered Kale.

"Eloped?"

"We eloped. Would you like me to spell it out for you?" Carl snorted at Kale.

"You have known each other for not even a month!" Kale belted out.

"Yes, and you have known Devan for more than half your life. I knew what I wanted when I saw it, and I didn't procrastinate. Life is too short. Maybe you should take a lesson from your old grandpa."

"That's not fair and you know it, old man!" Kale snapped.

"We wanted you to be the first to know, and that's why we had you come here," Antoinette attempted to calm them down.

"When? How?" Veronica was trying to make sense of the situation.

"We changed Carl's destination on his plane ticket to Boston. He has been staying with me."

"You claimed you got home safely. I saw you go through the gate."

"As soon as you rounded the corner, I came back, and we switched the plane ticket. I did make it safely home—to my other home." He and Antoinette smiled at each other.

Veronica put her head into her hands, and after an awkward moment of silence, she burst out laughing. Kale stared at her as though she had lost her mind.

"What is so amusing?" Antoinette scowled.

"You! I knew it! You were totally checking him out at the store. You loved his playful banter and pretended to hate it. And you—" she cocked her head towards Kale. "You are now my family in some weird way. I don't know exactly if you are my cousin by marriage or what, and who really cares? It's funny as hell. And you—" she pointed to Carl. "You are a sneaky devil. However, I am pleased to call you Grandpa."

"Grandfather," Antoinette corrected Veronica.

"No! She will call me Grandpa. I love you, but I'm not going to pretend to be a snooty hoity toity grandfather."

"Are you saying I'm snooty?"

"No dear, not at all. I'm saying you pretend to be."

"Hmmph. Anyway, we are going to go to Carl's place for a few months, and we would like to invite your families including the Montgomerys and Jamesons to come for the holiday."

"Minus Jeane and Devan's husband obviously," Carl snuck in.

"Grandpa, really?"

"Well if it was my choice, they'd both disappear." Kale grinned. He felt the exact same way his grandpa did.

Veronica's eyes grew big. "Wait!! Do you mean Christmas in Hawaii?"

"Yes, we will have a special dinner tonight and invite the rest of your families. Well, our family!" Carl and Antoinette looked at each other lovingly. Kale and Veronica were both in awe that Antoinette possessed the ability to be affectionate with anything, let alone another human being.

❧ ❦ ☙

"I hate that Nate couldn't come," Devan picked up her bag from the trunk of the taxi.

"Death doesn't wait for anyone," Kale said taking the bag from her and grabbing Veronica's as well.

"Dude's my kin now. That's so weird," Veronica laughed. "So, one day you and I will be related too."

"Shhh," Devan scanned the area making sure no one heard Veronica's big mouth.

Kale glanced over his shoulder and smiled sheepishly at the girls. "I heard that," he chuckled.

"Keep moving, Iakona!" Devan urged. As usual, Jeane and Justin were side by side. And as expected the kids were all together in a group.

Carl's house was just up ahead. As they walked, it came into view. It was a modern building at the top of the road. It had large picture windows and a wrap-around porch. The view, if you were standing on the porch at the front of the house, was overlooking the other houses in the complex. The view at the back was grass, palm trees and the street they had to travel to get to the beach. The porch was built this way to take advantage of Hawaii's beautiful weather. Devan, Veronica, Kale, and the kids were planning to stay with Carl and Antoinette. Jeane, Justin, the VonStrosses, the Iakonas, and the Montgomerys were planning to stay at the hotel.

"I see *my* bed." Kale trotted out the back door onto the wooden deck where a hammock swung in the warm salty air.

"I wanted that," Devan griped.

"Good thing Grandpa installed another one," Kale smirked. There was a hammock on the other side of the porch.

"I admit I would have given it to you if there was only this one."

"You lie!" Devan exclaimed.

"I would never lie. Well, not to you anyway," he said taking things out of his bag. She saw him put something under his pillow, though she couldn't tell what it was.

"What is that?" She pulled the pillow off exposing the strange object.

Kale lifted it up and handed it to her. "It's a dream catcher that Nate made for me."

She took it out of his hands and touched the silky black and teal feathers that were attached. "Oh, it's beautiful. Have you been having nightmares?" she was truly concerned and handed it back to him.

"You see what I'm married to. I have nightmares and bad daydreams."

Devan gave him a half-hearted smile before she changed the subject. "Shit, I didn't get to finish my gift wrapping before we left. Tomorrow when the kids go to bed, will you help me?"

"Of course."

The next day they all explored part of the island. Veronica was in complete awe as she had never seen anything like it. Her parents and Vinnie marveled at every lush green thing they saw. The Iakonas felt at home and commented on how they had thought about moving back. The Montgomerys had always enjoyed Hawaii. They attempted swimming in the Pacific, although it was a little chilly for most of them. After the kids went to bed that night Kale and Devan wrapped the majority of the remaining Christmas presents. She had to quit because she was so tired.

"Thanks, Kale. Let's hit the hammocks. I'm so tired I can't keep my eyes open. We'll do the rest in the morning." She left the room and climbed in her hammock. She saw Kale coming over to her.

"Kale, no. We both aren't gonna fit in here. It's going to break!"

Kale ignored her warnings and squeezed in next to her. He propped her head up with his bicep. Though it felt like her head was on a pillow made of concrete she was very comfortable. "See, it's all good."

As soon as he crossed his feet the ceiling groaned, two seconds later the rope holding up the end dropped. They tumbled to the floor in a giggling mound. Carl threw the door open with Antoinette behind him. "Are you kids okay?"

"I told him it wouldn't hold both of us," Devan said trying to catch her breath.

"Sorry Grandpa, I can fix it."

Carl saw the new hole in the porch ceiling and shook his head. "You'd better! Go get my camping hammock and the stand, and *you* sleep in that. Let Devan have yours. You're lucky the kids didn't wake up. What were you doing?" Carl squinted his eyes and with a frown on his face he said, "Never mind, I don't want to know."

"Good friends, my ass. Good friends don't lay in the same bed," Antoinette closed the door behind herself.

"Hey Monty, you asleep?"

"Not anymore," she grumbled.

"Let's take a stroll."

"Kale, it's too late."

He got up, put his shoes on and lifted her hand to help her out of her hammock. "I'm not taking *no* for an answer."

She took the sweatshirt that was lying on the floor by her hammock and slipped on her flip flops. She followed him down the road to the stop sign and stepped into the grass that led to the beach.

"Kale Kai Iakona, don't even think about getting in that water. It's way too cold."

Kale went back to her and took her hand. "But I have you to keep me warm," he pleaded dragging her to the water's edge.

"No, no, no!"

"I'm kidding Monty I'm not going in the water. I just want to take a stroll on the beach with my favorite person." He let go of her hand and put his arm around her. They walked in silence for a bit. It was calming and dark, there were lights here and there and the moon was extraordinarily bright. The waves rolling upon the shore were cool but not cold. "Do you remember the last time we were here?"

"Uh, yeah, it was seven months ago," Devan yawned.

"No, not Hawaii. This beach right here."

She inspected the beach ahead and could see the fishing pier and beyond that lights from a resort in the distance. Devan's mind let her go back in time.

She took off her shoes, fastened them together and swung them over her shoulder as he tied his and did the same. "Beautiful night," she said looking up at the stars in the clear sky.

He placed his hand on hers. "Not as beautiful as you are."

She smiled. It was so romantic. The water was coming in over their feet washing away their footprints. Her hand was in his. It was something straight out of a romance novel. They walked a little farther until Devan came to a grinding halt. She let go of his hand and stood in front of him face to face. "I need to tell you something," she said with a hesitant sigh.

He got a little worried. "Well, let me say something first." She let him continue. "The past few weeks have been amazing and..."

"I love you," she blurted out.

"I love you too."

She didn't think he was really listening. "No, Kale, I love you. I really love you."

He grasped both of her hands. "I'm madly in love with you Devan Marie. I have been trying to work up the nerve to tell you and you just blurted it out," he chuckled.

"I'm sorry, I didn't mean to ruin your game." she said apologetically.

He leaned down and kissed her ever so passionately. "Now that we have that squared away..." he picked her up threw her over his shoulder and ran into the surf. He stopped when the water was up to his waist.

In his arms she gazed in to his bright green eyes. "All these years, it's only been you. The others were just decoys. I have loved you since the moment you rescued me from the cliffs."

"Well, you sure had a funny way of showing it. Wait. There were others?"

"Well, no, I was just trying to make it sound dramatic."

Kale laughed threatening to drop her.

"Shut up, you liked it," she said kissing him.

"I will always rescue you, always."

"I know we are supposed to be *friends* and all, so forgive me for what I am about to say." He put his hands on her shoulders and spun her to face him.

"I know I promised to behave, and I plan on it—for a while. But one day I am going to break that promise, and you won't be able to get mad at me for it."

"Oh, I won't, huh?"

"No. One day I will kiss you again the way I want to kiss you and the way you want to be kissed," he knelt down to her face, his lips too close for her comfort.

"You won't push me away, and you won't tell me *no*." His beard tickled her chin as he spoke. "One day, Devan Marie, you will be mine again. Until that day comes, and I promise it *will* come, I will wait not so patiently on the sideline. So right here in the same place when I told you I was madly in love with you all those years ago, now I am telling you that I am still madly in love with you." He gave her a peck on her cheek, removed his hands from her shoulders and stepped away from her. She reached for his hand as he walked away. He turned back.

"You promise for right now to not do anything?"

He tilted his head down towards her and gave a sad smile. "Yes, I promise."

"So, what if I was to kiss you the way I wanted to—" She put her other hand behind his neck and pulled him down again, so his face was level with hers. "Would you dare push me away?"

When her lips finally touched his, he swept her up in his arms and kissed her as intensely as she kissed him. When the kiss was over, he set her down and lightly pushed her away from him.

"Yes," he smirked. He headed in the direction from which they came.

"Come on, *wahine*, let's go back before you regret what you might do next."

When she woke up, she caught a glimpse of Kale who was still in a deep slumber. *If only that walk and that kiss had* really *happened*. To her he appeared to be cold. She took her blanket and put it on him before going to the front. She found her way to the front and saw Carl with his arms resting on the railing taking in the green scenery that surrounded the area. She went to stand next to him.

"You know, I figured by this time you would officially be my granddaughter." Carl put his hand on her shoulder.

"Is everybody still sleeping?"

"Yes, my dear, you can speak freely. We didn't get to have a little chat like I wanted back in November. Why haven't you left that loser of a husband yet?"

"Wow, this is what you wanted to talk to me about?"

"The second you drop that asshole—"

"I'm sorry to disappoint you."

"That's it? That's all you are going to say to this poor ancient man who could die any day?"

"What do you want me to say?" she was stunned that he had said that.

"I want to hear the truth. I want to hear that you still love my grandson." He had a serious tone in his voice that Devan wasn't used to.

"Carl—"

"Call me Grandpa, and don't tell me it's irrelevant."

"But it is."

He grabbed ahold of both of her hands tightly.

"You know I do,"

An ornery grin spread across his face. "Now, you tell him that."

She pivoted to see Kale standing right there. She came out with, "Merry Christmas."

He stretched and draped an arm over her. "Tell me what?"

"Merry Christmas," she repeated.

"I'll go put on a pot of coffee," Carl said heading back in. "It's okay, Devan, he knows. We all know. You and I will finish this conversation later."

"What is he talking about?"

"Nothing. Oh, hey, we'd better finish wrapping the gifts before the kids wake up." They went back inside and finished the remaining gifts and hid them under the tree.

It was complete chaos. There was wrapping paper everywhere and happy children playing with their new toys. The adults had made out as well. Antoinette VonStross was extremely generous this year. According to Veronica, Christmas gifts were always plentiful coming from Antoinette. This year was special, there were so many new people in her family. She didn't leave anyone out including the Jamesons and the Montgomerys. They began cleaning up the kids' mess while Antoinette finished passing out the adults' gifts.

"And Veronica, your gift is—Carl, where is Veronica's gift? I set it right here next to Vincent's."

"Oh, you know what? I moved it. Veronica, I think I put it in here," he rummaged through some things in another room. The doorbell rang. "Oh, there it is."

"Carl you are a strange man! Why would you put our granddaughter's gift on the porch? I told you last night—"

"Hush, Toni! Veronica, go ahead and get it."

Veronica bounced up and opened the door to see her tall handsome suitor wearing a smile and a bow. She jumped up on him and squealed. "I thought you had to work?"

"I did. Carl called me when he found out I wasn't coming and insisted that it was very important that I still come even if I can only stay a few days and not the whole week. Mrs. VonStross had already purchased the ticket with everyone else's. They just had to modify the dates."

"I'm so glad you came, my boy," Carl slapped him on the arm.

"Thank you for being persistent, Carl," Nate said as he sat down next to Veronica.

"Grandpa! You call me grandpa!" Carl demanded.

"Hey! Why is it that you insist everybody calls you grandpa except me?" Jeane asked.

"It's simple really. You are much too sophisticated to call me grandpa." He didn't even crack a smile.

"Well, that makes sense." Jeane was quite happy with his response.

They finished cleaning everything up and headed over to the hotel for the feast Antoinette had set up. When they walked through the doors to the private banquet area, the families were impressed. The room was festive with Christmas decorations everywhere. There were several tables. Three of the tables were set up as a buffet. There was a mix of traditional holiday food and Hawaiian dishes. On one buffet table there was ham with fresh pineapple coated in brown sugar, turkey, cornbread stuffing, mashed potatoes and gravy, green bean casserole, candied yams, and steamed broccoli. On another buffet table there was rice, lomi salmon, crab legs, poke, kalua pig, and tuna tataki. The last buffet table had bean and lentil soups, salad, deviled eggs, celery with cream cheese and peanut butter, potato salad, and Hawaiian coleslaw. Devan headed straight for the bread table totally bypassing the dessert table without even a glance and swiped two croissants. Kale mocked her and placed two croissants on his plate as well. "I figured I better get some before you eat them all."

Devan couldn't wait. She took a bite of one and almost melted to the floor. "Oh my god, Heaven in my mouth. They are so warm and buttery. You cannot find croissants like this anywhere at home."

The kids went straight to the desserts. "No. You will eat a full plate of non-sugary food before even looking at that table," Kale warned all the children.

"What all is over there?" Veronica sat down next to Devan.

Devan couldn't see everything that was there, so she nudged Kale who was sitting closer. "What I see is, peanut butter fudge, Christmas cookies, ambrosia salad, pineapple upside down cake."

"Oh my god, stop, Kale! You just made me gain five pounds," Jeane claimed sitting down across the table from them.

"I doubt that. You never gain weight," Justin commented making everyone roll their eyes.

Kale continued, "I also see haupia cake, malasada, butter mochi, and candy canes."

"What is malasada and butter mochi?" Nate questioned putting his napkin on his lap.

"Malasada is pretty much like a doughnut, and butter mochi is a golden-brown rice cake made of mochiko rice. I think it's got coconut milk and eggs in it." Kale said.

"I can't wait to try all these foreign foods." Veronica took a bite of ham.

"Foreign?" Kale was being a smartass.

"Sorry, I mean Hawaiian foods,"

"That's better," Kale snickered.

When they were eating dessert, Carl stood up and requested everyone's attention.

"I cannot thank all of you enough for being here. I am so excited to bring these families together. You are all our family now, and I love each and every one of you. I can die happy now. I have a beautiful bride and a wonderful large family like I have always wanted." His eyes started glistening.

"You are not allowed to die anytime soon, my love," Antoinette stood up. "I agree with my husband, except for the dying part. I am very happy you are all here. I haven't been near children at Christmas since Vincent and Veronica were little. It was magical to see their little faces light up." Her voice cracked, "You all are going to soften this old hard heart of mine. I ask you to lift your glasses and toast to Family. I hope we can spend many more holidays together. Merry Christmas!"

"Merry Christmas," they all said back.

Carl came up behind Kale and Devan and whispered, "Almost a perfect family, I wonder what is missing, hmmm?"

"Grandpa, don't push."

Antoinette came up next to Carl and was behind Devan. "I know most of your story now, missy. Carl told me everything. One of these days you and I are going to sit down and have a private chat. Not now, but sometime soon. I told you I don't like liars." Antoinette said under her breath. Devan wasn't sure what kind of threat this was, regardless, it made her uncomfortable.

"Chat about what?" Devan turned and stared up at her. Antoinette gave her a warm smile which really threw Devan off.

"Your future."

Chapter 11

New Year's Eve 2011

Everyone was exhausted from the trip to Hawaii, but Jeane insisted that they throw a New Year's Eve party. Jeane and Justin were in Cleveland for work for the day, so Devan told Kale she would help him get ready that afternoon. That morning when Devan went to the grocery store to get food for the party, she ran in to Veronica who was doing the same thing.

"Fancy meeting you here," Veronica buzzed past her.

"Hey, I was gonna call you before tonight. I want all the juicy details from the two nights you got to spend with Nate."

Veronica looked around to make sure no one was near. "He's here with me, so I gotta make this quick. Listen very carefully…" She paused taking a deep breath building up to a climactic answer that had Devan in suspense and then plainly stated, "Nothing happened."

"What?" Devan was shocked.

"I know, right? I'm trying to understand it myself. I don't think we have even had a real make out session since I was drunk."

"You are joking…"

"I wish I was. He's such a—such a *gentleman*. It's insane. I am beginning to wonder if he has ever even had sex."

Devan snickered.

"Dee, don't laugh. I'm dead serious." Devan could tell by Veronica's eyes that she wasn't kidding.

"Okay, well, maybe he is waiting for the right time. What do you guys do?"

Veronica looked again before speaking. "We cuddle, which is nice, but damn it I want him to ravish my body. I started changing clothes in front of him in Hawaii and he quickly turned away. He was obviously uncomfortable. Maybe he doesn't like me like I thought he did."

Devan spotted him coming up the isle and whispered, "I highly doubt that. Let me see what I can find out."

"Hey Devan," he walked up to the girls with his arms full. "Are you excited for tonight? I am. It will be so nice. I haven't celebrated the New Year with the living in so long. I always chose to work, however, this year I have a beautiful date to ring in the New Year with." He smiled at Veronica and put the items in the cart.

There is something strange about this. He is totally in to her. Maybe I should say something to him. To buy herself some time to think, Devan stretched up to get a bottle of sparkling juice that was just out of reach.

Nate stepped over to where she was. "Please allow me," he picked up a bottle. "How many do you need?"

"Five, please, and thank you," she replied.

He set them in her cart, "Is there anything in particular you'd like us to bring tonight?"

"Just yourselves. Oh, a little bit of a warning…" she pushed her cart aside so that she could stand closer to Nate in order for him to hear her better and lowered her voice, "Justin and Jeane tend to drink a lot more than the rest of us. I'm hoping that is not the case tonight, or hopefully they will pass out early."

"Thanks for the warning," Veronica said. "I guess we will see you tonight then."

That afternoon Devan and her children, Callie and Cyrus, went to assist Kale with preparations for the party. Devan told him about her conversations with Veronica and Nate at the grocery store.

"I bet there were a few wild nights in Hawaii," Kale said with a chuckle as he put a pork roast in the crock pot.

"Well…" Devan hesitated. *Should I really tell Kale? I did tell Veronica I would see what I could find out.*

Kale glanced over at her and could see she was deep in thought. He took a bag of sauerkraut out of the fridge and as he cut it open to pour on top of the roast she began speaking again.

"Veronica claims nothing happened, and I believe her. You should have seen the disappointment on her face."

Kale turned back to face her still holding the sauerkraut bag. It was dripping juice all over his shoes. He was so stunned at what she had said, that he didn't notice the mess he was creating. "What? I thought for sure they would have…I mean, Veronica would have…are you sure?"

Devan grabbed some paper towels and pointed down at Kale's feet. "Great! My shoes are going to smell like fermented cabbage for a year." He dumped the bag in the pot and closed the lid. Devan started wiping up the floor and his shoes. She looked up at him at the exact moment he looked down at her. They both laughed. He reached down and pulled her up. They were chest to face, the way they both preferred it. He could smell her fragrant shampoo, and she could breathe in his signature scent, pleased that he hadn't changed it. *Ahhh Nautica.* She wrapped her arms around his waist. He rested his chin on her head. "I'd hug you back, Monty, but I don't want you to smell as bad as I do."

She snatched his hands and put them around her. "I plan on taking a shower," she squeezed him even tighter. "I'm just so glad you are back."

"Me too, Monty, me too."

"What are you guys doing?" Joey, Kale's son, came into the kitchen.

"Come here, Joe." Devan opened her arms to him when he went over. "I'm so glad you are back," she hugged him, and he hugged her back.

"Group hug," Callie yelled from across the room and ran over. Her yelling triggered Kale's other two kids, Sage and Kai, and Devan's son, Cyrus, to run in and join in the fun. "I love you guys!" Devan said still hanging on to everyone.

"It's like one big happy family," Sage commented. The little girl was right. They were like one big happy family, only there was no *like* about it. They *were* family and together were happy.

When the hugging subsided, and Kale and Devan were back to preparing for the party, Kale questioned Devan again about what really happened with Veronica and Nate.

"According to Veronica her attempts to turn him on were unnoticed."

Kale rolled his eyes in disbelief and washed the potatoes to make the loaded mashed potatoes that were in front of him. "I highly doubt they were unnoticed. Veronica is smoking hot!" Devan slapped his arm. "Ow—not as hot as you of course."

"She's your cousin now or something. Just remember that," she reminded him.

"It's Veronica. She doesn't seem like the type to…ugh that sounds bad, even in my head. Let me rephrase…" He thought for a second then continued. "She seems like…nope. I give up."

"I think I know what you are trying to say," Devan replied, smiling. "I just don't think there is a way to describe it."

"I'm not saying she is slutty by any means. However, I'd be willing to bet she has a full body latex cat suit for special occasions. Maybe even some floggers and whips. Hell, I bet she had a body harness with matching ball gag already branded with Nate's name on it."

Devan smacked his arm for the second time. "Kale Kai Iakona!"

He shrugged his shoulders. "Out of all of our friends if you had to guess who would be involved with bondage you know damn well it would be Veronica."

Devan didn't have to admit anything, he could see it on her face. "Well, I'm sure she has some handcuffs somewhere."

"Poor Nate," Kale shook his head. "I'm kidding, I don't think Veronica is really that way, although I'm sure she wouldn't mind if people assumed she was." He handed her a potato to peel.

After peeling the rest of the potatoes and cutting them up, they were ready to go in the pot. As she went to put them in, she passed Kale who was attempting to make a cheese ball. "What are you doing?" she asked.

"Making a cheese ball." Kale replied while chopping pecans.

"Why ruin it with nuts?"

Kale stared at her like she had completely insulted him. "Um… haven't you ever had my mom's famous Hawaiian cheese ball?" She peeked over and turned her nose up at the concoction of cream cheese, shredded cheddar cheese, crushed pineapple, green peppers and spices.

"Yes, I have, and that is not it. She doesn't use peppers, and she doesn't roll it in pecans. She rolls it in shredded cheese."

"Fine, let's call mom." He washed his hands, pulled his phone out of his pocket and made the call. When he got off the phone, he put his hands on Devan's shoulders, and leaned down to look directly in to her eyes.

"You are right,"

"Told you so!" she smirked at him.

"And *I* am right," he smirked back.

"We can't both be right." She placed her hands on her hips.

He let go of her, went to the refrigerator and pulled out two more bars of cream cheese. "I have mom's recipe right. She always makes you a different one since you don't like peppers and nuts on or in your food."

"Oh, I never noticed," she said and went over to stir the potatoes.

"Neither have I. So, either we are both that dense or…"

Devan interrupted him. "Oh, my god, I know what I was going to ask before I got sidetracked with the cheese." Devan scooted over to where Kale was, so she didn't have to scream it across the kitchen. "What do you know about Nate's and Veronica's relationship? She seems to think that he's not in to her as much as she is him. The whole Hawaii trip I think set her off."

Kale sighed as he rolled the first cream cheese mixture into a ball. "All right, I have no idea what happened in Hawaii, but I can tell you he liked her enough to get on a plane for seventeen hours, spend two days with her and then take a seventeen-hour flight back home. I'd say he more than likes her." Kale brought up a good point. That was a lot of travel time for a measly two days of fun.

"Okay, then why do you think *nothing* happened?" Devan started to unwrap the extra cream cheese.

Kale quit what he was doing and took the cream cheese away from her. "I'm going to make it for you. I need to see if I make it the way you like it. Now, to answer your question, I think Nate is old-fashioned, super old-fashioned. For some reason he has a lot of respect for Veronica," Kale chuckled and sprinkled the pecan pieces on the ball and then rolled it over the remaining pieces. "I do know for a fact, he really likes her. After all, he thinks about a future with her."

"Ohhh," Devan smiled.

Kale grabbed the Saran Wrap, covered the cheese ball and put it in the fridge.

"Now, don't go and say anything to your little friend. I don't think Nate divulges much personal info to anyone, and I think if you tell Veronica how long it took us to…"

"To what?" Jeane came strolling in and set her bag down in the middle of the kitchen.

"Uh…" Kale wasn't sure on what to say.

Devan took over for him. "To get along. Kale and I hated each other for years." Kale shot her a look as if to say *Nice save!*

"Oh, I didn't know that. Haven't you guys been the best of friends since you were tiny? What changed?"

"It was the Summer of 1994, and this cute blonde girl tripped and fell for me."

The salty scent of the ocean mixed with the chlorine scent of the pools. The sand and the fragrant native flowers intoxicated her. To say it was beautiful was an understatement. The walk to the beach seemed like it took forever because of all the resort's amenities, but she finally saw an arrow-shaped sign that said: "Beach Straight Ahead." She headed down the last set of stone steps, and then it happened. Her left flip-flop broke and she tripped on the second to last step. "Damn it!" she exclaimed, as she was stopped mid fall by something hard.

"*Whoa, you okay?*" *the guy who'd caught her asked. He steadied her and helped her down the final step onto the sand, with Devan's face smashed against his warm chest the whole time.*

'*That was his chest I hit?*' *she realized in awe as she looked up. He smelled of sunscreen, coconut and lime. The scents were swirling all around her.* "*I'm so sorry! My stupid shoe broke and...*"

He leaned down to get a closer look at her. "*But you're okay?*"

"*Uh, yes,*" *she stammered.* "*Thank you. I'm sorry to have, uh fallen for...on you. I mean on you.*"

"On you," she corrected him with the biggest smile on her face thinking back.

"I fell *on* you."

"It was you?" Jeane scoffed as she took her shoes off and threw them into the foyer. "No offense, Devan, I think you are um… pretty now, yet I just can't picture you as anything other than plain when I think about you at a younger age."

Kale and Devan both gave her a nasty look.

Jeane picked up her bag. "I'm going to go lie down for a bit, I'm exhausted. Wake me when it's time to start the party," and she left the room.

"Wow," was all that Devan managed to say.

Kale followed and hugged her. "Don't mind her, Monty. She's just a jealous bitch. The pictures I saw of her when she was young are bad. She was a homely girl. She could have never measured up to you. You weren't just cute, Devan, you were beautiful. I remember the first thing I thought when I caught you. *An angel has fallen from Heaven right into my arms.*" Kale smirked at Devan.

"Oh, shut up, Iakona. You never thought that." She laughed, forgetting about Jeane.

"Okay, maybe not, still I thought you were hot!" He laughed with her, then released his hold on her and cupped her chin with his hand. "You will always be the most beautiful girl I have ever seen. Jeane doesn't have a leg to stand on next to you." That made Devan blush.

When Devan got home, she noticed the laundry room light on. She went to hit the switch when she saw the entire floor covered with clothes. There were boxes that had been in storage in the room that had been torn into, even the holiday totes had been ripped open. There were Easter eggs, cob webs, old Christmas bulbs, mixed all in with the clothes. It looked like a tornado had destroyed her once organized room. As she started picking up the pieces she cut herself on one of the broken glass ornaments. Blood gushed from her hand. She ran into the kitchen and put it under cool water then wrapped it with a paper towel.

"God damn it Dee, you got blood all over my favorite shirt. What the hell?"

She looked over at the light grey tee-shirt Justin was holding up. There were about four drops of blood on it.

"I'm sorry, it's not like I planned on cutting myself. What the hell happened to my laundry room?" Justin went over to Devan and shoved the shirt in her face. "Get the stains out!" She could smell the alcohol on his breath. Her heart sank into her stomach. Maybe he felt the need to drink because he was coming home, and he didn't want to be there. Maybe he did it just because he wanted to. Maybe, just maybe he did it to piss her off.

"Why did you drink this time Justin?" She made the mistake of asking when he was walking away. He turned around and yelled, "Maybe because I had to come home to this shithole where I can't find anything to wear. I hate what you did to that room."

"Yeah, that's pretty obvious, but you didn't have to destroy it. I worked hard…"

He stopped her. "I don't give a flying fuck what you did. I want it back the way it was."

"Fine but you need to clean up the mess you made." She said glaring at him.

"That's the woman's job." He said and walked away before the tears started stinging her eyes. She had looked so forward to tonight. Now, she didn't even want to go. She didn't want to have to babysit Justin. She didn't deserve to be humiliated again in front of the people she loved.

Later that evening Devan pasted a smile on her face and walked over with Justin and their kids to Kale's and Jeane's new house. She was going to make the best she could out of the night. The Montgomerys and Iakonas were already there along with Pete, Kristy, Veronica and Nate. Devan met Veronica and Cassandra in the kitchen and she unloaded the treats she brought onto Kale's island.

The second Cassandra left the room Devan spoke quietly in Veronica's ear. "I didn't get much info from Kale, but what I did find out is Nate is very serious about you."

"Really?"

"Come on Roni, the dude flew all the way to Hawaii to be with you for only forty-eight hours."

Veronica snatched the bottle of champagne that was sitting on the counter beside her and poured them both a glass. "You're right," she handed the glass to Devan.

"I am positive this next year will be a good one," Devan smiled.

"Cheers to that!" Veronica said as they tapped their glasses together.

A few hours had gone by, and it was clear Jeane and Justin had been hitting the bottle hard. Devan quickly became annoyed with them. She had hoped since the kids were all there the two J's would have been less likely to become completely sloshed. Devan wasn't exactly surprised though, especially with Justin. His drinking had been increasing over the year. She was glad all the kids had gone to bed aside from Cyrus. She had no idea how her little man could still be awake. It was already past eleven o'clock. Cyrus was used to going to bed at eight o'clock.

"Hey, sooo when are you guys going to have a baby?" Jeane quizzed Kristy like it was her business.

Kristy was polite, "We are talking about it and thinking maybe sometime next year if everything goes as planned."

Justin came up behind Jeane and leaned over her shoulder.

"Dude, get her done," he said to Pete and clanked glasses with him.

Pete chuckled, "Feeling good, are we Mr. Jameson?"

Justin glanced at Jeane from the corner of his eyes then back at Pete. "Always…man!"

Cyrus ran up to Justin. "Daddy, Daddy, I want a drink!" Kale saw Justin handing his cup to Cyrus, and he ran over.

"No, no, no, buddy, you can't have Daddy's drink," he removed the cup from Cyrus's little hands. "Follow Uncle Kale. I will get you some kid-friendly juice." He shoved the almost empty cup into Justin's chest hard. "Come on, man, think before you act."

Devan was in the kitchen getting a plate and talking to Cassandra. Kale came rushing in, "The booze hounds are back at it. We need to keep an eye on them. Your dumbass husband just gave your son his drink, and I am pretty sure he and Jeane are not drinking wine or champagne," suggested Kale.

Devan set her plate down and was about to leave the kitchen to find Justin when Kale put his hand on her arm. "Monty, I got it. Cyrus didn't drink it. I caught it before it happened, so you don't have to worry." They both whirled around when they heard loud laughter from their spouses.

"Uh oh! Look who's under the mistletoe."

Devan tilted her head up towards the ceiling and groaned then heard, "De…van you have to do it," Jeane said then winked at Kale.

Kale glared at her. "Who is she going to kiss, herself?"

Jeane shoved him closer to Devan. "No! You, you big oaf. You are the one closest to her."

Cassandra could have easily intervened, of course, but she didn't. Kale kissed Devan on her forehead.

"No, no, no! You gotta do it like this…" Justin put one arm behind Jeane's back and one on her cheek and bent her over backwards just slightly and kissed her. The drunks giggled then crumbled to the floor. "Do it…do it," they chanted.

Kale didn't wait any longer. He did exactly what Justin did and then he placed his lips on Devan's. Even though it was just a peck, it was enough to make Cassandra smile a wide-toothed grin.

"Happy?" Devan was pissed.

"Wait…you did it?" Justin frowned. "I didn't see it. Now you gotta do it again," he downed the last of his drink.

"No, we don't, you jackass!" she retorted brushing past Jeane and Justin.

"Come on Dee, we are just having fun. Take that stick out of your ass and have a good time for once," Justin said behind her.

Devan wanted more than anything to smack him and she might have, had Kale not stepped in. "You two just go sit down." Kale followed her. "I'm sorry, no I'm not sorry," he said touching her shoulder.

"The problem is not you, Kale. It's Justin. I am so sick of his drinking. I begged and pleaded for him to behave tonight and not get drunk. Every time we go somewhere I have to babysit him, or my night will be ruined…and it usually is anyway."

Kale tried to make her feel better. "It's okay. He's not being that bad. I will keep him in check. I promise."

Devan rolled her eyes. "It's not your problem. Besides I'm sure you will be busy enough with…" she nodded her head toward Jeane who had draped her arms on Justin. Kale shrugged. They appeared smitten with one another.

"You want me to take care of that?"

"No, if you don't care then I don't care." Kale thought her eyes said she did care.

"I'll take care of it," he said and turned to walk over to them.

She gripped his arm. "No, if they are distracted by each other, then maybe the rest of us can have a good time." *Oh, she was serious.* "Unless you are worried about it since she *is* your wife."

"Only on paper," Kale commented. "The kids are all asleep except for Cyrus, and I'm pretty confident he is on his way out."

Devan looked to see Cyrus with his head bobbing and finally resting on Pete's arm. Kale went over, scooped him up and took him upstairs with the other kids. He tucked him in the bed with Kai. When he stepped out of the room, he saw Devan standing in the doorway. "I'm sorry," she apologized.

"For what?" He approached her in the hallway and shut the bedroom door, so their conversation wouldn't wake the kids.

"I was kind of bitchy downstairs. I had a rough evening."

"What happened?" Kale was concerned.

She shrugged her shoulders. "I came home from your house and walked into a huge mess in the laundry room. He had everything everywhere and he was just a complete asshole. Nothing I couldn't handle, but this shit just gets so old. I have two children, yet I feel like I have three. He makes matters worse. He doesn't even help with the house when he is home. I sometimes wonder if he was put on this Earth just to bug the hell out of me. He stresses me out so bad. I hope Alistar makes them travel a lot again. I could use some peace in my life."

Kale put his arms around her. "I'm sorry. I do think they will begin traveling more. Jeane made some kind of comment a few weeks ago about not being able to be home much to help after the start of the New Year. I had to laugh. She *never* helps. You and I did this today, the only finger she lifted was to untwist the cap off her drink."

"I don't know how you do it Kale."

"Those last three years were really rough, nevertheless, I've got you back now, and you have me. Monty and Lettuce Head take on 2012. The dream team is back."

Devan forced a smile, but Kale could see the tears welling up in her eyes.

"Please don't be sad, Monty."

"It's just…it's so frustrating."

"He's really not that bad tonight."

"Sure, he didn't throw a shit fit and leave yet like he did at Thanksgiving."

Kale recalled Justin leaving early but didn't know about the fit. Devan could see the confusion on his face and explained how Justin embarrassed her in front of Carl and how Carl stood up to him. Tears flowed down her face, and he wiped them away.

"I don't want to see you cry. I didn't even realize it'd become such an issue. I really, really want to hurt him." Kale felt bad for Devan. He was so angry with Justin for treating her with such a lack of respect and causing her so much stress.

She wiped her face and stood up straight. "This next year everything will be better. It has to be." He grasped both of her hands and placed them in his. When he felt the bandage on her hand, he lifted it up to take a good look at it.

"Why is there a bandage on your hand?"

"One of the boxes he had torn into was old Christmas ornaments that we didn't use this year. As I was cleaning up the mess, one of the shards of glass went into my hand." She looked down at her feet.

Kale took a deep breath and tried his best to hide his sudden anger from Devan. He didn't want her to feel any worse. "I promise, Devan Marie, I will do everything I can to make this year great!"

He meant every word that he said, and she knew it. Her eyes, staring at the ground, very slowly lifted up to meet his. There were so many words that were said between the two without opening their mouths to speak. His heart ached for her as much as her heart ached for him.

Devan was thinking, *Jeane is never there so Kale has to work full time, clean the house, get the kids to school, attend all the school functions and parent-teacher conferences…all by himself.* She knew they both got the short end of the stick.

"Hurry up guys…ten minutes until 2012!" Pete shouted up the stairs. They both jumped and separated quickly.

"Um, you go ahead. I am going to make sure all the kids are still asleep," Kale told her. When Devan left, Kale backed in to the wall and slammed his head back hoping to knock some sense into it. He inhaled a long slow breath and held it for several seconds. He exhaled slowly and let out a low groan. He had so many emotions going through his head. Part of him wanted to go downstairs and rip Justin to a million pieces. Part of him wanted to sweep Devan off her feet and run away with her. Part of him didn't know what to do while another part was anxious. "Just breathe, Kale," he whispered to himself. He took another long breath and exhaled while heading down the stairs.

Jeane and Justin were already passed out on the loveseat slumped over on each other. Bottles of champagne were opened and being poured. Veronica put one goblet in Kale's hand. Everyone now had a glass and they were all standing by their significant others. Everyone, other than Kale and Devan who stood on opposite sides of the room awkwardly. "Ten…nine…"

"You are not allowed to enter the New Year without a kiss," his mom said pushing him over towards Devan.

"Five…four…three…two…one… Happy New Year!" Kale tilted over and aimed for Devan's cheek, but she moved her head and his lips met with hers. Time came to a standstill for them both. Her lips appeared to merge with his. Once together they did not move a muscle. They were two pieces fitted together, creating the perfect puzzle. They were complete. When they parted, every single person, who was there, was staring at them. Kale looked at the time 12:02.

"Happy New Year! Cheers!" he downed every last drop of the liquid.

<h1 style="text-align:center">Chapter 12</h1>

February 2012

"Dee, I have a problem. Pete, Maggie, and I are chaperoning the Sweetheart Dance tomorrow night. Maggie just called me and told me that four of the teachers who were coming tonight were out today with some type of virus that's going around and won't be able to make the dance. I am begging you, *please*, is there any way you could help?" Kristy pleaded.

Devan contemplated, "Let me see if my parents can watch the kids. I will ask Veronica if she is available as well."

"Okay, good. Pete is calling Kale as we speak."

Devan groaned to herself. She knew she would have to see Kale soon.

"If Roni agrees, do you think she will bring Nate? That would help a lot."

Devan really wanted to go to the dance, but she was nervous. After that kiss on New Year's, Kale and Devan had only seen each other in passing and at Sunday Family dinner night. On Sundays she felt so awkward being near Kale, his family and even her own parents. Everyone who was there on New Year's, who wasn't passed out cold, saw that kiss. Those amazing two minutes had more emotion and passion in them than she knew was even possible. Butterflies swarmed in her stomach just thinking about it. Devan smiled and closed her eyes. She could feel her heart flutter and a comfortable warmth spread across her body.

"Hello…Devan…are you still there?" Kristy's voice over the phone brought her back to reality.

"Yes, I'm sorry, um…what were we talking about?"

"You said you would check with Veronica, and I asked if she would bring Nate."

"Oh yeah, I will tell her to bring Nate. I'm sure they will both agree."

"Thank you so, so much! I need to let you know that it is formal. Please tell Roni she can't wear something too short or too low-cut. I keep picturing what she wore to Prom." Devan laughed at the memory of the dress that Veronica had worn. The black dress was floor length with a slit going up to her mid right thigh and a neckline that was a bit lower than it should have been. It reminded her of something Elvira would wear. Devan assured Kristy she would make certain Veronica was dressed appropriately.

When the call ended, Devan sent Veronica a text telling her about the dance.

Veronica sent a text back inviting her over that afternoon to see what she had in her closet. The two were close in size and would be able to borrow each other's clothes, although Devan was about two inches taller—not enough to really make a difference.

When Devan arrived, Veronica led her down a hallway to a room. Veronica disappeared to the back of the room and opened doors to reveal a large walk-in closet that was the size of a small bedroom. Devan was impressed. Veronica had vintage clothing, casual clothing, a lot of steam punk clothing, and in the very back she had formal gowns. There was not much color to her wardrobe. For the most part she had black with a sprinkling of blue, purple, and the occasional red. Veronica pulled out all the gowns and laid them on the bed. Devan went over and pulled one out of the pile. She held it up. It was black satin with a plunging neck line and a completely open back. *The Elvira Dress!*

"Isn't this what you wore to prom?" Devan ran her hands over the silky material.

Veronica turned around. "Yes. That will be perfect!"

"No! No! This is a high school dance. We can't excite all those poor hormonal teenage boys."

Devan's face was priceless. "Oh my god, Dee, I was only kidding. I don't even know if I would wear that to a Halloween party," she laughed. "I really should donate some of these."

Veronica searched through the rest of the gowns. Nothing really seemed appropriate for chaperones, so the girls decided to hit the thrift store in town.

Devan stepped out in the first dress she had picked. It was a 1990's decade style. The dress was crimson velvet. It had a V-neckline in front and in back. There was ruching in the front under the bustline to the waist. The skirt part of the dress came to a few inches above the knees.

"Oh my god! Put all the other dresses away. That is perfect! Is that velvet?" Veronica rubbed the fabric. "Oh, it is. Kale is going to freak out! Have you seen him at all since—"

Devan's face was almost as crimson as her dress and she blurted out, "No!"

"Hmmm, well, this should be interesting. It looked like one hell of a smooch you guys shared."

Devan knew she could trust Veronica and therefore explained exactly what had happened on her end.

"Well, I honestly don't know what to say to you. It's beautiful and sad all at the same time, but I know what will make you feel better."

"And what's that?" Devan headed to the register.

"A latte! Let's pay for these and get one on the way home."

Devan put the crimson velvet dress on the counter. Veronica put her black dress on the counter. It had a scooped neck and back and was floor-length. The dress was form fitting and hugged her perfectly.

"That sounds like a lovely idea."

On the way to the coffee shop Veronica went into detail about some of the work that was going on at the funeral home. "I bet I have seen Kale more than you have. Now that he's family and all, I guess—" She stopped in mid-sentence. "Oh, holy hell! Did you just see that billboard?"

Devan stretched her neck out as far as it would go, but the sign couldn't be seen anymore.

"No. What was it?"

"Oh, I can't even begin to tell you. You have to see it for yourself." Veronica turned on to the closest road then turned around. "Okay, get ready for it. It's coming up on the left."

Devan spotted it and frowned. Veronica snickered at the scowl on Devan's face. "James Crenshaw, Attorney at Law, Specializing in Divorce and Domestic Cases." James Crenshaw was Devan's high school boyfriend before the Iakonas moved to Ohio from Hawaii. *James the Great! Or so he wanted everyone to think.* She crinkled her nose just thinking about him. There was someone he reminded her of the more she remembered things about him. He was so superficial and extremely conceited. If an idea wasn't his it was awful. James was condescending to every person he met including Kale who towered over him in many ways, not just height.

"Hey, what was it he used to say all time? I think he even put it as a quote under his senior picture in the yearbook," Veronica pulled in to the coffee shop parking lot and got in line for the drive thru.

"I eat, I drink, I sleep and I breathe football!" Devan mocked her old boyfriend.

Veronica snorted—she was laughing so hard. "Oh my god, yes. He was so lame." Her tone changed. "He was awful to me. He would pour milk in my locker every Friday after school so Monday morning I would come in and open my locker to the smell of sour milk."

"I'm so sorry Roni. I wish I had known that. I did get him to finally stop picking on Nate. I really called him James the Terrible in my own head when I realized how horrible he really was."

"Remember that little Goth kid Brandon that was a year or two younger than us?" Veronica questioned.

She had to think. "Oh, yeah Swenson, didn't he have him stripped down to his boxers and tied to the flagpole? I wonder what happened to him."

"It was Swanson, and yes something like that. Rumor has it that he left and had to be put in the nut house."

Devan gasped, "That's awful!"

"Yeah, he was a nice kid too, we used to play together when we were little. His grandpa worked for Antoinette."

"You probably turned him goth," Devan giggled.

"I probably did. Hey, let's play a game. Who's worse James, Justin or Jeane?"

Jeane! That's who James reminded her of, though she couldn't see her hanging anyone from a flag pole or pouring milk in someone's locker. "That's tough."

"I know, right? Well, you don't need to decide anything. We can agree that they are all *terrible*, but—now you can leave Justin. Just give ol' James a call. He will hook you right up. Man, he looks almost the same, doesn't he? I bet he reeks of that same cologne." She paused, "Oh, what was it?" She pretended to be thinking very hard. "Ah yes—complete ASSHOLE!"

"I think I could have gone the rest of my life without seeing that billboard. Ugh! Thanks for wasting two minutes of my day on that bad energy."

"Sure, that's what friends are for."

Devan giggled at Veronica's sarcasm. "Smart Ass!"

⁂

An hour before the dance started, Kale and Pete were helping the DJ set up. When the gym doors opened, Kale looked up from the set list. His mouth almost dropped to the ground.

Pete looked up as well and his eyes flew over to Kale whose mouth was open. Pete leaned forward so only Kale could hear him. "Now they are some of the most beautiful women I've seen in a long time. You might wanna wipe the drool off though," he snorted. Kale finally tore his eyes off the women and touched his mouth to make sure there was no drool. He, however, could not help but look back at Devan. The crimson velvet dress fit her body like a glove. The tiny bit of cleavage gave him a peek of what lay beneath the smooth fabric. Her dress ended a few inches above her knees, and the red stilettos cradled her feet perfectly. Her long dark hair was parted to the side and curled under. She was without a doubt breathtaking. He jumped up and greeted each woman with a hug and a peck on the cheek marveling at how

139

lovely they looked. When he came to Devan, he bent down and whispered in her ear, "I hope you can save a dance for me, beautiful."

Devan smiled slyly, "Is there anyone else for me to dance with?"

As the night went on, the students were behaving so the adults were able to enjoy themselves. The DJ spoke, "We are going to slow it down a bit. This next song is an oldie but goodie and fitting for some of you ladies out there."

"Lady in Red." by Chris DeBurgh began playing.

"Oh, this is totally your song tonight," Kale dragged her out on to the dance floor without even asking. He peered down and grinned before pulling her close. "Wow, I don't think the top of your head has ever been so close to my face. Those must be some shoes you have on." He gave her a squeeze.

Devan looked in to his eyes. It *was* nice being closer to his face. *I could kiss him so much easier now.* She did, on the other hand, feel a little uncomfortable as his eyes did not leave her face. They looked directly in to hers. Dancing with Kale was one of her favorite things—the warmth of his body, the smell of his Nautica and one of his strong arms encompassing her while his other hand carefully held hers. She, of course, enjoyed that he was so much taller than her. Devan loved everything about it. Anytime they danced it was like no one else was in the room, just Kale and her. In the middle of her reminiscing and their dancing, her left heel broke. Kale held her tight so she wouldn't fall. She decided to take off both of her shoes and set them on the stage.

He was sure their dance was done, but she came right back in his arms. He rested his chin on the top of her head. "Now, this is how I remember it," he said. "You know what I have missed the most?"

"What's that Kale?" She rested her head against his chest.

"Kissing your head."

She looked up at him, "Kissing my head?"

He gently pushed her head back to his chest. "Shhh, don't talk. Yes, kissing your head. Your hair always smells so nice, and it feels like satin on my lips."

He kissed her head, "Plus it's easy access being this tall."

Their dance was disrupted with a loud slamming of the heavy doors. The entire gymnasium looked in that direction and saw a man dressed in a sharp suit holding two dozen roses in his arms. He noticed everyone had quit dancing and talking and was staring at him.

"Hello…um, is Miss Jenkins here? I have a delivery for her."

All the kids pointed to Alison standing by the punch bowl. Her mouth dropped open as Will walked over to her and handed her the flowers. She hugged and kissed him. Some kids whistled, most clapped.

"Oh, stop it!" she exclaimed with a huge grin.

Devan looked up at Kale who was smiling from ear to ear. "You knew about this, didn't you?" Devan squinted her eyes at him.

He shrugged, "I might have had an inkling."

"An inkling, my ass. I bet you planned the whole thing yourself." She smacked his chest.

"No, that was all Will. The only thing I did was tell him the date and gave him directions."

When the dance was over, Devan pulled out a pair of canvas shoes from her bag. The adults cleaned up and put things away. Devan was getting ready to leave and was saying goodbye to her friends and started toward the door. Kale was helping the DJ pack his equipment when he noticed Devan's shoes sitting on the stage. He followed after her calling, "Hey Monty," waving one of her shoes, but it was too late. She was already leaving the parking lot.

Pete laughed. "I see Cinderella left her shoe and Prince Charming found it," he commented to Kristy.

"Shoes," she corrected Pete.

A few days after the dance, Justin had picked up the mail and handed an envelope to Devan. She opened the card. It was a formal invitation to her high school reunion.

"What is it Dee?"

"It's an invitation to my fifteen-year high school reunion. The theme is prom."

"When is it?"

"April 13ᵗʰ."

"Do you want to go?"

Devan was surprised by what appeared to be his interest.

"Yes, I think I do," she replied.

"Well, you'll have to take Kale. I'll be out of town, I'm sure he will go with you." He abruptly left the room.

That was just like Justin.

"I'm a big girl. I don't need anyone to go with me. I can take myself!"

When Sunday dinner rolled around Justin brought up the invitation. "Hey, so Dee got an invite to her high school reunion," he said with a mouth half full of food.

"Oh, neat. How many years is it now?" Cassandra questioned.

"It's the fifteen-year reunion." *God, I feel old!*

"Anyway, it sounds pretty cool, but I can't go, and I don't want any of those guys hitting on my wife. She might think the grass is greener on the other side." Justin seemed like he was sincere.

Jeane almost spit out her food trying not to laugh as Devan was fuming knowing full well that the grass was truly greener on the other side.

"It's when Jeane and I will be in Vancouver. I know I won't have anything to worry about if she goes with you, big man," he said to Kale. "I know you can protect her and keep her in line." Devan was thoroughly pissed now.

"Well, I have to check my calendar," There was a tinge of sarcasm in Kale's voice.

"Like you have any plans," Jeane nudged him.

Kale looked at Devan and said, "I'd love to take you."

And he meant it with all his heart. "What is the theme?" he asked.

"Get this…it's PROM," Justin said.

Kale and all four parents stopped eating and stared at Devan.

Jeane looked at all of them and said, "Oh don't tell me you never went to prom."

"Oh, I did go." She could still feel everyone's eyes on her.

"Who was your date?" Justin was curious and shocked at the fact that she went at all.

Devan's father Chris, answered for her, "Kale was."

"Really? What happened? Did no one ask you?" Jeane sounded so condescending.

"And your big brother came to save the day," Justin continued for her.

Elaine, Devan's mother, almost choked.

"Actually, she had two invitations. This guy Jose and Pete," Chris stated.

"I thought Pete and Kristy were together then." Justin was confused, and the look on his face was priceless.

"They were, but she ended up with…" Chris continued.

"Mono!" Cassandra blurted out.

"Kristy had Mono, and Devan felt the need to stand in for her and that's why she told the other guy no," Cassandra lied through her teeth.

"So how did you end up going with Kale?" Justin wanted to know.

"He came into town to visit us, and Kristy was feeling much better so she asked Kale to go," Nahoa claimed.

"And then you traded dates?" Jeane asked trying to piece it together.

"Yeah something like that," Kale quickly said.

"That's unbelievable…" Justin said stunned.

"Oh, you have no idea!" Chris exclaimed.

The next morning Kale unlocked the funeral home and made his way over to the corner where all his plans were. Nate came in a few minutes later with a full drink carrier and large bag.

"I didn't know what you liked, so I ordered a few different things." He started pulling things out of the bag and naming them. "Eggs, ham, bacon, sausage, um—what else is here. Oh, pancakes and biscuits and gravy."

"Wow! That is a lot of food. You didn't have to go and do that."

Nate grabbed some paper plates and forks out of the bag and placed them on the table.

"It's my pleasure. I am indebted to you," Nate handed a coffee to Kale. "Black just the way you like."

Kale was thoroughly impressed. Nate had to be the nicest person he had ever met. He took a plate, opened the container with meat, took a piece of bacon and put it in his mouth. He chewed most of it before he swallowed.

"Say, did you get an invitation to your class reunion?" he brought up the subject to Nate who was splitting a biscuit in half.

"Yes, I did, but I kind of already made plans for that night. I doubt Veronica would want to go anyway, being the rebel that she is," He chuckled and poured gravy over the biscuit.

"Devan's husband requested that I take her," Kale said nonchalantly.

Nate coughed, practically choking on the food in his mouth. "Did you just say Devan's husband wants *you* to take her to the reunion instead of him taking her?"

"Basically, yeah."

Nate gathered himself together and took a drink of his coffee to clear his throat.

"I'm sorry, I just find it odd that he would do that, knowing the past you two have."

"I guess I never really explained that to you. He and Jeane don't exactly know our relationship. They've always assumed we had more of a sibling bond."

"I see. Are you going to take her?"

"I hate getting all dressed up in a monkey suit again, but it will totally be worth it to see her all gussied up. You really should consider changing your plans. I think the four of us would have a good time."

"If Veronica wants to go, I will. However, if it's up to me, no. I have no intention of seeing anyone else from school. That bar brawl in October was more than enough for me. I'm not sure if you heard the things that Jasper was saying. They don't bother me now, but in high school I heard those things every day and it did bother me."

"I get that, but look at you now."

"Yes, I would prove everyone right. 'That bean pole, Nate Cavendar, really did become a mortician.' While I don't *play* with dead bodies, I really do like helping those left behind by helping to make their loved ones look good."

"What I'm trying to say is, that you aren't that scrawny, tall kid anymore. Hell, if we weren't friends, I might be scared of you."

Nate gave him a look that that basically said "bullshit."

"Okay maybe not, but it's only because we have a similar build. We are both big guys. We are supposed to be scary."

"Great. So, I was scary then, and I'm scary now."

Kale rolled his eyes. "Okay. Let me try this again—and this time you can't respond. No one is going to mess with you like they did back then. They will be afraid that you would crush them. You should dress up in your Sunday suit with added confidence, and you will have a gorgeous woman on your arm. You are going to be owning your own business, and not many people can say that at your age."

Nate sighed, "I will go only if Veronica insists. That is my final answer."

"Okay, fair enough, speaking of your 'mistress of the dark' and my newest relative, can you still see a future with her, or is she getting on your nerves?" Kale had his phone under the table and sent a text to Veronica as Nate was talking.

> 4-13-12 class of '97 reunion, theme prom. Devan and I are going. You need to convince Nate to go. Don't tell him I said anything.

She returned his text promptly.

> Fuck, Yeah! I love dressing up.

Kale smiled and put his phone in his pocket.

"She's great. I really enjoy what we share, but—"

Oh no, not a but!

"I think it's time to take the next step in our relationship."

Oh good! Wait—what? Kale looked at Nate with raised eyebrows and a questioning look on his face.

"How would you feel about adding another member to your family? I have a ring already picked out."

Kale was so excited he got up from the table, went to where Nate was sitting and gave him a huge bear hug. "That would be awesome!" Kale let go of Nate and stood up. "There is one downfall though." He frowned.

"There is?" Nate questioned him.

"Yeah, I won't be the tallest one in the family anymore." Kale sat back down in his seat with a faux frown on his face.

Nate chuckled. "We can make you some platforms if you'd like." Nate put his coffee cup to his lips and then set it down. His face was serious. "This has to be kept between us. I haven't decided exactly how I'm going to propose yet. You are one of only four people who know, and I plan on keeping it that way."

"I promise, Nate, I won't say a word to anyone."

"I just have one request, no make that two," Kale said.

"And what are they?"

"You get her father's permission, and you name your first child after me."

Nate laughed, "I really don't think Veronica wants to have children, and I already did. He is one of the four."

"Oh good! I think that is an important old tradition. It shows respect and honor."

"I agree wholeheartedly." Nate had a huge smile on his face. Kale knew it reflected the same smile he had.

Kale was so happy. He grabbed Nate and hugged him again.

"Wait, do you have any idea what you are getting yourself into? Veronica is pretty spicy."

"That's one of the many things I love about her. It's funny, her dad asked me the same thing then said and I quote: *'If you are looking for a woman who is going to cook and clean all the time and keep her mouth shut—Veronica is not that person. She needs to wear a sign that says, 'Danger Ahead Proceed with Caution.'"*

Kale laughed, "All women should have warning labels."

That same day, Devan received an email from Alison. It read...

> Devan,
>
> Last night was wonderful. I think Kale had a hand in Will's surprise. Would you please thank him for me? Will was very tired from his drive and fell asleep about an hour

after we got back to my house. I was so excited and could not sleep, so I finished the story. I know there is still a lot more to our story, but for now this is enough. Please read it and tell me what you think.

Alison

Devan opened the attachment and read it thoroughly. The last page made her cry.

When we got back to my house, he handed me a little blue box. I was scared and delighted all at the same time. As he handed the box to me he said: "Alison, you are the light in my life that I have been missing all these years. I promise that I will never let you go again. Please promise me that one day, whenever you are ready, you will be my wife."

Chapter 13

April 2012

*T*he day before prom, Devan stared at herself in the mirror. 'I'm sick of my blonde hair. I look like half of the preps at school. I need a change, and I know exactly what I'm going to do.'

That evening Kristy came over to drop her dress off for the following day. Devan was just getting out of the shower when she got there. She unwrapped the towel covering her hair, and Kristy said, "oh-my-god! What did you do?"

"You don't like it?" Devan asked as she started combing her fingers through her thick dark hair.

"I mean, I don't know. I…uh…it's 'black', Devan—jet black."

"Yep, it was time for a change."

"That's a big change."

The girls had only thirty minutes before Pete was supposed to pick them up. They were putting final touches on their makeup and making sure their hair was perfect.

"I have to admit, Devan, I didn't think the black was going to work, but you look like you were born with it. I love it."

"Aw, thank you, bestie."

"Well, how do I look?" Kristy asked, fluffing out her dress.

"That green really looks great with your red hair. It's beautiful. You look gorgeous." They hugged.

"It's too bad Hawaii isn't here to see you. We'll take a ton of pictures to send to him so he can see what he missed," Kristy promised.

"That's a great idea. Let's start now." Devan pulled out a Polaroid camera and snapped some pictures of the two of them.

A short time later, the limo pulled up and Pete and the driver got out. "Your chariot awaits," he said when they answered the door. The driver was huge. He looked like he was taller than Kale. He opened the door and helped Devan in, while Pete helped Kristy.

'There's something strange about that driver. He held on to my hand a little longer than was appropriate. Kinda creeped me out.' She tried getting a look at his face, but he turned his head too quickly.

'Well if I'm going to get kidnapped, the only description I could give is that he had dark facial hair and a dark ponytail,' she thought. "Ew…"

"Ladies, I have faux champagne. Peach Orchard sound okay?" Pete asked. He'd gone all out with the limo, the drinks and the corsages. Kristy's was made up of red rosebuds and ferns with green and white ribbons. Devan's had purple and white orchids with tiny peach rosebuds and dark purple and black ribbons to accentuate her dress.

When they got to the prom, the first two songs the DJ played were fast. Pete danced like a pro, swinging both girls around like they were floating on air. They had so much fun. When things started to slow down, Devan excused herself so Kristy and Pete could have a slow dance. Someone came and sat next to her on the bleachers. "There's something about this song," she heard a familiar voice say. She looked over, and it was the creepy limo driver. "Would you like to dance?" he asked.

'Who does this guy think he is? He was paid to drive, not flirt with the clients.' "Um, no thanks. I think I'll sit this one out," she said and fake smiled.

He set his hat down and rubbed his goatee. "Come on, I won't bite," he said and grabbed her hand.

She tried pulling away, but his hand was huge. "Excuse me. I said, no." She looked up at his face and all her anger subsided. "Kale? What are you doing here?" She smiled, trying her hardest not to cry.

"Rescuing you from being a wallflower." He got up and led her out onto the dance floor where Mazzy Star's "Fade into You" continued playing. She wrapped her arms around his neck and he held onto her waist.

"I thought you were mad at me. I haven't heard from you in two months."

"I was too busy working a few extra jobs so I could take you to prom."

She gave him a nasty look. "Wait, so this was planned?" She looked over at Pete and Kristy. Kristy was looking right at her with a surprised smile on her face. Pete winked at Kale. "That jerk," she said and laughed.

"Hey, now, it was really hard for him to keep such a big secret. I told him I'd kill him if he told Kristy."

"Thank you," she said hugging him tight.

He kissed the top of her head. "I almost didn't recognize you," he said touching her dark hair.

"Well, I didn't recognize you with your beard and longer hair, plus I swear you're even taller than last time I saw you."

"Well, I grew an inch and gained ten pounds of muscle. I can't look like the boy next door forever, Monty."

She'd missed those green eyes and long eyelashes. And those lips, those plump, pouty, perfect lips. She grabbed his chin and kissed him. His lips were just as soft as she remembered. Being in his strong arms brought on a flood of emotions — safety, passion, love, happiness.

"It killed me not responding to you for two months, but I couldn't ruin my surprise. I did, however, still answer your letters. You'll get them, I promise."

"I missed you so much," she said, kissing him again.

Devan put down the picture that she was holding and came back to present day. Prom '97 had been magical. She ran her fingers through the dark hair lying on her shoulders, then went in to the bathroom and stared at her light roots. She took a closer look and could see a few gray hairs staring back at her. "Oh, hell no!" She was mortified. She knew how hard it was to cover up gray. Her mom complained about it all the time. "Man, I was not expecting to see you guys this soon. Well, I guess it's time to lighten up the situation. Fifteen years have gone by." Devan called her mom, got the name of her hairdresser, called the salon and made an appointment for the next day. She had two weeks left until the reunion. She was glad that Sunday dinner had been canceled after the first hair lift. It was going to be a two-week process of lifting the dark from her hair. It wasn't so much the shock value she was worried about but more so leaving the house with orange hair. The first lift of the black hair left it a medium reddish orangish to light brown. The second lifting was much better leaving her hair a light blonde with only undertones of orange, creating a bright strawberry blonde. The hair dresser combated the orange that was left from her second visit with an ash toner. Her hair was now a perfect medium blonde with a few highlights.

When she walked in to the Iakona's house for Sunday dinner, all the parents commented on her hair—how it was nice to see it so bright again, how it seemed healthier and made her appear younger. When Kale arrived, he was very quiet. She wasn't quite sure what he was thinking. He walked right past her and loaded up his plate. Then he sat down at the table across from her and began eating. Cyrus accidentally spilled his fruit punch all over her and himself half way through dinner. Devan excused herself and took Cyrus to the bathroom to clean them up. When she was in there, she peeked in the mirror and noticed several bumps on her crown. As she pulled the hair tie out of her hair, it broke. She smoothed her hair down and went back out to finish her dinner. When she sat down Kale quit eating. His fork had food on it and was only inches away from his mouth, but he just kept it there as he stared at her.

"What?"

He put the fork down, something she was almost positive he was incapable of doing.

"Your hair—It's—blonde?" he blurted out.

"Yes, it is."

"What happened?"

She couldn't tell if he really wanted to know, or if he was disgusted by it. She decided to be nice, although she wanted to bitch back. "I saw mom's stylist and had the color removed from it."

"How?"

"With bleach, Kale."

"Why?"

"It was time for a change. It's my damn hair. I'll do what I want with it. I don't need your approval," she snapped at him. The adults all stopped their conversations when they heard her raise her voice.

"I think it's perfect." Kale told her.

No one spoke a word, not even Devan. She was not expecting him to say that and didn't know how to respond.

"Don't get me wrong, I appreciated the dark too. This just looks more natural. It's a very pretty color on you."

"Thank you," her voice was quiet. Everyone went back to their conversations.

"You're welcome. So, let's talk about Saturday. Pete had mentioned something about getting a limo. He spoke with Nate and Vinnie too. Nate already had something planned and Vinnie is on duty." He began eating his food again.

"Oh no, Maggie was so looking forward to him coming." She grabbed her glass of water and took a drink.

"I know, but if he gets off early, he is going to surprise her. Do not say anything. I don't want to get her hopes up if it doesn't happen." He gave her a scornful look.

"I won't," she promised.

"Good, then Pete, Kristy, Maggie and I will pick you up at five-thirty." He took another bite.

"Actually, Kristy wanted all us girls to get ready here," she remembered.

"Cool. That makes it a lot easier."

That Saturday, Maggie, Veronica and Kristy showed up at Devan's house to get ready. "This is really kind of cool, Dee," Kristy commented plugging in her curling iron.

"Yeah, it is. Too bad you can't come with us, Roni," Devan said as she offered them all a glass of wine. Veronica refused since she had to drive over to Nate's house. Kristy refused, complaining about heartburn due to break-fast. Maggie accepted gratefully.

"I know," Veronica began to explain, "I'm sorry, but when Antoinette calls, you don't ignore her. We haven't seen her since Christmas, so this will be nice. Don't worry we will be there. I'm so glad those assholes, the two J's, are out of town. I can't see them being there. It would have been awful."

Devan agreed. Veronica stayed another hour until she had to leave. Shortly after, the girls were finishing with their final touches when they heard a knock on the door. Kale and Pete were each holding a dozen roses for their dates. Kristy's were a deep red and Devan's were a lovely peach. Kale also handed red roses to Maggie and said they were from Vinnie.

"Peach? I haven't seen peach flowers in a very long time. Thank you."

"I'm guessing the last time was at your wedding," Kale responded.

"No, there was no peach in my bouquet." Devan said thinking back.

"I beg to differ. When you get back tonight, take a good look at your wedding pictures." He linked his arm in hers and led her down the porch stairs to the sidewalk. When they reached the limo, the driver had already opened the door.

"I'm disappointed, Kale! I thought you were going to drive us," Kristy joked as she got in the car.

After dinner they arrived at the reunion expecting to see Nate and Veronica, yet they were nowhere in sight. Maggie's former cheer mates gathered around her as soon as they walked through the door.

"We will see you in there," Devan said to Maggie as she pulled Kale into the dance hall. As soon as they walked in, Devan heard a familiar voice.

"Excuse me, Devan?"

Devan cringed and turned to see Desiree. "Oh Desiree, please, not tonight," she begged.

"No, no. I regret what happened. I'm not here to start anything."

"You what?" Devan could not believe the words that came out of her mouth and she turned back around to face Desiree.

"I am terribly sorry for my behavior at Alumni Night in the fall. I was strung out on—well, you don't want to know, but I'm clean now. Getting arrested that night was the best thing that ever happened to me."

Devan was taken aback. "That is wonderful, Desiree," Kale said and squeezed Devan's shoulder to make her say something.

"Yes, uh, congrats," Devan managed to say.

"It took getting in trouble to finally realize I had a problem. I wanted to apologize to Veronica as well. Plus, I needed to speak with her about something else too."

"Well, she isn't here yet." Devan studied her. She had color to her cheeks, her hair was done up nicely, makeup was nice, and she appeared healthy.

"Hey, man," Jasper walked up to them. They didn't even recognize him. He filled out some, changed his hair, and was clean cut. "Jasper," he felt the need to remind them who he was due to the fact Devan was just staring at him. Once again Kale squeezed her shoulder.

"I'm sorry. I don't mean to stare. You look really great. You both do," Devan stated.

"Thanks. I finally got rid of the hair bleach and cut my mop. Bet you had no clue I had really dark hair."

"No, I didn't," she chuckled.

"Listen, I'm sorry for the way I acted…"

"It's okay. Hey, we all make mistakes." Kale cut him off and shook his hand.

"I'm so glad you guys came tonight. We both were hoping to see the two of you and Nate and Veronica. I don't know if Des told you or not, but I'm sober."

"No, I didn't get that far. We both started going to AA and NA meetings and found our way to each other."

"Congrats. I think that's great!" Kale shook Jasper's hand again and then Desiree's.

"Thanks, but we need to speak with Roni and Nate. Step nine is making amends."

"They should be here shortly. I think they will be as pleasantly surprised as we are." Kale said.

An hour or so had gone by, and they still hadn't seen Veronica or Nate. They walked around and mingled with people. Devan cringed a few times when people questioned her if she had heard James had become a lawyer.

She tried desperately to not think about the ginormous billboard she and Veronica had seen last month every time his name was brought up.

"Where are Nate and Veronica?" Pete finally asked.

Devan shrugged, "I was wondering the same thing. This afternoon she made it sound as if they would still be here about the time it started. I'll shoot her a text."

The music was turned down and one of their fellow graduates took the microphone. "As a special treat tonight, we have some of the playlist that was played at Prom, and we would like Maggie Frasier, student body president and 1997 Prom Queen, to come up."

"What? Why?" Maggie said trying to hide behind Devan and Kristy.

"Go up there, Mags." Kristy pushed her towards the front of the room where the DJ was.

She slowly walked up the steps and was presented with a bouquet of flowers and a sash that said "1997 Prom Queen". They placed a tiara on her head and then moved back to the microphone. "We are starting off the dance tonight with a special song that the King and Queen danced to at our prom. Will the King please come up?"

Someone yelled from the crowd, "He's not here tonight."

"Oh well, Miss Frasier, go ahead back to the dance floor and your date can share this dance with you."

She didn't want to say that she didn't have a date, so she stepped down to the dance floor and did her best not to show her embarrassment when the spot light shined down upon her.

"Would Miss Frasier's date please join her in a dance?"

Kale was ready to go up and dance with her when the doors opened, and the spotlight was moved on to that person. "May I have this dance?" requested the police officer who had just entered through the doors and was now walking towards her.

It was Vinnie. The music began playing as he put his arms around her. "Sorry I'm late. I came straight from work."

"I see that," Maggie rubbed her thumb over the name on his badge.

Devan took a picture of the dancing couple with her phone and sent it to Veronica. It was odd that she still hadn't heard from her. "Can you text Nate and see if they are okay. It's not normal for her not to respond."

Kale nodded, sent the text and then walked to a table that was empty and pulled out a chair for Devan.

When the song was over, Maggie and Vinnie went over to where Devan and Kale were sitting. "Hey, have you heard from your sister?" Devan asked Vinnie.

"Don't worry, they will be here. I just got confirmation before I came here tonight."

"What is taking them so long?" Maggie looked at the time on her phone getting concerned then sat down at the table.

"Don't worry about it, they will be here," Vinnie promised. It was clear Vinnie knew what was going on.

Maggie's, Kristy's, and Devan's phones rang all at the same time. It was a text from Veronica.

Come outside.

The girls didn't even tell their dates. They proceeded out the front doors and saw Veronica and Nate elegantly dressed as though they had stepped out of an early 1900's Gothic novel. Veronica's dress was a cobalt blue velvet with a sweetheart top that was slightly off the shoulders with ribbons hanging down. Under the bustline of the dress was a ribbon fringe. The dress was fitted from the bustline to the hips. There were two slits from the thighs to the floor that had embroidered edges. The back of the dress was longer than the front and lay on the floor as a train. With this she wore long black satin gloves. Nate wore a black coat with decorative nonworking buttons on both sides. The long sleeves ended at the wrists in six-inch cuffs. The bottom of the coat flared out and came to mid-thigh. Under the last buttons on both sides was black lace on the inside edges from the buttons to the bottom of the coat. Nate's vest was cobalt blue wide spaced double breasted in brocade with wide overlapping lapels. They looked exquisite.

Just then the men came out looking for their dates.

"Can you help me pull this glove off? I have such a hard time with it. It keeps getting stuck." Devan tried to assist, but the glove wouldn't budge. She tried loosening up the fingers when she saw it.

"Oh my god," Devan exclaimed.

Veronica pulled the glove off herself and flashed a beautiful antique engagement ring.

"It appears that I'm going to be Mr. Veronica VonStross!" Nate said with a huge grin. Kale, Devan, Kristy, Pete, Maggie, and Vinnie congratulated the newly engaged couple. After a few dances, many hugs, and several pictures the group decided to go back in and enjoy the remainder of the reunion.

When it was over, the gang decided to go out to a late-night restaurant. While they were waiting for their food, Veronica was telling them how Nate proposed.

"I headed straight over to Nate's after I left Devan's house. He was standing next to his 1951 Cadillac Hearse. Oh, she's beautiful and so shiny. Anyway, he was dashing in his attire with his hair tucked behind his ears..." She was looking directly at him with complete admiration and adoration. "He's so tall and handsome and when the sun hit his eyes at a certain angle they lightened to an almost dark honey brown..."

"We know what he looks like, Roni, get to the good stuff," Kristy interjected.

"Yes, sorry. Okay, so he said, 'We have to stop somewhere before going to your parents' house.' He took the long way to the cemetery. We got out and went to the Cavendar Mausoleum. He lit the sconces on the wall and there on his great-great-great however many great-Grandfather Nathaniel Josiah Bryant Cavendar's crypt..." She took a deep breath while grinning from ear to ear. "There were rose petals everywhere and an off-white box in the middle. He asked me to open it. I did and there was nothing in it. I was going to make some smartass remark—you know me. Anyway, he was holding the ring in his fingers. He basically told me he couldn't live his life without me and wanted to marry me. I obviously said *yes*. Then we kissed, we hugged, and then drove to my parent's house. They had planned a special dinner for the occasion."

"So that's why Antoinette was visiting." Devan commented.

Veronica nodded.

"Wait, are you really going to take her name?" Pete had to know.

"If she wants me to," Nate smiled.

Veronica scoffed and rolled her eyes. "Um no. You have a legacy to uphold. It will be an honor to take Cavendar as my last name."

After the food arrived, Kristy stood up and cleared her throat.

"Not now Kristy," Pete reached for her hand to pull her back down. She ignored him and began speaking.

"I have good news and bad news." Pete tried to get her to sit again.

"Stop, let me do it. If I don't do it now…"

"Speak Kris, what is it?" Veronica egged her on.

She cleared her throat again. "Pete and I are expecting."

Everyone cheered, then came the hugs and congratulations for the second time that evening.

When it got calm again Pete stood up this time. "I also received an offer for a position working with my cousin on an oil rig in Alaska."

Kristy interrupted her husband. "The pay is unbelievable."

"Did you take it?" Kale asked before taking a bite of his food.

"Yes, we leave May 30th." Pete frowned.

"That's a chilly place to raise a baby," Veronica stated.

"Yes, but we will make it work." Kristy replied.

That night they all left the restaurant with bittersweet feelings. They were happy for the news of Kristy and Pete's pregnancy, and Nate and Veronica's engagement but very sad that Kristy and Pete were leaving their town.

When Kale took Devan home, she invited him in for a cup of tea. While the herbs were steeping, he requested that she pull out her wedding album. He was right. There were two peach roses tucked away in her bouquet.

"How did I not notice this?"

Kale shrugged his shoulders. "Oh, I don't know, maybe the excitement of getting married had something to do with it." He smiled half-heartedly, but Devan didn't notice. She stared at the picture. Memories of that day flooded her mind. *I wasn't excited to be marrying Justin,* she thought. Devan paused before replying, "I don't think that was the case."

"No?" Kale questioned.

"I think I was too focused on trying not to run away with you when you begged me to," Devan looked up from the album. Her eyes met Kale's, and she couldn't turn away.

Kale gazed deep into her eyes. He never expected either one of them to end up married to different people. Kale always imagined his life with Devan and only her. He wanted nothing more than to run away with her and all their kids. Knowing that it wasn't possible at the moment, he kept staring into her eyes, placed one of her hands in both of his and said to her, "Understand this," he leaned in so close, he could smell the coconut scent left by her shampoo. "We will have our happy ending. I promise you that."

"What makes you so sure?" Devan inquired. She had her doubts—everything and anything always seemed to get in the way of their happiness. Wanting a life with Kale was one of the only things she had ever truly wanted.

"I just have a feeling. I can't describe it. Just know, we will be together someday. Until then…" He finally looked away from her beautiful blue eyes, kissed her hand, and took his leave. Devan gazed at her hand where he had kissed her, eyes brimming with tears as she prayed that he was right. *We deserve to be happy.*

Chapter 14

May 2012

Kale decided to throw Kristy and Pete a going away party on Memorial Day. The weather was nice but hot for May. Kale had opened the pool the previous weekend, so it was ready for the party. He and Nate were grilling the standard Memorial Day staples—hot dogs and hamburgers. Veronica and Devan were poolside watching the kids. Pete and Kristy were on their way over.

Veronica sat up and tried squeezing more lotion out of the tube, it was empty. "Hey, can I use some of your sunscreen?"

"Didn't you just apply a bunch?"

"I did, but I forgot my feet." Veronica whined.

Devan sat up and turned to Veronica. "It is 90 degrees out and you are wearing a huge sun hat, huge sunglasses, and a long sleeve cover-up." Devan laughed while pulling her sunglasses down to the tip of her nose.

"It's sheer," Veronica pointed out.

"I forgot, the dead do not like the sun." Devan giggled and pushed her sunglasses back up.

"Oh my god, fine…" Veronica took her hat off and set it on the concrete under her lounge chair and put her sunglasses in it. She pulled off the cover up to reveal a black and white hypnotic two-piece swimsuit which was covered in skulls. The skulls were all types of fluorescent colors.

"I didn't know you had skin," Kale shouted to her while flipping a burger on the grill.

Veronica stuck her fist in the air, put up her middle finger and flipped him off.

"Hey! That's my fiancée." Nate opened the package of hot dogs, then handed them to Kale.

"That she is sir. I still can't believe it. I think you guys make a great match. I am very happy for you."

"Thank you, I think so too. Man, it's getting hot," Nate took off his black t-shirt and put it on an Adirondack chair close to him.

The girls cocked their heads at the perfect time. Nate had just taken off his shirt, exhibiting his fit and sexy body. He was a tad darker skinned than Kale.

"Oh my," Veronica exclaimed. Devan leaned over close to Veronica, so no one could hear the conversation.

"Have you guys uh…"

"No."

"Seriously?"

"Yes."

"I'm sorry."

"Thanks, I need all the sympathy I can get. I knew he would be hot, but I didn't exactly expect him to have pecs the size of Kale's."

"Are you telling me this is the first time you have seen him without his shirt on?"

Veronica kept silent and put her sunglasses back on, so she could gawk at him without getting caught.

"Oh my god, it is!" Devan stared at Kale, who took his shirt off next. "Oh my god, how I miss having my hands all over that body." She spoke a little too loud.

"Dee, children." Veronica reminded Devan of the kids swimming within hearing distance. "Oops. I'll just stare at Nate then. He really is a fine specimen. How are you not attacking him?"

"I want to. I want to sooo bad it hurts," she whispered to Devan, so the kids couldn't hear her. "Jesus Christ, just look at him. I want to go over there right now, grab his hand, take him in the house, yank off his swim trunks, push him down on the floor, jump on him and glide my fingers down that rock-hard chest. Oh my god, I'm getting hot flashes." She waved her face with her hand. Devan couldn't help but chuckle. Veronica was sweating and turning red.

"Go jump in the water and cool off."

"This isn't the kind of thing water is going to take care of." Veronica threw her sunglasses at Devan and dove into the pool.

Meanwhile back at the grill Nate was in awe of his future wife.

"Wow! She is voluptuous." Nate said it in a way that made Kale question their intimacy. They watched as Veronica emerged from the pool. She smoothed her long dark hair back and out of her face.

"You say it as though you have never seen her before."

"Well, I've only seen her fully clothed." Nate was flustered, embarrassed that the truth was coming out.

Kale was stunned, "Wait! So, you are saying you guys haven't…"

"No."

"Not even a little…"

"No."

"But you are engaged!" Kale was amazed. He took the burgers off the grill and put them on a plate.

"I asked that we wait. It's a type of respect that I want to show her and that she deserves." He took the plate from Kale, set it on the picnic table and covered it with another dish so the flies wouldn't bother it.

"Wow, man, I am shocked and impressed. That willpower…I can't even imagine. Look at her, she is smokin' hot!"

"Yeah, it might be more of a struggle now," Nate admitted quietly as Veronica strutted over towards them.

"Hey, do you need any help?" She tipped her head to one side trying to get water out of her ear.

"No, but would you like a drink?" Kale looked her right in the breasts.

"Eyes up here, Cuz, as in cousin," she sassed.

"I'm sorry, I'm just dizzy from your swim suit," Kale used as an excuse.

Veronica tilted her head down and then jumped once and laughed.

"It is kind of hypnotizing. I didn't plan on being a hypnotist today." She squeezed past the guys and went to the cooler. She bent over very seductively and glanced back at them both staring at her. "Anyone else want one?"

They both shook their heads no. She took a water for herself and one for Devan. She moved extra slow past Nate grazing his chest with the cold bottle.

When she sat down, Kale could hear Nate exhale loudly.

"All that is yours," Kale smacked Nate on the arm.

"Not yet."

"Not yet what?" Justin came up behind them and smacked them both on the back.

"Veronica isn't mine yet," Nate answered. Justin leaned over the table in front of him almost touching the food. "Damn! She is bangin'. I never even imagined…"

"I don't think you should start now." Kale pulled him away from the food.

Justin looked back at both Nate and Kale. "I'm sorry, bro. I don't mean any disrespect," he told Nate and patted his shoulder. "I bet your nights are wild." He bit his lip. Kale smacked him on the back of his head. "All right, all right." He started to unbutton his shirt then got a glimpse of Nate and Kale and how large they were compared to him. He felt inferior. "It's not that hot yet. I think I'll keep this on a while. Besides you both make me look extra white." He walked away towards Jeane with his tail between his legs.

"That's not all we make him look," Kale puffed out his chest. Nate laughed.

Pretty soon everyone had arrived, so they sat to eat. Kristy was telling the girls what her new house looked like, while Pete was explaining his job to the guys. No one had even bothered to see that another person had shown up until Veronica tapped Devan on the shoulder and pointed to the tall man with white hair coming through the gate.

"Who's that?" Veronica asked her.

"That's Alistar Cadence, Jeane's uncle."

Veronica's mouth dropped. "*The* Alistar? He's real?"

Devan nodded her head. Alistar stood about six-two. He had salt and pepper hair, with way more salt. There was never a single hair out of place. His clothes were always crisp and clean and never anything less than a sport jacket and tie. Devan figured he didn't even own a pair of jeans. He was pleasant towards Devan, but his professionalism took over his personality. When he would smile, she never knew if it was real or fake. Every once in a while, however, she would see a glimpse of a real human being in his piercing blue eyes. He reminded her of Donald Sutherland, especially his voice. He was handsome for a much older gentleman.

"What's he doing here? As far as I know he's never been seen in public."

Devan laughed, but Veronica wasn't far off. Devan had only seen Alistar about ten times in her entire life.

"I have no idea," Devan said then left Veronica behind to find out.

"Hello Devan. It's so nice to see you. How have you been, dear?"

"Very well, thank you. And you, sir?" He put his hand on the top of her back.

"That's good to hear. I am quite well myself. I am here looking for a Mr. Peter Monahan. I was told I could find him here."

Devan led him to Pete. Before she had a chance to introduce him, Alistar introduced himself. "Do you know who I am, son?" Pete said *no* then put his plate down. "I am Alistar Cadence."

Pete grabbed his hand and shook it. "It is so nice to meet you, sir."

"Likewise. I heard you just accepted a position with a potential client of mine, Mr. Carter."

"Yes sir, on his oil rig." Pete picked up his plate.

"I heard that he often visits his fields and his rig. If you meet him, I'd like you to put in a good word for us. He is a very important person that we want to have in our corner. He needs to know how reliable we are and what hard work we can do. Especially how dedicated and talented our main architect is." He gestured towards Kale.

Pete swallowed the food in his mouth. "Absolutely."

Alistar reached into his pocket, pulled something out and handed it to Pete. "This is for your troubles. Buy something nice for your new place." He walked away leaving Pete standing there to see what had been placed in his hand. Pete opened his hand and stared at the nicely folded cash. His eyes grew large as he counted it. He mouthed to Devan *"ten thousand dollars."*

"Go put it in a safe place," Devan urged him. He looked down at the money, then back at Devan and shook his head. He went over to where Alistar was standing. "Sir, I can't accept this."

"Sure, you can son…I almost forgot," he pulled something else out of his pocket and handed it to him. "Start a college fund for your child." He smiled at Pete and turned back around.

Pete trotted over to Devan. "Tell me you saw that?"

Devan nodded. "Yes, now go put it in a safe place until you leave."

Kale came over to Pete before he had a chance to do anything. "Dude, why didn't you tell me you will be working for Carter Petroleum?"

"I didn't think it mattered." Pete shoved the money into his pocket.

"How did he find out if you didn't even know?" Devan butted in.

Kale and Pete looked at one another and then over to where Jeane was standing.

"I told her what your new job is, and I guess she did the research. You'd think she would have told me."

Pete and Kale looked back at one another and said "nah" at the same time then chuckled.

They watched as Alistar was talking to Jeane and Justin. It looked as though it was a heated discussion. Jeane pointed over to Kale and then to Devan. She shrugged her shoulders and then walked with her head down over to Kale. "Justin and I can't go to the lake in July. Uncle Alistar has a full schedule for us the week before and the week of the vacation." Kale couldn't tell if Jeane was actually upset or putting on a show. "I tried explaining that it was our first actual nonwork related vacation in a few years. He says either we change it or cancel it."

"Jeane we are all looking forward to that trip. There is no way they are going to have any other dates available this late in the season." Kale told her.

"Well, then you'll have to go without us. What about your friends Nate and Veronica? They could go in our places."

Kale looked at Jeane and tried his best to sound disappointed.

"Yeah, I guess I could ask them. Hey, Nate can you come here a second?" Kale yelled to Nate who was on the other side of the yard. Nate walked over and asked what was up.

"Do you guys have any major plans in July?" Jeane asked.

Nate thought for a moment then shook his head. "No, just work for me and Veronica is a teacher so she is off."

"Is there any chance you would be willing to go to Tennesse with mine and Justin's families for vacation? Justin and I have to work. I'd like you to go in our place." Jeane said taking ahold of his hand practically begging him.

Nate looked over to where Veronica was and called her over. When she got there Jeane gave her the same spiel. Veronica looked at her calendar on her phone.

"What week?" She asked.

"The 22nd through the 28th." Jeane replied.

Veronica scrolled down to the dates then looked back up at Jeane. "I'm free."

Jeane was delighted. "That is wonderful. Everything is already paid for, so you'll just need to pack your bags. Don't forget sunscreen, we redheads are so fair."

Veronica watched Jeane walk away. "Why does she consider me a red head?"

Kale looked down at her head. "Well, it does have a reddish tint to it in the sun."

"It's not real, and I would hardly consider it red. Anyway, vacation sounds fun. I wonder why Devan didn't say anything." Veronica asked.

"That would be because she doesn't know yet. Why don't you go inform her." Kale suggested.

Veronica went back over to where Devan was and explained everything. She was, of course, excited. She would much rather have Veronica and Nate there than Justin and Jeane. She knew everyone would have a great time.

"I keep forgetting to ask, did Desiree ever find you?" Devan asked Veronica changing the subject.

Veronica took another bite of her hamburger and began talking with her mouth full. "Yes, I meant to tell you this. First let's discuss the transformation she and Jasper had. Good God! I had no idea he had dark hair did you?"

"No. I was shocked to see them both and hear them apologize," Devan told her.

"I know, that's crazy shit right there, but…they do kind of make a cute couple."

"Yeah, I thought the same thing. So, what did Desiree *have* to talk to you about? Was it just she apologizing or what?"

"Well, she did apologize. They both did, but she didn't just apologize for the bar, she also apologized for the shit with my ex-husband."

"Really? That's interesting," Devan said unscrewing the cap on her water to take a drink.

Veronica leaned in. "It gets even stranger. Get this, Tom is back."

Devan made a face like she had no idea who Tom really was, so Veronica continued. "My ex-husband, you know the guy she went and screwed?"

"Oh, why?"

"She isn't sure. But she saw him at the bank the other day. He was in town for a bit. Had some family business to attend to." Devan took a swig of her water. "She seems to think he's *really* here to get me back,"

Devan spit out her water.

"That was my reaction too," Veronica laughed.

"Well, he can try all he wants. I can't see you leaving that gorgeous man over there." Devan pointed at Nate who was talking with Pete and Kale.

"Oh hell no! I have no idea why she thought that. It is strange that he came back though. I was told he moved to Florida, and that his family moved there shortly after. I'm not sure what family business he would have left to handle."

"Hmmm…"

Kristy came up to the girls and gave them hugs.

"Are you leaving?" Devan asked getting up.

"Yeah, thank you so much for doing this. It was really nice."

"I didn't do this, it was all Kale." Devan said pointing to the man.

"Well you helped, and I appreciate it. I'm going to miss you so much." Kristy squeezed her again.

"And I really hate to miss your wedding Roni," Kristy hugged Veronica.

"I know, but you will see pictures and I will call you and tell you all about it." Veronica promised her.

Pete came over and hugged the girls as well. Kale and Nate soon joined the group of friends.

"I feel like I just got *you* back and now *I'm* leaving," Pete said to Kale.

"You know I'm only a phone call away my friend," Kale said giving him a big bear hug.

"Nate, I am so glad I finally got to really know you. You are pretty cool guy."

Pete hugged him as well.

"Let us know that you get there safely," Devan said while grabbing on to Kristy one last time.

"We will. I love you guys!" Kristy said letting go of Devan.

"We love you too," Devan said as she stepped closer to where Kale was standing. They watched them go out the gate and get into their car and leave the driveway.

"There they go, off to the next chapter in their life." Kale said as he put his arm around Devan's shoulder.

Chapter 15

The Lake 2012

It had been four years since Kale and Devan and their families had been to the lake. The kids were older now, would appreciate it and they would be able to have a little more freedom. Thanks to Kale's pool, all of them knew how to swim. Though the adults wouldn't let them swim without supervision, the resort was small enough they would easily be able to keep tabs on the kids on land.

Devan was excited for Veronica and Nate to be there. She knew they would all have a great time without the negativity of Jeane and Justin. It was going to be a great vacation.

The ride was long as usual, traveling with that many kids was never an easy thing. All the bathroom breaks alone would make any adult frustrated, yet Veronica and Nate didn't complain once.

When they arrived at their cabin, Kale had Joey take the kids over to the basketball court to play so the adults could unpack and set things up without the little ones getting in the way. When they were finished, the guys decided to take the kids swimming out behind the cabin which left Veronica and Devan free to take a walk and explore the grounds.

"This is the infamous *willow tree!*" Devan pointed to a giant old weeping willow tree with long green tendrils hanging down, some even close to the ground.

"Well, it is very beautiful." Veronica tried wrapping her arms around the trunk, even though it was too thick. "Pleased to meet you Mr. Willow. I will be stopping by later to introduce you to my fiancé." Veronica continued, "You know Devan, I really could introduce Nate to the tree, and he wouldn't think I was a total freak. He loves nature and would enjoy the fact that I do too. I think he will really love it here."

When the girls got back to the cabin, they were greeted by Will and Alison who had five large pizzas in their hands. "Your dinner is ready," Will said to Devan as she unlocked the door.

"We didn't even order it, yet." Devan motioned for them to come in.

"*We* did. Dinner is on us tonight," Alison said as she set the boxes down on the table. Devan yelled to the guys and the kids to come up to the cabin to eat. After dinner Veronica and Nate offered to take the children to the playground that was nearby.

Kale and Devan sat down at the table with Will and Alison as they watched Nate and Veronica follow the kids out the door.

"That is going well," Will commented.

"Oh yes, aside from you two I have never seen a better match," Kale replied, and Devan nodded in agreement.

"I have!" Will winked at Devan making her blush.

The kids, Veronica and Nate came back a half hour later red faced and sweaty.

"Hey, do you guys want to see an old broken-down houseboat?" Will asked getting up from the table.

The kids all yelled, "Yeah!"

They all climbed up the hill to a building that said McGrudle's Garage. Inside there was a tattered large vessel. Rust peeked through the peeling paint on the railing. There were marks from it sitting in the water for a long period of time. Holes were in the screens on the windows and what curtains that were left were in shreds. The inside showed cupboard doors hanging from hinges that had let go several years earlier. The cushions on the furniture and mattresses on the beds were split with tufts of stuffing hanging out.

"Hey Mark, can you step out for a minute?" Will kicked at something under the boat.

"I can slide out," a deep southern voice said coming from under the boat. A man, on a creeper, scooted out from under it. Devan could tell he was quite tall. As he moved out from under the boat, it was as though his legs had no end. Will introduced the man, "This is my cousin, Mark. He owns this garage. He works on boats most of the time with an occasional car or two."

When Mark stood up, he was only a few inches shorter than Kale. He put his hand out to Devan then retrieved it quickly. "Sorry ma'am. I don't want to get grease on ya," he apologized.

"It's cool. You can call me Devan."

"Pleased to meet you," he nodded.

"And this is Kale," she introduced.

"Ha, yes, Kale, the man not the vegetable."

"That would be me," Kale grinned as he stepped closer to the man, grabbed his hand and shook it. "I'm not afraid of a little dirt."

"I have heard a lot about you, sir." Mark chuckled as he handed Kale a towel to wipe the grease off.

"These kiddos are Joey, Sage and Kai, my children, Callie and Cyrus, Devan's children and our best friends, Nate and Veronica," Kale said gesturing to each of them as he said their names.

"Nate? Your real name Nathaniel?" The man questioned as he stepped up to him.

"Yes."

"By any chance, are you a Crane?"

"Yes, sir. How—"

"Who's your mom?" Will was curious.

"Willow Crane," Nate told him.

"Your mom is my second cousin which makes you somehow related to Will here as well."

"Our native American cousin! Well that makes sense. You do have a lot of her features," Will commented as he walked over to Nate. He looked him up and down as though he were remembering something. "You know who he really reminds me of?" Mark thought but didn't have an answer. "Nick,"

Will said nodding his head. Mark wiped his hands and set the rag down on the tool box. He got a better look at Nate.

"Damn, they could almost be twins." Mark asked, "Do you remember a big family reunion sometime back in the '80s? You would have been a little guy."

"I don't think he was ever a little guy," Will grinned.

Nate had to think about it before he responded. "Vaguely, I do remember a big lake with lots of people, and there was one kid close to my age that I played with who was darker complexioned like me."

"This would be that lake, we were some of the people and that kid was Nick," Mark said slapping Nate on the back.

"Wow, this is a lot to take in. It's nice to finally meet family," Nate said as he shook Mark's hand.

"Wanna hear somethin' else?" Will asked Nate with a smile on his face. "You aren't the only undertaker in the family. We got four of 'em other than you. I bet you are the tallest though."

"Yup there's Bennie, Sasha, Nick and Timmy. They work together at the family funeral home. They would really enjoy meeting you," Mark said and put his hand on Nate's shoulder. "We are going into town on Tuesday. Why don't you and the future Mrs. come with us? We'll take you to the Gregecevic-McGrudle Funeral Parlor. You'll meet them all."

❧❦❧

They looked into each other's eyes for a long time before Kale moved his lips over hers. 'I'm in heaven', she thought. His arms were wrapped around her, and the softness of his beard tickled against her chin. It was so nice, but it wasn't smart.

She pushed him away. "Even as much as I hate Justin right now, and as much you hate Jeane, this is still wrong."

He picked her up and set her in the tree. "Come on, Monty. You can't tell me you aren't enjoying this. All of these memories from when we were kids—"

"Kale, we aren't kids anymore."

"No, but we can pretend." He tilted her chin down so he could kiss her lips. She didn't fight back. He put his hands around her lower back and she draped her arms around his neck and wrapped her legs around his waist. He picked her up and gently set her on the clay pebbles beneath the tree. "I miss this," he said brushing her hair out of her face.

"So do I, but it can't happen anymore, Kale."

"Okay, but how about one last kiss—"

"No."

"Just one little peck—" He kept getting closer to her face.

"No." She smiled.

He kissed her anyway. "Okay, I'm done," he said as put his hands in the air.

Devan sat up for a few minutes and stared at the moon shining through her window. She loved when she had dreams that were actual memories especially ones like that. As much as she wanted to, Devan knew she would not be able to go back to sleep. She didn't remember seeing that tree down by the dock. She peeked at her phone. It was 5:07a.m. Everyone else was sleeping, so she decided to get up and go to see if that tree was still there. Quietly, she stepped out of the door and headed down to the dock. Devan was extremely disappointed when she saw the tree was no longer there. She sat down on the pebbles and sighed. The moon was beautiful, bright and full. It's reflection in the water was starting to ripple, and she heard splashing in the distance. Devan got up to investigate. When she turned the corner, she saw someone in the water. She was worried they needed help.

"Are you okay?"

"What?" It was Veronica.

"Roni, what are you doing?" Devan was somewhat irritated.

"You'd better not be standing on my clothes."

Devan looked down to see what appeared to be a pile of clothing beside her feet.

"I'm not standing on your clothes. Now what in the hell are you doing out here at five o'clock in the morning? No offense, but you aren't the type of person to swim laps in a lake." She was standing with her hands on her hips.

"No offense taken. I'm doing a cleansing," Veronica said as though it was a normal thing.

"Please don't tell me you are naked and taking a bath in the lake."

"I'm not taking a bath. It's not like that. I'm doing a spiritual cleansing. There are many ways to do it, but my favorite is with water. You could use a good cleansing yourself. You should do it with me."

"Why would I want to do that?"

"It can remove negative energy and replace it with positive energy. I always feel better afterward."

Devan considered it. "All right, what do I do?"

Veronica was very happy to share this moment with her friend.

"Okay take all your clothes off," she instructed.

"What? No, don't tell me you are naked—"

"Okay, I won't tell you."

"Seriously?" Devan rolled her eyes.

"It's going to be dark for another hour, so no one will see. I won't watch."

Devan groaned, nevertheless she did as she was told. She was already having second thoughts.

"Now, close your eyes, and picture a white light surrounding you. See the light from the top of your head throughout your whole body, going down your arms into your fingers, all the way through your toes. Can you feel the energy?"

"I think so."

"Good, now gently go under the water, and as you go down ask the universe to wash away all of the negativity that has been surrounding you. Be specific when you ask."

Devan did as she was instructed. As she sank to the bottom, she asked that all the negativity be taken away. That wasn't all, she also asked that the vacation be wonderful without too many emotions. She did feel lighter when she surfaced.

"How do you feel?"

"Surprisingly better, we should do this all the time."

Veronica laughed at Devan. "So, what's going on in your mind now that we are here?"

Devan swam for a few seconds then answered. "I'm fine. I think since we didn't bring Satan and her disciple with us it helps. However, it's just the first day. As long as feelings, hands and lips stay out of it, we will be good." Devan dove under the water and came up near Veronica. "I have to say swimming naked is amazingly freeing."

A bass boat flew by in the distance. It was starting to get light out.

"Time to go, Dee. The fishermen are heading out."

When the girls advanced towards the shore, they saw Kale holding their clothes with a smirk on his face.

"These wouldn't be yours, would they?" He knew damn well they were and answered his own question, "Of course, they aren't. Fine ladies such as yourselves would never go skinny dipping." He turned away from them.

"Hey, asswipe, give 'em back," Veronica demanded.

He started walking up the hill.

"Kale, come on," Devan shouted after him, but he just kept on going. "Kale Kai Iakona, if you don't come back here right now—"

He was completely out of sight. Veronica and Devan looked at one another with open mouths.

"Do you think he's coming back?" Veronica worried she would have to get out of the water nude.

"If he knows what is good for him, he will," Devan huffed.

Kale came back a few minutes later with towels. He pulled something out of his back pocket and threw it at Devan. She snatched it and held it up. It was a bikini top. He threw something else at Veronica. It was the bottom. "You can decide who wears what. I'll leave these towels right here."

"Come on, dude, that's it?" Veronica pleaded.

Kale laughed and took something out of his other pocket. It was another top and bottom. "What do I get if I give these to you?"

At the same time Nate walked around the corner of the cabin. Devan wasn't sure who would be more embarrassed if he saw her naked—him or her.

"Hey, breakfast is ready," he said as he stood next to Kale and checked out the garments Kale had in his hands. "Um—"

"What do you want?" Devan bellowed.

Kale smiled really big, "I want a big fat kiss on the cheek from both of you at the same time wearing your bikinis, and I want Nate to take the picture. Then I want you to do the same with him."

"Deal," Veronica grinned.

Nate shook his head, "No, you don't have to do that."

"He's first!" Veronica pointed at Nate.

Kale threw the pieces in the lake to the girls. They put them on and started slowly walking out of the water trying to avoid any sharp shale rocks that could slice their feet. The tops barely fit exposing just a little more than intended but not enough to cause worry. Nate almost looked away. Almost.

The girls posed on each side of him. Kale pulled his phone out of his pocket and held it up.

"Okay, now I want backs toward the water." He stepped in front of them, moved Devan so her front was to Nate's side and put her hand on Nate's chest. Then directed Veronica to do the same thing. He stood there shaking his head. "Something is not right…" He thought for a moment. "Nate, take off your shirt."

Nate bowed his head down. "Is it really necessary?"

Kale nodded his head. Nate shook his. Veronica gave Devan a look, "Should we?"

Devan snickered. She knew Nate would turn bright red if they did it. Devan nodded and the girls each took a side of his shirt and lifted it up trying to take it off.

Kale snapped a few pictures as he laughed. When Nate's shirt was finally off, the girls went back to their stances.

"Wow Nate, I knew you looked good, but your chest feels as hard as it looks," Devan commented.

Veronica didn't say anything. She was ecstatic finally touching her fiancé's bare, warm, tan chest. Kale was thoroughly enjoying Nate's bashfulness and Veronica's gratification. So was Devan. When it came time for the kiss on the cheeks, Nate was forced to squat down. Next up was Kale. He didn't have to be forced to take his shirt off. He took it off and threw it on the bank. "Let's do this, ladies." He squeezed them as he crouched down when they kissed his cheeks. "This is the life, my man!" Nate chuckled and took the picture.

After breakfast, Nate and Veronica left with Alison and Will to meet the rest of Nate's family. Kale and Devan took the kids out in the boat for the day. When they came back to start dinner, Nate, Veronica, Will and Alison were already there.

"We were wondering if we could take the munchkins off your hands tomorrow?" Will asked Devan and Kale. "There is a carnival in town, and we'd love to take them," Alison said.

Devan and Kale glanced at one another then looked at the kids pleading faces.

"You sure you want to? Five kids *is* a lot," Devan stated.

Alison and Will both answered "yes".

"Okay, if you are sure." Kale shrugged his shoulders.

Bright and early the next day Alison and Will picked up the children, so Veronica, Devan, Nate, and Kale all piled in the boat. Kale showed Nate and Veronica the waterfall. It seemed as though it had been completely decimated by people and the environment. It was a solemn sight to see. On the way back, Devan shouted something to Kale. He couldn't understand over the loud roar of the motor, so he stopped the boat.

"What?"

"The stone house," she pointed to the shore.

He beached the boat on land and tied it to a tree. They walked up the short hill to an abandoned stone house that was slowly crumbling. "Ugh, this is just as eerie as the day we found it years ago."

Devan was really excited to show it to Veronica. She knew she would love it. "Oh, I hope Edith is still there." She said hiking up the hill as fast as she could. She didn't bother to go in the house, instead she walked around it to the other side. She squealed as soon as she found what she was looking for. Nate, Kale, and Veronica walked through the tall yellow blades of grass to where Devan was. She was standing by a headstone that read, "Edith Lenter, 1878–1889, Beloved daughter."

"Now, did you honestly think someone would have dug her up?" Kale asked trying to reach her.

"Funny you would even mention that. Veronica and I learned yesterday that digging up graves was something that did happen in this area," Nate remarked.

"Um…"

"No, it's true. This area was…well, still is a big flood plain. The Army Corps of Engineers decided to build a dam, so they made people relocate, burned down houses and barns, moved graveyards, all to create this lake, and counteract flooding to keep people safe," Nate explained.

"That's horrible," Devan stated.

"It was, yet it continues to save lives," Nate said inspecting the stone.

"So, you are saying that down at the bottom in the middle of the lake there are towns?" Devan moved on from Edith's headstone.

"Were," he corrected. "There wasn't much left. There are probably some remnants of foundations, that's about it."

"We aren't swimming with *dead bodies*, are we?" Of course, it was Kale who needed to know that.

"No, they dug up the graves and took whatever was there including different colored soil and relocated it to a higher level that wouldn't be underwater." Nate tried not to laugh at Kale.

"Yeah, I still bet…" Veronica began.

"La la la…" Kale cut her off and covered his ears, so he wouldn't hear the rest of what she was going to say.

"I bet they missed some is all I've got to say. Especially the old ones. I mean even some of the bones would be decayed." Veronica said yelling up to Kale.

"I *thought* I heard voices. Can I help you?" An older gentleman approached the group. It startled all four of them.

"I'm sorry, we just assumed this was an abandoned…" Kale started.

"It was, but even so, it's private property." He gestured to the faded, ripped *No Trespassing* sign on a tree thirty yards away.

"I'm so sorry," Nate apologized.

"Is that you Nick? Well, why didn't you say so, introduce me to your friends," the man said coming up to Nate.

"Sir, I'm sorry. I am not Nick, but he is my cousin. My name is Nate."

"Oh my, you resemble him quite a bit. I just heard about you today when I was in town. I'm Hershel McGrudle, one of your other cousins." He extended a hand to Nate.

"I am so pleased to meet you Mr. McGrudle. This is my fiancée, Veronica, and our friends, Kale and Devan."

"Family, not friends, Nate," Veronica corrected him.

"Yes, I'm sorry…our family," Nate said with a smile.

"Well, son, if they are your family, and I am your family…that makes them kin to me too. Follow me, I have some fresh sun tea waiting in the house."

They followed the man into the no longer empty cottage. Devan and Kale were both shocked to see all of the improvements that he had made. The peeling wallpaper was gone and the plaster repaired. A whole new floor had been put in along with electric and plumbing. The fireplace was still there, and so was the picture of the girl with her parents.

"I love what you have done. I can't believe you kept the portrait," Devan said walking up to it.

"Yes, ma'am. A few years back, I checked the house out and found it had good bones. Since it belonged to family, I decided to take a chance on it. A lot needed to be done to it and still does, but each time I finish something, it's nice knowing I'm restoring a piece of history. Naturally, I couldn't get rid of the picture. It's of my great aunt Edie. She's buried out back," Hershel said as he met Devan at the fireplace.

"I knew it was her. I told you Kale."

"Who? That dead girl in the picture?" No sooner had he said it, he could feel all eyes on him, and it wasn't a pleasant feeling. "I'm sorry, I just meant because it was a postmortem photo. I meant no disrespect." Kale said trying to save his ass.

"That's okay son. How did you know that she was dead in the picture?"

"She told me," Kale said pointing to Devan. "She said that the girl most likely was dead due to the way she was leaning awkwardly on her mom and her eyes were looking somewhere else, almost as if they were frozen."

"She was correct. Poor Edie died the night before this was taken. She had malarial fever." Hershel explained.

"Is that the same thing as Malaria?" Veronica inquired.

"It is, she was the only one in our county to get it, too. Poor thing."

"I thought that was a tropical disease." Devan stated.

"Yes, however it wasn't back then. The CDC spent a lot of time trying to eradicate it. They finally succeeded between 1920 and 1940." Nate spoke up.

"The CDC was around then?" Kale was surprised.

"Somewhat but it didn't actually become the CDC until the late '40s I believe." Nate answered.

"Well, aren't you a bucketful of knowledge," Hershel chuckled.

"That's so hot. It's nice to finally be with someone who has a brain," Veronica whispered in Devan's ear. "Remind me to talk to you later about something," she added.

After their visit with Hershel they went back to the cabin and had dinner with Will, Alison, and the kids, who were waiting for them. Devan and Veronica decided to take a walk after cleaning up the kitchen, the rest stayed back to play games.

"I wanted to tell you what happened last week. My ex came by the house."
Devan's eyes grew big. "What?"

"I think Desiree was right about him wanting me back," Veronica said.

Devan quit walking. "What did he say?" She wasn't sure she could walk and listen at the same time. A conversation like this clearly needed her full attention.

"He apologized and tried to kiss me. I backed up and told him I was with Nate. It was funny though, he questioned me three times who Nate was, almost as if he knew him. It was weird. Anyway, he said he was sorry and left. It was very awkward." She kept walking not even having noticed that Devan had come to a complete halt.

"Did you tell Nate?" Devan was hoping she hadn't.

"Yes, I did. I didn't do anything wrong." She backed up and grabbed Devan's arm, "Keep moving, Dee."

"But what if …"

Veronica interrupted, "That schmuck would not have a chance even if Nate was not in the picture. He's damned lucky I didn't clock him—or rip off his balls,"

"Well, I do believe you. I believe that no one measures up to Nate."

Both girls giggled at the comment. "He definitely measures higher than most men at six-foot-seven."

"That tux fitting is going to be fun. Speaking of tux fitting um…I want to know if you would be my Matron of Honor?"

Devan was stunned. "What about Maggie, you guys have been best friends forever."

"Well, she is my Maid of Honor. I spoke with her before we left, and I told her that I was going to ask you to be the Matron of Honor. She was glad. She thinks you should be the one standing next to me since we have become so close. I told her order doesn't matter, I love you both."

"She should be standing next you, not me, but yes, I would be honored."

"Thank you so much. I do agree with her though. I want you by my side. Maggie and I don't see each other as much, and you and I talk a lot more. If I'm going to be honest, I really want to see you walk down the aisle with Kale. I don't give a shit how trivial that sounds. Plus, I know Maggie wants to walk with Vinnie."

"I didn't know Kale was in the wedding. He hasn't said anything to me about it."

"Nate is going to ask him this week. He already asked Vinnie last week. It's a damn good thing tuxes don't take four months to come in like our dresses."

"True,"

"He already had his mind set. I can't believe he didn't say anything to Kale when I mentioned something to you girls about being bridesmaids. He's going to ask him to be his best man. I swear, they are almost as inseparable as you and I." What Veronica said was true. Kale and Nate were together a lot and had a meaningful friendship.

"I think that will be great. I was already excited for your wedding. This is just icing on the cake."

"You know what is really cool?"

"What?"

"We will all be related one day." Devan scrunched up her face which showed Veronica she was not following what she was saying at all, so Veronica went on. "Kale and I are related now. When Nate and I get married he will be related to my brother. My brother will marry Maggie, then she will be related to all of us. Finally, when you and Kale get married…all six of us will be related by marriage one way or another."

Devan laughed and hugged Veronica. "I like where your head is—maybe one day your assumption will become a fact."

"It will, I've seen it." Veronica was certain.

Chapter 16

fter they docked, she grabbed his hand and led him down a path into the woods, instead of going straight to the cabin. Nothing was said as the rain kept pouring down.

The trail led to an opening near the willow tree. She pushed him against the tree just like she'd done years ago. He leaned down, his hair dripping water on her as she met his lips. She kissed him like it was the last time she'd ever see him.

He wrapped his arms around her and held her close, but she broke the embrace.

"I let you go…" A bolt of lightning lit up the sky and the thunder roared.

"What?"

"Kale Kai Iakona, I release you from my heart and from my soul," she said as tears streamed down her face.

"You aren't making sense."

"I can no longer love you, I can no longer care about you. You're free to live your life without me."

"Devan, don't…" He dropped his arms and stepped back.

"This is my goodbye. I can't keep doing this to myself. The same goes for you. Things went way too far today. I won't be able to look Justin in the eyes for a long time." She was trembling, and the rain wasn't letting up.

"Devan, nothing really happened."

"It did, though. Once again, we stepped out of bounds. This whole trip has been nothing but us going out of bounds. You might be okay with it, but I'm not."

"Then what was that kiss?"

"That was goodbye, Kale. After today, I think it's best if we don't talk for a while." She looked away from him.

"Devan Marie…"

"You're moving, and I think maybe that's the best thing for us."

"Well, I'm glad this is so easy for you, because it fucking sucks for me!" He took another step back.

"It's what's best for you, for me and for our children." She was right, and Kale knew it.

He got in her face. "You know, you've constantly complained about me rescuing you over the years. Well I'm sick of you making decisions for me! You don't want to see me? Fine!" He started walking away, and a cold gust of wind chilled him to the bone.

"Kale!" she yelled. He slowly turned around. "We can't keep our hands off each other. I'm not saying it will be forever".

"Poof…I'm gone," he said and turned around.

Streaks of pure white danced across the sky and thunder echoed all around them.

Kale opened his eyes and stretched. He knew he wouldn't be able to sleep anymore after having that nightmare. *I might as well get up.* That time long ago nearly destroyed him and his family. Kale's hate for Jeane intensified. Because of the move, he couldn't even turn to his parents for help with the kids. He could have used the assistance since they were having problems in school and at home. The only good part was that Jeane was gone most of the time. Three long years he and Devan were separated with absolutely no contact. What should have happened was his family unit got closer, but it didn't. The kids were sensing his pain, and in turn, they acted out. Jeane continued to be Jeane—out for herself. That time was bad enough, but it was over so what was the point of dreaming about it? He got out of bed, tiptoed to the back door and was able to slip out without waking anyone. He sat down on the picnic table and stared out at the water trying to get the horrible dream out of his head. It wasn't working very well. The sun would be rising soon though, and he would no longer be alone with his tainted memories, or so he thought.

The door creaked, "I didn't think anyone else was up." Veronica sat down beside Kale at the table. He almost breathed a sigh of relief that his alone time came to a rather quick end. Almost. "Did you know the last time we were here Devan and I didn't talk for three years?" He didn't even say good morning. He was too worked up.

"That's what she told me."

"Are you aware of the reason?"

"I know it was a heightened emotional time and that you tried your hardest to get her back…"

"I should have fought harder," he stopped her.

"No. The timing was off. After meeting Jeane, I'd have to say Devan made the correct decision. I'm sorry, but she was right."

"Fuck the timing. It's never going to be the correct time." He glared at her. She could see the anger and frustration simmering in his emerald eyes.

Veronica leaned her head on Kale's bicep and put her hand on his. "At some point the time will be right…I don't know when, however, I know that you guys will be together again, the way you both want to be."

"She still wants me?" His question made Veronica lift her head to look at him. He had a smirk on it.

"She never stopped wanting you, not that you need to be told that."

"It's nice to hear," he grinned.

"Now, if I make coffee, will you drink some?"

Kale glanced down at his watch. "I have a better idea. Let's take a stroll down to the marina. It will be open soon. I'll buy you a cup."

On the way to the marina, he slowed his pace when the old willow tree came into view.

"Go on, Hawaii, give it a hug. It's been a while since you have seen your old friend." Veronica nudged him.

"Oh no…she told you that too?"

"Only her version! I'd *love* to hear yours." Veronica winked at him.

Kale proceeded to tell her while they walked, how he and Devan had made plans after dinner one day to meet at the tree. One thing led to another and they ended up in the woods by the tree out of sight in a heavy make-out session. That's when they heard their parents close by.

"Devan had a bad case of the giggles. I just knew we were going to get caught." Kale laughed at the memory as he opened the door to the marina. He grabbed two cups of coffee, paid the cashier and headed outside to a table overlooking the lake.

They sat down, and Kale handed her a cup. "So, are you ready for the wedding?"

"Yeah, I think so, got the caterer, and the music…"

"What song are you having for your first dance?" Kale interrupted her.

"Shit!" Veronica looked like a deer in headlights.

"Shit? I think I'd pick something a little more romantic," Kale harassed her.

"Oh, shut up! I can't believe I didn't think of that. I have no idea." She placed both of her hands on her cup and sighed.

"Every couple seems to have a song they call theirs. What is yours?" Kale took a sip of his coffee and quickly put it down again, complaining it was way too hot.

"We don't have one." She panicked, "How could I not think of that? I have everything planned down to my underwear."

Kale snickered and then narrowed his eyes at her. "I didn't think you owned a pair of underwear."

Veronica smacked his arm. "This is no time for jokes."

"It's okay, I will gladly help you through this. We will find a song. I promise."

She was almost in tears. "I'm about to marry a guy that I don't even have a song with."

"Jeane and I didn't have a song. I told her to pick one out, I didn't care."

"You can't compare your wedding to mine, Kale. I am actually in love with Nate. You never even liked Jeane," Veronica threw out.

"You got me there, kid."

She fiddled with her cup while trying her best to not let the tears, that were welling up in her eyes, escape. "I want a song that means something. I don't want to just pick one. Do you and Devan have a song?"

Kale sat back and stroked his beard. "Kinda,"

"What do you mean kinda? You aren't being very helpful."

"There is this song, "Fade Into You,". It's kind of haunted us through the years."

"Haunted you?"

"Yeah, first time I heard it I was slow dancing with Devan at the Homecoming dance in 1994. Then I believe it was at your guys' Prom. I'm surprised they didn't play it at the reunion. Anyway, it's happened several times over the years when I'm dancing with Devan. That damn song always finds a way into our lives."

Kale sat back and chuckled, "Does that help? Are there any songs that stick out?"

He could tell by the expression on her face that she was thinking very hard.

"We danced to a few songs at the reunion. There was one that I really liked, but I don't remember what it was. I don't normally listen to that kind of music."

"You were preoccupied that night. You were freshly enga…"

"Wait," Veronica exclaimed, "there was this song that was playing on the radio…we had stopped to stargaze, and we could hear it in his car. It's an old one from the '50s, I think. Anyway, he took my hand and we danced. What the hell was that song—I only something, something for you."

"Oh, I know that song." Kale began singing it, "I only have eyes for you."

"Maybe, let's look it up." Veronica pulled her phone out. Kale beat her to it.

"Here," he set the phone down and the music began to play.

"That's it!" She jumped up and down. Kale grabbed her hand and started twirling her around. It was the end of the song when Kale dipped Veronica backward. Will was standing there with his arms crossed.

"Listen…I can't handle another complicated relationship, let alone another damn secret especially from you," Will pointed at Kale, "and she's betrothed to my cousin. Now you are messin' with family." He pretended to get angry.

"No, no, it's not like that. She needed a wedding song and…you know she's my cousin now, right?" Kale questioned.

"I'm kidding. I know neither of you is that stupid. Besides your relationship comes off as more of a sibling kind of thing. Wait…did you just say cousin?" Will scratched his head.

"Yes, our grandparents married each other in December of last year," Veronica said and took a seat.

"Well, isn't that something," Will smiled. "Hey, it's going to rain today. They aren't calling for it, but trust me it's going to rain. I wouldn't venture too far from the cabin if I were you," he warned them before walking in to work for the day.

When Kale and Veronica got back to the cabin Devan and Nate already had breakfast made.

"Where did you guys go so early?" Devan asked setting milk on the table.

"Are you jealous?" Veronica teased.

Devan grasped Nate's hand, pulled herself close to him and hugged him. "Nope."

"Did I miss something?" Nate looked down at the top of Devan's head and then over at Veronica.

Veronica and Devan both laughed. Kale wasn't paying attention. He glanced over when he heard them and saw Devan's arms draped over Nate.

"Oh, I see how it is…" He gave Devan the evil eye. She couldn't help other than to laugh even harder. Kale could see the confusion on Nate's face, and he chuckled too.

"They are just messin' with you, bro."

During breakfast, Veronica mentioned what Will had said about the weather.

"Well we could go out for a bit and come back as soon as it starts raining."

The kids quit eating and shouted "No!" in unison.

"Why not?" Devan wanted to know.

They all began talking.

Joey put his hands up to hush the others, "I got this!"

"Before you guys got back yesterday, we were watching a movie about a ship on the ocean that sank and everyone died."

"You want to know why everyone died, Mom?" Cyrus shook his fork at Devan, "because it rained in the boat."

Veronica lost it. "Guys, that's completely different. Storms on the ocean can be very scary, but we are on a lake. That would never happen," Devan promised them and shot Veronica a dirty look.

"You go ahead and go out there then. I'm not going to get on any boat if it's going to rain," Cyrus told her.

"How about I stay here with you guys and we play Uno, then your parents can go out for a little bit?" Nate suggested.

"I don't want them to die either!" Sage had a worried look on her face.

"I promise we won't." Kale leaned over and hugged her.

"Are you sure?" Devan asked Nate.

"Yes, he's sure. Go skiing, have fun," Veronica answered for him.

"Thank you," Devan said and got up from the table to clean up her mess.

"Dee, go get ready and leave before it does start raining. I will take care of this, just go."

Devan and Kale thanked Veronica and Nate and went down to the boat. When they got out on the open water the sky wasn't too dark. Kale put the boat in neutral and asked Devan if she wanted to chance it. She put on her ski jacket and ski gloves and jumped in the water. He waited until the boat had drifted far enough away from her, then put the ski in the water and shoved it toward her. Devan waited for Kale to throw the rope. The moment he threw the ski rope, it started pouring. There was no warning at all. He reeled the rope back in, and she swam with the ski and handed it to Kale.

After he took the it, he helped her up onto the platform and into the boat. He stood near the driver's seat and waited for Devan to get situated. She took off her ski jacket and headed to the front where Kale was, and, as fate would have it, she tripped. Naturally he caught her. With both of their bodies slippery from the rain, they held their embrace and stared into one another's eyes until a colossal wave hit the boat rocking them and knocking them on the seat. Their eyes were wide from the initial shock. They looked at each other and began laughing hysterically.

"Nothing like a little *déjà vu* to start your day," Kale laughed. Devan wished she could go back to that magical day. It was the first kiss they had ever shared. She had been flirting with some motorcycle-riding, bad boy-type guys. Kale didn't like it one bit, so he interfered after one of the guys agreed to take Devan for a ride. Kale called her his little sister. Devan remembered how much it pissed her off! She also remembered, just how amazing that first kiss was…

The rain was coming down in sheets. At the speed their boat was skimming across the water, it felt like hail was pelting their skin. Kale threw the towel at her again. "Use it!" Devan obeyed this time. She didn't want to admit it, but it did help. Suddenly, the boat stopped. Kale looked both frustrated and confused. "What the…" He put the boat in neutral and turned the key off and back on again. The motor sputtered, then nothing. "Damn it!"

"What?" she hissed.

Kale threw his arms up in defeat, "We're out of gas."

"Dad told you to get gas," she said giving him a cold stare.

"No, he told 'us' to get gas."

"Well, what are you going to do, Hawaii? Can't rescue us now, can you?"

"Is that what this is about? Yesterday with those motorcycle guys who were very willing to give you a ride?"

"Hmph!" was her only response.

"Jesus, Devan! Our dads would've kicked my ass if I hadn't gotten you out of there."

Devan glared at him. "I didn't need rescued, asshole!"

"Maybe you didn't think so, but I'm a little more educated about how guys think than you are."

Devan's temper ignited and she stood up. Throwing the drenched towel down, she got in his face and poked his chest with her finger. "Stop rescuing me! I'm not as stupid as you think when it comes to boys." She was so cold and angry that she was shaking.

"Really?" he asked taking a step closer to her.

"Yes!" she spat at him.

Kale grabbed her head and pulled it back so he could reach her lips. She was stunned and initially tried to push him away, but that urge quickly faded as she began to return his fiery kiss. Her hands found their way from his chest to the back of his neck, deepening the kiss.

With his fingers tangled in her hair, he pulled away. "No, you don't! You had no idea I was going to do that," he said angrily.

"Oh, so you're into incest?"

"What?"

With her hands on her hips she sassed, "You told those guys I was your little sister."

He rolled his eyes and said in his best hillbilly imitation, "Yep, if I had a sister I'd kiss her just like that. Mmmhmm."

"Well, your sister would be disappointed in your kiss…if that's what you want to call it," she said sarcastically and laughed.

"You think you can do better?"

"Oh, I know I can," she said with a devilish grin. She shoved him down onto the driver's seat and straddled his lap. She grabbed the back of his neck and tangled her hands in his hair pulling him to her. She touched her warm lips to his and gave him the best kiss he'd ever had. He put his arms around her waist and pulled her in even closer. His powerful arms engulfed her as his lips began searching hers for more.

A horn blew and Devan jumped off his lap, startled. Another boat from the resort had pulled alongside. "You kids need a tow?"

"Um, yeah, thanks. We ran out of gas," Kale said.

"You been out here since this started?"

"Yes, sir."

The man tossed a towrope to Kale and he tied it to the boat's bow. "You kids are probably freezing. Let's get you back to the dock." Devan and Kale exchanged glances. They weren't so cold anymore.

"Do you forgive me?" Devan asked snapping back to the present while trying to balance herself and get off Kale.

"Forgive you for what?" Kale was completely unaware of her quick change to a somber mood.

"For letting you go…"

He pulled her back down on top of him and held her there. "I was angry, I was hurt, I may have said some not so nice things about you, but…"

"But what?"

"You were right, and I discovered something when I came back," he paused trying to be more suspenseful.

"Which was?" Devan was losing her patience.

The ends of Kale's mouth turned upwards, and he had a huge smile on his face. He then released his tight grip on her. "You never really let me go," he finished.

Devan stood up and backed away from him. "And who told you that?" She put her hands on her hips.

"No one, it's written all over your face every time we are together." He smirked, sat all the way up and put the keys in the ignition to start the boat.

"Ohhh…so that's what you think huh?" She scoffed at him and picked up a towel.

"There is no thinking about this, Monty, I *know*!" He turned the key and the light sputtering of the motor seemed to echo in the hollow they were in.

"You know nothing, Kale Kai Iakona. Nothing!" She sat down in the seat and folded her arms across her chest. She knew that Kale *did* know. Still she wasn't going to give him the satisfaction of admitting it.

When they reached the dock it was dark, and the lightning had just illuminated the sky. Devan jumped out and pulled the boat in while he turned it off. She held the boat steady for him. He reached over the side but his wet shirt stuck to the wood. He took his shirt off and this time he bent over the side still trying to tie it. Devan could see all his shoulder and arm muscles move. She was enjoying the sight until she got caught.

"Is this better?" Kale flexed for her.

"Shut up Iakona," she growled and peered out into the storm. Lightning lit up the sky again. She picked up her towel and headed towards the end of the dock. He jumped out of the boat and chased after her grabbing her arm.

"You need to wait until that lightning dies down. Go have a seat in the boat," he instructed. She glared at him and went back to the boat and sat down. The rain was loud on the tin roof of the dock. Devan wasn't about to talk to him, while Kale was being smug. When the rain slowed to a steady rhythm, she hopped out of the boat. He followed her up the hill. Right before they reached the cabin he snagged her arm and turned her to face him.

"You aren't seriously mad, are you?"

"Why, does it matter?" her tone indicated that she was.

"Come on Monty, I was just having fun with you." Kale held her there with his hands on her shoulders. She stared up at his gorgeous face and smiled. She stood on her toes, raised one hand, stroked his beard, then moved her other hand to the back of his neck. He didn't look away from her eyes. She slowly moved her hand through his hair to where it was tied. She had to stretch her arm farther to get ahold of the band. Devan concentrated on keeping eye contact with him as her face kept getting closer to his. He gazed at her lips then back at her eyes. He moved even closer making it easier for her to grab the band holding his hair. It was fairly loose. She pulled it out releasing his thick wet curls and scooted away from him.

"Thanks," she said and tied up her hair with it.

"What was that?" Kale asked her while moving his hair out of his face.

"I lost my hair tie in the lake, and I needed one," she pursed her lips and then took off. He caught her, threw her over his shoulder and walked in the cabin that way. Veronica nudged Nate and nodded towards Devan and Kale.

"I'm glad to see they had fun today," Nate smiled.

Friday morning came early when Sage woke up the whole cabin with a nightmare.

"It's okay, Sage, we are here," Devan tried consoling her.

"What happened?" Kale asked.

"I had a bad dream," she said cuddled in Devan's arms.

"About what?"

"I don't want to talk about it," she answered her father. "Can I come lie in your bed?"

"Of course," Kale couldn't say no to her tear-streaked face.

Devan squeezed her tight then released her hold on the little girl. "Go, get some sleep."

"Aren't you coming too?" Devan couldn't ignore that pouty face.

"Yes, she is," Kale spoke for her. The three of them crawled into Kale's bed.

Sage took Devan's and Kale's hands and put them together with hers on top. She looked over at each of them and grinned. "Now isn't this nice?"

They snickered.

Kale and Sage fell asleep. Devan's mind was going a mile a minute. Her hand was still in his. His sheets had his scent—coconut, lime, and a hint of Nautica. She studied the features of his face. His eye lashes were long, his eyebrows were arched just right. His nose was perfect, his lips were pink and plump, excellent for kissing. His facial hair was a bit straggly. His dark, thick, curly hair was pulled back. She noticed the sun had put a few light reddish-brown streaks in it. Kale really was beautiful even with an overgrown beard and mustache. He opened his eyes and saw her staring at him. He smiled his magnificent smile. Devan sighed and watched him raise his eyebrow. *Oh God that was out loud.* Kale had heard her sigh. She tried letting go of his hand and slip out from underneath Sage's arm. Devan was only half success-ful. He was not letting her hand go. Kale shook his head *no* and refuse to let go until, she mouthed she had to use the bathroom.

An hour later everyone had awakened, and breakfast was being cooked. Sage sat down next to Nate at the table. He asked how she was feeling. The little girl claimed she was fine. "I was thinking, Sage, why don't we make dream catchers today?"

"What is a dream catcher?" she asked Nate as she took a drink of her milk.

"A dream catcher catches all your bad dreams and only lets the good ones come through to you."

Sage clapped her hands, "YES!" She loved the idea.

"Okay, after breakfast why don't we search for things that we can use to make it?"

"What will we need?"

"Something round to make the circle, some string and, if we can find any, feathers to decorate," he told her.

Sage stood up. "Okay people, chop-chop. We need to hurry and eat so we can get to work."

The day was spent swimming, boating and searching for items that could be used to make dream catchers. They had found fish bones, an occasional odd shaped stone, and different types of feathers. When everyone got back to the cabin the boys took the buckets that had the items gathered and poured them out onto the picnic table on the deck.

Nate checked out what was there and scratched his chin, "We did good today, but we still need things to make the frame and string." He went in the back door of the cabin and out front and looked around. He came back with a smile on his face. "I found something, follow me."

They followed him out to the old willow tree. He took a knife out of his pocket and cut off nine wispy pieces and handed one to each person. "Okay before we start, I want all of you to thank the tree for the use of its tendrils." Devan grinned at Veronica who was beaming at Nate's request.

"Why do we need to thank it? It's just a tree," Callie said.

"It is not just a tree, my little friend, it is a living organism. Trees help give and sustain life. They give us the oxygen we breathe. They can provide food, shelter and even medicine."

"Oh wow!" Callie jumped up, hugged the tree and thanked it.

Veronica and Devan giggled as all the kids did the same. When the kids were done, Kale went over and put his arms around the tree. "I thank you for your branch and all of the memories you have provided." He winked at Devan.

Veronica, Devan, and Nate thanked the tree as well. Nate suggested that they sit in a circle surrounding the trunk of the tree, and he began to show them the first steps to making the hoop for the dreamcatcher. He held out his tendril and slowly made a circle with it about the size of his hand. He took the remaining part of the branch and wrapped it around three times creating the hoop. He then moved the remaining length in the center of the hoop then out. He kept doing that as well as twisting the hoop around securing its shape.

"Then you tuck the end in," he explained as he slid it in between the already intertwined part. Sage was having a rough time with it and requested his help. While he was working on the frame, she asked quietly if she could call him Uncle Nate.

"Of course, you can." Nate handed her the hoop.

"Does that mean I have to call Ms. Vonstross Aunt when you get married?"

"Well, no, you don't have to," Nate said.

"I want to, even if she is a teacher at my school," Sage whispered.

"I'm sure she would like that," Nate smiled. "but you should ask her first if it is all right for you to call her that."

When everyone was done with their hoops, Nate asked if anyone had ideas for the web. Joey jumped up, ran to the cabin and came back with a handful of dental floss that he handed to Nate.

"That is very resourceful, Joey. Great idea." Nate took the floss and showed them how to weave a web in the hoop. "And then you leave the string out that you tied on the hoop last. You take two or three more pieces and tie it on to the bottom."

When they did that, they went back to cabin to choose what stones, feathers, and bones they wanted on their dreamcatchers.

Later, Kale thanked Nate. "That was a cool thing you did. Thank you, because of you I have a happy daughter."

"Good, hopefully she will sleep well tonight. Hey, I was going to ask you something," he said to Kale.

"Yeah?"

"You are the brother I never had," Nate put his hand on Kale's shoulder.

"Likewise," Kale nodded.

"I would like to know if you would mind being my best man?"

"Mind? Are you kidding me? I would love to be your best man." Kale hugged him.

"That means a lot to me, thank you."

After they packed up to leave, Nate pulled Devan aside. "Can I talk to you for a second?"

"Yeah, sure," she told him.

"I was wondering if you would help me with something? Kale tells me you are an excellent singer." Nate stated.

"I don't know if I'd say that." Devan blushed.

"The way he talks about it, I'd say you can sing very well. I have a baby grand piano that's at least 100 years old. My grandmother taught me to play when was six. It needs tuned up," he spoke quietly and took a quick look around to make sure no one was listening.

"I had no idea you played." Devan was quite impressed.

"I don't think anyone does, but I was thinking if you are willing to sing, I will play the accompaniment."

"To what song?"

"It's 'A Thousand Years' by Christina Perri."

"I'm not familiar with it, but I'll give it a try," Devan said and put a hand on his arm.

"Thank you. If it's okay with you, I'd prefer to get started on it shortly after we get home from this trip." Devan agreed. Nate embraced her. "Thank you so much! This will be very good."

"What will be very good?" Kale, being nosy, walked around the vehicle to where Nate and Devan were.

"Just a little surprise for Ver—" Devan cut him off then put her hand up to stop him from saying anymore.

"It's none of your business, Iakona. You'll just have to wait." She gave Kale a look and brushed past him.

"You know, Nate, sometimes her sassiness is so sexy other times I'd like to strangle her," Kale chuckled.

Chapter 17

Fall 2012

Veronica's and Nate's wedding was less than a week away. After the piano had been tuned, Devan met Nate at the funeral home two days a week to work on their song in secrecy as per their agreement on vacation. It was their second to last rehearsal when Nate stopped mid song.

"Damn it!" He noticed Devan was staring at him with large eyes and her mouth dropped open. "I'm sorry, the pedal just broke," he apologized.

"Oh my god, you just cursed! Are you going to spontaneously combust?" Devan joked.

"You have been around Veronica too long. That is exactly something she would say."

"If you are swearing, then you've been around her too long as well," she laughed.

"I will have you know, I have been saying 'damn' for at least two decades."

"Nathaniel Raven Cavendar, you just swore again!" Devan pretended to be shocked.

"No, I was just saying it, not cursing. However, I will probably say 'damn' and a lot more if I can't get this pedal replaced by Saturday. It's going to be difficult when I work until six and they close at four."

"Not a problem. Make the call first thing in the morning, and I will make sure I am available to be here when they can fit it in."

"You would be willing to do that for me? Oh, thank you! By the way, how did you know Raven was one of my middle names?" He looked up from the piano.

"Wait! You have more than one?" Devan asked with one eyebrow raised.

Nate nodded his head. "Yes, Bryant is the other one. All of the Cavendar boys have had the middle name Bryant at least since Nathaniel Bryant Josiah Cavendar, the man who came over from England."

"Wow, that's neat and creepy all at the same time." Devan commented.

"I'm assuming my 'bride to be' told you that."

"Well, it's kind of funny now that I think of it. A while back we were talking about John Cusack and Veronica had mentioned how she was more of an Edgar Allen Poe fan from the movie, *The Raven*. Then she found out Raven was your middle—well one of your middle names, and flipped out."

Nate smiled. "That is amusing. I never thought about that. She *has* stated how Poe is her favorite author." He glanced down at his watch. "I have to go pick up her birthday gift before the store closes. I know it's a little early, but I really wanted to give it to her on our wedding night." He got up from the piano.

"Where are you headed?"

"To an antique bookstore near where I work. It just opened a few weeks ago."

"Do you mind if I tag along?" Devan picked up her purse and keys and headed for the door.

"Of course not. I'm glad you want to go. I want you to meet the owner, and I would like to know your opinion on the gift."

When they arrived at the book store a woman about their age came up to them. She was about Devan's height, had long, dark, thick hair and chestnut eyes that matched Nate's.

"Nathaniel, I am so glad you came in today. I was hoping to see you before the wedding. I don't work the rest of the week." She looked at Devan and stuck her hand out. "Hello, I'm Rachel Lakeland."

Nate introduced Devan and the woman gave her a hug.

"Oh, I am so happy to meet you. I hear you were the matchmaker," she said as she brushed her long hair out of her face.

"I wouldn't say that. They pretty much matched themselves."

"Well, I hear you had a hand in it." Rachel turned to Nate, "Are you excited?"

Nate nodded his head, and his eyes lit up like a little boy at Christmas. "I am. You and Lucas are still coming, right?"

"Absolutely, my brother finally might have found that date."

Devan found it a bit strange that Nate invited someone he just met to his wedding but wasn't going to question it too much. Veronica hadn't said anything about extra guests. She wondered if Veronica knew.

"Rachel and I are actually related. We found out when we met."

Now I see why she was invited.

"Lakeland, as in Lakeland Estates?"

"Afraid so, my great-great-great-great-great grandpa killed this guy's great-great-great-great-great uncle."

"That's right. Jonetta was cousins with Oswald and Nathaniel."

"Oh, she knows her town history." Rachel was impressed.

"Well, I just learned that last year. This is so cool," Devan said.

"Come back here, I want to give the book to you," Rachel nodded towards a door.

They went in the back of the shop where the kitchen was. Rachel pulled something very carefully out of a box and placed it in Nate's large hands. Devan tried to get a closer view of it.

The Raven, by Edgar Allan Poe. The cover was light brown and the letters were fading. It had to be exceptionally old.

"This is a first edition. It was illustrated by Gustave Dore. Harper and Brothers published it in 1884, thirty-five years after Poe's death."

Nate really *was* the perfect match for Veronica. Devan couldn't think of a better gift he could have gotten her. This book was ideal. She looked up at Nate whose eyes met hers.

"You amaze me, Mr. Cavendar. Veronica is going to be beside herself. Nothing is going to top this. Now what am I supposed to get her?"

"Follow me—" Rachel led her to a smaller room in the store. There were candles, antique dishes, jewelry, and stones.

Something caught Devan's eye and she went over to it. "This!" Devan pointed to a beautiful dark blue object.

Rachel smiled. "I just picked that up from an estate sale. It's blue goldstone. It is said to have been created by Italian monks in the 17th century."

"What is it?" Devan held up the pendant and studied it.

"It is more like a glass bead. It has copper in it. See the little flecks of light? That's the copper. Everyone was trying to find gold back then. It's considered a lucky gemstone and can be helpful with migraines and detoxifying the system. It has a lot of good properties."

"Well, I love the fact it's a lucky stone. I'd like to get it for her."

Rachel picked it up, took it to the register and placed it in a small silver box.

The next day, Nate called Devan and told her that the piano repairman would be there later that afternoon. She sat in the parlor of the funeral home and waited patiently. Vinnie had done a really nice job renovating the place. Nate was hoping to open officially after the start of the New Year. The rich deep burgundy carpet had hunter green and beige sprinkled throughout. The pale wallpaper had thin gold stripes running up the wall to the baroque crown molding. The ceiling had a large brass candelabra dangling in the middle creating an eerie glow. Some of the pieces of furniture were replicas and some were reupholstered originals. She got up and sat down on the slick surface of the piano bench. Her fingers glided across the keys. There were some keys that were in perfect condition while others had cracks in the ivory. Devan wondered whose hands had touched those keys. She knew it had been in Nate's family for years, but she didn't know how old it really was.

The chimes rang, she got up and peeked through the thick, red, crushed velvet drapes that were hanging over the window by the front door. It was the piano repairman. She greeted him and showed him to the location of the piano. He replaced the pedal and a broken string. He tuned it then played scales, chords, and a song. He left and Devan made sure the lights were all off then went out the door carefully locking it. As soon as she had locked the door, her phone rang. "Hello?"

"Hey, can I come pick you up in five? I have a few last-minute wedding errands." It was Veronica. Devan had to think quickly. She couldn't give up her location."I'm already out, how about I pick you up?" Devan offered.

"That works, see ya in a few."

When Devan got to Veronica's house, she was already waiting outside.

"I have to pick up the picture of Nate's dad and stop at the florist. Thank you for going with me. I want to know what frame I should get," she said as she got in Devan's car.

"Why do you have a picture of Nate's dad?" Devan asked pulling out of Veronica's driveway.

"I wanted to honor him, and I thought that Nate would appreciate that. I plan on setting up a table with a candle and an arrangement of flowers with his picture on it at the wedding."

"Roni, that's awesome. Nate will love it. How did you get it without his knowledge?" Devan was curious.

"His mom sent it when I asked her how to get one, and I had a copy made," Veronica said, while fidgeting with her purse.

"That is very sweet. Mrs. Cavendar is coming for sure, right?" Devan was slightly worried since Nate's mom lived so far away.

"God, I hope so, since she is officiating. Veronica put her purse on the floor.

"She is?"

"Yup. I'm stoked! Oh, Devan, just wait until you meet her. Willow is mystical and welcoming and nice. And beautiful! Oh, my god, Devan, she has to be one of the most beautiful women I have ever seen."

"Mystical?" *That's an odd word to describe someone.*

"You'll see when you meet her," Veronica promised.

When they arrived at the store, Devan helped Veronica pick out the perfect frame. Then the girls headed next door to the flower shop.

"Oh, Miss VonStross, I was just getting ready to call you. Your shipment came in damaged. Not one single sunflower can be used. The roses are all fine, though. We will replace them at no charge to you. In fact, we won't charge you for your order at all, but may we suggest using daisies in place of the sunflowers?" The woman behind the desk asked as soon as Veronica walked in the door. Devan was worried that Veronica was going to blow up. She kept watching her face waiting for the terror to strike.

Veronica was pleasant to the woman. "No, I will pay for them, and I think daisies will work. Only the arrangements and my bouquet had sunflowers. I'm sure it will be just fine." Veronica replied calmly. She and the florist lady went over the change in the arrangements and the bouquet. Veronica thanked her as the lady apologized once again. She and Devan then left.

When they got in the car, Devan commented on how well Veronica had taken the news.

"Sure, I'm disappointed, but, Dee, I'm marrying the perfect man. At the end of the day I'll be Mrs. Nathaniel Cavendar. What's a few missing flowers?" Veronica said buckling in.

"Good point!"

The date was October 27th 2012. It was finally Veronica's and Nate's wedding day. Everything seemed to be in place. The bridesmaids' dresses had come in on time, and Veronica and the girls were pleased with the quality and appearance of the Edwardian replicas. The girls' dresses were made of two layers. The under layer was a cream-colored satin dress. The front bodice and the top layer of each dress was covered with lace which gave each dress the appearance of being made totally of lace. It resulted in a deep V in the front and the back and went over the shoulders to create cap sleeves.

As Devan put the last pin in her hair, she noticed someone else in the mirror. She turned to see a beautiful woman with long, dark hair. Her eyes were a light brown surrounded by thick dark eyelashes. Her high cheek bones lifted as she smiled. She was stunning. "You must be Mrs. Cavendar."

The woman stuck out a long tan arm to meet Devan's hand. "I am the one and only, for a few more hours anyway. Please call me Willow."

"You are just as beautiful, as Veronica said you were." Realizing how strange that sounded Devan apologized. "I'm sorry that was weird, but your hair is so long and shiny." *Really, Devan?*

"You are sweet, Devan."

Wait how does she know my name? I never told her.

"I'm glad I am finally getting to meet you. You have made my little Raven very happy."

"Me?" Devan was surprised.

"You found him, you introduced him to his bride, his best friend, and you have made his dreams come true."

"I can't take all that credit." Devan was overwhelmed.

"If it wasn't for you, this day would not be happening, and this building may not even be standing. You did this, Devan. You may not have made the wish, but my dear you planted the dandelion." Mrs. Cavendar smiled at her.

"A weed, I planted a weed." Devan scoffed.

"Oh, Devan, the dandelion is a magical plant. The leaves and the blooms provide nutrition, make a terrific salad, make a nice wine, a delicate tea, infused oil to soothe and heal chapped skin, vinegar, jelly and a pain reliever. The roots are used for medicinal purposes, teas and wines. It is a magnificent plant not a weed that is a nuisance."

"I don't know what kind of dandelions you have but mine have always been weeds."

Mrs. Cavendar grabbed her hand. "Devan, beauty is in the eye of the beholder. Dandelions are amazing plants that can be resourced for food several months out of the year. They bloom a few times a year usually from May to October. Every once in a while, they will surprise you and pop up in the strangest place and at the wrong time of season. The Dandelion will become your friend." Willow leaned in and embraced Devan then whispered in her ear, "When you see the field of green that is spotted with yellow, you'll know the time is near and your wait will soon be over. When the howling north winds meet the warmth of the south winds, a long awaited, desire will arrive with the force of a beast. The truth will prevail right before the second full bloom. Things you have wanted will come to fruition as the last seedlings travel through the air just before the first frost appears on the ground. There the seeds will wait through the winter to be warmed by the sun in the spring, where the plants will renew. That's when your life will take on a different meaning and a new cycle will begin."

"Why are you telling me this?"

"The Universe wants you to know."

Devan wasn't sure what to think. Her intuition told her Nate's mom was right. Now she understood why Veronica called her *Mystical*, because Willow Cavendar was exactly that!

"Hello Mrs. Cavendar, so nice to see you again. If you'll excuse me, I need the matron of honor." As soon as Devan felt the cold hand on her arm, she knew it was Antoinette. She pulled Devan into the hallway and checked to make sure no one was listening.

"I need to speak with you sometime before the night is over."

"Can't you do it now?" Devan asked.

"No, there isn't time. Just make sure you see me before either one of us takes our leave. Now go finish your face, it only looks half done," Antoinette remarked.

Ugh, what does this woman want?

Devan walked back in the room to finish her makeup and apologize to Mrs. Cavendar, trying not to worry about the upcoming conversation.

"It's quite all right dear. What Mrs. VonStross has to say to you is vastly important. You will need that knowledge for the future."

Devan gave her a strange look, then asked how she knew what Antoinette wanted.

"She's not the woman you think she is. She's something—magical."

Devan was dumbfounded. Before she could ask Mrs. Cavendar questions, Maggie bumped into her. When she turned back around Mrs. Cavendar was gone. Devan shook her head and looked in the mirror. Antoinette was right, her face needed attention. She pulled out her makeup bag and began putting on her makeup for the wedding.

"Has anyone seen her wedding dress yet?" Maggie tried to fix a loose strand of her hair.

"Only her mom," Devan said applying her last coat of mascara.

"Hey, is my *nonna* here yet?" Veronica yelled from the bathroom.

Devan searched and located Gianna. "Yes."

"Is everybody here?"

Devan made sure that everyone was present that needed to be. "Yes," Devan replied.

Veronica slowly opened the door and emerged. Her gown was an Edwardian era dress made of satin with lace and elegant beading over top. A brooch made of pearls and tiny diamonds set in silver lay between her breasts. The sleeves were short and adorned with intricate beading throughout the embroidery. The bodice was tapered at the waist. The material then flared out all the way to the floor. Devan couldn't tell if it was cream colored or if it had been yellowed with time. The chatter stopped, and mouths were agape. Devan was the first to say something.

"Oh my god, Veronica, you are absolutely gorgeous."

Veronica smiled at Devan and scooted past her to where Gianna was standing and fidgeting with her purse. She hadn't even been paying attention. When Veronica placed her hand on her grandmother's shoulder, Gianna looked up, gasped and covered her mouth with her hand. Tears started streaming down her face.

"Oh, *mia dolce e Bellissima nipotina. Non avrei mai pensato di rivedere quel vestito di nuovo.*"

"*Nonna*, slow down," Veronica said.

"I said my sweet beautiful granddaughter I never thought I would ever see that dress again." Gianna spoke in her broken accent.

"I know, Mom surprised me with it. Great Aunt Sophia sent it over a few months ago."

"Let me see you, *bellissima*," Gianna circled Veronica continuing to wipe her tears. "My heart, *Nonno*, would be so happy. I wish he was here to see this."

Veronica hugged Gianna. "He is *Nonna*, he is."

"Thees dress was made in 1906 for my grandmother, my mother wore it in 1927, and it was last worn in 1948 when I married your *Nonno*. You are wearing a one hundred and six-year-old dress."

"Yes, I am, *Nonna*, and it didn't need a whole lot done to it. I had to replace a few beads and patch a hole. I did have to replace the lining, that was it."

There was a knock on the door. It was the florist with the bouquets and corsages. Veronica passed out the bouquets to the girls and put the corsages on her grandmothers, mother, and soon to be mother-in-law. Each girl had three red roses wrapped with cream ribbon. The corsages all had red roses and baby's breath in them as well. When she reached for her box, it wasn't there.

"Um, I think he forgot a box. Mine isn't here."

"No, yours is right here," Willow said with a box in her hand.

"It is Italian tradition that the groom gives the bride one last gift before she becomes his wife. The gift is her wedding bouquet. He made this himself." She opened the box and presented the flowers to Veronica.

"How did he do this? I was told there was a bad shipment of sunflowers," she said holding up the large bouquet of red roses and sunflowers.

"Nate made some calls—"

"Does this mean—" Veronica ran out into the hall and half way down the stairs to see sunflower arrangements everywhere. Kale caught her.

"You better high tail your ass back up there. Nate is right behind me."

She nodded and ran upstairs. "They are everywhere. It's just how I imagined."

"Okay, I think it's about time. Is everyone ready?" Veronica's mom asked.

"Wait, not yet," Antoinette pushed past everyone in the crowded room to get to Veronica. She pulled something out of her purse and held it up. It was a vintage pearl choker. "I am assuming you don't have anything borrowed, I wore it when I married your grandfather."

Veronica snatched it out of her hands, "I have always admired this." She hugged Antoinette who returned a warm hug. "Now, I have something borrowed, something old, something new, oh no, I don't have anything blue!"

Devan ran to her purse and came back with a box. "I was going to give it to you for your birthday."

Veronica held up the silver necklace with the oval dark blue gem stone and laughed. "I have wanted a necklace just like this since I was a little girl. There was this lady that—"

"Honey, everyone is waiting for us downstairs," her mother interrupted.

"You know what, we will save that story for another day. Thank you, Devan, it's perfect. Let's do this!"

Devan once again walked down the aisle to Kale on the other side waiting for her. Kale standing in his black tuxedo, black bowtie and black vest with his dark curls swirled around his face and resting on his shoulders was quite a sight to see. His green eyes sparkled at her as she took her place. This was the fourth wedding they were in together that wasn't theirs. Maybe one day it would be theirs, but for Kale that day was not soon enough.

Veronica's father walked her down the aisle. Her veil was as long as her gown.

He lifted it and kissed her on the cheek and placed her hand in Nate's.

Willow Cavendar's words were beautiful. The ceremony was a perfect mix between the Native American and Italian cultures. The Native American part tied in life and love with nature while the Italian part emphasized the importance of family.

"Nathaniel Bryant Raven Cavendar do you, my son, take Veronica Lenore VonStross to be your mate, your wife, your love, your life?" Willow asked Nate.

"I do," Nate answered with so much emotion the guests were in awe.

Willow turned toward Veronica. "Veronica Lenore VonStross, do you take Nathaniel Bryant Raven Cavendar to be your mate, your husband, your love, your life?"

"I do," Veronica answered with a broad smile as she held back tears of joy.

"By the powers vested in me by the state of Ohio, I pronounce you husband and wife. Nathaniel you may now kiss your beautiful bride."

Devan watched Nate's face when he was told he could finally kiss Veronica. It brought tears to her eyes. She had never seen anyone so happy in her life. She imagined that the that same look would be on Kale's face if she were to ever walk down the aisle to him as his bride. *That is what true love is* she thought to herself. *It's not that I don't have true love, it's just that I can't have my true love yet.* There was still some hope left in her for a future with Kale.

After the food was served and the cake was cut, Nate and Veronica had their first dance as husband and wife. When the song was over the DJ requested that the bridal party come out on to the dance floor as well. Devan tried turning around as soon as she heard the beginning of "Fade Into You" by Mazzy Star. Kale took her hand and led her out on to the dance floor. "It's the bridal party dance, Monty. As Best Man and Matron of Honor we have no choice."

Kale glanced over at Veronica who winked at him as he shook his head. "You little shit," he mouthed. She gave him a smirk then buried her head in Nate's chest.

"What was that about?" Devan asked Kale.

He looked down at her and smiled. "Nothing," he shook his head.

"Did you get her to play this?" Devan narrowed her eyes.

"I did not. I may have told her about the song back when we were on vacation since she was having a hard time finding the perfect song."

"So, you told her this one would be good?"

Kale laughed, "No, I ended up explaining how this song had somehow become our song. The lyrics don't match, but the music does. I can't hear this song without thinking about you."

She stared up into his green eyes. "I happen to have a love/hate relationship with this song," she sighed.

"Me too," he grumbled. She scooted in closer and put her arms around his waist and squeezed him tight. They remained that way for the duration of the song.

When the song was over, the DJ handed the microphone to Veronica's father. Vincent VonStross senior was a man you didn't mess with. He seemed like a cold, hard person until you got to know him well. He was actually pretty funny yet he was an intelligent hardworking man. "I want to officially welcome Nate into the family. I used to chase guys off with my old buddies Smith and Wesson but not this guy. Maybe I haven't because he's a good guy, or maybe I'm afraid that he's the only one in this town that could kill me and bury my body and no one would ever know." He had the wedding guests in stitches. "I'm kidding, of course. Most Dad's would be a little hesitant if their daughter brought home an undertaker. No offense, son." He looked apologetically to Nate. "Not this dad! I swear this guy is the most respectful man I have ever met that I am not related to by blood. Nate not only asked me for my permission to ask Veronica to marry him, he asked my wife and my son as well. At first I wanted to say no, for *his* safety and wellbeing." The guests were quiet. When he saw their expressions he questioned, "Have you not met my daughter?" Again, the crowd roared. Devan quit listening and nudged Kale. "I would be shocked if Nate had not asked her dad. Did you know?"

Kale nodded. "Yeah he told me the story. I thought it was pretty cool. After all, I asked your dad and well, Justin asked me thinking I was basically your brother." He chuckled and shook his head at the same time.

Devan had often wondered what the conversation was like that Kale had had with her father. She turned her attention back to Veronica's dad.

"But I told him how honored I would be to have him as my son-in-law, and I meant it. Veronica and Nate, we know that you had not planned on a honeymoon, but your mother and I would like to send you away to a little place called Salem, Massachusetts for a seven-day honeymoon. Honey, I know you have wanted to go there since you were a little girl, and I found out from Nate's mom that he has always had an interest in the place too." He started walking over to the dance floor. "I didn't get to do this at your first wedding, and I'll be damned if I don't get to do it this time. Sweetheart, this better be your *last* wedding. I really like this guy. Anyway, as I was saying I didn't get to do the father and daughter dance last time as I had a broken ankle, but I am good to go now. I love you, Roni. You will always be my precious little girl. So, Roni may I have this dance?"

After the father and daughter dance the music sped up quite a bit. Everyone was having such a good time. Jeane and Justin were in their own world as usual probably getting sloshed, yet Kale and Devan were not bothered by worrisome or embarrassing thoughts. They, too, were in their own world dancing the night away.

The music stopped, and people quieted down. "That's my cue," Devan said and went over to the other side of the room as the piano began playing "A Thousand Years" by Christina Perri. Kale watched her walk over and pick up the microphone.

"Oh my god—" Veronica stepped out of the crowd to stare at her new husband playing the old piano.

"So, this is what she has been working on?" Kale rested his arm on Veronica's shoulder.

Veronica leaned up against him, "I heard this song for the first time at the reunion. I told him I didn't normally like songs that were sappy, but there was something about this one."

"I think you finally have a song, cousin. Well, let's not waste the music. Shall we?" Kale took Veronica's hand and led her to the dance floor.

Devan smiled at Veronica and Kale and kept singing. She scooted closer to Nate and motioned for him to look. He lifted his eyes up from the ivory keys for a split second and a huge grin spread across his face. His new best friend dancing with his new wife made him very happy.

"She really has a beautiful voice," Veronica commented.

"Yes, she does," he agreed then looked over at Devan who happened to be looking right back at him.

"To be honest, I think you are right. This may be Nate's and my song now…however, the lyrics scream Devan and Kale." She teared up and tilted her head back to see Kale's face. "I'm sorry for you guys. You are in shitty situations and are meant to be together. I don't care what cards were dealt to you. You belong with her!" He wiped a tear from her cheek.

"I know," he said with a half-smile trying not to tear up himself. "We are so lucky to have you and Nate as our close friends and now family, and we are both very happy for the two of you. Don't worry about us, we will get our happy ending one of these years."

The song ended, and Veronica hugged him tight, "You will, hopefully sooner rather than later."

As Devan set the microphone down, she saw Antoinette near the door motioning for Devan to come to her. She walked over to where she was standing.

"I told you that we were going to talk," Antoinette was stern.

"Yes, you did, but do you really think this is the time and place?"

"Considering what I just witnessed tonight, yes." She held the door open and practically jerked Devan out of it.

"I'm sorry, I don't want to be disrespectful, but I do not understand why you want to talk to me so badly."

Antoinette was fidgeting with a lighter and cigarette. "Do you smoke?" She offered one to Devan. Devan shook her head no. "It's for the best. It's a nasty habit. Anymore I only do it if I drink." She finally got her cigarette lit and put the lighter and box back in her purse. "Carl was right. You and Kale are madly in love with each other even after all these years."

"Oh no, please just stop." Devan rolled her eyes.

"I most certainly will not! How many times have you walked down the aisle to see him standing there?"

"Today makes four," Devan answered.

"And how many times have you wished it were the two of you getting married?" Antoinette asked before inhaling the smoke.

Devan figured she had no reason to lie. "More times than I can count."

"I understand the situation that you are in."

"If you understand then why are we talking about this? You know that nothing can be done." Devan said irritated.

"What I do know is money can fix a lot of things…"

"Money can't fix this," Devan cut her off.

"No but it can help. I'm just offering an out for you. I can afford the best lawyers."

"Have you told Kale this?"

"According to Carl the key to Kale is you. The second you say you are ready, he will do anything he can to be with you. I didn't believe him until tonight."

"Why tonight?" Devan wished she had taken a cigarette at this point.

Antoinette dusted off a step on the stoop and sat down grabbing Devan's hand to make her sit down next to her. She kept hold of her hand. "I knew from the moment I met you two, you were something else—um twin souls you could say." Devan had heard this before, but she couldn't remember where. "I didn't realize how much in love you were until tonight. He is stupid in love." *Well that was rude.* Antoinette picked up on the judging vibe Devan was throwing off. "Don't take it in a bad way. What I'm saying is—he would pick up and leave everything to be with you without even considering the consequences."

"No, he wouldn't!" Devan argued.

"Devan, he would, and he has tried, but you won't let him."

"If he did, she would end him! He wouldn't be able to see his kids, and he wouldn't be able to work in the field he loves. She would take everything and tear him apart. I can't let that happen to him." She had tears in her eyes.

"My dear, I know that you would never forgive yourself if something like that were to happen, but I'm here to tell you—it won't. So, what is really holding you back then?"

"I don't understand."

"I can handle that trollop. I can make sure Kale sees his kids, is able to work and gets what is owed to him. However, I can't make you do something that you are afraid to do. You need to ask yourself what it is that you are really afraid of because it's not just Kale losing his kids, there is more to it. Figure it out and get back to me." She handed Devan a card.

"Why are you doing this?"

Antoinette let go of Devan's hand, stood up and peered down at her. "Devan, even I can't ignore true love. I know I come off as this hardcore bitch, and believe me I am, but there is this softer side that I don't let show often. Besides Carl loves you, and I am willing to help and accept anyone into my heart that he loves. That includes you too, missy. Fear can be an evil thing. Find out what you are so afraid of and face it. The offer is on the table. It will be there for a year or even ten years. You call me when you are ready." With that, she walked into the funeral home and shut the door behind her leaving Devan alone with her thoughts.

I'm not afraid of anything. I just don't want Kale to have his kids taken away. That's my biggest fear. I have no idea what she's talking about. If that was all taken care of there would be no issues, aside from Justin. He's an easy fix. The kids would be happy, Kale would be happy, I would happy. Fear! I have no fear. What's the worst that could happen? It wouldn't work out? Like that would happen. Yet in her subconscious, that was what scared her. Devan had envisioned this perfect life with Kale, but what if it was too good to be true? She brushed the thought out of her head and went back to the reception.

After the reception Devan and Kale decided to stay and help clean up. They were the only ones left except for the bride and groom who were locked in a room somewhere. They finished cleaning and headed for the back door. They said loudly that they were leaving and slipped out. When they got outside, they noticed that neither of their cars was there.

"Are you kidding me?" Devan was pissed.

"They couldn't think to carpool?" Kale was angry. He quit walking, looked at Devan and grabbed her hand to bring her down to a sitting position on the back stoop.

"What?" She was clearly agitated.

"I just thought of something…" Kale smiled.

"Oh? And what is that?"

"This was the first wedding we have been in that we didn't kiss."

She loosened up a little, "Yeah, this is the first one for sure where you didn't attack me with your lips before it started."

"After our weddings I got smarter."

"Really and how is that?"

"I kissed you the night before Pete's and Kristy's."

"So, what made this one different then? I must have gotten uglier in my old age," she laughed.

He gave her the evil eye and got up. "Never! The truth is, I promised myself that I would never kiss you at a wedding again unless it was ours."

She got up and walked to where he was and looked up. A single drop of rain fell onto her face. When he looked at her it appeared as though she had a tear. He moved his thumb to her face and wiped it away.

"I'm sorry. I wasn't trying to make you sad," he apologized. "I can kiss you right now if you really want me to."

"That wasn't a tear, silly, it was rain." She no sooner finished her statement when it began pouring. It was a nice warm rain and quite frankly it felt great.

Kale took her hand to lead her back to the funeral home, but she didn't budge. "Come on," he tried tugging her hand again.

"The door is locked Kale. I locked it on the way out." She laughed hysterically.

"It just figures," he laughed with her.

She finally calmed down. "You promised yourself that you wouldn't kiss me at a wedding unless it was ours?" As if it had just registered.

"Yes."

She moved closer to him and gently picked up his hand and intertwined her fingers with him. "Well, I didn't make that promise, and anyway the wedding is over." She found her way into his arms and moved her free hand up to his cheek. Kale didn't say a word, but she didn't need his permission. He leaned down as she got on the tips of her toes and raised her lips to meet his.

Little did they know they had an audience. Nate and Veronica were silently watching with smiles on their faces.

Kale ended the kiss rather quickly. "What was that for?" she asked disappointed.

He pulled her underneath the willow tree for a shelter as the rain came down harder. "Devan, I made you a promise. As much as I don't want to keep it, it's a promise I plan to keep." Devan nodded her head and he continued. "Our circumstances right now really suck, we just have to deal with them. In order for this to work we don't have a choice other than to be friends. However, you and I both know that the truth is *we* will never be just friends. I am confident as the kids get older our time will come. There will be a day when you will walk down the aisle to me for the last time. At that time, you will be mine forever."

"I already am yours forever. Since we are being honest, I've never been anyone else's."

"Oh God this is weird. I feel like we are breaking up, after all, the last time we had a discussion like this near a willow tree it ended horribly."

"But this time we won't stop speaking for three years. I propose one last pact."

She took a step back from him.

He leaned up against the tree. "Okay, and what would that be?"

"That we be the team that we have been talking about. We do it well. We really don't have a choice at the moment anyway. No more stolen kisses, no more undressing each other with our eyes—"

He cut her short, "Wait, you undress me with your eyes?"

"Shut up," she giggled. "I'm human too, and I know what the whole package is." She eyed him up and down.

"Oh really?" He took a step toward her.

"Stay on the subject Iakona. No more tight embraces, and no more longing looks."

"So, no kissing, no wanting, no touching, no looking. Got it. Maybe you should make a list of what I'm allowed to do. It will be much shorter and easier to remember."

She wrapped her arms around him. "You can be there for me and let me be there for you. You can love our kids and have faith that this is the last pact. After this everything, and I mean *everything*, awaits us."

"How do you know this?"

"I just know." Devan shrugged her shoulders.

"Is there a goodbye kiss at least?"

"There is no goodbye Kale, but we will seal this pact with a kiss." She stood on the tips of her toes and put her hands on the back of his neck. Their eyes met and only a second after, their lips met as well. His full lips felt soft and warm on hers. Devan had been aching for this for over a year. She parted her mouth and invited him in. *What am I doing?* She twirled strands of his hair with her fingers and tugged at them slightly. He let out a low groan. *Oh, this is how she wants to play?* He grabbed both sides of her hips and picked her up never stopping the kiss. She enveloped his waist with her legs and continued caressing his tongue with hers. She pulled tighter on his hair. He kissed her even harder. There was too much excitement. It had to stop, but he couldn't stop. Devan sure as hell didn't seem like she wanted it to stop. He pulled his mouth away from hers. She smiled a devilish grin and kissed him again. *Why is this so difficult?* He gathered his strength and pulled away, this time lowering her till her feet touched the ground. When she let go of his hair, he backed away from her. She had a puzzled expression on her face.

"I'm sorry Monty, if I hadn't ended it, I wouldn't have been able to control it. I barely could control myself as it was."

Devan watched as his feet shuffled back. She took a deep breath. Kale was worried that he had upset her until she spoke. "No Kale, I'm sorry. I took it to the next level and even though I don't regret it, I do apologize for my actions. It was totally the opposite of what we are trying to do."

Kale laughed, "It's gonna be tough to come back after that one."

Devan pulled the pins out of her hair and giggled nervously. "Yup, still if anyone can do it—it's you and me."

He walked back over to her and put his hands on her shoulders. "Now, how are we going to get home?" The door opened, and Nate threw his keys to Kale.

"You can drop it off tomorrow," he said and shut the door.

Kale and Devan glanced at one another then back at the door.

"Do you think they heard all that?"

Devan looked to the left and saw a curtain move next to an opened window.

"I think they heard and saw everything—Goodnight newlyweds!" she hollered.

"Goodnight!" Devan heard Veronica say.

"All right Monty, let's get you home."

As Kale opened the door to the hearse, he paused and leaned over. "You aren't going to attack me when I get in are you? I'm quite fragile and you are scary."

Devan reached up, tugged on his tie and pulled his face down to her level. "No but if you don't hurry up, I'm going to turn into a pumpkin and the big bad wolf is going to come get you."

Kale shook his head. "I don't think you can mix fairytales." She let go of his tie.

"Just get in the vehicle, Lettuce Head. It's late and we are both tired."

"As you wish!"

Chapter 18

August 2015

Three years had gone by and Kale's and Devan's relationship had surprisingly remained calm. Everything appeared to be going smoothly on the surface. Alistar had been building resorts near the Great Lakes so Jeane and Justin had been in town a lot more than normal, which was unfortunate for their families. Devan and Kale were still a team though and helped each other whenever they could.

School was going to start in a few weeks. It was Sunday family dinner and Devan's turn to host it. After dinner Kale offered to clean up, which really meant making sure there was no leftover food. Devan was in the kitchen washing dishes and Kale was making decisions on the leftovers. If he felt there wasn't enough in the bowl or on the plate to save, he ate it. If he thought Devan could get another meal from what he was seeing, he would put it in a container and put that in the refrigerator. She laughed as she watched him.

"What?" Kale took the last roll and shoved it in his mouth.

"I just don't know where all the food, that you eat, goes. I wish I could eat like you do and not gain an ounce. I have about twenty pounds of fat I need to lose." She squeezed the little bit of extra skin around her middle to emphasize her point.

"Nah, you are fine the way you are. I don't see any of the fat that you are talking about." Kale squinted at her abdomen.

"I'm disgusting, I can't even look at myself in the mirror anymore," Devan frowned.

"I think you are perfect, but if you are that unhappy with yourself, why don't you run with me in the mornings?" Kale asked before eating the last bite of leftover pasta.

"You run?" Devan was surprised. It was odd that she had never seen him run before, considering they lived in the same neighborhood.

"Four days a week. I get up at five and jog through the entire allotment. You should join me," Kale smiled.

"What do you do on the other three days?" she questioned.

"I meet up with Nate at the gym."

"How did I not know any of this?" Devan was surprised.

"I have no idea because you sure as hell have stared at my body enough to know that I work hard." Kale raised his eyebrows and had a mock frown on his face.

"Well, yeah back in your football days—"

He cut her off. "Oh, please, Devan. If I took my shirt off this very second your tongue would fall right out of your mouth," he taunted smugly.

While she tried to play it cool, she was getting excited just thinking about *that chest, those arms—wait no what is he doing?*

Kale stood up, lifted his shirt over his head and threw it on the floor. *Oh my god, oh my god, OH. MY. GOD! Would it be so bad to just go over there and…*Crash! The plate Devan was holding slipped right out of her hands onto the floor. Cassandra ran in to see what had happened.

"Are you okay?" she asked Devan then turned to Kale. "Why is your shirt off?"

Oh, this should be good. He's going to embarrass me I can tell. Devan could already feel the redness creeping into her cheeks.

"I got spaghetti sauce on it," he said while smirking at Devan.

"Gimme' that, I'll try to get it out. Go help Devan clean up that mess." Cassandra held the shirt up and looked at the red spot. "I thought you outgrew missing your mouth when you were five." She walked away shaking her head.

"What were you saying before you dropped the dish? Something about my body in my football days?"

When Kale stood up from picking the pieces off the floor, Devan grabbed his arms and pulled him close to her. His skin was smooth and warm. There was a faint scent of Nautica teasing her. She turned and pushed him toward the wall with all her force. Her hands went straight for his chest then to his biceps. He just stared at her letting her feel her way. When he couldn't take it anymore, he moved Devan so her back was against the wall with such a swift movement she didn't even know it happened. He placed his hands on the sides of her face and gently lifted her head up so he could look her in the eyes. When their eyes met, he gave her a firm but gentle kiss. He moved his hands to her waist, lifting her, and she wrapped her legs around his hips. Her hands were on his shoulders. He turned with her in his arms and moved the things that were on the table out of the way causing more crashing of dishes on the floor. Kale continued kissing her while setting her on the table. He stopped and licked his lips. There was a hunger in his eyes that made her even more aroused. He ripped her shirt open. Buttons were flying everywhere.

"What in the hell is going on?" Justin had his hands on his hips.

Devan looked down at the remaining shards of glass on the floor, then over to Kale, who had a broom in his hand, and finally at her husband.

"I dropped a plate," Devan said coming back to reality.

"Well, don't make Kale clean it up. He's our guest." Justin took the broom from Kale and handed it to Devan. As Justin was leaving the kitchen, he smacked Kale on the chest. "You are putting me to shame."

He sure is. Devan silently agreed.

"Maybe you should come run with Devan and me, sometime," Kale suggested.

"Devan, run? Yeah, good luck with that one. It would probably be good for her to get rid of some of that pudge, though." Both she and Kale glared at him.

"You're an asshole, Justin!" Kale said as he walked over to Devan and took the broom out of her hand. She was still in a daze but had a frown on her face and was staring at the spot from where Justin had disappeared. Once again, her husband ruined a good dream—even if it was only a day dream.

"Mom," Cyrus called. Devan didn't respond.

"Mom, mom, mom, mom—Devan!" Cyrus shouted pulling her out of her own head.

"What?"

"Can we go play on the computer?"

"That's fine," Devan told her son.

"Where did you go?" Kale asked as he finished sweeping up the mess. He laughed, "Maybe I should take my shirt off more—"

"Shut up Kale Kai," she exclaimed as she threw the dish towel at him.

While the boys were downstairs playing their computer games, the girls were out playing in the yard. It was a good time to have an adult discussion.

"So, we wanted to talk to you guys," Jeane looked at Devan and Kale. "Uncle Alistar is going to be building over in Europe for a few months. We will be there for one month, then home for two weeks and we'll go back and forth until the job is done."

"Okay and what will I be doing?" Kale asked.

"Working from home and being a dad," she answered him. "We suggest that you help each other as you have in the past when we weren't home."

"And when you are home," Devan said under her breath. Kale glanced at her and tried not to laugh. He was thinking the exact same thing. Justin and Jeane made it a habit to leave Kale and Devan to deal with *everything*.

"You say a few months?"

"Give or take," Justin commented.

There was pounding on the stairs coming up from the rec room. "Aunt Dee, Daddy—I'm sorry. I'm sorry." Kale and Devan jumped up quickly.

"Mommy! He didn't mean it, I swear," Cyrus cried.

"What happened?" Devan hoped it was nothing big.

"I got out your old laptop, the one with the frog game on it. I just wanted to show Kai, because it's so much fun—"

"And?" Kale asked going over to the boys.

"And we were playing the game and— I hit a key and it said deleting files. Then it shut down," Kai had tears in his eyes. "I'm so sorry Aunt Dee—"

"Kai, it's okay, buddy. We will figure this out, and I'm sure we can fix it." Devan wasn't too worried. She never used that computer anymore.

"Sounds like it might be a Trojan virus or something. I have a system recovery kit at home. It might take some time, but I should be able to fix it." Kale sat back down. "I'll take it home tonight."

"Okay. If you can't fix it, it's no biggie. There isn't really anything too important on there," Devan sat down on the other side of the room. "Go on, Jeane, tell us everything we need to know." Though she didn't really care, she sat there and listened to her talk.

That night when Kale got home, he opened the laptop to work on it.

"I'm gonna pack," Jeane said as she walked out the door.

"Yeah, whatever. I'll be doing this for a while." He started going through things on the computer and downloaded a few programs. After a few hours, Devan's laptop was restored, and it seemed as though everything was working correctly. He was about to turn the computer off when a message popped up on the screen that Word needed to be updated. He had time so why not? As he was going through the motions, another message popped up. *Do you want to save the changes to Aloha Paradise?* He hit yes and then got out of Word and hit the power key but stopped. *Aloha Paradise sure sounds interesting.* He opened Word back up and found the document. He began reading.

It was the summer of 1994, and I was about to embark on a struggle that would last the rest of my life. Kale continued to read.

"Daddy?" Kale lifted his head from his desk. "Yeah?"

"What can I have for breakfast?" Kai put his face only an inch or so from Kale's.

"Where is your mom?" Kale asked yawning.

"She left. Uncle Justin picked her up early. She told us when you woke up, you'd make us breakfast." Kai stated as he danced around his father.

Kale rubbed his face. "What time is it?" He did not want to be awake yet.

"It's noon," Sage said coming in from the hall.

"What? Shit, I'm sorry. Why didn't you wake me up?" Kale jumped up from the office chair.

"I tried a few times." Sage folded her arms over her chest sporting her attitude.

"Damn it, Devan," he trotted down the steps, his mind racing as he remembered the story he read last night.

"Dad, I'm Sage," she reminded him who he was talking to as she followed him.

"I know, Sage, I'm sorry." Kale shook his head, trying to wake up and clear the cobwebs from his head. No amount of shaking was going to make him forget the words he had seen. Devan had a magical way with words and the way she told their love story was mesmerizing.

During brunch Sage wanted to know why Kale had mentioned Devan.

"I was working on her computer and, well, I was just up really late," Kale explained.

"Can we go over there today?" Sage asked and then kicked Joey under the table.

"Ow! What was that for?" Joey was not expecting that.

"You said *you* were gonna ask so I didn't have to," she kicked him again.

"Stop being a little bit—"

"You'd better not say what I think you were about to say Joseph Iakona." Kale shot Joey a threatening look then turned his attention to Sage. "Sure, let me call her, but—I will not let you go if you kick your brother again," he warned her.

"I'm sorry, Daddy. I'm sorry, Joey." Sage lowered her head.

Kale picked up the phone that was sitting on the table and called Devan. "Hey, Sage wants to know if she can come over? I have some important work to do. I'll buy dinner if you watch the kids." Devan agreed to the plan.

Kale watched as the kids skipped all the way down the street to the Jameson's. As soon as they were in the house, Kale shut and locked the door, then went over to the computer again. He read from the beginning. When he was done, he checked his phone and saw he had missed a few texts from Devan.

It was already six o'clock in the evening. He had been reading for hours. He couldn't tell what astonished him more—the fact that their entire love story was typed up, that it was Devan who wrote it, or the fact when she told the story, it was as though he was reading what was already in his own heart.

When he arrived at the house, Devan stood on the porch with the door open waiting for him. He walked up the steps, his mind still in his own little world, thinking about the story—their story—on *her* computer. He looked her up and down, then went closer to her. He grabbed the handle of the door and shut it. They were merely inches apart, standing on her enclosed front porch. He focused on her eyes. *Her gorgeous silver blue eyes.* He breathed in the coconut scent that the shampoo left on her hair.

Devan was paralyzed by his stare. Something inside her stirred. She was just waiting for him to press his lips against hers. He kept gazing deep into her eyes. Neither one of them could move.

"Daddy." They both jumped. Kale stepped back and blinked a few times. *What the hell was that?*

"Daddy," Sage tried to get his attention again.

"Yes, I'm sorry. We're coming," Devan apologized as she turned around and opened the door.

"He's coming in the front door, sweetie," she yelled to Sage, who was going toward the back of the house.

Kale snapped back to reality and followed Devan through the front door into the house. "I'm sorry, I'm really tired. This work has me—"

"In a trance?" Devan asked shutting the door behind him.

"You could say that." He didn't know if he should say anything to her about his findings, or if he should take it to his grave. He didn't know what to do. All he could think about was what he read. Then he went into the kitchen and sat down at the table. "Shit, I forgot I was going to bring dinner."

"That's okay." Devan followed him. "I already made it. Would you like some?" She headed to the counter to get Kale a plate.

"No thanks, I'm not really that hungry." Kale said. He could tell he had said the wrong thing because Devan froze on the spot.

"Kale Iakona not hungry? Are you sick?"

He was staring at her again. *Does she really feel the same way? Even after all these years, is she still in love with me?* She noticed he was watching her every movement not saying anything. Devan thought he did look a little pale and was wondering why he was acting so strange. She sat down in front of him.

"Kale?" He seemed out of it, and Devan didn't know what to think.

"Hmmm?"

"Are you okay?" She got up then walked over to him and put her hand on his forehead then his cheek. Her touch almost sent an electric shock through his body. Kale jumped about a mile as she touched him. *How can I be anywhere near her now and be neutral after I've relived our story? Our entire story!!*

"What?"

"Are you okay?" Devan was genuinely concerned.

"I…I didn't get much sleep last night." Which was true, but she didn't need to know the real reason why. Kale couldn't tell her that he read the story she had written about them. What if she got really mad? What if she quit talking to him again? What if he lost her once more? He couldn't let that happen.

"Can I get you anything?"

"No, no, I'll be all right," Kale responded. Then he raised his voice. "Come on, kids, let's go home." He got up from his chair.

"Wait, can you guys come over on Friday for a slumber party?" Devan asked.

"Uh, yeah, that's fine. Let me take care of all the food and snacks. I need to make up for dinner tonight. I'm so sorry about that." His head was still racing with all that he had read and he kept going back and forth about whether or not to say something to Devan about it. *I need to get out of here before I slip.*

"It's fine and you don't have to." He put his hand on her shoulder and leaned down, his face close to hers, "I want to."

"O…Okay," she stuttered.

Kale took a deep breath to inhale her scent, then walked through the kitchen and headed towards the front. *If I don't make eye contact everything will be okay.* "Bye," he said as he shut the door behind him.

Devan stood there for a second and peered out the back window. Kale's kids were still out there. She looked back at the front porch and saw him just standing there. Before she could reach the door, Kale had come up the steps and opened it.

"I forgot my kids." He walked to the back of the house, opened the door and told the kids it was time to go and headed back to the front where he brushed past Devan and stopped. He walked back over to her and wrapped his arms around her. *Should I say something?* There was one hell of a fight going on in his brain. He held her there for a few seconds then pushed her back and put his hands on her shoulders.

"I...I," he stammered. Kale took a deep breath. Should he or shouldn't he say something? What he really wanted to do was take her, both of their kids, and start a new life, just the seven of them. There was an ache in the pit of his stomach. He wanted to be with her even more now that he had read what was on her computer, but he didn't think that was possible.

"You what Kale?"

What are you doing Kale? He chided himself. *What do you think you are going to say, dumbass?*

"I will see you Friday." He hugged her, took a deep breath in and smelled her hair again. He let her go and went out the door to meet his kids who were waiting for him in the front yard.

The next day Devan ended up in the line at the grocery store right behind Nate.

She tapped him on his arm. "How are you doing?"

He turned around, smiled at her and said, "Hello. I am quite well, how are you?"

"I'm all right."

Devan knew she could trust Nate, she just didn't know if she wanted to say anything or not. Yesterday had been so weird, she wasn't sure if it was her imagination.

Nate put his hand on Devan's shoulder, "You are thinking too hard to be all right, so why don't you tell me what's going on?" If anyone knew what was happening with Kale, it would be his best friend.

Devan sighed, "It all started Sunday." *Really? You are going to tell him everything?* She ignored the voice in her head and carried on. "I hosted Family Sunday dinner and we were talking about working out, and then one thing led to another and Kale's shirt was off—"

The confusion on Nate's face made her stop.

"Oh, nothing happened. He was just teasing me about how I used to be obsessed with his body. Then he said something like if he took his shirt off my tongue would fall out of my mouth or to the ground. Anyway, he took his shirt off and my tongue stayed in my mouth, but the dish I was holding slipped out of my hands and broke into a million pieces on the floor. Oh my god, he looked so good. Then I fantasized about what should have…I mean what could have happened." *Good God, you had to tell him everything.*

"Well…"

"Wait, there's more! The next day Sage wanted to come over, so Kale called to see if it would be okay, which of course, it was. Around six o'clock Kale came over to pick up the kids. When he got to my house, there was this strange aura about him. I can't even describe it, I just know I wasn't sure what I was feeling, and definitely didn't know what was going on in his head. Something was *different*. I thought maybe he was sick. He was watching my every move yet barely talked. No flirting or anything. He just wasn't himself. He seemed almost shocked as if he received some bad news or something, but I…I can't describe it. All I know is something was definitely off about Kale last night."

Nate pulled at his dark goatee, "Maybe…"

Devan interrupted him a second time. "We were getting along so well. I just don't want all this stuff to ruin our friendship. We both know this is how it has to be for now."

"You say *for now*, so you do have hope for there to be something more in your future with Kale?" He asked trying to get it out before he wouldn't have a chance to speak.

"Come on Nate, you know that answer. Of course, I want a future with Kale, but now isn't the right time. When the time comes, I'll know."

"Maybe that time is coming sooner than you think. I would not ignore these feelings you are having," he said while loading his groceries on the belt.

"I'm not ignoring them, I just can't act on them right now. I'm going to use my brain."

"Sometimes we need to follow our hearts instead of listening to our minds." He took the last item out of his cart and turned his attention towards the cashier.

If only it were that easy.

Chapter 19

Kale shut the computer. What was he doing? He had read and reread *Aloha Paradise* over the past three days. Nothing else was getting done. He needed to talk to someone, someone who wasn't *Devan*. He grabbed his keys and shouted for the kids before he remembered his mom had picked them up earlier. Kale drove extra slow past Devan's house looking for a glimpse of her. He almost passed the stop sign. "What is wrong with you Iakona?" he asked himself out loud.

When he arrived at his destination, he jumped out of the car, ran to the door and started pounding on it.

"Kale?" Veronica questioned, surprised to see him.

"Oh, thank God you are home." He hugged her and kissed her on the cheek.

"It's nice to see you too, please have a seat." She motioned to the long couch, but he had already taken a seat.

"I need to talk to someone, I'm going crazy," he said putting his hands on his head.

"I'm sorry. Nate isn't home yet." Veronica apologized and sat down on the chair that was across from Kale.

"That's fine. I'm actually here to see you."

"Me?" Veronica seemed a little taken aback to see him.

"Yes, I found something. Boy, did I find something, Roni!"

"What did you find? Is it bad?" Veronica was not sure if she should get excited or be worried.

He shook his head no, then closed his eyes. "I don't know, maybe, I just don't know."

"Oh my god, did you finally catch Justin and Jeane?" She really hoped that he had. He didn't say anything. There was a long pause and still, Kale didn't say anything.

"For the love of the gods, tell me, what did you find?" She was ready to smack him.

"I found her book," Kale spoke in a low voice.

"Her book?" Veronica had no idea what he was talking about. "Whose book?"

"It was in one of the documents that I recovered in her laptop."

"Whose laptop? What is it about?" She opened her bottle of water that was sitting on the end table next to the chair and took a drink.

"Us, our story, from beginning until right after Pete's and Kristy's wedding."

Veronica spit out her water creating a little puddle on the hard wood floor. She knew exactly *who* and *what* he was talking about now.

"Oh Kale, I don't think that was meant for you or anyone else to see."

She went into the kitchen and grabbed some paper towels to clean up the mess.

"Have you read it?" He asked curiously as she walked back into the room and began wiping up the mess she made.

"No! No one has," she stated and finished cleaning up the floor.

"Then how do you know about it?" he said loudly after her as she went to throw the paper away.

When she came back into the living room, she looked at Kale and wondered, *should I or shouldn't I?* She contemplated for a moment. "If you ever tell her I told you, Kale, I swear to God I will kill you and embalm your ass alive and I won't know what I'm doing!" Veronica threatened.

Kale nodded knowing full well that she did have access to the equipment if needed.

"Devan was having a really hard time in Hawaii when you were all there for Pete's and Kristy's wedding. I told her to sit down and write about it. She wrote practically the whole thing in one night." She picked up her water then and set it back down. *I might end up spitting it out again at this rate.*

Kale rubbed his chin, "Go on."

"I'm done that's all I have. I'm assuming you aren't, though. Did you read it? All of it?" Veronica chanced taking a tiny sip of water so she could swallow fast, if she needed to.

"I haven't *stopped* reading it. I must have read it five times by now." He wished he hadn't just said that but then realized who he was talking to and blabbed away.

"I went over there to pick up the kids and when she opened the door, I pulled it shut so it was just the two of us on the porch. I was so close to her I could smell her coconut shampoo. I almost kissed her. Something happened inside me, Roni. I can't even explain it. When I saw her, I wanted to kiss her and beg her to run away with me. It was so overpowering I couldn't look away from her."

"Did you kiss her?" Veronica was hoping the answer was yes.

"No, but I don't know how I didn't." He obviously had some willpower. "I don't think I can be around her. I'm afraid of what I might do."

"So, you read her book about your love life with her, and now you are experiencing all those old feelings that have just been lying dormant inside your soul?" she guessed.

"Well, I wouldn't say they were lying dormant," he admitted. "We've had a couple close calls. So, what do I do now?" He got up and paced the room.

Veronica sighed, "I really don't know what to tell you. Why did you come to me?"

"You are her best friend, and you are basically the little sister I never had. We are practically blood now, and I know I can trust you." Kale quit pacing long enough for Veronica to see the desperation on his face.

"This…fucking…sucks. I want to march over there, pick her up, throw her over my shoulder and carry her out of that house. I just finished reading it again right before I came over here. Every time it just makes things worse. The emotions just keep getting stronger."

"Kale, for Christ's sake don't read it anymore. You are torturing yourself." She knew it was true, and Kale knew it as well.

"I just keep thinking, 'Look how far we have come, and how well we are doing by being a team.' My head and my heart are more conflicted than ever before. It's like I have confirmation that she has felt the same way I have all these years. I don't know where she stands now, though. Damn it, I thought I had buried all this shit." Kale ran his hands through his hair in frustration.

"No, Kale, you never had it completely buried. You just told me ten seconds ago that the feelings never went dormant." She folded her arms on her chest.

"Well, I had it under control. Now, I'm a complete mess." He started pacing again. All these memories and emotions clouded Kale's head.

"What do you want to do about it?" Anyone else would have shown sympathy and questioned him. Anyone but Veronica, and probably Antoinette. Veronica was known for her bluntness.

"I want to tell Jeane to fuck off and beat the shit out of Justin, but—it doesn't matter what I want. It's not going to happen."

"Kale, it does matter what you want."

"No, it doesn't. Devan is never going to go for it. She is scared to death that Jeane is going to take the kids and leave." Kale threw his hands up in the air.

"I think she is right about that." Veronica said, although she didn't want to say it.

"Maybe, but I know I'll get them back. Jeane can't stand anyone but her uncle, because he has money, and Justin, God only knows why. But she truly only cares about herself." Kale's explanation was more to himself than Veronica. "You know this is Devan's fault. I would do this right now…"

"I know. Personally, I say go for it," Veronica had a hint of sarcasm in her voice. "What do you have to lose other than—oh, say, *everything*?"

She was right. If he did something now, he could lose everything including Devan. "Fuck! How did I get here?" He sat down on the couch and cradled his head in his hands.

"I'd love more than anything to tell you to be patient, but if I'm going to be honest, I would say you have been patient for years." Veronica's voice was sympathetic this time.

"Her essence surrounds me even when she's not really there." He balled his hands into fists. "I don't have any clue as to how she even feels anymore."

"Oh please," Veronica was calling his bluff.

"Do you know something I don't?" he asked. "Has she talked to you about this, about us?"

"Not for a while, but that doesn't mean…" She got up out of the chair and sat down next him. "I'll say this—never in my life have I seen so much chemistry for so long. I can see the pain in your eyes, and it hurts me to know that people I adore are so miserable. Sometimes the way you look at her alone is enough to make anyone blush…and she does almost every single time." Kale smiled a little. Veronica continued. "This little pact you guys have made is horse shit. Sure, you are all cool as a cucumber on the outside but inside you are on fire. Well, you *were* cool as a cucumber. If I can understand this, you bet your sweet ass, she can feel it and so can most of Ohio."

"What do you suggest I do?"

Veronica put her arms around him. "Be you. Be the irresistible Lettuce Head she fell in love with. I understand with spouses and kids it's not easy, but if you do it, I think you will break her. I want nothing more than a happy ending for you two. I'm not known for my sappiness, but I admit I am in love with *your* love, almost as much as I am in love with my own."

"Am I interrupting something?" Nate walked in.

"Oh, this—isn't what you think. I'm sorry bro—"

"I come in here, my wife has her arms draped around you and I hear her say she's in love with you." Veronica dropped her arms from Kale's waist and they both stood up.

"No, it's not—Oh God—Nate, I would never…" Kale was stuttering and tripping over his words in effort to convince his best friend that nothing was going on.

"I'm just teasing," Nate smiled. "I have to give you a hard time. So, what's really going on?" They all took their seats, with Nate sitting down next to his wife.

Kale brought Nate up to speed and then asked what Nate thought he would do if he was in the same situation.

"Normally I'm a person who says you need to play by the rules, and when the time is right it will happen. However, I'm not going to tell you that now. I think Veronica has a good point. I don't think Devan ever fell out of love with you either, but if you keep doing what you are doing without going overboard it's going to spark something in her that she won't be able to come back from. Think of it almost as a tease."

"What do you mean when you say what *I'm* doing?" Kale asked.

"I ran into Devan on Tuesday at the store. She mentioned the shirt incident that happened Sunday night," Nate explained.

"The shirt incident?" Kale didn't know what he was talking about.

"The shattered plate," Nate tried to get him to remember.

"Oh…"

Nate didn't think Kale was understanding exactly what he was saying, so he decided to spell it out for him without going into exact detail of everything Devan had told him. "When you took your shirt off, she was so flustered she dropped the plate."

Kale laughed. "No, it just slipped out of her hands and…" he paused. "Did she tell you otherwise?"

"All you need to know is, it was weighing on her mind enough for her to tell me."

"Well, why didn't she tell me?" Veronica frowned. "Or better yet, why didn't you tell me?" She smacked Nate's arm.

"That is their business, not yours, my dear." Nate put his hand on her shoulder.

She shoved it off and sneered at him. "You have that all wrong, their business is *my* business!"

Nate ignored her. "She also told me about Monday night. How she could feel something had shifted. From what you just told me I'd say something broke free. I think everything is about to get a lot more interesting for both of you."

"I can't believe she felt it too." Kale was awestruck.

"So, if I were you, I would be myself and only hold back the obvious things like kissing her. I know the temptation is there, and it's bad. Do everything but kiss her. Crossing that line might make her mad. If she's not exactly where you are regarding her feelings for you, it will push her farther away."

"I think you should almost kiss her. You guys seem to do that a lot," Veronica said. Kale and Nate had confused faces.

"Here, I'll demonstrate." She sat up straight and moved Nate's head, so he was facing her. She put her hand on his thigh just above his knee. She scooted in closer to him and moved her other hand to behind his neck and pushed him closer to her. He held her gaze for longer than a few seconds then she went in as if she was going to kiss him but instead kissed his cheek.

"Or—here, stand up," she instructed Nate. She stood up and faced him then wrapped her arms around him. He reciprocated. Then he let go.

"My dear, I see what you are doing. I think he needs to see it from a man's perspective." He straightened her up and put his hand to her face to move the few strands of hair that had fallen near her eyes. Then he cupped her chin and pulled it up when he lowered his head to be closer to hers. His chestnut eyes peered deep into Veronica's light blue ones. He touched his nose to hers then looked down at her lips then back into her eyes. Nate took his other hand and brushed back her hair and put his lips even closer to hers. "And that's one way." He stepped away from Veronica who was left disappointed even though she knew it wasn't real.

Nate moved his eyes to Kale whose attention was on Veronica. Her face said it all. Kale looked back at Nate and pointed at Veronica who was standing there with her hands on her hips. Nate turned to look at her. He wasn't even turned all the way when she leaped on him. He almost fell backwards but swiftly caught his balance. Her legs were now around his waist. He held on to her as she moved her hand through his thick hair. She took a handful and tugged lightly then placed her head on his shoulder and winked at Kale. Veronica gently kissed his neck. She moved to his ear and nibbled on the lobe for less than a second.

Nate groaned, "That is not playing fair, Veronica." He tried to put her down, but she wasn't about to let go.

Kale chuckled and stood up. "Okay, guys, I think that's enough for today." He headed to the door so they could have some privacy.

"Just tease her Kale. Remember she's weak when it comes to the biceps and pecs." Veronica yelled so he could hear her. Kale turned around to say goodbye, but they were no longer there. He heard Veronica giggling as he shut the door. *Poor Nate.*

On Friday, Kale and Sage had gone to the store early and bought so many things they couldn't carry them all to Devan's. Add to that the kids' pillows and sleeping bags, it would have been an impossibility, so he chose to drive.

Callie was waiting at the door for them. She was quite animated, jumping up and down and giggling. "This is going to be so much fun. We have the tent," Callie told them.

"Wow you have a tent? You girls really ready to sleep outside in the wilderness all by yourselves?" Kale followed them into the house.

"Yes, and we are going to have a fire too!" Callie said with an overabundance of excitement.

Kale walked into the kitchen and put three overflowing grocery bags on the counter.

"You realize they are just going to be in the backyard, right?" Devan laughed.

Kale smoothed back his hair. "Try telling my daughter that. She requested every junk food she could think of, but I brought us some food too."

Cyrus came running in to meet them. "Hey, mom got us a movie for tonight."

"Can we sleep in the tent too?" Kai asked.

"Maybe next time, buddy. This time it's the girls' turn. Why don't you camp out in Cy's room tonight?"

"Okay!" the boys exclaimed and ran upstairs.

"Where is Joey?" Devan hadn't seen him come in.

"Oh, he's playing some stupid video game at home. He's beyond all of this, I'm afraid. He's a teenager you know."

"That's sad. I know kids grow up, but it seems like yesterday he was calling me mem." Devan commented and opened a bottle of wine. She offered a glass to Kale, but he shook his head no. "More for me," she shrugged.

They went out to the deck. Kale had tried to set up the tent for the girls, but they refused the help. He and Devan decided to go back into the house since they were not needed.

"It's kind of weird to be over here without Justin trying to get me interested in work." Kale stated.

"And Jeane not letting me get in a word edgewise." Devan added.

"So, when you gonna start jogging with me?" He pulled the food out of the bags.

"Mom…mom…" Callie was calling her. She ran up to her with her hands in fists. "I have four lightning bugs…please get me a jar."

"Okay, but you need let them go in the morning, first thing." Devan went in the house and grabbed a mason jar, a rubber band, a fork, and a piece of foil.

She promptly put together a perfect enclosure for the insects' short stay. The girls pulled a handful of grass each and put it in the jar, then added the bugs. Devan closed it up with the foil and rubber bands, then stabbed the foil a few times for air holes.

"Thank you!" The girls were so excited they took the jar into the tent with them.

Kale and Devan listened to them talking. It was hard not to giggle.

"So, I have been thinking for a bit, and I'm going to marry your brother." Callie told Sage.

"Ew—" Sage replied. "Well, I am not going to marry yours." Kale laughed out loud.

"Dad! Go away." Sage yelled.

"Okay, okay we are going in the house."

Kale and Devan watched a movie and then went outside to check on the girls. It was quiet. He unzipped the tent slowly trying not to wake them. "Uncle Kale take this please. They are keeping me awake." Callie yawned while handing him the jar.

When he went back to the deck, Devan was walking down the steps with a blanket in her arms. "Cold?" he asked and set the jar on the table on the deck.

"No—I wanted to star watch." She spread the blanket out on the grass and sat down on it. Up to this point he was doing well avoiding eye contact and keeping his distance. He apparently debated too long on if he should sit down next to her because Devan grabbed his hand and pulled him down.

"Come on, lie down with me." The sky was clear, and even though there was a veil of light from the city, they could see every constellation from their vantage point.

"Uh oh. It's a full moon." Kale tapped her on the shoulder.

"So?"

He flipped over on his stomach. "People do strange things when there is a full moon," he winked at her.

What is he doing? At least tonight he hasn't been acting strange like he did a few days ago when he almost forgot his own kids.

"Let's do something crazy," Kale had a wild look in his eyes.

This time she raised an eyebrow at him. *Is he flirting with me?* They had done so well masking their feelings for so long.

"Such as?" she turned on her side and was face-to-face with him. *Oh my god, am I really entertaining this?*

He smiled. Devan's face was lit up by the moonlight. Damn, she was even more beautiful than the day he had met her! He was staring too long, and she was getting nervous—nervous that something could happen and nervous that it wouldn't.

"Does Justin ever tell you how beautiful you are?"

"Uh… no, not recently." She managed to say, still anxious as to where this was going.

Kale lifted his hand and brushed Devan's blonde hair from her face. It was silky and smelled delicious. "If you were my wife, I would tell you all the time." He spoke softly yet seductively.

Shit! No, no, no, no, no this is not happening.

He leaned in closer his hand still on her hair. He knew it wasn't right. *Damn it we were doing so good.* He couldn't help it. It was almost as if other forces were at work.

Devan knew there was just something different tonight. Maybe it was the moon, maybe it was the fact their spouses were away—maybe, it was just because it was *them.*

He looked back up at the stars and didn't say anything else. They both stared at the night sky. He turned back to gaze at her. Her eyes were closed this time. He leaned in a little closer remembering the day he met her in Hawaii. She was so very young and beautiful then but not as beautiful as she was now.

She opened her eyes to see his face a little too close to hers. "Kale, what are you doing?"

"I just—was going to push the hair out of your face." The truth was, there was no hair there. A light breeze slowly danced a few strands of her hair onto her cheeks as he was talking. He moved them back into place then put his hand lightly on her cheek. He could kiss her right now he was so close. She lifted her head and her lips were even closer. One slight move and they'd touch. They delved deep into one another's eyes. Kale could tell her how much he loved her—how much he was *in* love with her. So many words were unspoken. "Devan, I—" The back door flung open. Devan jumped up almost hitting Kale's head with hers." *Wow! That was awful close*, Kale thought to himself. *Too close.*

"Do everything but kiss her. Crossing that line might make her mad if she's not exactly where you are and push her farther away." Nate's voice echoed in his head.

Thank God for Kai. Kale could have totally screwed up.

"Dad, can I sleep in my own bed tonight?" he asked.

"Sure buddy," Kale got up and held out his hand to Devan. She took it, and he helped her to her feet. He didn't let go of her hand until he was walking out the front door. He stopped and glanced down at her hand in his then back up to her face. "Sorry." He kissed her forehead and gently let go of her hand, but she was still holding on to his. He looked down at her hand then back up to her face and smiled. *That's what I thought!* He gripped her hand again and pulled her in a tight embrace. Neither of them willing to let go.

"You guys are so weird," Kai groaned. "I'm sorry, Aunt Dev, I'm tired. Can you hug on my dad tomorrow maybe?"

Devan squeezed out of his embrace. "I'm sorry Kai! Goodnight." She closed the door and locked it. She leaned back on it with the back of her head against it. "What just happened?"

"I'll tell you what happened. Kai is right. You guys are weird all hugging on each other and stuff," Callie claimed as she stepped out of the bathroom and passed her mom on her way back out to the tent. "You guys act like you haven't seen each other in fifteen years." With that said Callie went back outside.

Devan followed her daughter out. "What?" Devan asked and sat down on one of the chairs at the table.

"Mom, if you can't figure it out, I'm not going to tell you. Goodnight, I'm going to bed." Callie unzipped the tent and crawled in, but before she zipped it back up she stuck her head out. "Please let the lightning bugs go. I don't want them to die."

Devan took off the makeshift foil lid and watched them fly out. The last one seemed to linger flying near the table. It finally took a seat next to her. She set the jar down. "What's wrong little guy? Don't you want to go with your friends?" It walked over and climbed up her arm and sat on her shoulder then it flew back to the jar. "You are free. Don't go back there." She went to lift it from the mouth of the jar when she saw a faint light inside. "Oh no," She took the insect off the jar and set it back down on the table. She reached inside and pulled out the leaf that was covering part of the bottom. There was another lightening bug. If it wasn't for the one that lingered, she would have never seen this one, so it would have died. The poor creature needed assistance. She put her hand in there and gently scooped it up. She lifted her hand out and studied the insect. It lit up three times in a row but did not fly away. She hoped it was not injured. "Come on little guy, go be with your friends," she whispered. It walked around on her hand, up her arm, to her shoulder and lit up three more times. The lightning bug that was on the table flew over and landed on her upper arm to crawl his way up to his friend. Their antennas touched, then they flew away.

"Awe, you rescued your friend." Devan smiled as she watched them fly off together. She knew what it was like to be rescued.

Chapter 20

Sunday family dinner was at Kale's house this time. He did his best to not be alone with Devan. He didn't trust himself. Every time he would catch her eyes on him, he would smile at her yet didn't engage in much conversation. After both sets of parents left, the kids were playing outside. Kale went into the kitchen and grabbed a snack. Devan had followed him. When he closed the refrigerator door, she was standing on the other side of it. She startled him. "Oh my god, Devan."

"Sorry, do you need help with anything else in here?" she asked.

"Nope it's all taken care of, thank you." He finished wiping the table with a wet rag.

"You are quiet today, what's up?"

"I'm fine, just got a lot of work stuff on my mind. I can't concentrate lately, and I have a lot more work coming my way that I'm not looking forward to." He put the rag in the sink.

"Well with the kids going back to school Wednesday, you should be able to get more done."

Kale grinned at her and contemplated what to say or do next. He walked past her and sat down in the living room.

"God damn it," he heard Devan exclaim from the kitchen. He got up to see what she was angry about and found her with a plastic bag that was torn and a large pile of garbage on the floor.

"What were you trying to do?"

"Take the garbage out," she said through her gritted teeth.

"What? Why? That's a man's job."

She gave him a dirty look, "I take offense to that."

"Oh, get over it," he knelt down to help her.

"I'm sorry." She tried to get a new garbage bag but slipped on the floor and ended up on her bottom. Kale burst out laughing. She got up and snatched the rag that Kale had thrown in the sink. When Kale bent back over, she snapped it right on his ass.

"What the—" he popped up and made a face that let her know she was in trouble. He reached for the dish hose in the sink. Devan scooted back towards the living room, unfortunately for her she wasn't fast enough. He turned it on soaking her and half the kitchen. She tried charging at him and instead slid over to him, snagged his pants and dragged him to floor with her. They were toppled over each other laughing so hard that neither of them heard the kids come in.

"Guess we'll be checking out old folks' homes sooner than we planned," Joey told Callie.

"They will get kicked out if they do this crap," Callie commented.

"I guess we'll just have to take turns taking care of them," Joey said as they tiptoed over the mess.

"Hey, you realize we aren't even forty yet, right?" Kale piped up.

Callie stopped before entering the living room and whirled around. "We are quite aware of your age, more than you seem to be. I swear you act like you are four. I don't know what has gotten into you two lately, and I don't care. You'd better clean up this mess."

"Okay mom," Devan yelled to Callie. Kale and Devan laughed for a while longer before cleaning up.

The week school started Devan asked Veronica out on a lunch date.

"How are things?" Veronica was expecting Devan to come clean about Kale.

Devan took a sip of her drink, "Well, things are—interesting."

"I bet it's nice to have the jack asses out of town so much again."

Devan nodded. "Yes, that is nice, but…"

Veronica smirked. She knew there was a *but*.

"Things have been weird with Kale."

"How so?" Veronica questioned before taking a bite of her sandwich.

Devan took another sip of her drink. "For the last three years, things have been back to normal. Maybe not back to normal, calm though. Kale and I have been getting along great. No almost kisses, or heartfelt embraces, or lingering too long. Nothing has happened since the night of your wedding."

"Something happened the night of my wedding?" Veronica tried to act surprised.

"Oh please, Roni, I know you saw and heard everything."

"Well—there wasn't that much to see or that much to hear," she smiled slyly.

"Anyway, nothing has happened since then," Devan paused. "That all changed the other day."

"Oh?"

"Two weeks ago, we had Sunday dinner and he teased me as he normally does, however, this time it was as though something snapped inside me. He took his shirt off, and I haven't been the same since." She took a sip of her drink, embarrassed.

"You go swimming over there a lot, doesn't he take his shirt off then? Surely in the last few years you have seen him topless."

"Yes, I don't know. He had his shirt off and next thing I know I'm having this wild daydream about him and me getting it on, and he's standing right in front of me. And that's not all—"

"Oh, there is more?" Veronica was intrigued to hear Devan's side of the story.

"Since then, anytime we are alone things get intense, or at least it *seems* intense to me."

"I need details, woman," Veronica demanded.

"The almost kisses have happened several times."

Veronica interrupted her, "What would you do if he really did kiss you?" She was trying to feel out the situation.

"I don't know." Devan looked down at her partially eaten sandwich.

"What would happen if *you* kissed *him*?" Veronica tried a different approach.

"I don't know," she lifted her eyes up from the plate.

"Fair enough, just think about it. What would you do if he kissed you?" Veronica tried to put the idea in her head even more.

"I don't think I could not kiss him back, honestly, but then I'd hate myself or do something stupid such as not talk to him again for three years."

Nope, she's not ready yet. He will have to keep trying. I think he will wear her down. "Well, don't worry about it right now. Just enjoy it." Veronica took another bite of her food.

"I can't not think about it. I think he might be flirting with me again."

Veronica shook her head in disbelief, "Devan, he never quit flirting with you. He can't help himself. It's quite comical."

"No, he hasn't done it in three years—"

"You are delusional. Hell, he even does it near your spouses, yet they are too wrapped up in their own affair, or whatever it is they have going, to pay even the slightest bit of attention."

"I disagree."

Veronica laughed again. "Disagree all you want, my friend, I know the truth."

Devan shook her head '*no*' and finished her sandwich.

On the way out to their cars, Veronica grasped Devan's arm.

"Maybe the Universe is trying to tell you something."

Devan shrugged, "And what would the Universe be trying to tell me?"

Veronica let go of her arm and unlocked her car. "It's trying to tell you your time has come. Bliss is right around the corner. Stop interfering with your fate! Love you, bye." She jumped in and shut her door immediately so that Devan wouldn't have a chance to say anything else. Before pulling out of the parking lot she rolled down her window and shouted at someone. "Hey handsome," she waved and sped away.

The moment Devan saw Kale come around the corner she dropped her keys on the driver's seat and accidently shut the door. She tried opening it with no luck. The car was locked with her keys in it. It was almost as if Veronica had made her do this. *Bliss is right around the corner.* Veronica's voice danced in her head. *Yeah, and it's just a coincidence that Kale happened to show up at the exact restaurant I'm at.*

"Fancy meeting you here. I saw Veronica. Did you ladies just have lunch?"

Devan nodded. "Great minds think alike, huh? I'm here to pick up my carryout. Then I have to run to Cleveland for a meeting of the minds." He rolled his eyes.

"Oh yeah, have fun with that. Enjoy your food," she called after him. He continued walking to the front door. She didn't want him to know how stupid she was, so she tried remembering the lock combo on the door that she never used. She tried ten different combinations. *Shit!* She called Veronica. She couldn't be that far away she just left. When Veronica answered, Devan explained to her what had happened and asked her if she could come get her and take her to her house so she could get the spare key.

"I just saw Kale, have him do it."

"No, I don't want him to know how dumb I am, and I don't want to be alone with him right now. Plus, he's got a meeting to get to."

"Suck it up buttercup. You know he will do it, and he won't think you are dumb. Besides I have things to do!" She hung up.

"Damn it!" Then she remembered Justin had put a key hider that had a strong magnet that would hold the key under her car. She got down on the weathered blacktop and searched the underneath of the car. She couldn't see a thing, so she squeezed farther under then pulled her phone out and turned on its flashlight. She shined the light as far as it would go and couldn't see the hidden key case anywhere. She was there when Justin placed it on her car. *Where did it go?*

"Hey, weren't you leaving?" She heard Kale's voice and lifted her head which hit the bottom of the car.

"Ouch!" She scooted out and rubbed her head.

Kale set his bag of food down and helped her up. "What were you doing under there?"

She sighed, put the phone in her pocket and looked up at his beautiful face. A breeze lifted a few of the dark curls that were resting on his broad shoulders. He was wearing a heather grey tank top, and she gulped as she took in his large biceps and strong forearms. He pulled his sunglasses down a little exposing his emerald green eyes. "Well?"

"I locked my keys in the car, and I knew Justin had put one of those key hider things underneath. So, that's what I was searching for, but it's not there."

Kale stroked his goatee and chuckled. "Come on Monty, I'll take you home to get a spare."

"How do you even know I have other keys?"

"Your husband has multiple keys for everything, and when I say multiple, I mean five per lock. I bet I even have copies of your keys. Come on, I'll take you home to get an extra set."

As she walked with him to his truck, she asked puzzled, "You have copies?"

"When he lost his keys about two years ago, he made a ton of copies. I believe he gave a set to his dad, your dad and me." Devan rolled her eyes. "Yup, that's what I thought too." Kale unlocked the truck door for Devan and opened it.

When they got to her house, she jumped out of the truck, ran up to her front door, stood there for a moment, then threw her head back laughing. She came back to the truck shaking her head. "Yeah, so, my house key is on my key ring with my car key."

Kale snickered, "To my house it is." Devan got back in the truck. "I guess it was a good thing he gave me a key then, huh?"

"No, now you are going to be late to your meeting."

"I didn't really want to go anyway," he said pulling in to his driveway.

Devan got out of the car when he put it in park, "Won't you get in trouble?"

"Nah. That's the joy, and maybe the only joy of being married to the boss's niece." He pulled his phone out, dialed a number and put the phone to his ear.

"Hey Jan, I'm not going to make the meeting. Can you forward the notes to me later? I had some car trouble—okay great—Yes, I'm fine, thank you for asking—No, I'll be there Friday—Yup, it's an easy fix. Thank you—all right—bye."

He looked at Devan who was shaking her head at him. "See, no problem."

They went inside and he grabbed the key. On the way to get her car he asked what she was doing for the rest of the day.

"Cleaning," she stated.

"That doesn't sound like any fun. Let's go to the matinee," he suggested.

Devan knew there was a way to get out of it. "Well, the only thing that seems even remotely interesting in the theater is a romantic comedy, and you wouldn't want to see that."

"That sounds good. I haven't seen a good romantic comedy in a while. Let's get your car back, and I'll eat lunch and see if the grandmas can pick up the kids."

She thought for a moment. "Can't, my mom has to work late today." *Good one Devan!*

"Okay, not a biggie—my mom will get all the kids. She'll love that!" *Well, it was worth a shot.*

At the movies Kale pulled the old trick where he stretched and nonchalantly placed his arm on her shoulders. She found herself leaning in to him. She quickly straightened up, the second she did, Kale pulled her back. It's not that she didn't want to be that close to him. Hell, sitting in his lap wouldn't be too close for her. It was nice. They hadn't done anything like this in a long time. It almost felt like a date, as if they were teenagers again. The movie was quite enjoyable. She wasn't sure what she appreciated more, his laughter at the funny parts or the love story itself. When the movie was over he held her hand all the way to his truck.

"Hungry?" He unlocked the door.

"I have to get back, I can't take advantage of your mom that way," she said as she slid onto the seat.

He shut her door and went to the other side of the truck and got in. He buckled his seat belt and turned his head towards her. "Well, that's convenient then because I just got a text from mom saying dinner is ready." He smiled at her. He drove her to her house, so she could get her car and follow Kale over to his mom's house.

Dinner was wonderful as always. Cassandra was an excellent cook. After dinner, Cassandra brought out a bag and handed it to her. "It's daffodil bulbs. You mentioned in the spring how nice mine were, so I dug some up for you."

Devan opened the bag and peeked inside. "Thank you so much, Cassandra."

"You are very welcome, dear. I would plant those in the next two weeks. They say between September and late November, but the earlier the better from my experience."

That Friday she decided to plant the bulbs before she forgot about them. After half the daffodil bulbs were planted, she was dripping with sweat. It was so hot! When she was finished, she got a bright idea. *I know he told us we were welcome anytime.* Devan looked over towards Kale's house. *Nothing would feel better than jumping into that pool.* She walked over to his back yard and unlocked the gate. She viewed the clear water, emptied her pockets and jumped right in with everything on. It was so nice. It was cooling on her hot skin. She saw the time on the clock hanging on the outside wall. She still had time before the kids got home.

Kale arrived home and went upstairs to the bathroom to take a quick shower before he had to pick up the kids at school. He threw his shirt on the floor and figured he would call Devan to see if she wanted him to get her kids too. He heard a ring tone. He checked outside and saw there was someone swimming under water. It was Devan in the pool in her clothes. He stood there watching for a few minutes and realized how this reminded him of a popular scene in *Fast Times at Ridgemont High* and laughed. He put his shirt back on and headed down the stairs. When he got to the bottom of the steps, he thought about what Veronica said the other day and pulled the shirt back off. Devan was on the float by the time he got down there. He tiptoed out the door and stood by the pool. "Is this a common thing for you, jumping in my pool with all your clothes on when I'm not home?" It startled her so much she fell off the float. "You told me to come swim anytime whether you were home or not."

"That I did."

"I'm sorry. I was planting the bulbs your mom gave me, and it was so hot. I saw no one was home so I trotted over here and slipped in the back."

"I see. Well, do you mind if I join you?"

"It *is* your pool." She got back on the float.

"Yes, I know."

"Oh my god, will you get in already?" She splashed water to where he was standing.

"Hold on, I have to get my shorts on," he went back in the house. He came out a minute later in his swim trunks and went over to the diving board and slowly walked to the end. The sun was shining on his deep tan. His silver necklace sparkled in the light. He bent over and got into form and remained that way for longer than necessary. He stood all the way up and pulled his hair out of its enclosure nice and slow making sure she didn't miss one single twitch of his biceps. His hair tumbled down onto his robust shoulders. Her mouth opened slightly, and she took a deep breath. He smiled just enough without her noticing then dove in.

They swam around each other, play fighting, and just having a good time. The 2:30 alarm went off on her phone. She had no idea that it had gotten that late. She jumped out of the pool and stood there. She didn't bring a towel or a change of clothes.

He surfaced. "Where are you going?"

"The kids," was all she managed to say.

"Oh shit," he had completely forgotten. He was too busy trying to get Devan all hot and bothered. She headed for the gate. "Just wait." She watched as he very slowly emerged from the pool. She bit her lip. She remembered how hard his chest was and could almost feel her hands gliding down it. *Oh my god, Devan, what is wrong with you? Snap out of it.* She shook her head a few times to get rid of the naughty thoughts that were entering her mind. He saw that. "You okay?"

"Uh, yeah, just water in my ear."

"Well, listen I actually tried calling earlier to see if you wanted me to get your kids when I picked up mine."

"Today is Thursday, right?"

"No, it's Friday."

"Oh, well then my mom picked them up. I swear there was something I had to do today." Something registered in Devan's mind, "Shit, I am supposed to meet Roni at my house in ten minutes."

He threw a towel at her. "Just relax a second. Let me get you some dry clothes."

They walked into the house, and she stood there freezing in the cold air conditioning. He returned with a fresh towel and one of his t-shirts and basketball shorts. He saw her shiver, took the wet towel and placed a dry one on her shoulders as he rubbed them for a minute. Then he hugged her trying to warm her up. His bare chest against her face felt so warm. The front door swung open. Joey dropped his bag on the floor in shock when he saw them.

He finally smiled. "Hi."

Kale let go of Devan. She excused herself to change. When she came out Joey gave her a look of interest. She immediately explained herself.

"Man, you guys get to have all the fun while we are at school," and he walked away.

She thanked Kale and jogged home to see Veronica with her hands on her hips.

"Why didn't you go in?"

"Door's locked."

She reached in her pocket to get her keys. "I left them at Kale's."

On their short stride back to his house Veronica drilled her asking every little detail. Devan rolled her eyes a lot. She knocked on the door and Kale opened it while pulling on a tank top. Veronica licked her lips, "MMM! Hello, sexy. Your girl, here, left her keys." He held his arm out in the direction of the pool.

Devan went to find the keys while Veronica talked to Kale.

"You know we are cousins, right?"

Veronica winked at him, "Only by marriage. I can say you are sexy if I want."

Kale chuckled then asked quietly, "Has she said anything?"

"She has. Keep up the great work."

Devan walked back in with a raised eyebrow as if she knew they were talking about her. Veronica grabbed Devan's arm and headed for the door.

"Thank you," Devan yelled back to Kale who was watching them leave with a smile on his face.

Veronica stopped at the door and turned around. "Hey, Antoinette is having a fall masquerade party or something at Lakeland Estates in the middle of November. Official invites will come in the mail in about a week. She just told me about it today. So, you two should make sure your asshole spouses are out of town, so you can have a good time. Okay, bye," she shut the door behind her.

Chapter 21

November 2015

October had come and gone quickly. It was the second week of November which always meant Conferences at the schools. Justin had been home all week which put everyone on edge. The day they had to go to the school Devan's phone buzzed, and she looked down at it to see a text from Justin. He claimed he would be a few minutes late getting home, and Devan needed to wait for him so they could go to the conference as a family. The second he stepped through the door she could smell the alcohol on him. Justin stumbled past her and loudly told her he was going to take a shower and then be ready. She turned around to see Callie whose face was solemn. "Mom, I don't want him to go."

"I don't want him to go either, honey." Devan had to think. Maybe if the kids could hurry and get ready, they could leave before Justin got out of the shower. She told them to get ready and be in the car in five minutes. They did as they were told. As they were starting to pull out, Justin ran out and pounded on the window.

"You can't leave without me," he said opening the door yelling. "We are going as a family, or none of us are going."

"We were just running to the drug store to get some aspirin," Devan lied through her teeth. "I know you are tired so why don't you go ahead and stay here. We will only be gone for an hour, tops," she tried convincing him.

"Devan, there is a whole bottle of aspirin in my bathroom. I'm not gettin' outta the van. We're all goin'," he slurred.

She put the car in park and opened the door to get out, "I'll be right back." She shut off the car and took the keys in case Justin would leave with the kids. She ran in the house and called Veronica.

"Roni, I have a problem. Is there any way you can work it so we see you instead of Mrs. Chandler tonight?"

"What's going on?"

"Justin came home drunk. He is sitting in the car right now and refuses to get out. He says we are all going to meet the teacher tonight or none of us will go."

"Ugh…yeah, I'm sure I can do something. It's a good thing I moved up to the next school, for emergencies like this. When you come in, go through the other door and come straight to my room. I'll get the information from Janet, I mean Mrs. Chandler." Devan was so thankful Veronica had taken the middle school art teacher position when the other teacher retired.

During the ride to the school, Devan was praying that that this would work and that there wouldn't be any type of scene at all. Aside from the fact Justin reeked of booze, if he could keep his mouth shut and not sway or show any signs that he was drunk, it would be okay. When they stepped outside of the van she grabbed the perfume that was in her bag and sprayed him. He wasn't happy, as usual.

"Mom, why are we going to Aunt Roni's room…Mrs. Chandler is over…"

"Mrs. Cavendar, which is how you will be addressing her tonight and anytime you are in school, is taking over for Mrs. Chandler tonight," Devan told her as they walked through the door.

"But Mom—"

"Callie, she called me and told me," Devan lied again.

"Hello, Callie, Mr. and Mrs. Jameson, I'm filling in for Mrs. Chandler."

Justin scoffed, "Mr. and Mrs. Jameson."

"I have to be professional," she assured him.

The Jamesons sat down at a table. Veronica pulled out the folder, that had Callie's name on it, and began to give a nice report. When she was in the middle of explaining, Justin interrupted her.

"What can we do to make 'er get all A's or whatever you guys call 'em these days?"

"She's getting all A's and B's. Callie is doing very well," Veronica told him.

"Yeah, still it's not straight A's. She nee's to do better," he slurred.

Devan was getting pissed. Callie was on the verge of tears. Justin continued on. Veronica excused herself, moseyed over to her desk, and picked up her phone to see the time.

"I'm sorry, guys, the next conference is coming." She went back and told Callie what a great job she was doing.

As soon as they got back in the car he started. "You need to work harder. You should be a straight A student, none of this B shit," he slumped into his seat.

"Callie, I think your report was wonderful. I am so proud of you," Devan said hoping Justin would shut the hell up, but he didn't.

"It's not good 'nuff. Ya know you can do better," he shook his finger at Callie.

Devan could hear sniffling, and she was pretty sure she could see Callie was crying when she looked in her rearview mirror.

When Justin spoke again, Devan told him it was in his best interest to shut up. He finally did. When they got home, Callie ran into the house crying. Justin opened the car door and could hardly get out. Devan told Cyrus to go into the house and he did.

"What the fuck is your problem?" Devan slammed her door shut and went over to where Justin was swaying. She got in his face, "Your daughter is doing a beautiful job in school. You have no reason to complain."

"Yeah, well she can do better," he sneered at her.

"Justin! You were rude, and you hurt her feelings."

"So wha'! She's a fuckin' kid. She'll get over't," he said pushing past her.

"Oh my god! Why did you insist on going?"

"I have ev'r right to know how she's doin'. I'm 'er dad."

"Oh, now you decide to be her dad. It's pretty fucked up that you got drunk off your ass knowing that you had this conference tonight. I'm so sick of this shit!"

"Yeah, well wha' kinda life do I have? I go to work and come home and go to bed. So, what if I wanna drink." He got in *her* face this time. His nasty booze breath nauseated and infuriated her even more.

"You couldn't have picked a better day? Why the hell did you have to do it today?" She lowered her voice to a normal level.

"Yeah, I should'a thought 'bout that, but I din't. I drank because I wanted to, damn it!"

She walked past him into the house. "I don't know why you can't even be sober for your kids."

"It's not 'bout the kids. I do it for m'self, and I don' fuckin' wanna be sober. I feel good bein' fucked up. No, I feel fuckin' great! It's amazin'." Justin stated as he came up behind her.

"It's amazing to be drunk…too drunk to be there for your kids?"

He leaned down close to her face. "I. DON'. CARE. wha' you or my ungrateful kids think." She wiped the spit off her face and did everything she could to not haul off and hit him. As he staggered into the kitchen, she grabbed his arm.

"If you make my sweet little girl cry again tonight, I will castrate you!"

He scoffed at her words. "Know wha'? I won't say a goddamn wor'…to anyone. Fuck this…I'm goin' to bed."

The next day Justin called around three o'clock and asked what was for dinner. Devan told him—thinking he sounded strange on the phone. He already sounded drunk. When he told her he would be home at five o'clock she said dinner would be ready. At six o'clock he called saying he was on his way home and wanted to know if she wanted anything from Taco Bell. She told him *no* that dinner had been ready at five o'clock so they ate. Justin got pissed and screamed at her. She hung up. He texted her an hour later saying he was going to a hotel for the night.

"Where's Daddy?" Cyrus asked when she put her phone down.

"He's working really late tonight," she said in a calm voice.

"Why does he always work late? Doesn't he love us anymore?"

Devan wanted to scream. She fought back the tears, and she lied to her child.

"Sure he does, buddy. Daddy sometimes has to work extra hard so he can make sure we have a roof over our heads and food in our bellies." She put her hands on his cheeks.

"Then why is he always drunk?"

Devan was shocked by the words that came out of his mouth and dropped her hands from his face.

"What did you say?" she was hoping she had heard him wrong.

"Why is he always drunk?" Nope, she heard him correctly.

"Where did you hear that word?"

"Callie told me. She said when daddy acts weird, or he doesn't talk right that he's drunk. That he drank beer or something."

Devan's heart was hurting. An eleven-year-old shouldn't know what that actually was, and a seven-year-old should not even know the word.

That following week Justin was home again and drank most of the days. Some days were tolerable while others were not.

"Why are you drunk again?" Callie asked when Justin stumbled in.

"What the…who d' you think you are talkin' to, li'l girl?" He was attempting to take his shoes off but not succeeding.

"It's true. I can smell it from here." Justin gave up trying to take his shoes off and walked closer to her. Devan intervened worried about what could happen.

"This is your doin'. You 'r tellin' the kids this. You 'r such a bitch," he pointed at her.

"No, Dad. She didn't say anything. You do this all the time!" Callie shouted at him.

"Your mom is a tot'l bitch for teachin' you kids this." He headed towards Devan.

"Dad! She's not a bitch! You are a drunk loser. That's what you are. Mom does the best she can on her own, and you treat her like shit!" Callie screamed at him.

"Calista—"

"Mom, you know it's true. It's not fair you have to do *everything*, and he makes it so much worse for you. I hate you, Justin Jameson. You are a terrible person!" She was going closer to him. Devan put herself between Justin and Callie.

"Fuck it!" Justin left slamming the door behind him. She looked at Callie's red face and Cyrus, in the corner, who was terrified. She tried desperately not to cry.

"You think we don't see things. You try to cover it up, but Mom, we see. I have known for a few years that Dad was a drunk. I just…I didn't want you to know that I knew. I figured it would make things harder for you. I'm sorry, I couldn't hold it in. I had to yell at him. I hate the way he treats you. I hate the way you have to do everything. I hate that you always have to clean up after him and try to cover for him. I hate him, Mom, I really do."

Devan couldn't hold it in anymore either. She crumpled to the floor in tears. Not because what Callie said was true, but because Callie was the one who said it. Devan hated Justin even more now. She hated that she settled for a loser who chose alcohol over his own children. She blamed herself. She couldn't give her children a loving and caring father that they deserved.

Callie hugged her tight. "I'm sorry, Mommy. I didn't mean to make you cry."

Devan sat up and wiped the tears from her eyes. "Oh honey, you didn't make me cry." She stood up and wrapped her arms around Callie. "Who wants ice cream?" She was trying to change the mood as fast as she could. Both kids lightened up immediately.

At the ice cream shop, they saw Kale and his kids. He noticed right away something was wrong. Even though her eyes lit up when she saw Kale, the redness in her eyes didn't go away. Kale didn't want to pry for fear of upsetting her.

"How was your day?" he asked before shoveling a spoonful of his sundae in his mouth.

She took a sip of her malt and set the cup on the table and took a deep breath.

"Same old shit, different day. You?"

Kale smiled at her, "I, uh, went shopping today for my masquerade outfit."

"Oh yeah what did you get?" She picked up her malt and put the straw in her mouth.

"It's a surprise, so I'm not telling you. Unfortunately, I did get confirmation that Jeane is going, and they will both be in town. However, I say we don't let it spoil our fun."

The spark in her eyes disappeared and she turned away from Kale. He thought he saw her eyes start to water. She got up and excused herself to go to the restroom.

Her face was red and her eyes were glossy when she came back. He didn't want to upset her, but he had to find out what was wrong.

"Okay, Monty, what's going on?" Kale reached across the table and grabbed her hand. She smiled weakly and looked up at him.

"Nothing."

"That's not what I see."

"Oh, yeah, just having some issues with my contacts. It's time to change them," she rubbed her eyes.

He decided to let it rest. She wasn't going to talk about whatever it was, and he knew her well enough to know if she really wanted to tell him what was bothering her, she would. "Okay, so listen, we have a few nice days this next week, wanna come jogging with me?"

She sat there for a second, lifted her eyes from the table and met his. "Yes!" Devan said surprising Kale.

"Really?"

Devan stared at him and he noticed her eyes had changed again. She had determination written all over her face.

"Do you have a punching bag?"

He was intrigued by her question. "Why?"

"I need one, no, I need a punching *dummy*!" Her eyes grew wide.

Kale tried not to laugh. "Why don't you come to the gym with me once. I think you'll find all you need there," he smirked.

"Okay sounds like a plan…but I want to run for a week or so before I go to the gym." She picked up her malt and looked at it. "Guess, I don't need you anymore." She chucked it in the garbage can that was near their table.

"Ugh, Monty…you wasted it. I would have finished it for you," Kale frowned.

"Sorry."

That night after the kids had gone to bed, she called Veronica and told her what had transpired since the conference.

"Then we ran into Kale and the kids at the ice cream place, and I felt better."

Veronica giggled, "Of course you felt better. Your knight in shining armor was there to brighten your day."

"No, I mean, yes. I had an epiphany," Devan told her.

"Do tell." Veronica couldn't wait to hear what Devan had cooked up.

"Kale has been trying to get me to go running with him, and he brought it up again tonight. I've been avoiding the subject, but tonight when he mentioned it, I thought it was a great idea so I agreed. At that point I decided to start taking my frustration out physically."

"Yeah, I bet that's what Kale has been doing for years to get that physique. Sexual frustration and horrible wife…now it all makes sense," Veronica teased.

"Then what's Nate's excuse? He's bulked up a lot since high school."

"That's easy, he did it in case he needed to defend himself from all those assholes, and now he does it to be sexy for me," Veronica said as though it was a fact.

"I see. Well, I've gotta get ready for bed. Five a.m. comes early."

"Why do you need to be up at five?" Veronica asked.

"I can't let Kale see how horrible I look when I wake up. He'll be at my house at six o'clock to run."

"He's seen you plenty of times when you wake up. You are running for exercise not walking down a runway during fashion week." Veronica couldn't help but harass her friend.

"Well…I just…I want to appear presentable, okay?" Devan stumbled on her words.

"Oh, it makes sense, perfect sense. Goodnight, my friend." Veronica hung up the phone and smiled to herself. Naturally, Devan wanted to look good for Kale.

The next morning Kale showed up at her door at exactly six a.m., and he did that every day for the rest of the week and the week after. They even went running on Thanksgiving Day. Devan was beginning to get better both physically and mentally. Seeing Kale daily helped her as well. Between the endorphins from the exercise and being around Kale, she felt amazing. Her confidence was building back up, and she began to recognize the person in the mirror staring back at her.

Veronica noticed and even commented on it. "I must say, Dee, you are glowing."

"Well, it is a little warm in here," Devan fanned herself.

"No, I mean your whole being is glowing. You seem happy, and I sense this positive energy radiating from you," Veronica stated.

"I do feel better. No, I feel a *lot* better since I have been running with Kale in the mornings. I might have to get a treadmill since it's getting too cold."

"Or you could just join the gym."

"Gym—Shit! I gotta take Cy to karate." Devan jumped out of her chair and told Cyrus to get ready.

"Can I go with you so we can check out that gym?"

"You…want to check out the gym?" Devan was convinced she heard her wrong.

"Well, yeah. Nate's invited me a few times, but I always decline."

"Okay, let's go." Devan put her shoes on and picked up her purse, then followed Cyrus and Veronica out to the car.

After dropping Cyrus off at his karate class, Veronica and Devan checked out the gym then sat down and watched the kids finish the class. "I'm gonna go get a water. Do you want anything?" Devan got up from her seat.

"Nope, I'm good. Thank you."

Devan found the vending machines and put her money in. When the bottle fell from its slot she reached in, pulled it out and twisted the cap off. She put the bottle to her mouth and turned to head back. She stopped dead in her tracks when she saw Kale through the glass working out in the gym. He was hot in his sleeveless t-shirt. She had no idea what he was doing, and it didn't matter because he looked good doing it. She kept watching as Kale got off whatever machine he was on. He threw his shirt down on the bench, grabbed the hand towel, and wiped the sweat off his face and his gleaming chest. He took his water bottle, that was near the shirt, and started drinking. Never had someone looked so sexy drinking a water. He put it down and went over to the squat machine. She didn't even notice the people passing by, or hear Veronica say the class was over.

"What are you staring at?" Veronica looked to see why Devan was so captivated. She herself got a little hot and bothered when she saw her husband working out. Kale noticed them and waved then walked over to Nate and pointed to Veronica and Devan. To the disappointment of the girls, the guys put their shirts on and met them in the hallway. Nate greeted Veronica with a big hug and kiss on the cheek. "I never thought I would see you here, *ever.*"

"Actually, Devan and I were talking about getting a membership." Veronica told him and winked at Kale. Nate and Kale both raised an eyebrow. "Where do I sign up?"

"Oh shit, you were serious," Kale said to Veronica.

"Devan told me how good she has been feeling since she's been running with you in the mornings, and it got me thinking that maybe I should be more active as well. Forty is coming up in a few years. I probably shouldn't wait till then."

"Okay, let's sign you up." Nate ushered her to the counter where people were checking in. Devan and Kale followed. The person working the desk explained that due to the fact Veronica and Nate were married, she didn't have to buy a membership and printed out a card for her. The man then asked Devan for her first name, thinking that he was going to search for her because her kid was enrolled in karate, she spelled it. He printed something and handed a card to Devan. She read it and opened her mouth to say something and Kale stopped her. "Thank you," he told the man and put his arm around Devan and walked her out to her car with Nate, Veronica, and Cyrus behind them.

"Okay, I feel like I am missing something," Veronica said to Devan.

Devan handed the card to Veronica, who had a smart remark.

"I think Devan Iakona sounds a lot better than Devan Jameson."

Devan smacked her arm.

"Can I be Cyrus Iakona then?" Devan's son asked.

"Oh shit, sorry," Veronica said under her breath.

"Uncle Kale is a good dad, and then Kai and Joey can be my brothers."

"What about Sage?"

"Eh, I already have a sister. I really don't want another one." Everyone chuckled except Kale. He squatted down in front of Cyrus.

"You know I love you, buddy, right?"

"Yes."

"While I would love more than anything in the world to be your dad, you already have a dad, and I know that he loves you very much. Is it okay if I'm your best friend instead?"

"I guess." Cyrus got in the car, but before shutting the door, he peeked his head out. "Hey, Uncle Kale?"

"Yeah?"

"Some dads are best friends too you know. When you and Mom get married, you can be my best friend and my dad too." He shut the door.

Devan's mouth dropped open.

Kale laughed, "Kids say the darnedest things. I'll see you guys later." He hugged Devan and kissed her forehead then got in his truck and left.

"Are your ears cleaned out?" Veronica asked Devan before getting in Nate's SUV. "Your new gym membership card, your own kid. The Universe is talking to you again. Maybe you should listen." Nate waved and Veronica got in the car and shut the door. Devan opened her door and got in her car. She looked at Cyrus in the rearview mirror.

"Why did you say that?"

Cyrus shrugged his shoulders, "I dunno...I wanted to?"

"Cyrus, why would you think that Uncle Kale and I would get married?"

"I used to think you were already married until Callie told me I was stupid." He rolled his eyes.

"Well, why did you think we were married?"

"Cause, you guys do stuff married people do, duh." He rolled his eyes again.

"And what's that?" Devan asked worried what his answer was.

"I dunno, you take care of your kids together, and help each other, and you hug…only married people hug. You guys hug *a lot*."

Devan didn't say anything. She buckled her seatbelt and turned on the car.

"Don't worry, Mom, I'm not gonna tell Justin anything."

Chapter 22

Kale stood outside of Nate's and Veronica's house waiting for them to answer the door. Veronica opened the door and let him in. He sat down on their long plush couch, slipped his boots off and plopped his feet on the ottoman.

"Do you have your suit for tomorrow?" Veronica asked sitting down in the chair across from him.

"No, I have a tuxedo."

"Wow, that's…shocking. I thought you hated those things."

"I do, but this is a special occasion, and I even got a real bowtie this time." He nodded his head proud of himself. "So, how do you think I'm doing with Devan?"

"I don't know Kale," Veronica leaned back in the chair and sighed. "I think you are wearing her down. You should have seen her at the gym the other day. She was quite flustered."

"The gym?"

"Yeah, before you saw us—she saw you. I have no idea how long she was standing there. She was gawking at you with her mouth open when I walked up to her," Veronica replied.

"What?"

"Um…" she pointed to his chest and arms and shrugged.

"Oh stop." Kale was getting embarrassed. "I don't get it. How can it be sexy to a woman watching a guy work out and get nasty and sweaty?"

"Okay, let's reference a famous TV show from the '90s—women in bathing suits running on a beach in the hot sun."

Kale shrugged not catching on to what she was saying.

"Bouncing up and down," she said slowly.

"Ohhhh…" Kale finally understood. His face grew red as he realized how he had made Devan feel.

"Yeah, that's basically the equivalent of watching a sexy man work out."

Veronica jumped up off the chair. "I'm gonna get a water, want anything?"

Kale shook his head no.

Veronica came back in and sat down in the same chair. "I think you are doing a superb job. Dee has to break, dude. There was the whole thing with the gym card and Cyrus. Wow, it couldn't have been more perfectly timed. You even had me going when you were talking to Cyrus." She took a sip of her water and put the lid back on then set it in her lap.

"That was crazy. When he said that to me, I wanted to grab Devan and him, get my kids and Callie and run away with them."

Veronica gave him a half smile, "I know. You are more of a father to those kids than Justin has ever been and probably could ever be." Kale knew what she was saying was true.

"Speaking of Justin, has Devan mentioned anything about him lately?"

"No—why?"

"Hmmm."

"Why? What is he doing now?" Kale sat up and put his feet on the ground. "Veronica, tell me…what is that asshole doing?"

"To make a long story short, he was drunk at conferences, then the next day he left and didn't come home until the day after. Then the week after he was drunk again, and this time it was worse."

Kale looked like he was going to fly off the couch. "Worse?"

"The other two times he had words with Devan, this time he had them with Callie and Devan. Callie called him a drunk."

"Did he touch either of them?" His eyes darkened about two shades.

"No, but Devan was pretty upset."

"When was this?"

"The night you ran into one another at the ice cream place."

"I knew it wasn't her contacts." Kale was fuming.

"No, it wasn't, yet running into you and seeing you made her feel better."

"Ugh, I want to kill that asshole."

"That's a great idea, Kale. Violence always makes everything better." Her sarcasm wasn't enough to stop him.

"That dickhead. Can I just go beat his ass now?"

"Sure, if you want to get arrested."

"Why wouldn't Devan tell me this?" Kale already knew the answer to his question.

"Probably because she doesn't want you to get arrested, and don't you tell her I said anything," Veronica threatened.

The next night was the masquerade party that Antoinette was hosting. While Devan and Justin were driving to Lakeland Estates where the party was to be held, Justin *incidentally* mentioned that he and Jeane would be in Texas while the kids would be on Winter Break. Devan could have cared less except it was a reprieve from Justin's drinking and demoralizing comments. She was thrilled to have something to look forward to. Finally, they reached the parking lot.

Kale pulled in and saw Devan stepping out of the car. Her hair was in a beautiful upsweep—her gold and black mask was in her hand. Her dress was a strapless burgundy mermaid style dress with an overlay that had a scooped neck and sleeveless sheer black lace. From the knee down, both pieces went in to a flare that swept the floor. She was stunning.

"Are you just going to sit here all night or are you going to open my door?" Jeane complained, drawing Kale's attention away from Devan.

Kale got out and opened her door. Jeane stepped out in her black slinky serpentine scale-look strapless dress. At mid-thigh the dress dropped into a black sheer chiffon with cutouts.

"Hey Justin—" Jeane headed towards him rather quickly. Justin stopped and eyed her over.

"Wow, you are hot tonight, Jeane."

"I know…Oh, Devan, you," she paused, "are adorable in that burgundy dress…it's so pretty." When she said *pretty* Devan cringed. Jeane's insulting compliments were always annoying. Justin ran up the steps and opened the door for Jeane, however, he let go of the door just before Devan got to the top step.

"What the hell, Justin?" Kale ran to the door and opened it for her. Justin turned around, "Did you say something?"

"You basically let the door slam in Devan's face. You couldn't hold the door open two seconds longer?

"Why? She has two hands," Justin remarked and followed Jeane inside.

Kale was annoyed at Justin's rudeness and was about to say something else then he noticed again how beautiful Devan looked. He took her hand and helped her up the stairs. "You are absolutely stunning, Devan."

"Thank you, you are quite handsome yourself, but you don't have to tend to me tonight, Kale, I appreciate it though." Devan still seemed a little sad.

"Let me get you a drink."

While Kale found the bar, Veronica came up behind Devan.

"Wow, he is looking fine tonight. I'd say he was the hottest guy here—if I hadn't already seen my husband." Devan turned to see her wearing what appeared to be a full skirt dress, but the appearance was deceiving. It was actually a black satin sheath type dress underneath with the top covered in lace. The front was a sweetheart style with wide straps made of lace while the back began at the end of the lace straps forming a U shape. Sheer black chiffon was gathered into the waist seam and billowed out from the waist to the floor. Veronica was striking.

Nate came walking up to them dressed in a tux, handsome as ever. His tux jacket was black with satin lapels that had a single button closing. His vest was a black floral brocade which had a deep V and three buttons. He wore a stark white long-sleeve shirt with black onyx cufflinks to close the sleeves. The buttons of his shirt were black faux onyx. His black bowtie was satin also. His black pants had a satin stripe down the outside of each leg.

"Mrs. Jameson, you are a gorgeous sight to see."

"Why, thank you, Mr. Cavendar." Devan smiled at him.

"Ugh, please don't call her that, it's an insult," Veronica winced and took a sip of her wine.

When Kale saw Devan talking with Veronica, he went back to the bar to grab another glass of wine. He presented both glasses to the girls. They both thanked him.

"Well, aren't you beautiful, cousin," Kale said as Veronica kissed him on the cheek.

"Thank you. I was just telling Devan how you are without a doubt the second hottest guy here."

Kale laughed and put his arm around Nate. "Yeah, I'll always be second best to this stud."

Antoinette appeared out of nowhere. "Kale, your grandpa wants to see you. He's sitting over there. Excuse me, I'm going to steal Devan for a moment."

Devan knew Antoinette would want to talk to her. She always did whenever she saw her. "Devan, my dear, you look lovely." Antoinette placed a hand on Devan's shoulder.

"As do you," Devan returned the compliment.

"Okay, enough of the horseshit. You know what I want to talk to you about…so what's the status?"

"I'm still not ready." Even though seventy-five percent of her wanted to scream that she was ready. Ready to take her life in her own hands and tell Justin to fuck off for good.

"It's okay. I'm not going to hound you *this* time." Devan was surprised and asked why. "Because my sweet girl, I can feel the tides turning, and I know that one day, in the near future, you are going to come to me." Antoinette was sure of herself. "You can call me anytime, day or night, you have my number, right?"

Devan nodded.

"Good, now go enjoy yourself, but first, go see Carl," Antoinette urged.

They walked over to where Carl and Kale were sitting at a table.

"There's my beautiful granddaughter." He had a hard time standing up.

Kale helped him. "What's wrong, Carl?" Devan asked with great concern.

"Oh, I'll be all right, I'm just a little sore."

Devan thought he was a bit pale, and she didn't like what she saw. He didn't look quite right.

Carl noticed the distress in her eyes. "I'm fine, just a little jet lagged. How about a dance with this old man, providing my wife lets me?" He grinned at Antoinette.

Antoinette shrugged. "As long as I can have a dance with my grandson." She gestured to Kale.

"Of course, madam." Kale put his hand out for her to take. She took it and led him to the dance floor.

"Come on, missy, I'm not getting any younger." Carl grabbed Devan's hand.

When the dance was over, they switched partners. "May I have this dance Miss Montgomery?" Kale asked with an open hand.

Devan placed her hand in his. "It's Mrs. Jameson," Justin corrected him as he and Jeane passed them.

"Nah, she'll always be Miss Montgomery to me," he responded as he gazed in to her blue eyes.

"You can have her for now, but song after next we switch partners," Justin said and twirled Jeane over to the bar.

Devan rolled her eyes. Kale chuckled, "What? You don't want to dance with your own husband?"

"I don't want to stop dancing with you," was the answer she gave him.

Kale was surprised, "Um…I don't want to stop dancing with you either." She smiled back.

When the song was over, they went to get some appetizers. Half way through eating, Jeane and Justin came up and told them they wanted to dance.

"Sure, just let me finish this," Devan told Justin before she took another bite.

"Come on, it's just one dance. You probably shouldn't eat that anyway." He gripped her arm and pulled her out of her seat. Kale was about to say something, but Devan shook her head *no* at him.

"Let's go Kale," Jeane demanded.

He gave her a cold stare. "I will when I'm done eating."

Even Jeane knew not to mess with Kale and his food. She sat down and patiently waited for him to finish.

Meanwhile Justin was being an ass as usual. "I should be your hero."

"Oh?"

"I just saved you from extra calories that you shouldn't have."

"Excuse me?"

"I see you are toning up a little bit. I never thought you'd actually start running with Kale. Hell, I didn't even know you knew how to exercise." Justin laughed at his own joke.

Devan didn't find it funny. "I have been working my ass off," she told him.

"Okay, okay there is no reason to be a bitch. I'm just saying you might wanna work a little harder. What do you have about thirty more pounds to lose?"

"Eight! I have eight more pounds to lose, *asshole*." She smacked his arm and attempted to slip away from him, but he grabbed her arm tight and pulled her back.

"What the fuck, Devan. You should want to dance with your husband." Justin was angry, and Devan couldn't tell if he was drunk already or not.

Kale saw him grab her arm. He could tell Justin was arguing with Devan. "What the hell is he doing now?" Kale said out loud.

"Probably putting her in her place, like he should have done years ago," Jeane retorted.

"If anyone needs put in their place it's that prick." He set his drink down and got up from the table.

"Kale, stay out of it," Jeane shouted after him. Kale walked right up to them on the dance floor, took Devan's hand and pushed Justin out of the way. He didn't say anything. Justin fell back, and his mask came off. He stood up and dusted himself off. He was mad but didn't dare chase after them. Jeane was there to console him. Kale pulled Devan in close and then swung her around. They danced unlike they had ever danced before. The ballroom was dark enough to create a romantic glow. Everyone just watched the two of them. Some people had smiles where others such as Justin and Jeane were confused.

Kale and Devan didn't stop. Kale pulled her in a tight embrace when the song changed to an even slower one. He lifted her chin up to make her look in to his eyes. He didn't care who was watching. He didn't care what the consequences would be, and Devan didn't seem to mind.

Kale smelled so good. Devan was high on his cologne alone. His muscles moved under her fingers every time they took a step. His strong arms encased her. Even if she wanted to get away, she wouldn't be able to.

Antoinette and Veronica were standing by the dance floor discussing Veronica's coming Winter Break. Veronica was asking Antoinette if it would be all right if Nate and she visited during break.

"Of course, you may come. Carl and I would love to have you..." All of a sudden Antoinette's attention was drawn elsewhere. "Is that..." She began to ask Veronica, who was staring at Devan and Kale, who were holding on to one another very closely. They were gazing in to each other's eyes, completely oblivious to anything that was going on around them.

Veronica was shocked at Devan. She would never be that obvious in public, yet here she was showing the world that he was hers and she was his. "Yup," Veronica answered. Nate came up behind Veronica and Antoinette, and his mouth dropped open when he saw what they were looking at.

"Did Justin and Jeane leave?" He asked aware of Devan's and Kale's closeness.

"Nope." Veronica said.

"Oh my," Nate said and put his arms around his wife.

"Yup," she put her hands over his and started swaying to the music.

"Good, maybe she'll be calling me sooner than I thought." Antoinette smirked.

"Wait, why will Devan be calling you?" Veronica questioned her grandmother.

"Don't worry about it, dear. Nathaniel, would you mind dancing with this old witch?"

"Mrs. Von—"

"What did I tell you, boy?" she snarled at Nate.

"I'm sorry, Antoinette. I would be honored to dance with my wife's grandmother who is not a witch," he stated and released his hold on his wife and walked Antoinette out on the dance floor.

"That's what you think," Veronica said under her breath. No sooner had they left when Justin and Jeane came up and sat next to Veronica, who instantly regretted staying in her seat.

"Whatcha drinking?" Justin asked her.

"Moscato," she said.

Justin went to get the three of them a drink. While he was gone Jeane pointed at Devan and Kale.

"Whas' that all about anyway?" she slurred.

Veronica bit her lips and turned her head away from Jeane, so she wouldn't say anything stupid, like the *truth*.

"Seriously, I don't get it. Wha' does he see in her? She's so plain Jane."

Veronica whipped her head around to look at Jeane who continued.

"She's just blah. Okay, she's kinda cute tonight, I'd say she's a six at the most. Wait, why are you over here? Where is your husban'? You know, he's creepy but in a sexy kinda way. I'd do 'im." Veronica opened her mouth to say something just as Justin handed her the Moscato, so she thanked him.

"Thank ya. Look at 'em. I just, ugh, sorry. I just don't understan' what you ever saw in her. Why *did* you marry her?" Jeane asked and then downed her entire drink.

"She used to be cute, and I didn't really know you yet. You weren't available anyway." Justin spoke in a slow drunken manner.

"Wow!" Veronica managed to spit out. "You guys are seriously fucked up."

Justin and Jeane laughed until tears came out of their eyes. Veronica wasn't amused at all.

"No shit. You're a bright one, aren't ya little witchy girl?" Jeane snickered.

"No, I mean you are fucked up people not just fucked up from drinking." She got up out of her seat. "Excuse me."

"Be careful, Jeane, she might put a spell on ya." Justin threw out.

"He's right. I'd be careful if I were you," Veronica warned.

"Where you goin'? Tell your yummy hubby to get over here and ask me for a dance." Jeane tugged on Veronica's arm.

"Hey…" Justin whined, insulted that Jeane even entertained the idea of dancing with someone else.

"I most certainly will not," Veronica snapped removing Jeane's hand from her arm.

Jeane got up, "Fine I will go get him myself."

"You do and that will be the last thing you do tonight," Veronica threatened.

"Wha' are you even sayin'?" Jeane asked.

"Consider it a warning. If you touch my husband, you will regret it." She pointed her finger at Jeane's chest.

"You don' scare me," Jeane said while swaying.

Veronica put her finger on Jeane's chest just above her breasts. "Down." She pursed her lips, blew air at her and pushed her. Jeane fell back and landed on her ass right in the chair she had been sitting in.

"How'd she do that?" Jeane asked Justin.

He shrugged his shoulders and stated, "Well, I guess she really is a witch."

"An' a bitch," Jeane said trying sit up properly.

"Hey, ya wanna get outta here?" Justin asked getting out of his chair.

"Yeah, let's go—shit's borin' anyway." Jeane got up and walked in front of him.

"Good, 'cause I wanna see what you got on un'er that dress," Justin said while smacking her ass.

Carl had been watching the whole thing. He got out of his chair and met them at the door.

"Come on, old man, I don' wanna have to deal with your shit t'night," Justin said trying to move past him.

"I just came over to tell you I'd like to pay for a cab for you. It's clear you both have had a lot to drink tonight, and I want you to be safe. So, if you will kindly give me your keys, I will pay for wherever you want to go."

Jeane thought for a minute and surprisingly thanked him.

"Tha's really nice, Carl, thank ya, but Kale has my keys." She turned to Justin, "Give 'im your keys."

Justin mumbled something then dug into his pockets, pulled out his keys and handed them over to Carl. "Wha' if I'm not ready to go home?"

"That's fine, you can go anywhere you want in the city. I'll pay for your trip there. Wait…" He put Justin's keys in his pocket then pulled a wallet out of his back pocket.

"Here," Carl opened his wallet and pulled out a few twenty-dollar bills and handed them to Justin. "Why don't you grab something to eat while you are out, on me." He smiled and placed his hand on Jeane's shoulder. Carl called the cab and waited with Jeane and Justin until it got there. As Justin got in the car, he thanked Carl. Jeane hugged Carl and said, "Thank ya, Gran'pa."

"It's still Carl," he told her as she got in the car. When they left, Carl shivered and wiped his shoulders down where Jeane's hands had been.

"I saw that."

He turned around to see his wife standing there with her hands on her hips.

"You would wipe that hug off too."

"I'm not talking about that…"

"I didn't want them hurting anyone else," he defended himself.

"I get that, but why did you give them money?"

"I figured it would give Kale and Devan a longer break from having to deal with them tonight."

"You have such a good heart." She kissed him on the cheek as they went inside.

After about another hour or so, almost everyone had left, and people were starting to clean up. Kale and Devan were the only ones that were left on the dance floor, which had been empty except for them for the past half hour.

"It's time to wrap up. You want to go get your friends?" Antoinette asked Veronica. Carl touched Antoinette's hand.

"No, don't, Veronica. Toni, give them ten more minutes." Antoinette nodded and put her hand on Carl's. Veronica, Antoinette and Carl watched Devan and Kale dance.

"I don't think her eyes ever left Kale's," Antoinette commented.

"Well, I know his never left Devan's," Veronica said.

"They never do. If she is in the room no one else is. Been that way since they were kids. When are they finally…" Carl didn't even get to ask the entire question.

"Soon!" Veronica and Antoinette said at the same time and looked at one another and grinned.

"I hope to Hell you two are right. This shit has been torturing me for years. And when I say years, I mean *years*."

"Don't worry, love, it will happen."

"I know that, I just better be alive to see it."

"You will be!" Antoinette and Veronica said at the same time again.

The music finally ended. Kale and Devan stopped dancing and looked around to see that most of the decorations had been taken down and the only people left were staring right at them with huge smiles on their faces.

"Um…so I guess our time is done," Devan laughed and dropped her hand from his hand.

"Our time will never be done," he pulled her close to him. He hugged her tight.

Devan didn't know what to say. She felt ashamed that she had let what Justin said affect her self-esteem. "Thank you for rescuing me tonight."

"I hate seeing him treat you like that," Kale replied. "But," he gently put his hands on her cheeks and forced her to look him in the eyes, as he stared intently in to hers, "you know you have a safe place with me. No matter what, our time will never be done. I will never give up on you or on *us*. Our time will come. I can feel it." He sounded so sure.

Devan smiled at him. Deep down, she secretly couldn't wait for their time to come.

Chapter 23

December 2015

A few weeks later Kale received a call from Veronica who was visiting Carl and Antoinette. She had told him that Carl was in the hospital and very sick.

"I think you should come," The concern in Veronica's voice was enough to get him to start packing. "Antoinette is on the phone with your parents now," Veronica continued. "I'm sure Devan will take the kids."

"No, she's coming with me," Kale announced. "If need be, they will *all* come. I will call her. Thank you for letting me know," he told Veronica. He hung up, and immediately dialed Devan's number.

"It's fine Kale, I can come get the kids now. Get online and find a flight." Devan instructed.

"No, I need you to come with me," Kale pleaded. "Just pack for you and the kids."

Devan considered what he said, then hinted, "I have a better idea. I'll call you back!"

A few minutes later, Kale's phone rang while he was frantically grabbing clothes and shoving them into a suitcase. Devan said her parents would be over shortly to pick up all the kids in their van so there was room for everyone.

The flight was long as usual, but to Kale it seemed to take much longer than the normal seventeen hours. He tried to sleep yet only got a few winks here and there. When they landed in Hawaii, Veronica picked them up and took them back to the house. It was too late to go to the hospital as visiting hours were over.

In the morning Kale got up early and left the house before anyone was awake.

When he arrived at the hospital, he swung by the information desk to ask which room his grandpa was in. The friendly volunteer gave him directions and he all but ran to the room. Kale was stopped short at the entrance, overwhelmed by all the tubes, IV pumps, and medications going into his grandpa's body.

Someone walked up behind him, "Can I help you?"

Kale spun around to see a woman standing there in bright white scrubs, her dark hair up in a twist, a light blue stethoscope hanging from her neck, hugging a chart to her chest. She was petite, standing slightly over five feet tall, had a sweet face, brown eyes and a calming demeaner.

"Yes," Kale answered her. "This man is my grandpa."

The woman smiled, "My name is Luana. I've been his nurse the past few days. I just got here for the day and I'm going to check his vitals."

Kale smiled back at her, "Thank you for taking care of him. Is there anything you can tell me?"

She led him into Carl's room and proceeded to tell Kale that Carl had pneumonia. His blood pressure was low, so he was on a medication for that. He was also on antibiotics for the infection, a machine to help him breathe, Tylenol for his fever, and IV fluids.

"He is unconscious right now, however, he can still hear you. Feel free to stay as long as you'd like," Luana said. "If you have any questions, just let me know."

His parents came in to visit shortly after Kale had arrived. He explained everything that the nurse had told him. After a few hours Veronica, Nate and Devan showed up with lunch.

When Devan excused herself to use the restroom, she thought she overheard Antoinette arguing with someone down the hall. When she got closer, she was sure it was *her*.

"You don't want to mess with me, girl," Antoinette warned.

"You don't know who you are talking to!" It *was* Jeane. *Why is she here? She and Justin are supposed to be in Texas.*

"Yes, I do. You're a spoiled little bitch," Antoinette hissed back at her. "I know all about you and your family. I have a long history with the Cadences."

Devan walked over and inquired if they needed anything in hopes to break up the argument.

"Thanks, but I have a lunch meeting with Justin, my uncle and a potential new client," Jeane declared.

"Oh, Justin is here?" *Of course, Justin is here.* He was Jeane's puppet. If Devan had a normal marriage, she would have known that her husband was in Hawaii. He had only told her they were going to Texas.

Jeane glared at Devan as though she was an idiot. "You know we work together, right?"

"Yes, Jeane, I am aware. I just didn't expect to see you in Hawaii when I was told you were going to be in Texas," she sassed.

"We were—oh—I don't have time to explain things to *you*! Give Carl my love." And with that she stalked off nose in the air.

"Give Carl her love! Like she has any love to give to anyone other than herself," Antoinette sneered. "Even if she did, Carl sure as hell wouldn't want it."

"What were you guys arguing about?" Devan asked.

"Nothing to worry you, my dear. It's so nice to see you although I wish it was under other circumstances." She put her arm around Devan and gave her a squeeze.

"I thought he didn't look well at the masquerade," Devan frowned.

"Yes, I think it started right before then," Antoinette said. "He probably caught something on the plane ride there, and it turned in to pneumonia." Antoinette stopped and looked at Devan with glistening eyes. "I am really scared that he won't come back to me."

"He will," Devan hugged her and exclaimed, "he has to!"

"Okay, enough of the emotions for right now." Antoinette wiped her eyes just under her eyelashes so she wouldn't get mascara all over. The two of them strolled down the hall back to Carl's room to join the others. Devan, Nate and Veronica were the first to leave after another hour or so. Kale would have stayed the night if Antoinette hadn't insisted that he go home to get some sleep. After a few more hours and arguments, he finally gave in and left.

Kale went up to the hospital again early the next day. He heard Carl's door open and saw Jeane walk through in all her glory.

"Why are you here?" Kale was annoyed with her presence.

"We were in a meeting next door, and I wanted to catch up with you before we headed back to the hotel. Have you decided how long you are staying?" she asked.

"As long as I need to," he replied curtly.

"You don't have to have such an attitude, Kale," Jeane grumbled, equally annoyed.

"Why are you *really* here?" He was blunt.

Jeane grabbed a seat and sat down. "We need you to smooth some things over with Mr. Carter. He's refusing to speak to anyone but you."

"Why, what happened?"

"There was a design flaw that we fixed and he's not happy about it."

"There was no flaw. I made that design myself." Kale's discontent was giving way to suspicion.

"We had to cut a few costs and—" Jeane trailed off.

Kale put his head in his hands, looked down at the floor and sighed, "You couldn't give him exactly what he wanted because it was more expensive than you had planned. So, in order to still get your full cut, you had to make a few adjustments."

"Well—" Jeane attempted to tell him her story, but Kale didn't give her a chance to defend herself. He interrupted her instead.

"So, you come in here, invade my space and time with my grandfather to fix your fuck up."

"It's part of your job," Jeane argued. "Besides I wanted to talk to you about Carl as well."

"What about him?" A knot formed in his stomach.

"You need to convince Antoinette to sell us his land," she stated.

"Excuse me?" He could not believe his ears.

"I had promised that land to my uncle years ago," Jeane responded as though this explained everything.

"How can you promise something that is not yours?" Kale was pissed.

"Well it would be had he not married that bitch. You'd be getting all his stuff including his land when he dies," she surmised. "And he doesn't look like he's doing very well at the moment."

"Jesus, Jeane, he can hear you. I can't believe you are talking about that right now." Kale was frightened that he could lose Carl, and Jeane wasn't making this any easier. She was acting as if the death certificate had been printed and signed.

"He's unconscious, and he can't hear anything," Jeane defended in a hurry. "I really wanted that land. Then all we would have to do is get rid of his neighbor on the left and we would be able to build."

"What in the hell are you talking about? First of all, his nurse told me he still can hear us. Secondly, that land IS NOT YOURS!" Kale was furious. He was staring at his grandpa, willing him to wake up. The longer the conversation went on, the more the knot in his stomach tightened.

"It doesn't matter anyway. That bitch is going to take everything and leave you nothing." Jeane was clearly enraged.

"Oh my god, Jeane, I don't care about that!" Kale nearly shouted at her. "I just want my grandpa around, and I want him healthy and happy. And Antoinette makes him happy. You really should be more respectful," he added as he lowered his voice. He didn't want the nurses or the doctors to make him leave for being disruptive.

"Fuck off, Kale. You are so stupid." She knew she wasn't going to get her way, so she got up and abruptly left. The second Jeane left the room, he called Kevin Carter and left a message in hopes that he could make right the wrongs that Jeane and her Uncle created.

That evening Carl woke up. Kale drove up there as soon as he could. He knocked on the door and was greeted by Luana, who had a smile on her face.

"I've just checked him, and he passed my inspection," she winked at Kale. "If you need anything, just hit the call light." She walked in to the hallway. "He will be very happy to see you."

"Not as happy as I will be to see him," Kale replied as he let her pass. He stepped in the room and shut the door behind him. When he turned around, he saw his grandpa, sitting up in the bed, looking a little pale and tired, but otherwise, he appeared to be better.

"Come here boy," Carl motioned for Kale to come to his bedside. Kale obeyed. "Pull up a chair," he instructed. Kale did as he was asked. "Kale, I love you," Carl began. Kale saw the dark circles under his eyes however, he was ecstatic. The ventilator had been removed, his voice was gravelly, and he was still getting oxygen via a nasal cannula in his nose, but he was awake and talking. "You are my favorite grandson."

Kale chuckled, "I am your only grandson."

"While that is true, I want you to know how much you mean to me," Carl smiled.

"I know, Grandpa," Kale replied. "You mean the world to me too."

"Now that we got that crap out of the way," Carl continued, "I don't have much longer."

"Don't say that!"

Carl cut Kale off, "Christ, son, I'm ancient. I was born in the Jurassic period and I'm in the hospital! We both know this is it for me." He closed his eyes as if to prove his point.

"Grandpa!" Kale was shocked. It sounded like his grandpa was giving up.

"I want you to make me a promise." Carl opened his eyes and lifted his head off the pillow.

"Okay."

"It's a bit unconventional," Carl stated.

"Oh Lord," Kale muttered.

"Just hear me out," Carl closed his eyes. Kale furrowed his eyebrows. It worried him how much it tired his grandfather just to have a simple conversation. "I want you to promise me you will not stop pursuing that girl until she has your last name."

He shouldn't have been surprised that Carl wanted to talk about Kale's relationship with Devan.

Kale murmured, "Pursuing her is not the problem."

"I know, I know," Carl stated his eyes still closed, "but I don't want you to give up, no matter how hard it gets—never let her go." Carl paused to catch his breath.

"A tiny bird told me that you brought her with you. I want you to bring her to see me tomorrow, please."

"I will grandpa," Kale promised.

"Now go back home and get some sleep. My wife is coming back soon and I'm hoping to get a little frisky with her," Carl smirked.

"Oh my god, grandpa…"

"Go on son, I can hear her clicking heels now," Carl urged.

He got up, bent over, kissed his grandpa on the forehead and hugged him gently, "*Aloha wau iā óe.*"

"I love you too grandson."

Kale and Devan went to the hospital together the next day. Devan was extremely pleased to hear that Carl was awake and off the ventilator. Kale, however, didn't have the heart to tell her how quickly he tired from just talking.

When they entered the room, Carl wasn't hooked up to anything—no tubes, no oxygen. He was lying on the bed, head on the pillow, eyes closed. Kale approached him and spoke softly in case he was sleeping, "Grandpa?"

Carl's eyes fluttered open. "Kale…" he spoke in barely more than a whisper.

"I'm sorry, Carl," Devan apologized as she stood beside his bed, opposite of Kale. "Did we wake you?"

Carl appeared to gather all the strength he could, closed his eyes and replied, "I…have…very…little time."

Kale and Devan exchanged looks of uneasiness. "What do you mean, Grandpa?" Kale asked.

Carl forced his eyes open again and grabbed both of their hands before stating, "My dying wish is…that you two…get together once and for all." He took a deep breath, "Do it for me…if you won't do it…for yourselves." Carl begged in his weakest, most pitiful voice. He held on to their hands then slowly closed his eyes and gently released his grip and held his breath.

"Carl, get up," Antoinette demanded walking in to the room with a cup of coffee.

"Antoinette, I don't know how to tell you this—" Devan couldn't muster up the courage to say the words.

"Carl, get your ass up. That's not funny," Antoinette said sternly.

Carl sat straight up, startling Devan and Kale. "I thought it was funny," Carl spoke in his normal voice. Apparently, he was feeling *much* better.

Devan and Kale sighed with relief. Kale put his hand on his grandpa's shoulder. Carl glanced up at him with big grin on his face, "Now, Kale, there are two photo albums at the house that I'd like you to bring to me."

Kale was confused. "Here to the hospital?" he wondered.

"I want to find a certain picture, and I believe it's in one of those albums," Carl clarified. Kale agreed so Carl described where he believed the photo albums were located. Devan said she'd help Kale find the albums.

Antoinette watched the conversation between Carl and Kale with amusement. It wasn't until Devan had piped up that Antoinette was reminded of something. "By the way, Devan," she began. "Since it's so close to the holidays, I took the liberty of putting your parents and all the kids on a flight. I meant to mention it last night, but I fell asleep early." Devan just looked at her, unsure if Carl was *really* as well as he seemed. When she didn't answer right away, Antoinette went on. "I spoke to your mom after you did yesterday. I hope you are okay with their invitation. I know the kids are off school for winter break, and I know Carl would love to see *all* his great grandchildren. They will be moving him out of the intensive care unit today since he's doing so well now, and he will be able to have young visitors."

Devan exhaled a breath of relief. "That is very generous of you, Antoinette. Thank you." Antoinette nodded her head in acknowledgment. "When will they be here?" Devan asked.

"You will see them sometime tonight."

When Devan and Kale departed from the room Antoinette asked, "Carl, why do you really want those albums?"

"I don't," he shrugged his shoulders. "I just needed to plant a little seed."

"My dear I think you may be going mad. We should probably ask for the oxygen again—it seems not enough is getting to your brain."

"Sometimes being reminded of the past in *color* as it was, can be a real eye opener."

Antoinette had to ponder his words for a few seconds. "Oh, I see what you did there. Such a smart island man." She kissed his forehead.

At the house Kale and Devan were looking for Carl's albums.

"Oh my god, Kale," Devan exclaimed. He went over to where she was, knelt down next to her and took the picture out of her hand. They had been going through a few boxes searching for the photo albums Carl wanted.

"I have never seen this before," Kale said. "Must have been a *sneaky* picture," he chuckled. It was a picture of the two of them looking in to each other's eyes, smiling in the sunset. They were in their early twenties.

"Young and in love," Kale stated. The way he said it gave her butterflies. He leaned over towards her. "Some things change, and some things never change." He kissed her cheek and stood up. After a few seconds, he handed it back to Devan and said, "I want that picture, set it aside please." She obliged and continued to sift through the box. Kale had found another picture that had captured his attention and was curious as to how his grandfather had acquired it. It was a picture that Kale had shot of Devan at a local hidden beauty that wasn't on any tourist maps. It was the first time he had taken her there. He remembered it like it was yesterday.

It wasn't a long walk, but the path was rocky. Kale stopped near a large moss-covered boulder, pulled off his shirt and handed her a pair of water shoes. "Get undressed. We're going in."

"In where?" Devan didn't see anything but rocks, and the ocean was quite a ways off in the distance.

"Come on," he said, and walked away.

"I don't see anything," she almost whined.

"You will."

The two of them rounded a corner and the view that came into sight was the most beautiful scenery.

"Here's Ol' Blue. Well, that's what I call it. Its real name is Nani Mau Loa. In English that means forever beautiful," he said.

"I can see why."

"The water here is cooler than the ocean, but it's not cold. Most tourists don't know about this little gem," he said proudly.

They slipped into the water. It was a little chilly for their liking, but they didn't care. The water was crystal clear, and they could see little fish swimming around them. "This is so awesome!"

"You wanna see something even better?" He took her by the hand and led her into what appeared to be a small cave. It was dark, but a blue light could be seen in the distance.

When they reached the light, it was coming from a small opening in the roof of the cave. The sun beamed down onto the blue water and created a gorgeous glow. The blue glow touched everything — even Devan, who was smiling at him.

"See why I call it Ol' Blue?" he asked her.

At that moment her smile was all he could see. "She's so beautiful," he thought. Her blue eyes sparkled up at him. The feelings that were overwhelming him were making him nervous. He felt her moving closer to him. He looked down at her lips and she looked up at his. His hand emerged from the water and barely touched her cheek as he moved a strand of her hair away from her face. Her lips were begging to be kissed—and he was aching to kiss them.

"Sorry, that's been bothering me," he said, as their eyes met and time stood still. Kale was so anxious, but the setting was perfect. It couldn't be more perfect. It would have been the most romantic first kiss ever, but he was too nervous!

"Next!" he shouted and took her by the hand again and led them to the next adventure.

Kale's attention was stolen away from his quaint memory when his phone rang. He looked down to see who it was. "Excuse me, Monty. I have to take this business call." He slid his finger across the screen, placed the phone to his ear and said, "Hello Mr. Carter, thank you for calling me back," as he stepped out of the room.

Devan continued searching and finally found an album towards the bottom of the box, she opened it and began thumbing through the pages. She stopped when a picture of Kale caught her eye. All Devan could do was stare, trying to take in what she was seeing. There was Kale down on one knee smiling from ear to ear. He had a tiny box in his hand. It was open and Devan could see a ring within. She pulled the picture out and read the back—'*Kale Kai practicing his proposal to Devan.*'

Devan contemplated, sneaking a glance at Kale, who was still on the phone in the other room. She hesitated only a second longer, then stuck it in her back pocket. There were many pictures in this book of her and Kale. Was this meant to be for them? Maybe a wedding gift? As Kale walked back in to the room she asked, "Everything okay?"

"Yup, come on Monty," he told her, lifting a second photo album out of the box. "We found them. Let's go."

When they got to the hospital with albums in hand, they asked for Carl's new room number. When Kale and Devan entered his new room, Carl requested that Kale go get him a drink, a snack and a magazine for his entertainment. "And I don't mean just any old magazine, I want the one with the hidden bunny on the front," Carl told his grandson. "Grandpa!" Kale bellowed

"Don't 'Grandpa' me, Kale Kai, you used to love searching for that bunny." Kale was embarrassed. He knew Devan would be curious, and he'd have to go into detail on exactly what the 'bunny' was.

"Hidden bunny?"

"That Mr. Hefner is a brilliant man." Carl grinned.

Devan giggled, she understood what they were talking about now.

"I'll bring you back something all right!"

"Grab something salty and sweet too, please. I know I have my sweetness right here," he winked at Devan making her blush, "but I have an immense sweet tooth today."

"Okay."

The truth was Carl wanted to talk to Devan alone. "I know Antoinette has spoken to you," he said as soon as Kale was out of ear shot.

Devan sighed loudly, "Yes, she has on more than one occasion."

"It's not just coming from her, girly." Carl reached for her hand. "You guys are meant to be together, Devan. You know that, I know that, we *all* know that. You deserve happiness whether you believe it or not. I know things have been rough for you and timing is an issue, but life is meant for living. You can't keep letting it pass you by."

Devan just stared in to Carl's deep brown eyes. She knew what he was saying was true.

"Don't you love him anymore?"

She was taken aback by his question and admitted, "You know I do. I can't believe you would even ask that."

"I need to hear you say it!"

"I love him, Carl," she confided.

"GRANDPA!" he corrected her.

"Sorry, Grandpa—I love Kale. I always have, and I always will."

Kale, who was approaching the room, his arm full of Carl's goodies, was in the hallway and heard Devan say that she loved him.

She said it out loud in the open! Kale couldn't believe his ears.

Devan slipped her hand out of Carl's when she heard Kale enter the room right after she confessed that she loved him. He decided not to mention anything he overheard on his way back.

"Ah what did you get me son?"

"Well, I've got some snacks here, but it was the craziest thing, when I went in to the gift shop, they said they had just sold the last *Playboy*."

"Damn the luck," Carl chuckled.

Three hours later, Devan and Kale were driving back to the house, both silent. Both were stuck in their own memories of their shared time together eons ago. When they pulled in to the driveway, there was an unfamiliar car parked next to Carl's.

"Who could that be?" Devan wondered.

As they opened the front door and entered the living room, they saw Devan's parents and both her and Kale's kids sitting with Veronica and Nate. After many greetings, stories from the kids and some catching up between the adults, Devan announced it was bedtime for the kids who were each yawning, one after the other. Kale was exhausted and headed to bed himself. She took her time tucking each child in. Finally, she closed the door to Cyrus' and Kai's room and went to her room. She turned her light off and slipped into bed hoping to have sweet dreams.

Chapter 24

Kale was restless, covers were off more than they were on. He was hot, he was cold, then hot again. It was the same pattern of his and Devan's relationship over the years. The memories of their past were flooding his mind. Seeing those pictures earlier was almost a glimpse of what his future should be. The more Kale replayed what he overheard Devan say to his grandpa, the more he wanted to hear her say it to him. He turned on the light on the bedside table and sat up. He was wide awake and knew he wouldn't be able to go back to sleep. Kale got up to get a drink of water and saw Devan in the hallway leaving the bathroom. *What are the chances?* With no warning whatsoever, he gripped her arm and pulled her into his room.

"I heard you this morning," he spoke quietly.

"Kale…" Devan attempted to speak. However, Kale was too impatient to let her utter more than one word. He wanted an answer, and he wanted it now.

"Tell me," he insisted as he moved closer to her, slowly inching his way forward.

"Tell me what you told my grandfather."

Devan looked away, but Kale kept moving in. He was only inches away from her. He grasped her chin.

"Say it!" Kale demanded. She gulped and stared in to his eyes.

Devan didn't have to say it. It was written all over her face. Kale could see *it* every time he gazed in to her eyes. "I love you," Devan said quietly. "I've always loved you."

"And you always will." He grabbed the back of her head and kissed her deeply.

"I want to show you something," Kale took a small box out of his pocket. He opened it up and it was empty. "Your ring will be in here again, and you will wear it one day," Kale told her.

"Jeane is not going to give you back that ring," Devan stated.

"She didn't get your ring. I still have it tucked away in a safe spot. Hell, I didn't even buy her that one. She bought it for herself way before she ever met me." He closed his eyes and tried to contain his composure. He was getting too worked up in the wrong way thinking about Jeane. He wanted to keep the sentiment flowing. "I don't want to talk about her. I don't want to talk at all."

He shoved the box out of her hand making it fall to the floor. He pushed her up against the wall. Kale leaned back and looked her up and down. Salivating, he wanted every piece of her. Kale kissed her again, deeper making her melt. Devan wrapped her arms around his neck. He instinctively picked her up and she encased his waist with her legs. Abruptly, he stopped kissing her lips and went for her neck. Kale knew she couldn't hold back her inhibitions when he did that. She moaned. "Oh god Kale, do me. Right here, right, now."

He discontinued what he was doing and lifted his head with a distorted face. *Devan would not say 'Do me.'*

Someone slapped his arm. "Wake up, I need you to do me up." Kale opened his eyes and rubbed them to get a better look at who was speaking. It was Jeane.

Oh Christ! "What are you doing here?"

"I heard my children were here, and I wanted to visit with them," she claimed as she turned her back toward Kale.

Bullshit! He knew better.

"And I had the kids pack this dress. I needed it for today's meeting."

And there it is.

"Now zip up the rest of the dress," Jeane commanded.

"Some manners you have!" Kale retorted.

She backed up closer to him. "Please," she added. He sat up and did as she directed. "Did you ever call Mr. Carter?"

"Don't worry I smoothed everything over," *As usual.*

She twirled around and smirked at him. "Good." She walked out the door, but before shutting it she said in a snarky tone, "She must have been good in your dream…whoever she was."

"What?" Kale was confused.

"Look down dumbass," she shut the door, leaving it cracked open.

He glanced down to see the tent in his shorts. "Shit!" He was embarrassed and remembered his dream. "Hey, it's called morning wood!" he shouted back.

The door flew open and Kai came running in. "I want some."

"You want some of what?"

"Morning wood," Kai exclaimed. "Where is it?"

Kale grabbed a pillow and placed it over the area. "One day you will buddy, when you're older."

"But I want it now!"

"It's not what you think…um let me get dressed, and we will make breakfast okay?"

"Okay, but I still want some," Kai pouted.

After breakfast Kale's and Devan's parents left to visit Carl at the hospital, so Kale, Devan, Nate, and Veronica decided to take the kids to the beach.

Nate and Veronica went for a stroll and the kids all followed them. Devan sat down in the warm dry sand and stretched out her legs. Kale joined her.

"I'm glad Carl is doing well."

"Yes, me too. He had me scared there for a minute."

Devan nodded her head. She knew the emotions were strong. Kale and Carl had always had a special bond. Then again so did she and Carl. He was the type of man that you were thankful to meet. His hugs were warm, his heartfelt talks were meaningful and if he didn't make you laugh there was something seriously wrong with you. He was a grandpa to her, and she had always felt that way. A tear slipped out of the corner of her eye and worked its way down her face. Kale glanced at her and saw it.

He put his arm around her shoulders. "He's going to be okay, Monty." He wiped the tear away with his thumb.

"I know, I just was…" She was cut off by Kai running and yelling.

"Daddy, is this morning wood?" Kai was so excited he tripped over a rock and face planted in the sand. Devan and Kale both jumped up to help him.

He got up and dusted himself off, picked up the piece of drift wood that he dropped and ran to Kale. "I think I really found it, Dad! I found morning wood!"

Devan glanced at Kale who was turning a slight shade of red.

Jeane could be heard cackling in the distance. Devan looked in the direction she heard it and saw Jeane and Justin walking on the other side of the beach headed their way. *I thought they were at a meeting.*

"Mom, Mom, I found morning wood!" Kai told Jeane when he saw her.

When they reached Kale, Devan and Kai, Kai showed her the driftwood, extremely proud.

"What did you find again? Say it loud and clear," Justin snickered.

"I found MORNING WOOD!!" Kai screamed, attracting the attention from other beach goers. A rather large elderly woman who was lying on a beach towel taking in some rays, sprung up and had a disgusted scowl on her face. She glared in Kale's direction as if he was being a terrible father. He put his hands in the air, "He's a kid." The woman planted herself back down as she grumbled.

"Great job little man. Now go find some more," Jeane told him.

Justin put his hand on Kale's shoulder, "Teaching them young, huh?"

Kale looked down at Justin's hand, and Justin quickly removed it after seeing Kale's not so friendly face.

"Did Kale tell you about the hot, sexy dream he had last night?" Jeane asked Devan.

"You know, Jeane, morning erections are not always caused by sex dreams." Justin tried defending Kale for fear that Kale would go off on him.

"Oh no, I heard him moaning and everything." Jeane sneered.

Kale rolled his eyes. "I thought you guys had a meeting this morning," Devan remarked.

"Yes, we did. It's over with, so we figured we would take a break before going back for another meeting," Jeane stated then glimpsed down at her watch. "Oh, I didn't realize what time it was. We best be going back." She went to leave, then turned back around. "Have fun guys, and Kale?"

"What?"

"Tell Carl, I said, hi."

When they were out of sight Devan decided to ask Kale what that was all about.

He explained without going into specific detail of everything that happened prior to breakfast.

"No, not that…"

Oh my god I just told her all of that, and I didn't have to.

"The way she said *Carl*, it feels like something is there."

Kale nodded and told her the conversation Jeane had had with him about Carl's property.

"So, that's what Antoinette and Jeane were arguing about the other day." She thought out loud.

"Come again?"

Shit! "The other day I overheard them talking. I didn't hear much other than Jeane questioned Antoinette if she knew who she was really talking to. Then Antoinette called her a spoiled bitch, and then something about she's had a long history with the Cadence family.

Kale shook his head in disbelief, "What a bitch. I can't believe she would talk to Antoinette about that while her husband…wait…yes, I can. What does the long history with the Cadences mean?"

"I don't know, but I think it's something we are going to have to talk about with Veronica." Devan said.

After lunch they cleaned up and went to the hospital and had a nice visit with Carl. Devan had a chance and pulled Veronica to the side and asked her what she knew about Antoinette and the Cadence family.

She shrugged her shoulders. "I have never heard her say that name before. She talks very little about people she has worked with, which I'm assuming that's what the word 'history' suggests."

"I just find it peculiar," Devan stated.

"I do too. Let me see if there is anything I can dig up." They walked back in the room to see Carl handing out gumballs to the kids. The children were quite happy with their treat.

On the way home from the hospital, Cyrus and Kai were fighting in the backseat.

"Cyrus, quit kicking Kai!" Devan sternly repeated for a third time.

"Mom," he whined, "Kai keeps threatening to put his gum in my hair!"

Devan looked back at Kai who smiled around a huge wad of gum. "Kai, if you do that, you will never chew another piece of gum for the rest of your life!" Kale threatened.

"Fine!" Kai yelled. "I'll spit it out when we get home."

After dinner, Devan agreed to let the kids play for thirty more minutes before it was time for bed. She checked the house searching for the boys after putting the girls to bed and found Cyrus and Kai sound asleep in Kale's bed. She picked up Cyrus and put him in his own bed, but Kale said he would just let Kai sleep there.

The next morning however, he regretted that choice. "Kai? Did you have gum in your mouth when you went to bed last night?" Kale questioned his son as he tried to lift his head off the pillow and failed for the fourth time.

"Um…" Kai stuttered.

"You said you were going to throw that out last night!"

"I'm sorry dad," Kai was practically in tears.

"Kai, my head is stuck to the pillow." Kale was struggling to move his head.

"Um…I'll go get Aunt Dee," He ran out the room as fast as he could. A moment later Devan stepped in the room wiping her eyes and yawning. "What's the emergency?" She moved closer to where Kale was.

"My hair is stuck to the pillow," Kale groaned.

Devan sat down and inspected. She tried pulling one piece and it didn't move.

"Okay." She was fully alert now. "There are a few things we can try." She tried ice and then peanut butter. It was almost as though his head was fused with the pillow. *How much gum did that kid have in his mouth last night?* Devan wondered.

"Kale, sweetie," Devan didn't want to say it, "um, I think we are going to have to cut your hair." She cringed at the thought but was trying to be gentle in her delivery.

"Do it!" Kale practically shouted.

"What?" Devan asked taken aback. Apparently, she loved his hair more than he did. "Do it!" he repeated. "I have a massive headache, and I have to take a piss. We have been working on this for two hours. Just cut it already!"

The only scissors she could find were in the kitchen. Devan cut his hair and when he got up, she just gawked at the pile of hair and almost cried.

"I'm gonna take a shower and get this peanut butter out," Kale practically ran to the bathroom.

"Would you see where Veronica is and have her come over to finish my hair please, unless you think you can do it?" he yelled from the bathroom.

"No way, you have her do it. She does a nice job on Nate's." Devan was still staring at the pile on the pillow, lost.

Veronica and Nate came back after sightseeing. Veronica gasped and put a hand over her mouth. Devan had said it was bad over the phone. Veronica, on the other hand, thought she severely underestimated how bad it really was.

"Shut up and just chop it," Kale instructed.

Veronica gave Devan a sympathetic look and went to work. After a few minutes, Devan had to leave the room. She could hardly stand to watch so she told them that she was going to pick up lunch.

When she got back, Veronica was sweeping up an even larger pile of hair on the floor than there was stuck to the pillow.

"He's still hot, Dee, just…um…different," Veronica told her.

"Where is he?" Devan asked her, trying to balance the bags in her hands.

"I told him he looked ridiculous with that creature on his face and short hair," she confessed. "So, he's in the bathroom trimming his beard."

"I hope you were nicer than that," Devan frowned.

"No, she wasn't," Nate laughed taking some of the bags out of Devan's hands.

"What's for lunch?" Kale wanted to know as he came walking out of the bathroom.

Devan dropped the remaining bags on the floor when she saw him.

"Is that my food you just let fall on the floor?" Kale was a bit irritated, not just at the food but how the overall morning had gone.

"Um—you shaved it all off," Devan blurted, no longer able to keep her shock to herself.

"Yeah, I didn't mean to it just ended up uneven. I figured it was easier to start over," he replied picking up the bags.

As they were eating, she couldn't help but stare. Kale kept glancing over at her too, feeling her eyes on him nonstop. Aggravation taking ahold, Kale finally couldn't take it anymore. "Jesus, Devan, ENOUGH!"

"I'm sorry I can't help it!" Devan said defensively. "You look exactly like you did when you were seventeen."

"God, it'll all grow back," Kale snapped.

"I didn't say it was a bad thing…" Devan began.

Veronica interrupted her, "It's not just her, Kale, I can't quit staring at you either," she admitted. "I'm not trying to be weird. I think you have always been a desirable guy, of course, but damn…dude, you are gorgeous. Why didn't you ever get into modeling?" Veronica marveled.

"I'm sorry, honey," she continued, addressing Nate now. "You know you are my number one and the most gorgeous man I have ever seen. "It's just… Kale is number two now."

Nate laughed, "I have to agree, Kale, you are probably the most attractive man that I have seen as well."

"You definitely don't look like Sasquatch anymore, Dad." Joey piped in.

Kale threw his hands up in the air, "That's it! I'm gluing it all back on." He got up from the table in a huff.

The rest of the day passed without anyone commenting about Kale's appearance. Devan had gone to bed early complaining about a headache. Kale, Veronica and Nate had stayed up a little later. Veronica had the great idea of going out and the guys agreed. Veronica quickly put herself together and threw on a midnight blue sundress that she had picked up the other day. She snuck into Devan's room and was startled to see a large figure hovering over Devan.

"Come on, Monty, wake up." Kale had beat her to Devan's room.

"What's going on?" Devan sat up in bed, rubbing the sleep from her eyes.

"We're going out, Dee," Veronica whispered. "Get up and get ready!"

A few minutes later, Devan still hadn't emerged, and Veronica was getting agitated. The men were waiting for them in the car. "What are you doing? Come on, you are taking too long. The kids are going to hear you."

"I'm looking for my stuff," Devan was still half asleep.

Veronica ran to her room and grabbed a few things then handed them to Devan. "Here, just put this on." She shoved the clothes into Devan's arms. Devan changed and met Veronica in the bathroom to fix her hair and apply make-up.

After she plugged the flat iron in, Veronica unplugged it.

"No time. Dee. Slap some mascara and let's go!"

Devan put on mascara and was about to flip the light off when she saw what she was wearing. She had not paid attention at all. Veronica had given her long black leather boots, a black halter top and a black short skirt. Ordinarily, Devan wouldn't wear these, and she even turned back to change her clothes, but Veronica pulled her out the door.

When they got to the club Nate and Kale went to the bar and ordered some drinks. While they were waiting, they heard someone talking behind them.

"You check out my *wahine* one more time, dude, I'm going to kick your ass!" Kale felt a tap on his shoulder, "Look at me while I'm talking to you, pretty boy."

"I think you may have me confused with someone else," Kale said still not moving. He figured it would be best to not engage. He assumed some drunk asshole picked out one of the biggest guys in the club to start something with for the hell of it.

A hand squeezed his arm infuriating Kale. He was here to have a good time not to be in the middle of a bar brawl. When he turned around, he saw a familiar large Samoan, round face smiling up at him.

"I knew it was you, Iakona!" Kuna chuckled and encased Kale in a bear hug.

"What would you have done if it wasn't me?" Kale asked.

"Run!"

"Smart choice. So where is this *wahine* you were talking about?" Kuna released Kale and stepped to the side to reveal a beautiful—Luana!

"No way," Luana giggled. "You are the great Kale Iakona I have heard about over the past six months. I can't believe I never put two and two together." Luana gave Kale a hug. "I feel as though I have known you for quite some time." She let go and peered up at him.

"Wait, you know him?" Kuna was stunned.

"I'm his grandpa's nurse."

"Mr. Kahalewai? Why didn't you tell me?" Kuna questioned her.

"Patient confidentiality, not to mention I had no idea you knew him," she said then glanced back at Kale, "You look much different than you did the other day."

Kale rubbed his jaw that only had a few stubbles on it. "Yeah I had a run in with gum and a razor."

"Oh, you so pretty, Iakona," Kuna snarked while he put his hand on Kale's cheek. "I don't think I've seen you like this since we were sixteen, man. Soft as a baby's ass yo!"

"Have you met my cousin?" Kale gestured towards Veronica who was walking over to them.

"Bro, when did you get a cousin?" Kuna inquired.

"My grandpa married her grandma," Kale explained, "And she married my friend here."

"Holy shit, man," Kuna exclaimed as he looked Nate up and down. "You *is* one tall mother…"

Kale interrupted his friend. "Six feet and seven inches. Dude has two inches on me." Kale bragged.

"Yeah, I see that. I'm gonna start calling you *Shorty* when I see you," Kuna laughed.

"You know I'm still a bit taller than you, right?" Kale reminded him.

"Yeah, yeah I know. So, who is the tall guy?" Kuna asked.

Nate extended his hand, "I'm Nate," Kuna ignored his hand and put his arms around him instead. "No formal handshakes here bro, I'm a hugger!" Nate hugged him back. "I'm good with that. This is my wife Veronica."

Kuna didn't hesitate and immediately embraced her. "I thought you were Devan for a second with that dark hair. You are both so pretty, you could pass for sisters."

"Not anymore," she said and pointed to Devan.

Kuna was surprised to see Devan with light hair. "*Wahine*! Gorgeous as always, get over here!" He picked her up and swung her around. When he set her down, Kale introduced Kuna to Veronica and Nate as Devan had met him when Kale was in college. "This is Kuna, he and I go way back to childhood. We played college football together and the last time I saw him was…"

"Your wedding to the wicked witch of Ohio!" Everyone cracked up. "Speaking of Satan where is she and her demon sidekick?"

"At the hotel, probably sharing a room," Veronica snarked.

Kuna raised an eye brow at her words then said, "They aren't here, and that's what matters!" He whispered in Veronica's ear, "You are a smart one, aren't you?"

She nodded and suggested they speak later.

For a few hours the six of them danced, laughed, joked, and enjoyed each other's company. When the music slowed down, they paired off in to couples. Instead of slow dancing like the others, Kale had plans of his own.

"Follow me," he took Devan's hand and led her off the patio onto the sand.

"Where are we going?" she asked trailing behind him.

He looked back and grinned at her, "Just follow me."

She was trying her hardest but walking in the sand in heels was not the easiest thing to do. She almost tripped. "Slow down Kale, I can't go fast in these damn Veronica boots." He stopped, let go of her hand and lifted her up in his arms then swung her over his shoulders. "What are you doing?" Kale didn't answer and kept going. Finally, they arrived just short of the water that was rolling onto the beach and he gently set her down yet didn't completely let go of her. He gazed down in to her eyes and smiled.

"What?" she asked.

"How is it after all of these years you are still the most beautiful woman I have ever seen when your face is lit up by the moonlight?"

Devan placed her hand on his smooth cheek. She couldn't run her fingers through his hair anymore like she could when it was longer, however she could run them through the top. She stood as far up on her tippy toes as she possibly could. He looked down in to her blue eyes and caved. The moment her lips touched his, it was magic. She could feel the entirety of his full lips for the first time in years. There was no scruff holding anything back. All the teasing had finally led up to this. She could easily lose herself in his kiss. It felt incredible after all this time to finally give in.

As much as he hated to do it, Kale pulled back. He didn't want Devan regretting anything. Not to mention Jeane and Justin could be lurking anywhere.

She looked up at him and smiled, it was almost as if she had read his mind.

"We should probably head back," Kale hinted.

She looked out at the moon reflecting on the water and sighed. It was the perfect back drop for romance novel. She got up on the tips of her toes and kissed Kale one last time.

The next morning Kale's parents took everyone out to breakfast. Nahoa had something important to tell them.

"Antoinette called me this morning and said that Carl will be coming home tomorrow. I think that we should all go back and start packing. He will need to get an adequate amount of rest to finish healing. Having all of us there would not be very relaxing." Everyone nodded in agreement.

"With Dad in the hospital and being here in general, Nahoa and I have decided that it is time to come back home to Hawaii." Cassandra said and then looked at Kale. "I'm sorry son, I know you just moved back to Ohio a few years ago. Seeing Grandpa like that, really scared me." Tears were forming in her eyes.

Kale got out of his seat and gave his mom a hug. "I know mom, scared me too."

"I just don't want you to be upset with us for leaving." She told him.

"Ma, I have known all along you'd go back to your roots. We can always visit. I understand completely."

"You know we will help you get ready," Chris told Nahoa. "How soon are you planning on moving?"

"As soon as the house sells. My sister and her husband have land for us that they would like us to build on. Antoinette said we could stay at the house until it is ready," Nahoa shared.

Kale knew exactly where they were talking about. His Uncle Russo and Aunt Noelani had told him that they would be sharing their land with his parents one day, and that he would eventually inherit all of it.

While he was sad that he would be far away from his parents again, he knew that he would never be alone like he was in Seattle. He had Devan and her family. Something inside him told him they would all be together again, Kale and Devan and their families.

Chapter 25

April 2016

On the way home from the store Devan hit a pothole and her tire blew. She called Justin, who of course, didn't answer his phone. She then called her dad who said as soon as he was out of his meeting, he'd be there to help her. She thought about calling Kale but decided it would be best to wait for her dad. Devan was parked on a dead end, side street. She sat in her car for about a half hour playing on her phone and then decided to get out and take a stroll through the field that was in front of her before her phone died. It was a good thing she had given her dad directions to her location. The field was covered in lush greens and recently bloomed dandelions. Devan ran through the sea of green and yellow like she was a little girl, each blade tickling her ankles.

She stopped and looked at her phone. She still had another forty-five minutes until her dad would be there. She decided to lie down and stare up at the vast infinite blue above her. It was a clear sky with the occasional fluffy cloud rolling through. She closed her eyes and the only thing she could see was Kale's gorgeous green eyes and his luminous smile. She sighed and imagined he was there with her. The sun was nice and warm against her face. She had no idea what had gotten into Kale since last August, but she loved it. Devan didn't want to admit the flirtatious behavior and constant attention had made her crave him like before, although truth be told, she never truly quit craving him. She had been able to contain most of her excitement, until now. All it took was a mention of his name and a smile would creep across her face. She took a few pictures and sent them to Veronica who called her.

"What are you doing?"

"I'm waiting on my dad to come get me, I have a flat," Devan told her.

"Where are you?" Veronica asked slightly concerned.

"In that field on Main and Mulberry."

"Well at least you aren't in a bad part. Are those dandelions?"

"I think so."

"Interesting. Listen, my class is coming in any minute, or I'd come get you myself. I definitely want to go to that field your picture is gorgeous."

"I bet you could create a beautiful painting of this." Devan told Veronica.

"That gives me an idea, if you are going to be there for a while, take advantage of it. Nature can be a wonderful tool for our brain."

"What do you mean?"

"Write, write anything. I gotta go, Dee."

She went back to the car and took out her notebook that had her grocery list on it.

She grabbed the pen, jogged back to the field and sat down. She viewed her surroundings. There were dandelions everywhere. In a month or so the yellow would turn to white puffs. Devan could almost see someone running through them. A girl, no, a young woman wearing white. All the seeds she'd run by would fly up in the air around her. Devan jotted down what she had seen in her head. Then above it wrote "Field of Wishes". She continued to write more until Kale entered her mind again. She flipped the page and started something new.

> *My Dearest Kale,*
>
> *Not a day goes by where I don't think of you. Hell—not even an hour goes by. I remember the moment I fell in love with you like it was yesterday. The way your green eyes looked into mine, I felt like you were star-*

ing into my soul. I remember after that day the whole world changed for me. The sun shone brighter, the sky was bluer— Life would never be the same.

She took a deep breath and smiled. Life *never* had been the same. She couldn't imagine life any other way. All the ups and downs, some how Kale was always involved. She continued…

I love the way your soft hair tangles around my fingers and how you tower over me with such great height. I love your strong arms around me. There is no place I'd rather be than in your embrace. Your lips are perfect. Just thinking about the way you kiss me gets me excited. It drives me crazy when we almost kiss. Just do it already! I want to kiss you in the rain, I want to wake up to your gorgeous face— every day for the rest of my life.

"What are you doing out here?" A familiar voice startled her.

She lifted her head up to see Kale coming toward her. She closed her eyes expecting to see him gone a second later. She opened her eyes and he was still there. "What are *you* doing here?" She answered his question with another question.

"I came to change your tire," he stated.

"I didn't call you…" She was cut off.

"No, your dad did. Oh, he says sorry, he tried calling to tell you his meeting ran over but your phone was off."

Devan picked up her phone, and sure enough it was dead.

"Come on," He held his hand out for her.

Instead of pulling herself up, she tried pulling him down. "Sit for a minute," she demanded.

"Um, Okay. What are you writing?" He asked as he sat down beside her.

"My grocery list, I was just passing time." She quickly flipped back the pages to where her list was.

"I see, why did I need to sit?" He leaned over trying to get a peek at her notebook.

Devan turned her book over and set it down in the grass. "Look everywhere…isn't it beautiful?"

Kale nodded. Devan reclined and he rested next to her.

"The sky is a perfect blue, and see how fluffy and magnificent those clouds are? It's a great backdrop for the cover of a book."

Maybe that's what she was writing that she didn't want me to see. He stood up and pulled his phone out of his pocket. He took a picture of her and then a few of the field. As he stretched out next to her, he took a selfie of them together which he showed to her.

"Oh, yuck, Kale, I look horrible. Let's do another one." Devan fixed her hair and got in what she thought was a better position until Kale ruined it by lifting her head and putting his arm underneath it.

"Damn it, Kale!" She fixed her hair again. He took a few pictures then leaned his head toward hers as she turned her head towards his. She was gorgeous. It was almost as though her blue eyes sparkled at him. He smiled at her.

"What?"

"You are so beautiful—"

"Oh, stop it." She smacked at him. "I'm not even close."

He dropped the phone in the grass and rolled over positioning himself over her.

"Damn it, Monty, if I say you are beautiful…you are beautiful!" Kale leaned in closer to her face.

This is it! It's finally going to happen. He's going to kiss me!

He hopped off her and helped her up.

"That's the shit I was talking about," she mumbled thinking about her letter to him.

"What did you say?" Kale asked turning back to look at her.

"Nothing." Devan watched as he changed her tire. She didn't realize she was hovering over him until he looked up at her and politely told her she was in his light. She apologized and moved back a few inches.

"Yeah, still in my light there, slick," he laughed.

Devan apologized again and walked back to the field with her notebook in her hand.

When Kale was done changing her tire, he got up from the ground and told her to pop open her trunk, so he could put the flat tire in it. When she didn't answer he looked out in the distance and saw her lying on her stomach among the grass and dandelions just writing away. He checked his watch. They both had plenty of time before the kids got home from school. Kale tried to open the driver's side door so that he could open the trunk, but it was locked. He didn't want to interrupt her, so he left the flat tire resting against the new one. Kale sat down and leaned back on her car and stared at her for a while.

Devan glanced up from her notebook and saw him sitting about a hundred or so feet from her. "Are you done?" She stood up.

"Yes ma'am. Are you ready to go or would you like to keep writing a bit longer? I don't mind," he said smiling at her.

"Let's go," she said as she jumped up.

That night Justin came home after the kids had gone to bed. It was clear once again that he was intoxicated. Devan tried her hardest to ignore it and went about her business, until he started following her.

"Whatcha doin?" he asked knowing fully well she was trying to clean up the kitchen.

"I'm trying to clean, Justin. Why don't you go ahead and go to bed?" She said as she was putting dishes into the dishwasher.

"I want to help," he started opening up all of the cupboards.

"No thank you, I'm fine."

He began pulling things off the shelves and setting them on the counter.

"What are you doing?"

He continued until the first cabinet was empty. He turned around and faced her.

"You have these all a mess. I'm tired of trying to find something to eat in here. Who in the hell taught you how to organize?" He threw a pack of bagels toward her. "It's got black mold on it, Devan, what the fuck?"

She bent down to pick it up and inspected it. There was no mold, they were onion bagels. The onion pieces didn't even resemble mold. She started to say something and then stopped. It wasn't worth it. She knew trying to reason with a drunk was a waste of time and would probably create more issues. Devan finished cleaning up the part of the kitchen she was in then went into the laundry room. When she came back, Justin had *everything* out of all the cabinets in the entire kitchen. They were completely bare while everything else littered the counters and the floor. She knew she should keep her mouth shut, but she couldn't.

"Are you going to put everything back?" Devan put her hands on her hips.

"No, that's your job. I make the money, you do everything else." He brushed past her, pulled out a bottle of wine from the fridge and poured himself a tall glass.

"That's my wine. You don't even drink wine. Haven't you had enough alcohol today?"

Justin looked at her, screwed the lid back on the bottle, set it on the floor and put it on its side. He smiled at her and rolled it towards her. "Here, you finish it! You obviously need it. Chill the fuck out, Devan. Damn! Why are you so angry all the time anyway?"

"Really?" Devan picked up the wine bottle and put it back in the fridge. "I don't need a drink every day Justin."

"I think you do, and that's why there is always a stick up your ass."

"Fuck off!" She walked away wanting to tear him into a million pieces.

He followed her. "Seriously, Dee, I don't know why you are always mad."

She stopped and glared at him. "Maybe it's because you are drunk the majority of the time. Maybe it's because our kids are afraid of you because you are drunk. I have to do everything, every damn thing. It's like you aren't capable of doing anything at all. I'm tired of cleaning up your messes, because of your being drunk. I'm tired of planning my entire life around *What if he's drunk?* I'm tired of wasting my energy on you. You can't be a father. You are not a husband. What the hell are you?" Devan could feel her ears reddening, and she was getting hot. "Christ, you couldn't even answer your fucking phone today when I got a flat tire. It's always my dad or Kale who helps me out. It's embarrassing!"

"Yeah? Well look in the mirror. You aren't that pretty face anymore. You are nothing, you are worthless…no guy is gonna want a single mom with two ungrateful children. Who is gonna want your fat ass?"

Her phone vibrated in her hand. Kale had sent the selfie he took of the two of them earlier in the day. "Someone will." She turned back and smiled to herself.

"You are delusional…" Justin shouted.

When she got upstairs, she grabbed her notebook, pillow and phone charger and went into the spare bedroom, shut the door and locked it. She pulled out the letter she had started writing Kale and continued.

I often imagine how our life could have been. I should have stayed…never left you in Hawaii that terrible day.

That would have been the right thing to do instead of fleeing like a coward. I think about it all the time. All of the chances I should have taken. I should have run away with you every time you asked. But if I had I wouldn't have Callie and Cyrus and you wouldn't have Sage and Kai. We have both been blessed with amazing kids. And Joey, my sweet, sweet Joey. If it wasn't for Jeane we wouldn't have him.

That being said, I hate Jeane and I hate Justin. The time has come to stop playing games… let's send them packing and start our life together. I love you, I always have and I always will. You are my sun in the morning and the moon at night. You are my everything!

The door knob jiggled disturbing Devan. When he couldn't open it he became angry and pounded on the door scaring her. He yelled some obscenities with added insults. Then finally gave up and left her alone. She assumed he went to bed.

I can't do this much longer. I'm tired of being treated like I'm nothing. I'm tired of the emotional abuse I put myself through on a daily basis. I'm done with Justin! I don't know when, I don't know how, but it's going to come to an end. My children deserve better. I deserve better. I'm ready. Come get me!

Devan set her pen down, wiped a tear that rolled down her cheek and gazed at the picture Kale had sent her again. "You are mine and I am yours. The time has come, my love, the time has come," she said.

The next morning, she went downstairs and was greeted by a disaster that was formally known as her kitchen. Justin had left everything out. The freezer door was open, and food was already thawing. Dish soap had been spilled all over the counter by the sink. The oven was on, luckily nothing was in it. And there was food from the fridge all over the floor. She looked at the clock which showed 7:57. Elaine, Devan's mother, would be there in a little over half an hour to pick up the kids. There was no way she was going to get it cleaned in time. She took a deep breath and slowly exhaled. Devan called her mom and asked if she would stop somewhere and grab a few breakfast sandwiches on her way over for the kids. She then took pictures of the mess and sent them to Veronica saying she needed to cancel their plans.

"What happened?" Callie asked as she walked into the kitchen. Devan's face said it all. "Let me help you, Mom." Callie started putting things back into the cabinets. Half of the mess was cleaned up when Elaine arrived.

"Should I even ask?" Elaine set down the bag of food on the table looking at the remnants of the mess.

"Dad," Callie said closing the last cabinet.

"Go wake up your brother and you guys get ready."

When Callie left the room, Elaine went over to Devan and put her hand on her shoulder. "Wash your hands since it looks like you are touching raw hamburger. Come sit down and eat a sandwich."

"Mom, I can't eat…"

"Devan, as your mom, I am telling you to sit down and eat." Elaine squeezed her shoulder.

Devan reluctantly washed her hands, went over to the table and sat down. Elaine followed and pulled a sandwich out of the bag and handed it to her.

"Does this happen often?"

Devan accepted the sandwich and started unwrapping it. "This particular thing? No."

"It's his drinking, isn't it?" Elaine pulled out a sandwich for herself.

Devan took a bite of her food and contemplated telling her mother the truth.

"We have seen it more lately than in the past. Your father and I are always here for you, Devan. We will help you in any way that we can. You don't have to live this way." She took a bite then asked, "Does Kale know?"

Devan sighed, "He knows Justin likes to drink."

"Does Justin physically hurt you?"

"Oh, God, no, mom, he doesn't. I don't think he ever would."

"Well, that's good because a fight would break out between your dad, Kale, and Nahoa as to who was going to kill him first." Elaine chuckled.

Devan smiled, she could picture the whole thing. The thought of any of them pulverizing Justin's face sent a sick sense of joy through her.

"Helloooo…" Devan's front door opened. It was Veronica.

"Didn't you get my message?" Devan asked. Veronica walked in and looked at the mess.

"Yes, I did. I thought I would come over here to help. What the hell happened?" She sat down at the table. Elaine tossed a sandwich her way. "Thank you. So, what happened, Dee?"

Callie came walking in with Cyrus and she answered, "Dad."

"Oh," was all Veronica said.

As soon as Elaine got the kids out of the house, Veronica drilled Devan who then told her everything from the beginning of the day before until the present.

Veronica jumped up from the table with her eyes wide. "I have an idea! Go take a hot bath and try your best to relax. I'm gonna clean up the rest of this so you don't have to. Then I'll run home and grab a few things and come back."

"No Roni, I will finish this."

"Don't argue with me. I need you as chilled as you can get. Cleaning this up will only piss you off even more. Go…Now!"

Devan went upstairs, and Veronica did exactly what she said she would. When Devan came back downstairs, she saw that Veronica had basically turned her kitchen table into an altar. There were candles of different colors, and a sage smudge stick was burning in a large shell. Stones were laid out in order from dark to light, and there was an empty pan in the middle of all of it completely out of place.

"Um…are we having a séance or performing some crazy black magic this morning that I need to be aware of?"

Veronica smiled, "I try to stay away from séances, and magic is neither black nor white. Go get your letter to Kale."

Devan was about to ask why when Veronica pointed for her to leave the room. A few minutes later she came back with the notebook.

"Rip the papers out, fold them and set them on the table." Devan did and also folded the grocery list she had made and put it in her pocket so she wouldn't lose it.

"What did you put in your pocket?" Veronica raised an eyebrow.

"My grocery list from yesterday. They didn't have everything I needed, so I saved the list to take with me to another store. Anyway, what are we doing?" Veronica reached over and pulled a strand out of Devan's hair. "Ouch! What the hell is that for?" Devan looked at her annoyed.

"I need a strand of your hair to complete the spell."

"Spell? What spell?"

"Well, I guess it's not exactly a spell. I guess it could be considered that, or it could really be…"

"What are you trying to do?" Devan asked.

"Okay, look. You are ready to be with Kale and get rid of those assholes, right?"

"Yeah…"

"I'm just trying to do a protection thing, to make sure things go smoothly and fall into place for you guys the way the Universe wants them to."

"And you don't think it would happen on its own if the Universe wants it to?"

"I know it will happen on its own or whatever. I just don't trust Jeane, so I want to add the extra protection. It won't hurt, and nothing bad will come of it…I'm careful with this shit now that I understand it better. We don't have to do anything if you don't want to."

"Is it going to make you feel better if we do?"

"Yes, I want to make sure you are safe from whatever evil Justin and Jeane are. I know it seems silly to you, but after seeing what Justin did, and knowing how Jeane can be…please let me do this."

Veronica had good intuition, and Devan trusted her judgment. If Veronica was concerned, maybe she should be as well.

"All right, what do you need me to do?"

Veronica smiled and opened the old tattered book that was sitting in front of her. She read over some details and then stopped in midsentence.

"What?"

"I need you to get a strand of Kale's hair."

Devan rolled her eyes, "How I am supposed to do that?"

Veronica got up from the table and went to the window by the front door. "Does he use a comb or brush for his hair?"

"Yeah, well, he did before he had to cut it. I imagine he still uses it."

"Well, I don't see anyone home."

"Jeane is at work and Kale is…" she looked the time. "Oh, he's probably at the office too."

"And the kids?"

"With his mom."

"Even Joey?"

"Yup"

"Perfect! Now's your chance. Get your key to his house."

"I actually don't have one."

"Go in Justin's office bottom right hand drawer."

Devan gave her strange look then went to Justin's office. It was exactly where Veronica had said. "How did you know that?" She dropped the key onto the table.

"I just did…don't waste any more time. Go quickly. I'll watch the house in case anyone shows up."

Devan picked up the note because she didn't want Veronica reading it, and the key then sprinted over to Kale's house. She checked to make sure the coast was clear then unlocked the door and slipped inside. She ran upstairs to his bedroom, went into his attached bathroom and searched the counter and drawers for a brush. She found one, pulled it out and inspected it. "Yuck!" she pulled off a long red hair. She put the brush back and kept searching until she found another one. Devan took that one out. It was pretty clean, so she held it up to the light, saw a few strands of dark hair, pulled them out and put them in her pocket. She thought she heard something fall but didn't see anything. She put the brush back and raced home. She took the hair out of her pocket and set it down in front of Veronica.

"Great, now get the note."

Devan reached into the side pocket she had put it in, but it was empty. So, she reached into the other one and her eyes got huge. "Oh, shit, I think it fell out in his bathroom. I have to go get it!"

"Just leave it Dee. So what if he finds it." Veronica stated.

"I'm more worried that *she* will find it."

"Ugh, all right… go back over and hurry."

Ten minutes later Veronica noticed a familiar vehicle heading towards Kale's house. She called Devan. "I think you need to leave, Dee. I'm pretty sure I see Jeane's car heading your way."

"I can't find it," she said frantically searching.

"Shit, she's pulling in, Devan. You have to get out of there."

"I haven't found it yet." She was retracing her steps.

The door opened to the vehicle, and Kale got out. It wasn't Jeane. She watched to see if anyone else got out of the car. It was only Kale. *Oh, this is too funny.* This was a perfect mistake. "Um, Dee, false alarm. Jeane is not home." She kindly left out that Kale was. He went to the mailbox, grabbed the mail and slowly walked to the door. Devan heard the front door open. *Shit.* She heard someone coming up the stairs. Veronica must have been mistaken. She had to think fast. What would her excuse be for being in Jeane and Kale's bedroom? She looked around…the bathroom. She pulled her clothes off, hopped in the shower and turned it on. Kale opened the bedroom door. "Uh, hello?" Devan didn't say anything. When there was no answer, he opened the door. He couldn't see through the frosted glass.

"Hello?"

She still didn't say anything. She almost started giggling she was so nervous. He walked closer to the shower and tried to open the door.

"Kale," she yelled and slammed it shut. He took a step back. "Um, what are you doing in my shower, Monty?"

She claimed that hers had broken and reminded Kale that he said she was welcome there anytime even if he wasn't home. "Now, can I finish please?" she was snotty. *Damn Veronica.*

"Yes, I'm sorry." He looked down at the pile of clothes on the floor, and in a swift motion he picked them up and briskly walked out of the room.

Devan quickly put some shampoo in her hair and washed it. After she rinsed it off, she dried herself and went to put her clothes on, but they were not there. "Damn it, Kale." She opened the door to the bedroom, he was not there and neither were her clothes. She ran down the stairs and saw her clothes scattered. Picking up piece by piece she couldn't find her pants. She finally found them on the floor next to Kale, with the note sticking out of the pocket. *Son of a bitch, I didn't check in the back pockets.* "Why did you take my clothes?" she asked.

"The better question is, Monty, why didn't you put them on as you found them?"

Kale had a good point. *Damn it!* "What?" She looked down at him. He sat there questioning her with a smirk on his face. Before she knew it, he had his hand on the towel. He could yank it any second. "Kale Kai Iakona, don't even think about it." Devan warned him.

"Too late. I already thought about it. When you find a beautiful, naked woman in your shower you can't think of anything else."

She smiled at the fact he called her beautiful. He said it a lot more than he should, but she didn't mind. She reached for the jeans and the towel slipped. Kale grabbed it before it exposed her completely and held it up for her. She picked up the clothes and ran into the laundry room to put them on. After that, she went in to the living room just as he picked up the note. She tried to snatch it out of his hands, but he lifted his arm up so she couldn't reach it. She tried and tried, he wouldn't give it to her. "What is it, Devan?"

"Don't worry about it."

"Well, apparently it's important."

"It's not, it's just…"

"How bad do you want it?"

She had one hand on his arm that was holding the paper and her other hand on his shoulder. He looked down into her eyes and moved the paper down to his other hand. She reached for it again, and this time he moved it behind his back making her wrap her arms around him. "Look at the predicament we have gotten ourselves into," he chuckled.

"Come on, Kale, just give it to me," Devan pleaded.

"What do I get in return?"

"What do you want?"

Still reaching for it, she groaned. He reached behind her back with it, so his arms were around her.

"You are violating my privacy."

"Excuse me? You come over to *my* house, go into *my* room, get naked in *my* shower, yet I'm invading *your* privacy?"

"Fine, keep it." Devan gave up.

She stepped away from him. He took her hand and placed the note in it. "I'm just having fun with you, Monty, chill out."

"Thank you, I have to go," she told him and headed for the door.

"Hey, do you wanna grab dinner with me Thursday? I think that's the day Justin and Jeane are leaving. I wanna try out that new place, and I don't wanna go alone."

"Okay." She walked back home and told Veronica everything and threw the note on the table. Veronica looked at it suspiciously and took it.

"Um, Dee," she unfolded it.

"Yeah?"

"This is your grocery list." Veronica handed it to her.

"What?"

She headed out of the room and started panicking. "Relax, if you couldn't find it, he won't be able to find it." Veronica tried to reassure her.

Devan came back in, sat down and tried to calm down.

"Okay let's try something different instead of what we planned." While Veronica took her through a guided visual meditation, she snuck the hairs and put them in her bag that she brought her things in. *I'll just save these for later.*

Thursday evening Devan went over to Kale's with the kids. She seemed distraught.

"Joey, here are the emergency numbers. Call me or your dad if there is any issue. Also, the restaurant's number is there as well," she said handing him the paper.

"Relax Monty, he knows what he's doing. It will be fine. We will only be gone for a few hours. Okay kids have fun and be good." Kale ushered Devan out the door.

"You okay?" He asked opening the truck door for her.

"Yeah, I'm fine. Something is just off today. I don't know what it is." She told him.

"Well, if you need to talk, I'm here. Let's go enjoy our dinner. I hear they have zucchini noodles."

Dinner was uneventful. It was a nice Mongolian grill. It was located on the main strip in town so they had a long walk to the car. When they got in the car Devan realized that it was her Grandma's birthday, and that was probably what was bothering her. She had been very close to her. Instead of going straight home Kale stopped at the florist. "I'll be right back." He grabbed a bouquet of flowers and set them in the backseat. Devan thought it was strange but wasn't going to ask about it. He went the opposite way which they had come.

"Where are we going?" He pulled up to the cemetery, shut off the truck, got out and pulled the flowers out of the backseat. He then went over to her side of the truck and helped her out.

"Where is she?"

"Who?"

"Your Grandma." Devan directed him to the grave. He set the flowers on the grave in front of him. "Happy birthday, Grandma Montgomery. You would be proud of your granddaughter. She grew into a beautiful woman with a good heart. She's a talented writer, a great friend and a wonderful mother, I'm sure that you know that. I'm sorry that I never got to meet you. I heard you were a terrific mother and grandmother. Oh, I'm so rude. I'm Kale Iakona…you might have heard of me but probably know me as Lettuce Head. I am the boy who harassed your sweet Devan and then fell in love with her." He put his hand on her shoulder. "I'll be in the truck take your time." She stood there in awe. When she heard the door open and close, she began.

"I know you know who that was. Oh, Grandma, I have myself in a mess. I'm sorry. I know it's been a while since I have visited, and to be honest if Kale hadn't brought me, I probably wouldn't be here now. I love him so much. This little plan we had, worked for a little bit. I don't know how much longer I can go on this way. I almost slipped the other day. I'm so afraid of doing something wrong and then Jeane will leave and take the kids. Deep inside I know we are meant to be together…it just seems like something happens, and it never works out. What do I do? Are we really supposed to be together? Can you give me a sign?" As she started to turn, she put her hand on the stone. "Oh happy birthday, Grandma." The moment her hand lifted it began pouring down a warm rain. The sky had been clear and there had been no forecast of rain. Devan chuckled. "Thanks Gram. Not sure what that means."

Kale got out of the car to meet her with his jacket covering his head. As he approached her, the heel slipped from her shoe making her stumble. He dropped the jacket and caught her before she actually fell, but he moved the wrong way and ended up falling with her on top of him. She laughed. He reached up and wiped the rain from her eyes. Devan moved his hair out of his face. He was perfect. She ran her thumb over his lips and placed her other hand on his chest. His hands moved to both sides of her face. She leaned in and kissed his lips gently and slowly. "Thanks for breaking my fall."

His eyes got wide. She got off him and stood up. "That's it?"

"No. Thank you for bringing me here too. It was very sweet of you." Devan was sincere.

"No. You don't get to do that. Not this time." He hopped up, grabbed her arm and pulled her to him. He rather forcefully captured her face.

"Kale…"

"No." He planted his lips on hers and kissed her passionately. It took her a second, but she reciprocated. The sky grew dark around them. Her hands found their way to his hair. It was much shorter now, but she was still able to twirl some around her finger. His hand moved to the small of her back and he pulled her into him. She felt a fire starting in the bottom of her gut. Kale kissed her so hard. He lifted her up, and she wrapped her legs around his hips. He walked to the truck like that, set her down against it and didn't stop kissing her. She reached for his belt buckle, and he grasped both of her wrists and held them over her head.

"But," she moaned. He bit her lip and traveled down her neck. Devan tried to free her hands.

He stopped. "I said no." He moved back to her lips, kissed her very gently, released her hands and stepped back to gain his composure. He was breathing heavily. She was about to say something, but he put his finger to her lips. She wrapped her lips around his finger.

"Okay, gotta go." He pulled her to the other side of the truck opened the door and practically put her in himself. As he buckled her in, his face was close to her breasts. Kale paused and shook his head. He shut the door and walked over to the driver's side. He got in the truck with a discouraged face. She put her hand on his as he buckled in. He stopped. "Please," he said removing her hand. He turned the key, started the truck and backed out. Devan didn't move. Kale kept his eyes straight ahead. When he pulled in her driveway she jumped out and slammed the truck door. He didn't even look at her and went home.

"What the hell was that?" She asked out loud. *He takes me to dinner, gets flowers for my dead grandmother, takes me to her grave, then attacks me…all to push me away.* She went in the house to sulk completely forgetting that her car and her kids were at Kale's.

A half hour later, she heard the kids come in. She looked out her bedroom window and watched Kale walk home, glaring at him the whole time. He stood at the end of the driveway and turned around to look at Devan's house. She was certain that he couldn't see her, but it sure felt like he could. He dropped his head and turned back around then walked up to the house. Devan shut the curtain just in time for Callie to walk into her bedroom.

"Here Mom," she handed Devan the car keys and walked back out. She held the keys in her hand staring at them. *After all this time, I finally had the nerve to go along…and the asshole shoots me down. Not okay, Iakona, not okay.*

Chapter 26

That Saturday Devan's phone rang. "Hello?"

"Hey, Devan, I wonder if you have a few minutes to talk? Would you come over?" It was Alison.

"Sure, what time?"

"Are you free now?"

"Yes."

"Great see you in a few."

Kale happened to look out his window to see Devan walk across the street to Alison's house. He wanted to talk to her, he *needed* to talk to her. Kale didn't mean for things to happen the way they did a few days ago. He lost control, and he was worried sick that he may have ruined any chance he had with Devan in the future. Kale put his shoes on and patiently waited for her to leave Alison's house.

Alison gave Devan a hug. "I have some exciting news to share with you. I wanted to tell you in person."

"Oh, what is it?"

"I'm going to marry Will!" Alison was ecstatic.

"That is wonderful. When?" Devan asked Alison with a huge grin.

"End of July!"

"That's soon…"

Alison cut her off, "Yes, and I want you to help me plan it."

"Okay," Devan agreed.

"I think it should be at the lake. Do you think you can make plans for a cabin or two? I'll get you a discount," Alison chuckled.

Devan pulled out her phone ready to call the resort, and Alison put her hand on Devan's phone. "Don't tell him."

"Don't tell him what?" Devan was confused.

"He doesn't know," Alison told her.

"Um, he doesn't know what?"

"That we are getting married." Alison said.

Devan sat there trying to figure everything out. "He's asked you a million times to marry him, but he doesn't know you are getting married?"

"I didn't tell him. It's more like a surprise," Alison explained.

"Alison, are you springing a wedding on Will?"

"Well, it doesn't sound that great when you say it that way," Alison smiled weakly.

Devan put her head in her hands. She looked up at Alison. "Before I say anything else. Do you have a plan?"

"Yes." Alison told Devan everything down to the part where she was going to request Kale's and Nate's assistance as well.

Devan let out a long sigh. "Yeah, I'll do it, with one stipulation."

"What's that?" Alison asked.

"*You* talk to Kale," Devan stated.

"That's not a problem. What's going on? Are you currently not on speaking terms?"

"I don't know what we are," Devan spoke truthfully. She had no idea what was going on and what would happen, but she thought it best that she stayed away from Kale as much as she could. Devan didn't go into detail and Alison didn't pry.

Alison called Kale while Devan called Veronica and Nate and told them about the surprise and what the plan was.

As Devan was walking out the door, she saw Kale coming out his front door.

He jogged to meet her in the street. "Hey, can we chat a minute?"

"I don't have time." Devan faced him with cold eyes and kept moving.

"Devan, I'm really sorry about the other day…"

"Kale, I said I don't have time." She put her hand in the air. "Now if you'll excuse me, I have to get home." Kale was taken aback by her rough tone. When Devan got home, she opened a bottle of wine and sat down in front of her computer and opened the email Alison had sent her.

> I forgot to mention I was self-publishing the manuscript you and I had worked on. If you have time, please add and change anything that needs fixed. This is my wedding gift to Will.

Fucking great! Now I have to read this shit. It certainly wasn't shit. It was well written. Between the two of them it had evolved into a wonderful story.

Devan added the last line—

> And they lived happily ever after.

It made her stomach turn. She couldn't help but think about the similarities her own love story had to Alison's and Will's. It made her sad and angry all at the same time. *What the hell happened Thursday?* She'd let her guard down completely. Oh, the mistake she almost made! Good thing Kale saved her from making that mistake. *He rescued me from myself and from him. Kale is always rescuing me.* Devan sent the manuscript to Veronica for a final edit and then sent it to the printer. Alison didn't send a cover so Devan and Veronica took care of it. The cover they decided on was a picture of the locket Alison had lost at the lake so many years ago.

Devan thought in detail about what had happened that day with Kale in the cemetery to the point she got butterflies. Then she got ANGRY! Sure, it was fine for Kale Iakona to make passes at her and *almost* kiss her every time he saw her. It was like she fell for his stupid game. *God, what an idiot I am!* Now she was going to be stuck with him every day for a week again. Well at least the spouses would be there, so she wouldn't have to deal with him that much.

When it came time for Sunday family dinner, Devan almost didn't go. Whenever Kale spoke, she would roll her eyes. She finally quit listening to him. She was already sick hearing about this trip to the lake. Devan really was happy for Will and Alison, but it was just a slap in the face for her. *True love prevails—yeah for them.* Three out of her best friends were married to their perfect matches, and they were very happy. The other one was in a serious relationship. She was sure any day she'd hear they got engaged, and the last one…well, the last one was Kale. "Guess we will go on being miserable together then," she said under her breath.

"I'm sorry, what did you say?" her mom asked.

"Nothing."

Kale was eating an apple and went over to her. "What Iakona?"

"We need to talk," he said before taking a large bite.

"I have nothing to say." Devan looked away. He was chewing annoyingly loud. "I swear you are always eating."

He walked closer to her. "What was that?"

"You. You never stop eating, and you chew so loudly it's disgusting," Devan winced.

"Is that so?" Kale got closer.

"Yeah," she rolled her eyes at him.

He took the half-eaten apple and shoved it right in Devan's face.

"Oh, that's real mature." She threw the apple at him hitting him in the back.

Kale swiftly turned around. "Downstairs, now!" His voice boomed.

"No!"

He grabbed her arm and pulled her down the stairs. Devan missed the last steps, and he caught her. "Are you okay?"

"Does it matter?" The attitude in her voice smacked him in the face.

"If it didn't, I wouldn't ask. Look, I know you are upset. Things got out of hand, and yeah, it was all my fault. I know that, and I'm sorry." Devan rolled her eyes at him again.

"Seriously? I'm trying to have a decent conversation with you, and you are acting like a kid." She pivoted to walk back up the stairs. Kale grabbed her hand, and she tried pulling it away from him.

"Let me be!" She raised her other hand as though she was going to hit him. He raised his eyebrow at her and took her other hand. Kale placed both her hands behind her back as though he was going to cuff her. His tight grip on her hands and the fact that he had his arms around her, angered her more. "I demand you let me go," she yelled at him not caring if anyone heard her.

"I'm not letting you go until you listen to me," Kale said sharply.

"Fine, will you let me go *then*?" she asked still trying to escape.

He squeezed her a little tighter. "When I'm done," he gritted his teeth, "I'll let you go." Devan rolled her eyes and let out a sigh of annoyance. "Enough with the eyes, Monty. I swear you have rolled your eyes a thousand times today."

"Drop the Monty shit! That's a childhood nickname, let it die!" She had had enough.

"Wow, okay, *Devan*, is that better?"

"Are you going to say what you need to, so we can get this over with? I have other shit to do." She *almost* rolled her eyes again. It was hard to tell whose patience was closer to running out, his or hers.

"Anyway, what happened the other day…I know my actions have led up to it, and I'm sorry. I've been out of line for a while now, and I think you have the right to know why."

"It doesn't matter. I don't want to know why. Can I go now?" Kale looked in her eyes and couldn't see the spark that had always been there before. He searched for a few seconds.

"What?" The anger just grew in her.

"Nothing. I guess we are done here." He had finally given up. Kale dropped his arms from her.

Devan headed up the stairs and stopped at the top and turned back towards him. "I have a question. Why was it okay for *you* to cross the line, but when I finally gave in, it wasn't okay?"

Kale didn't know what to say. He opened his mouth to say something, yet nothing came out. Devan shook her head in disbelief and opened the door.

That following Friday Veronica and Nate had invited everyone over for a movie night. Justin and Jeane were gone until Saturday night, and the kids were at their grandparents. Kale had originally offered to pick up Devan. When he arrived at her house, she had already gone. He drove to Veronica's and Nate's and saw her car in their driveway. Kale walked in, and Devan was in the kitchen waiting for the popcorn to finish popping.

"You could have told me you were driving," he said as he brushed by her to kiss Veronica on the cheek.

"Must have forgot," she shrugged.

Veronica gave a look to her husband that asked if he knew anything. His facial expression indicated he didn't. They often had a weird telepathic way of communicating. They all sat down in the living room and started the movie. Devan and Kale sat on opposite sides of the room. Every time Kale would glance at her she veered away in disgust. In the middle of the movie Nate got a call and had to leave to pick up a body. They decided to pause the movie until he got back. Kale went in to get some water and when he turned on the faucet, water began spraying everywhere. He reached under the sink and twisted the water valve off.

"Damn it, Kale, I'm sorry. That happened earlier and I completely forgot to tell Nate."

He smiled at her. His shirt was completely soaked. "No problem, I'll fix it, I just need a wrench and a flashlight."

"Of course, he'll fix it. Kale tries to fix everything," Devan muttered. Kale heard and shot her a dirty look. Veronica retrieved the items he needed and sat back down in the living room.

"What was that?" She asked her friend.

"What?" Devan was playing coy.

"What is going on between you and Kale? The animosity is so thick I'm surprised we are all still breathing."

"I don't know what you are talking about."

"You know damn well what I am talking about. Fine, don't tell me." Veronica was getting irritated. She'd never seen Devan act this way around Kale. There was always tension between Kale and Devan that was easy to feel. This was very different. It wasn't the longing for one another, or sexual tension. This was not good. It was almost as if Devan despised Kale. Something was seriously wrong.

Kale fixed the faucet quickly and even cleaned up the mess. He walked in the living room and took his shirt off exposing his statuesque physique.

"Jesus, Kale, can't you keep your shirt on? Yes, we all know that you work out." Devan scoffed.

"Dee, it's wet. What the hell is your issue?" Veronica was clearly getting frustrated with Devan's mood.

"I'm sick of him always taking his shirt off. Ooh check me out. I'm the great Kale Iakona. I have strong arms and am built like a God, so I have to show off my body every chance I get." She was mocking him.

"Why do you have to be such a bitch?" Kale snarled.

"Oh, I'm the one with the problem. Put your fucking shirt back on dickhead."

He looked at the wet shirt in his hands and without another thought tossed it, and it landed right on her head. Devan jumped up so fast she knocked her popcorn over. Meanwhile, Veronica seized a handful of her popcorn and started eating it watching the show unfolding in front of her.

Devan went to attack him with both hands out ready for a fight. "Don't call me a bitch!" she shouted at him.

Kale grabbed her wrists, put her hands over her head and pushed her against the wall. Veronica's eyes grew large as she watched with anticipation and shoveled more popcorn in her mouth.

"Stop this shit, Monty!" he told her.

"I said *don't* call me Monty." Devan struggled against his strength.

"Fine. You need to calm this attitude of yours."

She tried getting away. "I don't have an attitude."

He got closer to her face, and Veronica leaned over to try to hear what he was saying.

"Devan, this shit has to come to an end. I said I was sorry." His mouth was only a few inches away from hers. Devan calmed down and almost felt like putty in his hands. His signature scent swirled around her, his naked torso was wet against her shirt. Kale saw the spark in her eye resurface for just a moment. His pounding heart seemed to relax a little. Veronica was just sitting there waiting for the kiss, but the kiss never came. Devan realized what was going on. Kale didn't take his eyes off hers as he watched the light fade and anger replace it.

"You have three seconds to let me go, or my knee is going to meet your crotch," Devan threatened.

Kale released her and stepped aside. He went over and kissed Veronica on the cheek. "Thanks for inviting me. I'm sorry it didn't work out. Um, I apologize for our behavior."

"Don't apologize for mine," Devan spat at him. He glared at her which made her shut her mouth.

"Tell Nate I'm sorry." He stepped out the door.

Veronica opened the door and called, "Kale, your shirt."

"Oh, yeah." He walked back in going right past Devan as though she wasn't even there, picked up his shirt, thanked Veronica and left.

Veronica sat down and turned to Devan, "You gonna explain yourself?"

"There is nothing to explain."

"Um yeah, there is. You don't go from writing a letter where you are pouring your heart out to the man of your dreams to wanting to smack the shit out of him. What the fuck happened?" Veronica raised her voice just a tad.

"I don't want to discuss it." Devan shied away from Veronica, like a little girl that just got scolded by her mother.

"Devan, what is Kale sorry for?" Veronica asked in a softer manner.

"I have to go. I'm sorry about tonight." She didn't give Veronica the response she was looking for. Devan got up and marched out the door leaving Veronica in a bewildered state.

Sunday family dinner didn't happen that weekend. During the week Kale was leaving for a job and spotted Devan going for a walk. He considered talking to her then but quickly changed his mind when he saw her eyes shoot daggers at him. They both picked up the kids at the same time. Neither of them said a word to the other one. The kids could feel the tension.

"Daddy, why didn't you talk to Aunt Dee?"

"Mommy, why did you give Uncle Kale a mean face?"

Neither answered their kids. They just changed the subject.

At the next Sunday Family dinner, everyone was there. Devan and Kale went to grab the same tray at the same time which resulted in a mess on the floor.

"Damn it, Kale," Devan shrieked.

"I was just trying to help," he defended himself.

"I don't *need* or want *your* help." she snapped at Kale.

"You guys sound like an old married couple," Jeane cackled. They both gave her a look that made her shut her mouth and back away.

"We have an announcement to make," Chris, Devan's dad stated. "As you know they are widening our road and the city has offered us a considerable amount for our house and land. After thinking about it long and hard, we have accepted the offer."

"Alison is putting her house up for sale," Kale added, "I'm sure she'd let you guys put an offer out there before anyone else."

"Well, we already found a house," Elaine piped up.

Chris resumed for her, "We are going to be joining the Iakonas in Hawaii."

"What the hell?" Devan stood up, her face was becoming red. Kale couldn't tell if she was going to cry or scream.

"Honey, we figured you guys would be coming a little later anyway." Elaine tried to calm her daughter down.

"Why would you figure that?" Devan asked.

"I told them that my uncle has big plans in Hawaii, and that we would all most likely be moving there," Jeane stepped in.

Devan snapped her head around at Kale who had a shocked face. "I suppose you knew about this?" If looks could kill, Kale would be dead.

"No, I had no idea." He was just as angry as she was.

"So, you two," Devan pointed at Jeane and Justin, "planned this whole thing out with my parents?" she yelled.

"That's not exactly how it all went down, Devan."

"Shut up, Jeane. You disgust me!"

"Dev, it's not her fault," Justin tried to explain. "What happened was…"

"I don't give a shit what happened. Of course, it's not Jeane's fault. It's never her fault. It's not her fault my childhood home is going to be destroyed and that my parents are moving to fucking Hawaii and not down the street. It's not her fault that Kale's and my life turned to shit. How does it feel, Jeane, to take everything away from me? You destroyed my dreams why not the rest of my life? Do you want my first born as well? You are un…fucking believable." Devan grabbed her keys and headed for the door.

Chris's, Elaine's, and Kale's mouths dropped to the floor.

"What is she talking about?" Jeane asked completely confused.

"Like you don't know," Devan said as she looked back over her shoulder. "I can't be here." She walked out the door.

Kale jumped up, "I got this."

"Maybe you should leave her alone, Kale," Justin suggested.

"Maybe you should shut the fuck up."

"Dude, you don't know how to handle her when she's this way. She's crazy."

"Handle her? She doesn't need someone to handle her. She needs someone to listen to her and help her, and I think I know. I've known her a hell of a lot longer than you have!"

"Sounds like she needs to go to the psyche ward," Jeane commented.

"Are you really going to talk about our daughter that way in front of us?" Elaine asked getting angry.

Justin stood up in Jeane's defense, naturally. "Jeane's right. Devan has been psychotic lately. I don't know what her problem is."

Elaine scooted closer to Justin. "*You* are her problem. You think we don't see it? You think we don't know how you treat our daughter?"

"How you hurt her and your kids," Chris put himself between Elaine and Justin.

"Listen, old man, you have no idea what you are talking about. Your daughter has lost her fucking mind. You can't believe anything she says."

Kale pushed Chris out of the way and heisted Justin by his shirt collar and lifted him an inch off the floor. "I told you I would fucking kill you if you ever hurt her."

"I didn't lay a hand on her."

"Kale, put Justin down. He would never touch her," Jeane screamed at him. Kale ignored Jeane and pulled Justin closer to his face.

"He didn't hurt her physically, Kale," Elaine said.

"I don't care. I have warned him several times. Hurting her mentally is still hurting her."

"Son put him down. It's not worth it," Chis tried to reason with Kale.

"Honest man, I didn't touch her," Justin managed to say.

Kale let him go and walked to the door. He looked back at Chris and Elaine, "I want the kids to stay here tonight, please. I'm gonna go find Devan."

"Please message us when you do. The two of you need to blow off some steam before you come back. Don't worry we will take care of the kids. Just do what you have to do." Elaine said.

It didn't take Kale long to find Devan. She had gone home. He pulled in her driveway just as she was getting out of the car.

"Oh, God, why are you here? Can't I get any peace? I guess I'll go somewhere else then." She opened the door to her car to get back in. He grabbed her and spun her around to face him. Kale put his giant hand on her hair and smoothed it back. He could tell she had been crying which made him want to kill Justin even more.

"Just let me go, Kale. It would be in your best interest," she threatened.

"No, I can't let you leave, Devan. Not like this, you are too upset."

She knew he was sincere, however, she couldn't hold back her anger. "Well, I can't stay here."

"Let's talk about this." She continued to get into her car, but Kale pulled her out.

"For Christ's sake will you leave me alone?" Devan practically begged him. Kale knew she was not about to change her mindset. There would be no compromise.

"No!" He threw her over his shoulder, walked to his truck, opened the door and put her in. She was not amused and cursed showing her protest. Kale shut the door, locked it and hopped in the other side as quickly as he could.

"Where do you want to go?"

Is he serious? "Nowhere with you," she sneered.

"Well that isn't an option right now." He opened his phone and sent a quick text to Chris saying that he had found her. They were going for a drive, and he would text back later. He put the phone back in his pocket, turned the key and backed out of the drive.

Devan glared at him. They drove around in silence until her phone went off.

He grabbed it from her saying, "It's not important."

An hour later Devan couldn't take it anymore. "Where are we going, Kale?"

"Any place where you are willing to talk with me," he said and kept his eyes on the road.

"I don't want to talk. I thought that was pretty obvious," Devan stated.

"Then I'll keep driving," he told her.

"Well, I hope you have enough gas then."

"I filled up on the way to your parents'. We should be good for quite some time, Devan, quite some time. Just gonna keep driving until you speak to me," he smiled at her.

"You know I have kids that I have to take care of, and I don't exactly trust them with my husband," she barked at him.

"Don't worry, it's all taken care of. As for your husband, though, I'd like to discuss him for a bit."

"Well, have fun with that conversation. I won't be participating." Devan leaned her head against the window and watched the trees pass by.

"Monty, we need to talk!"

"Humph" she folded her arms across her chest.

Kale continued driving. It got darker and soon Devan was asleep. After another hour or so Kale pulled in to a rest stop and took out his phone to call Chris.

"Where are you guys? Your spouses are beginning to worry," Chris told Kale.

"I doubt that," Kale said. "Just tell everyone we are okay."

"When are you coming home?" He looked over at Devan who was still asleep.

"Sometime tonight or tomorrow, I guess. Can you make sure all the kids get to school? I'm sorry to bombard you with this, but I don't trust Jeane or Justin with any of the kids, and we all know Devan doesn't either."

"Where are you?"

"Honestly, Chris, I don't even know. I told Devan I'd stop when she decided to talk to me. She's not being very cooperative," Kale sighed.

"Yeah, good luck with that. We may not see you for days," Chris chuckled then changed his tone and said, "We didn't mean to hurt her, Kale."

"I know. I'll keep you posted." He hung up the phone and looked at Devan again. She was still asleep. Kale drove for another hour then pulled in to a gas station, filled up his tank and grabbed a large coffee. He was exhausted and didn't know if the coffee would even be able to help him at this point.

When Devan woke up, it was dark outside. "Where are we?" she yawned and stretched her arms out.

He glanced over at her. "Oh good, are you ready to talk now?"

"No."

"Damn it, Devan. I'm really tired and hungry."

"You are always hungry."

Kale ignored her comment and persisted, "Please work with me here."

Devan clamped her mouth shut and watched the road. The next sign she saw said Welcome to Virginia.

"What the hell. Virginia?"

He ignored her question. "Do you need to use the restroom?"

"What do you think?"

He found an old service station and pulled in. She went into the restroom. When she came out, he was waiting for her. "Do you want a drink or something?"

"I'm starving."

"Miss, there is a twenty-four hour café just down the road about fifteen minutes out. They have the best Rocky Mountain Oysters that I've ever had, and the liver and onions melt in your mouth," the attendant claimed.

"What are Rock..."

Kale cut her off, "Thank you, sir."

When they got to the truck, she asked Kale what Rocky Mountain Oysters were.

Kale laughed, "You won't like them."

"And why won't I?"

"Just trust me on this one."

They walked inside the café and sat down. "What's your angle here Kale?"

"I'm trying to get you to talk to me. I told you I would keep driving until you were ready to talk."

"I don't want to talk."

"Well, you are talking now." Devan rolled her eyes. "What do you want to order?" he asked her.

When the server came over, Kale ordered his food. Devan smiled at the waitress and said, "I'd would love an order of your Rocky Mountain Oysters."

"Devan…"

"Can I get some ranch with that?"

"Absolutely, darlin'. Do you want fries or onion rings with it?"

"Onion rings please."

"Alrighty." When the server walked away Devan looked smugly at Kale. She was determined to prove him wrong. She was going to eat every bite and enjoy it. They sat in silence until their food arrived. Kale was contemplating on telling Devan what Rocky Mountain Oysters really were, while Devan was thinking up ways to piss Kale off.

When the food arrived, Devan picked up a piece of her food and winked at Kale.

"Don't eat that…please." Kale begged right before she put it in her mouth.

Devan didn't mind the taste, but the texture wasn't something she enjoyed. She made a face while she chewed. Kale made a worse face. She finally swallowed. "It was delicious!" she told him.

"That's not what your face said," Kale chuckled and shivered at the same time.

The cook came out and went around asking everyone how their dinner was. When he came to Devan and Kale, he noticed Devan had only eaten one of the "oysters".

"I'm assuming your boyfriend here told you what these were, huh? Well, I can make you something else if you'd like."

"Oh, these are great," she said as she put another one in her mouth and began chewing.

"Well, I'm glad you appreciate them. They come in fresh from the farm down the road. Won an award at the county fair last year and a few years before, see?" The cook pointed to a plaque on the wall. *Tastiest Testes 2015, Best Beef Balls 2014,* Devan stopped reading and her eyes grew large. She glimpsed at Kale and then at the cook. With her mouth full she asked, "These are testicles?"

"Yes ma'am."

Devan spit out the meat, and it landed on Kale's plate. He turned his nose up and apologized to the man. "Can we order two double cheese burgers with fries to go?"

"Sure thing, I'll take these off your order," he said taking Devan's plate.

"Nope, we are paying for them. Thank you."

Devan was horrified. "Why didn't you tell me?" She was angry.

"I tried, but you didn't want to listen." Devan knew he had tried. She still wanted to argue anyway.

"You didn't try hard enough Kale Kai!" She put her hands on the table and glared at him. "Now what, Iakona?"

"Pardon?"

"What next? You drove all the way to freakin' Virginia. It's midnight or something. What now?"

The server came over with the food and the bill and asked if they'd like anything else. Kale handed her money and asked if there was a hotel nearby. She told him there was and explained how to get there.

"Thank you." Kale got up from the table and grabbed the food. Devan just sat there staring at him. He motioned for her to get up and she rolled her eyes again.

"I'm tired Devan, I've been driving for seven or eight hours."

"And whose fault is that?" She was being a real smart ass.

"Yours."

"No. You knew I wouldn't talk." Devan was not budging from her seat.

"Maybe, but…do you really want me to pick you up, throw you over my shoulder and haul your ass out of here?" Kale was sick of her shit.

Devan thought about it and looked around. She could see some of these people were carrying concealed weapons and she did see a cop over in the corner. She could probably get Kale in a lot of trouble. She squinted at him and sighed. She wasn't that much of a bitch, and she loved him way too much. *Stop thinking like that. We are angry!* "Fine, let's go." She got up.

The hotel appeared to not be open. Half of it was gone.

"Stay here," he told Devan, took the keys and locked the truck. Kale walked in and requested a room with two queen or even double beds.

"Sir, I'm sorry, with the construction we only have so many rooms, and we have one left. It's a King."

"Fine, I'll take it," Kale said regretfully knowing Devan was going to give him hell for taking it. He came out with his head down and unlocked the doors to the truck. Devan slipped out of the truck and followed him to a room. When he unlocked the door and flipped the lights on she rolled her eyes for the millionth time that day.

"Oh, that's convenient," she gestured at the large bed in the middle of the room.

"This is all they had. I promise you, I'll take the sofa," he assured her.

"No, you won't fit, Kale. I'll take the sofa."

"Jesus, do you have to argue over everything?"

"Oh my God, I'm trying to be nice."

"I didn't know you knew how to do that anymore." She didn't respond to him.

"I'm taking a shower and going to bed," he said and walked into the bathroom.

"Don't let me stop you," she replied.

After a minute he started throwing his clothes on the floor just outside of the bathroom door. He stepped out in a towel. She couldn't help but gawk. Kale was a magnificent piece of work.

"Do I have to worry about you running away?" Kale raised an eyebrow.

"Don't be stupid. Can I have my phone now?" Devan didn't even think about running away until he mentioned it. That got the wheels spinning in her head.

"I'll get it when I get out." He shut the door.

When she heard him run the water, she went over to his pants and pulled his keys out of his pocket. She snuck out the door shutting it behind her very quietly, then jumped in the truck. She sat in the truck seriously considering just driving away leaving him there. *Fuck him! He deserves for me to leave his ass here.* She put the keys in the ignition and turned on the vehicle. What was he trying to do anyway? He couldn't fix her problems, not this time.

"Hey, do you want anything?" Kale asked while getting dressed. When Devan didn't answer, he looked out and saw she wasn't in the room. He felt his pocket. "Shit!" He ran out of the hotel room with no shoes or shirt on. His truck was still there, but it was running. She was sitting in the driver's seat with her hand on top of the steering wheel staring out. *If I left him here, that would be a really messed up thing to do. What am I thinking? What am I doing?*

Kale approached the vehicle slowly, trying to not let her see him. He opened the door. Devan looked at him, shut the truck off and put the keys in the hand he was holding out. He put his arms out to help her out of the truck. She put her arms around his neck. When her feet touched the ground, she held on to him a little longer than she meant to. When Devan realized what she had done, she dropped her hands from his shoulders and headed to the room. Kale locked the truck and followed her. He sat down on the couch and faced her sitting on the bed.

"I wasn't going to leave you," she sulked.

"That's not what it seemed like." He leaned over and put his elbows on his legs. "If you want, we can go home right now," he yawned.

"No, you are spent, and I can't do that to you…"

"Yet you can scream and yell at me and throw an insult my way every chance you get, so why not make me drive eight more hours after being up for eighteen hours?"

"Look, maybe I have been a little testy, but Virginia? You know that I'm sorry. Let's just go to bed." Kale bust out laughing. "Um…did I say something funny?" She was shocked at his sudden mood change.

"You said *testy*," he managed to get out.

"I don't see why that's…oh, because of dinner." She shoved a pillow in in his face.

"Go to sleep Iakona!" She giggled and turned the light out.

Chapter 27

The next morning Kale woke up to Devan's hair under his chin. She was curled up against him. He had no idea when she had gotten in the bed, but he had no complaints. He gently lifted an arm and placed it over her. He was thankful she forgave him enough to be that close to him. Maybe she would be willing to talk today. He closed his eyes and enjoyed this peaceful moment that he had and fell back to sleep.

Devan woke up about an hour later feeling like she was being smothered. Opening her eyes, she saw her nose touching Kale's bare chest. She smiled for a second then tried to squeeze out of his tight embrace, he woke up when she did.

"I'm so sorry." He backed away from her. She gave him a look, and he wasn't sure what it meant. She got up went to the bathroom and came back a minute later. He watched her walk back over to the bed and sit down with her back facing him. *I can't do another day of this shit.* Then she climbed in under the covers and scooted backwards to him. Devan lifted his arm and put it over her and backed up into him until there was no room to move. He wasn't sure what to say.

"I'm ready to talk," she said.

Finally! "Do you want to go get breakfast first?"

"No, I don't want to move. I'm very comfortable."

Kale hated to do it, but he lifted his arm from her and started to get up.

She sat up and scowled at him. "Where are you going? I said I was comfortable."

He apologized, "I'm sorry, I promise I'll come right back."

She grabbed his arm. "No!"

"Monty, I'm sorry I really am. I have to take a piss and it can't wait."

She let him go and tried not to giggle. "Sorry," she reclined.

When he came back, she had the covers pulled up to her chin. "Are you cold?"

"Uh yeah, I lost all the heat from your body."

Kale got back in the bed and scooted right next to her. She snuggled up to him with her cheek on his chest. He was lying on his back, and she was on her side.

"Is that better?" he asked putting his arm on her back and lightly stroking her long hair.

"It'll do for now."

"You said you were ready to talk?"

"Yeah, what are we doing all the way in Virginia?"

"I admit, it's a little extreme, but you have me all kinds of confused right now. I wasn't sure what to do. I just know I had to get you alone with no other distractions."

"Hold up, *I* have you confused?" Devan lifted her head from his chest and looked him straight in the face. "Do you know what you've been doing to me the past few months? Not to mention all the flirting you have been doing, and the teasing, acting like you are going to kiss me, and the way you look at me. And *hello...* the cemetery? What the fuck was that?" She didn't wait for him to answer. "So, I finally cave, give up fighting my feelings and you tell me *no* making me feel like I did something wrong. So yeah, I got pissed. I got super pissed! It was so hard to not reciprocate everything you did prior, and then..."

He sat up and pulled her up, then took her chin in his hand and peered down into her sad blue eyes. The spark was back.

"I'm sorry. I truly am sorry. What I did was wrong, and I brought you down with me."

"Ugh you are doing it again," Devan sighed.

"What?"

"It's the way you are looking at me," she frowned.

"I don't know how else to look at you, Devan." Kale frowned back at her. He was glad she was ready to talk, but he didn't want to fight with her.

"That's the problem. When you look at me that way, which is most of the time," she paused "unless you are really pissed at me," It's…I don't know…I can't even describe it." She closed her eyes.

"Try," he insisted.

She opened her eyes and sat there just gazing at him. When she couldn't bear it any longer, she tilted her head up toward the ceiling trying not to cry.

"It feels like you only see me,"

"I do see you."

"I know, but it's like no one else is around. You and I are in our own little world where only *we* exist. I feel you embracing me, kissing my lips. I feel our love," she looked down, "how it used to be."

"What do you mean *how it used* to be?" Kale was intrigued and relieved that he was finally getting the truth at last.

"Back before Jeane and Justin. When we didn't have any worries, and I knew that we would be together forever. Back when life was simple and sweet." She had tears in her eyes.

"And that's a bad thing?"

"No," she shook her head, "I mean, yes. Our situation is not like that now, and it's not okay to feel that way. We're both married and have families. I shouldn't still feel this way about you."

He took her hand in his. "I disagree. Feeling that way about you is the only thing that keeps me sane most of the time." He wiped a tear from her cheek. "We are going to figure this whole thing out, with your parents, with me, with Justin and Jeane…"

"Ugh can we just leave them out of it for right now?"

"Yeah. Oh, I need to let you know that I kind of threatened Justin again."

"How bad was it?" Devan asked, curious.

"I yelled at him and picked him up by his collar, but that was it." Kale clenched his fist at the memory from yesterday, and the anger came flooding back.

"How bad did you want to hit him?"

"Really, really bad."

"Do I want to know why?"

"Nope." His stomach growled. "Are you ready to get out of here and get some food?"

"Yes," Devan replied with a smile. She really didn't want to talk about this anymore.

After they stopped for breakfast, they headed home. The drive was long and quiet, still they made it home right before the kids got off the bus.

"Is there anything else we need to talk about?" Kale asked her as he pulled in the driveway. "I want it out in the open right now! I don't want to have to go through this again."

"No," Devan replied.

"So, do we have a truce?" He waited to unlock the doors until she answered him.

"Yeah." She hugged him and hopped out of the truck.

"Oh, one more thing Devan…" She turned around. "I'm going to behave from now on. I won't be tempting you anymore," he promised.

Devan moved over to the truck, leaned in the window and kissed his cheek.

"As long as I'm alive, you'll always be tempting me," she said. Then she walked towards her house.

He watched as she unlocked her door and went into her house. *Maybe I should have told her about finding 'Aloha Paradise'. Maybe I shouldn't have brought her home yet. Maybe I should have kissed her one last time.* He pulled out of her drive-way. *Maybe I should turn my brain off and stop thinking about this.* Kale shook his head. *I don't think that's possible.*

A few weeks had gone by and everyone acted like everything was normal. Neither Jeane nor Justin asked where Kale and Devan had gone, and neither Kale nor Devan offered the information. It was odd, but it seemed that ignoring it was the easiest thing to do for all of them. Devan had been helping her parents pack up things. She still was not happy about it, yet she wanted to help them the best she could and spend as much time with them as possible. She was still sad that her parents were moving to Hawaii, but she understood why.

Finally, it was moving day. Chris and Elaine would be heading to Hawaii in a few short hours. When Devan stepped into the house, she heard laughter.

"What's going on?" she walked into the living room where she saw her mom, her dad and Kale looking at something that was in her mom's lap.

"Oh, Kale stopped by to see us off. We found a few things from when you guys went to school together, and we've been talking about old times," Chris said. He pointed to the thing in Elaine's lap. It was an old picture of her and Kale.

"Oh boy," Devan grabbed a chair and sat down.

"Do you remember when Pete and I were outside your bathroom window?" Kale asked her.

"When you were watching me shower? Yes, I remember." Devan gave him a dirty look. "Do you remember the smack I gave you?" She held her hand up ready to smack him. She was just teasing him but enjoyed watching the fear grow in his eyes.

"Actually, I wasn't watching you." He cowered down afraid she was going to smack him.

"You weren't? So, what do you call it then?"

"Well, we were going to scare you but…yeah…okay I started watching you. I could barely see anything." Kale said in a defeated voice.

"Well, I'm sure you saw enough. I can't believe you told my parents," she huffed and folded her arms.

"I can't believe you never told on us," he laughed.

"I figured my bite was worse than my dad's." Devan smiled.

"Hey, what time do you guys have to be at the airport?" Kale asked Chris.

"We really should be leaving here in about a half hour." He told Kale.

"Tell me where your bags are, and I'll put them in the car." He got up from his seat, and Chris showed him, so Kale put them in the car then came back in. He hugged Chris and Elaine and wished them a safe trip and left.

When they arrived at the airport, they walked to the security check point. Then Devan hugged and kissed them both.

"We are going to miss you," Elaine squeezed Devan tight, "and our grandchildren."

"I'm going to miss you too. I wish you didn't have to go," she pouted.

"I know. Listen, if you need anything you call us, and come visit us soon! Also, please be nice to that poor boy," Elaine pleaded.

"Are you implying Kale is a boy? Last time I checked he was six foot, five inches and about two hundred fifty pounds, Mom. He can handle himself," Devan retorted.

"Not against you he can't." Chris kissed her on the cheek and hugged her. "Take care of him, he needs you just as much as you need him."

"Dad…" Devan was beginning to get frustrated. She felt like she was losing her parents, and now they were lecturing her about taking care of Kale.

"Don't 'dad' me. You know I'm right. I love you sweetie."

"I love you too. Call me when you get in. I don't care if it's three o'clock in the morning, call me so I know you got there safely." She was doing her best to fight back the tears that had been waiting to fall, despite the irritation that was eating at her.

"Love you. See you both for the holidays," Elaine said as they walked away.

Both? Right then she felt two large hands on her shoulders. She turned to face Kale as the tears finally streamed down her face.

"What are you doing here?" She wiped her cheeks.

He pulled her in and wrapped his arms around her.

"I knew how hard this was going to be for you today. I didn't want you to be alone. I've been here the whole time."

"You didn't need to do that," Devan said.

"Yes, I did. Now be quiet and let me hold you a bit longer until you push me away." Kale held her a little more closely.

Devan didn't want to push him away. She was sick of pushing him away. She wanted to stand there in that moment and cry into his chest. She put her arms around his torso and held on for some time. He got a glimpse of her parents as they passed through security and waved. He waved back.

"Do you think the next time we see them they will finally be together?" Elaine asked Chris when she put her hand down.

"God, I hope so!" he said and put his hand on her shoulder as they boarded the plane.

Kale followed behind Devan on the way home. She invited him in and offered to cook. As he followed her in the house, he noticed a package on the porch and picked it up. He handed it to her, and she opened it when they went inside. It was a seedling in a pot with a card. "What is that?" Kale sat down in a chair at the table.

"It's a seedling from an oak tree," Devan explained. "I wanted to give it to my parents before they left. It figures it would show up right after they got on the plane."

"Why did you want to get it for them?"

"Because the house that they built their life in will be destroyed. We have that giant oak in the back, and they are just gonna tear that down too!" She started to tear up again. Kale got up and pulled her to his chest. She stayed there for a few minutes, then dried her eyes and walked to the refrigerator to make them both something to eat.

Kale sat back down and picked up the card that had come with the seedling. He read: 'The Oak tree: very common in America, the oak tree represents strength as it is a hard and durable wood, used in construction and furniture'. *Strong, just like Devan.*

❧ ☙

There were so many emotions Devan was feeling as she packed up her room. She spent practically her whole life here. It's a shame the houses were going to be torn down just to make the road bigger. *What a waste!* Her parents had built a life here. She knew the move to Hawaii would be good for them, but it was too far away.

She was putting the last box she had just packed into the bed of Kale's truck. That box was the last one that would fit. She still had to pack the closet in her room, and they had to move the bed as well. Aside from that the house was empty. Instead of feeling accomplished she felt lonely and angry. She closed the tailgate, walked around to the passenger side and hopped in the truck. The storage place was right next to the field where she'd had a flat tire a while back. The field was green, spotted with white now. When she got out of the truck she looked up at the sky. It had gotten dark and clouds were rolling by.

"We need to hurry Kale, I can feel a storm brewing right over our heads," Devan exclaimed. She picked up a small box, getting more and more aggravated. "Kale, you can't pile those boxes one on top of the other," she said lifting one.

"Monty, those are too heavy." He ran over and took the box out of her hand.

"Exactly, Kale, that's why you don't stack them." Devan's aggravation was clearly showing through her short temper.

"Fine, I'll take care of it." He gently moved her out of the way.

"No, I have it." She made her way in front of him and grabbed the second box.

"I swear you are the most stubborn person I have ever met," he said while taking the second box from her too. "Maybe you should go sit in the truck while I finish this."

Devan flicked him off and walked back to the truck to retrieve what was left. A huge gust of wind made her lose her balance and she fell, still holding the box.

"Are you okay?" he asked as he ran towards the truck and attempted to help her up.

She shooed him away, "I'm fine." She looked up and saw a million tiny things flying by her. "What is that?" Kale saw them too.

"Probably something off a tree. Dude, we need to hurry. I swear a rain drop just landed on my head." It had not been a fun day and Devan wanted it to be over with.

"You aren't made of sugar, so you won't melt," he laughed.

"Come on Kale, these clouds are a warning sign. Let's get this shit done and get back." They made a few trips from the truck to the storage shed, working quickly as Devan suggested. After her third trip to the truck, she glanced in the back. They were almost done.

After Kale put the last box in, Devan pulled down the door of the storage shed and locked it. Then she followed Kale back to his truck and climbed in the passenger seat once again.

"Oh my God, what is wrong with your stupid truck!" she asked struggling with her seatbelt after she had gotten in and shut the door. He reached over and released the belt. When it loosened back up, he realized how close his face was to hers. She cocked her head and looked at him. He looked deep into her eyes and then down at her lips. Their lips were less than six inches apart. She hesitated and almost trembled.

"You have to release it first." He forced himself to back away from her.

"Like you released me?" She said quietly. She had no idea why these feelings were coming up now, but she couldn't ignore them.

"What?" He put the truck in drive.

"You heard me," Devan said looking away from him. She couldn't look at him just yet. The truck began to move. Kale backed out of the storage unit parking lot and onto the road.

"Um, that was *you* at the lake all those years ago. Why in the hell would you bring that up now?" his tone was rough.

"It's bullshit!"

"You are right, it *is* bullshit. If you want to talk about this, I'm pulling over." Kale turned the wheel slightly to the right.

"I don't want to talk about it."

"I asked you a month ago, if there was anything else that we needed to talk about. Why didn't you bring this up then?" Devan didn't say anything, so Kale continued to drive.

"Why didn't you come after me that summer?" Her voice was quiet.

"You want to talk about this? We'll talk about it." He pulled the truck over to the shoulder of the road.

"No, just forget it." She looked out the window and saw the field again. She got out of the truck frustrating Kale even more. He put the truck in park, turned off the ignition and followed her. It was so windy. What the hell was she doing?

"Stop, Devan, this is stupid. I said let's talk about it, and you are running away from me."

"I said forget it," she shouted back to him.

"I've been trying to forget it for years. You pushed me away Devan, *you!*"

She flashed him an evil look and stopped dead in her tracks. Little white puffs were swirling all around her. As angry as he was, he couldn't help but think of how beautiful she looked right then, which made him even angrier.

"I have had nightmares about that fucking day for years. Hell, I didn't even want to go to sleep at night because I was afraid that I was going to have that damn dream again until Nate made me the dreamcatcher." He ran and caught up to her.

"Why didn't you chase me?" Tears were starting to well up in her eyes.

"Jesus Christ, Devan, I have chased you for years. I chase you in real life and even when I go to sleep. *You* wanted me gone so I finally took the hint and left." Kale looked up as big rain drops began to fall on him. "Let's go!" He grabbed her arm and practically dragged her to the truck.

"I didn't want you to leave," Devan said getting in.

"Really? That's not what I got from it. We meet again three years later. You make me promise to keep my hands to myself—then *you* jump on me." He pulled back on to the road and headed to her parent's almost empty house.

"What are you talking about?" She stared at him with no recollection.

"Really?" Kale sighed. "Hawaii, 2011, a few days after Pete's and Kristy's wedding, you broke your ankle. I took you to the hospital and then back to the hotel, where you proceeded to make a move on me and tied me to a bed."

"Oh please. I told Veronica that in confidence. It was a stupid dream." She rolled her eyes.

"No, it wasn't. Devan, it really happened."

"Shut up Kale!" She didn't believe him. So, he kept his mouth shut the whole way back to the house. When he pulled in to the Montgomery's former drive, he glanced over at her and told her in detail everything that she had told Veronica, but he didn't mention Justin.

"That's bullshit! I trusted her. Why would she tell you that?"

"Monty..."

"Didn't I tell you to stop calling me that?"

"Fine, *De—van*. Veronica didn't tell me anything."

"Whatever, so not cool! You are both assholes!" She got out of the truck and stormed towards the door. Kale jumped out.

"Really? This is how we are ending this today? I thought we were past this bullshit." He tried to grab her arm, but she was too quick for him. She unlocked the front door.

"Just go home, Kale. Thank you for your help today, but it is no longer needed." She basically shut the door in his face.

He grunted and went back to his truck. *I'm not fucking chasing her. She probably thinks this whole damn thing is a game.* It was raining even harder. He ran back to the truck and tried starting the engine. It wouldn't even turn over. After the fifth time of trying, he yelled in a fit of rage. "FUCK!" He got out and popped open the hood. It was pouring so bad he could hardly see what he was doing, and the wind was picking up speed. "Goddamn it!" He slammed the hood shut and tried to get back in the truck, however, the door was locked. The keys were staring at him from the seat.

Devan sat down on her old bed and stared at the remaining things she had in the closet. Right on the top shelf was Devan's and Kale's Prom picture. Maybe she was too hard on him. Did her dream really happen? Veronica and Kale had become close, but she wouldn't have told him. *Damn it, did I just fuck up again?*

"*You know one of these days he's going to stop coming back.*" She heard the voice in her head.

"I know," she answered. She picked up her phone and called Kale. It just rang. He didn't pick up. She pissed him off good this time. She set the phone down and looked back at the picture.

Oh, things I would love to tell the two of you. Why did you give up? Suddenly, she heard the door slam then the lights went out. It startled her. Thunder crashed loudly, startling her again. A few seconds later lightening lit up the room enough for her to see a dripping Kale in the doorway of her bedroom.

"My fucking truck…"

Devan didn't give him a chance to finish. She crossed the room, reached up, grabbed his head and kissed him.

"What you are doing?" She kissed him again, this time, however, she placed her hands behind his neck and jumped up on him, wrapping her legs around his waist.

He pulled away from her lips.

"Seriously, Devan, what the hell?"

"I was wrong."

"What?"

"I was wrong, I was wrong about everything. I shouldn't have made you promise to keep your hands to yourself. I should have never said those things at the lake. I should have told you *yes*, all the times you begged me to run away with you. I should have never left you alone in Hawaii all those years ago. I should have never doubted you. I should have never let you go! I'm yours. I always have been, and I always will be." Devan placed her hands behind his head forcing his mouth onto hers.

Kale walked with her to the bed. "It's about time!" He gently laid her down, but that is where the tenderness ceased. He ripped open her shirt. Buttons were flying all over the place. She fumbled with his belt while he took his shirt off. He was wet and cold, but that was about to change. There was nothing gentle about what going on. She clawed at his pants and boxers until they were off. She wanted him to ravish her body. He ripped off her panties. There was no waiting. He shoved himself straight into her. She let out a scream, half pleasure half pain. She didn't care if he was hurting her. She wanted this savage beast, all of him. He pulled out to her disappoint and stared at her long and hard for what seemed like eternity. She had never seen that look in his eyes before. She was slightly frightened and extremely intrigued. Without warning he flipped her over on her stomach and reentered her. It was so raw and barbaric. The mixture of pleasure and pain was explosive. Screaming into the sheets she was white knuckling. "Stop, stop, STOP!" she screamed.

He stopped and let go…afraid he really hurt her. She pulled herself away from him and got off the bed. He just stood there stiff as a board. She pushed him as hard as she could onto the bed and climbed on top of him. With her hands on his stone hard pecs she slammed herself down on him. He grabbed her hips and pushed her even farther down. Her nails were digging into his skin. They both yelled out in ecstasy. She then crashed down on him.

He woke up with her naked body lying on top of his. "Hey," he smiled and said quietly moving her hair out of her face.

She lifted her head and looked at him. "Hey," she smiled back at him.

"Do you have any idea what time it is? I locked my phone and keys in the truck."

She rolled off him and eyed her phone. "We have about ten minutes before we have to pick up the kids."

"That doesn't leave any time for you to run me home and get my other keys. Do you think we can all fit in your car comfortably?" Devan grabbed her clothes and began to put them on. "It seats seven so, it may not be exactly comfortable, but it will work. We will just put Sage, Kai, and Cyrus in the back together."

"What do we do now?" Kale asked putting his clothes on.

"We go get the kids, take them to your house, get your keys and then come back."

Kale laughed as he met her at the door, "No, I mean what do *we* do now that we have…"

"Oh, um…uh, let's go get the kids, and we will revisit this later." Devan pushed him out the door.

The kids were surprised to see Kale and Devan together.

"It's nice to see that you two are getting along." Callie set her book bag down on the floor of the SUV. Devan and Kale didn't say a word.

"Are you guys gonna start acting all weird again?" Sage asked from the back.

"Shut up!" Joey told her and smacked at her leg.

"You shut up. You like it when they act all weird." Sage smacked back at him.

"Just shut up okay?" Joey said giving Sage the evil eye.

"Well, I have a question," Kai cleared his throat. "Why are you guys wet?"

Kale and Devan laughed and explained that they had been moving stuff and how the storm came.

"Okay, but that was right after school started so why didn't you change. I just don't understand how you are still wet." Cyrus tilted his head waiting for some response.

"Does it really matter Cy? Can't you just accept we have weird parents?" Callie chimed in.

"Callie is right, Cy. You and she have a pretty weird mom," Kale chuckled.

"Gee thanks." Devan slapped his arm.

"Aunt Dee, I think my dad is much weirder than you," Joey said and slapped his father on the back.

After they dropped the kids off and Kale grabbed his keys, they went back to the Montgomery's old house. Before he got out of Devan's car, he took her hand and looked into her eyes. "Okay Monty, I don't give a shit what you say…I'm going to call you Monty if I want to."

"Fine," she raised an eyebrow at him knowing the question was coming.

"Okay, now are you gonna start running in the mornings with me again?"

She was surprised he didn't ask what she thought he was going to. "Um… sure."

"Good, because I miss someone watching my ass as I run."

"What in the hell are you implying?"

"You know you are always lagging behind me trying to catch up." He let go of her hand and slipped out of the car before she could smack him.

"You'll be watching my ass tomorrow, Iakona. Six a.m. be ready!"

"I don't mind slowing down for a sexy view like that." He unlocked his truck and got in. He put the key in the ignition and lo and behold, it started!

<h1 style="text-align:center">Chapter 28</h1>

July 2016

It was the week before Alison's and Will's wedding, and Devan was packing for the trip. "Callie, did you find those goggles?" she yelled from her room out to the hallway. A moment later Callie came in with a bag full of goggles, snorkels, fins, and other swimming gear. "Oh good." She took the bag and set it down next to the other bags that were by her door. She saw her phone lighting up on her way back to her bed where she was packing her suit case. She picked it up and looked at it. It was Alison. She accepted the call, "Hello soon to be Mrs. McGrudle."

"Are you ready?" Alison asked.

"*I* should be asking *you* that question," Devan replied.

"I am so ready," Alison responded, almost immediately.

"Does he have any clue yet?"

"No, and I'm trying to act normal, but I'm so damn excited, it's nearly impossible." Devan could hear the enthusiasm in Alison's voice.

"You are acting like you are getting married or something," Devan laughed.

"Everyone knows not to say anything, right?"

"No one knows aside from Kale, Veronica, Nate and me. I figured that was our safest bet."

"Good idea. Oh, please don't forget to pack the book," she reminded Devan.

"I have it already in the car. It was the first thing I took care of."

"Thank you, so much for that, and thank you for being a part of this. You have no idea how much it means—"

"I'm very happy to do it." Devan smiled.

"All right, well, I'll let you go. We will see you tomorrow. Have a safe trip!"

"Thanks Alison, bye." Devan hung up the phone and looked at the mess she had created in her room. "Better clean this up," she said to herself and zipped up her luggage.

The Lake 2016

The next evening, they arrived at the resort just before dark. Alison greeted them with open arms.

"Where's Will?" Kale asked hopping out of his truck.

"Closing up the marina. Why don't you guys go ahead and unpack before it gets too dark to see anything. Will and I will be up in a bit with dinner. Two deluxes, three cheese, two pepperoni, and two pepperoni and pineapple?"

"Oh, I stopped eating dairy," Jeane declared. "Do you have a salad?"

"Since when have you cut out dairy?" Kale raised his eyebrow at her.

"Probably five minutes ago," Veronica mumbled. Devan tried her hardest not to laugh, but she was unsuccessful.

"I just read an article on the way here, and I decided it was best for my body," Jeane stated.

"I'm impressed, I had no idea she knew how to read," Veronica snarked only loud enough for Devan and Alison to hear.

"We have salad, would you like chicken on it?" Alison was being nice trying not to grin at Veronica's remark.

"Yes, that would be divine," Jeane said in her sickening sweet voice that just made Devan's stomach turn.

Veronica and Devan both rolled their eyes and started to unpack. The kids even pitched in and did their part. Jeane and Justin didn't lift a finger.

The next morning Alison met Veronica and Devan for a walk. Everyone was still sleeping. "Are you sure he doesn't have any idea?" Veronica couldn't help but ask.

"If he does, he hasn't let me see it," Alison asserted.

"So, where are we doing this?"

"Right past those trees." Alison pointed towards the clearing in the woods that led to a gorgeous overview of the lake. "We go sit on that bench and watch the sunset almost every night. It overlooks the lake and the ground is flat. It is naturally perfect. He thinks we are getting our picture taken together as a family. I had to come up with something so he would dress semi decent."

"Do you have everything you need?" Veronica asked while stopping to bend down and tie her shoe.

"Yeah, everything is set up. The hardest part is going to be setting up the reception without him knowing. He's going in that morning to open but then will come home and get ready for the picture. Some of the staff agreed to miss the wedding to take care of it."

"I think it's all going to work out." Devan put her hand on Alison's shoulder, then looked back to see where Veronica was. "Hurry up slow poke, Kale is going to expect me to go for a run soon."

Veronica tilted her head to the left with a smile and lifted her right hand up and slowly raised her middle finger to Devan.

"I saw that Ms. VonStross." The teacher in Alison came out.

"Cavendar!" Veronica corrected and jogged her way to where they were.

"I think I will always call you Ms. VonStross in my head," Alison giggled.

"Actually, we are going to be related soon."

"Yup, another cousin by marriage." Veronica said. "Just waiting for this one now," she smacked Devan on the arm. Devan ignored her and continued inquiring about the wedding that was soon to take place.

When they got back to the cabin, Kale was awake and making coffee. Kale and Devan left for their run and Alison and Veronica poured two cups and went out back so they wouldn't wake anyone. Kale took off making Devan catch up to him. She hated when he did that. He finally slowed his pace to a moderate jog.

"How was your walk?" he asked.

It was still too much activity for Devan to carry on a conversation, so she slowed down her pace. Kale followed suit.

"It was fine," Devan uttered still trying to catch her breath.

"Did you tell them?" he blurted out.

He almost reminded her of a kid in school with his eager question. She knew exactly what he was getting at but decided to act as though she didn't.

"Tell them what?" Devan tried to keep an innocent look on her face.

"About you and me," Kale spoke as though Devan should have known what he meant.

"What about you and me?" Devan had to bite her lip to keep from smiling. She could almost hear the eyeroll.

Kale rolled his eyes at her then grabbed her hand and dragged her into the nearby woods.

"Stop playing coy with me. Did you tell them or not?"

"No—"

"Oh my god, you mean I'm this great big secret?" He teased her.

"What am I gonna say? Oh, hey, by the way, Kale and I finally had sex, and we occasionally make out now?"

"Speaking of—" He put his hand on the small of her back and pulled her close to him. "It's been a hot minute."

She gazed up in to his green eyes and then at his waiting lips. "It sure has," she said and then kissed him.

Kale stopped the kiss, "Are you going to at least tell Veronica?"

She wondered why this was so important to him. It was obvious he wanted Devan to tell Veronica what had transpired. It was unlike Kale to spill secrets, especially his own.

"Not planning on it anytime soon, why?"

He dropped his arms from around her. He seemed frustrated. Then Devan thought she knew why. "Did you tell Nate?" she asked.

"No, I didn't tell anyone. That's why I wanted you to do it so I could tell him."

Devan laughed, she couldn't believe her own ears. Kale was dying to tell his best friend about his forbidden love adventure.

"You know we are basically having an affair now, right?"

"So?"

"So, you want to go tell people that? It's looked down upon, it's a sin and you want to tell the world."

"I just want you to tell Veronica so I can tell Nate. They won't look down on us—they will be ecstatic for us."

What Kale said was most likely true, nevertheless, Devan didn't want it out there yet. She knew even though things were horrible in both of their marriages and their spouses treated them awful, it was still wrong. She wanted to end it with Justin first. She was disappointed in herself that she had let it get that far without taking care of the things she needed to. However, she didn't regret any of it. She stared back up at him.

"Not yet, there are things we both need to handle before a word is spoken to anyone. Even then, we have to be very careful. We have no idea how this is going to go yet."

"When are you going to tell Justin that you want a divorce?" Kale asked reaching out and brushing hair out of Devan's face.

"I haven't decided the exact day, but it's going to happen after I sit down and figure everything out and talk to a lawyer." She had planned on calling Antoinette to ask her to get the ball rolling and set up an appointment for when she got back. "What's your plan?"

"I'd do it right now if you'd let me. I'm just waiting for you." He was being completely honest with her and she knew it. She nodded at his answer, wrapped her arms around his waist and hugged him tight. She couldn't wait for the day they could tell their spouses to *fuck off*. IT would feel amazing!

"Let's go back," Devan said, pulling away from him. "I'm sure everyone is awake now."

When they got back to the cabin Nate and Veronica were almost done making breakfast. It was a nice quiche with cheddar cheese and spinach. Kale noticed the coffee pot was almost empty, so he made more. He knew how Jeane was when she didn't have coffee, and she wasn't even up yet. He figured he would spare everyone the discomfort.

As they were setting the table, Jeane came strolling out wearing a one-piece swimsuit in leopard print with a high neckline, and an oversized white sun hat with a matching white sarong and huge sunglasses that covered almost half of her face. She grabbed a coffee cup and the coffee pot though it wasn't done brewing. While she poured herself a cup the machine continued dripping. Kale was getting irritated watching the boiling liquid overflow on to the floor.

"Jeane, seriously? Clean it up!" Jeane put the pot back making an even bigger mess. The hot plate that the pot was resting on was sizzling and hissing. The smell of burnt coffee filled the cabin quickly. Jeane ignored Kale and went over to the fridge and pulled out the creamer. Veronica got a rag and cleaned up the mess while Jeane poured creamer in her coffee cup.

"Does that thing have dairy in it?" Jeane asked Veronica, pointing at the breakfast quiche she made.

Veronica waited to say anything until Jeane had downed some of her coffee.

"About as much as your coffee there." Veronica motioned to the cup in Jeane's hand.

"It has creamer not cheese," she replied coldly.

"Oh, I didn't know creamer was dairy free," Veronica sassed back and sat down without another word. When Nate was about to notify Jeane that the yogurt she was eating was dairy Veronica stomped on his foot.

Over the next few days Jeane continued to eat dairy and no one corrected her. For the most part they were all having a good a time. There were a few times where Jeane threw a fit about something. She refused to ride the tube because "she didn't want to do that kind of thing." Justin couldn't go a day without some type of booze. The others did their best to enjoy the trip.

On the fourth day Justin finally agreed to go fishing with the guys, which he had avoided the first two times. They decided to fish a little later instead of in the early morning while the women took the kids on an island picnic.

Justin grabbed a second beer from the cooler that he had brought and relaxed in his seat. "So, is this what we do? Just sit here drink beer and wait?" He cracked open the can.

"Well, it's not even noon yet, so no beer for me," Will said.

"Hey, it's five o'clock somewhere, am I right?" He nudged Kale with his elbow. Kale glared at him and moved to the other side of the boat.

"Oh, come on Kale, have a beer with me."

"I don't drink, Justin. You should know that by now," Kale gritted his teeth.

"Nate?" Justin asked turning his head toward Nate.

Nate shook his head, "I'm not much of a drinker myself, even though Veronica tells me I need to loosen up every once in a while and have some fun."

"How are things with your sexy little scary wife?" Justin was being nosy.

Kale reached across the boat and smacked Justin in the back of the head. "Ass! You can't talk about someone's wife like that! You are lucky he doesn't come over here and deck you." Kale was starting to get angry and super annoyed.

"I'm sorry, that was rude."

"Oh, she'd actually think that was a compliment," Nate laughed.

"She really is hot, dude," Justin attempted to redeem himself.

"Thank you. I think so," Nate smiled. "I think we all have beautiful women. Devan is looking quite fine these days herself, though I think she always has."

"Devan? Yeah, she's still pretty, but she appears as worn as she is. Now Jeane, there's a woman. She still looks young and…"

"She gets botox, dickweed," Kale said, his temper reaching a boiling point.

"Really? I wouldn't have guessed. Huh, maybe I'll suggest that to Devan. She sure could use it. She's got these big dark circles under eyes and those lines on her forehead."

Kale picked up his fishing pole like he was going to hit Justin with it. Nate grabbed it and shook his head no. Justin kept going on and on why Jeane was awesome and Devan was not. Kale looked down where Justin was standing; there was a large anchor attached to a rope. Kale took one step to cross the length of the boat, picked up the rope and swiftly looped it around his calves before Justin even realized Kale was there.

"Hey, what are—" Kale slapped his hand over Justin's mouth, snatched the duct tape that was sitting there and tore a piece off with his free hand and his teeth then put it over Justin's mouth. He picked him up and threw him over the side of the boat. Nate and Will turned their heads when they heard the splash. "*Bon Voyage*, mother fucker."

Nate put a firm hand on Kale's shoulder, bringing him back to reality. By the amount of the pressure Nate put on Kale's shoulder, he was pretty sure Nate knew exactly the type of daydream he just experienced.

"Hey, I got one what do I do?" Justin asked freaking out.

Will went over to help him. "Have you ever fished a day in your life?"

"No," Justin said.

"Well that explains a lot," Kale muttered under his breath.

Will reeled in the fish. It was a small mouth bass. "Here hold it like this and I'll take your picture with it."

"Ew, I'm not touching that slimy thing!" Justin was disgusted. "I don't want to smell like fish all day."

"Why did you even come?"

"Jeane told me to," Justin shrugged his shoulders.

"Didn't know Jeane was your boss," Will commented.

Nate sat there listening to everything but said nothing, his eyes traveling from person to person.

"She's not my boss." Justin was defensive and didn't stop talking for another ten minutes about how she was not his boss and tried to explain to everyone what his job was exactly to prove she wasn't his boss.

"For the love of God, will you please shut the hell up? You are scaring the fish away," Will finally said. The rest of the time while they were fishing was quiet.

The guys weren't back from fishing yet when the women and children arrived back at the cabin. The kids asked if they could swim so Devan and Veronica sat down by the lake and watched them.

"I can't believe how dark you are," Devan remarked. "It still amazes me how you get out in the sun for two hours and you are a bronzed goddess."

"Oh Dee, I'm half Italian, so it comes naturally," Veronica giggled as she watched the tiny ripples of water move across her tan toes. They heard a boat coming around the corner. Devan looked up and saw Will's boat slow down by the *no wake* buoys and head over to the dock. Will drove the boat close enough to the dock to drop off Kale, Nate and Justin. They thanked him and walked over to where Devan and Veronica were sitting.

"Hey Uncle Nate, come play with us," Cyrus attempted to splash water towards him.

Nate took his shoes off, handed his shirt to Veronica and went in the water to play with the kids.

"I've been thinking about kids lately," Veronica began.

"What?" Devan was truly surprised.

"Don't act all shocked and shit."

"I'm sorry, I am. I thought…"

"I know what you thought, but look at that," Veronica pointed at Nate picking up the kids and throwing them. "I can't deprive him. He would be a great dad. I would be taking away an opportunity—fatherhood."

"You are serious?"

"Yes, I am." Veronica was serious.

"When?"

"I don't know…not now, but maybe in a year or two."

"You realize you are thirty-seven?"

"I am aware, thank you."

"You just don't want to wait forever, that's all."

"I know," Veronica sighed. "Well you don't have forever either."

"I don't want more children," Devan said firmly.

"I'm not talking about kids Dee. You know what I'm talking about." Veronica stared at her.

"I'm working on it, things are—"

Veronica interrupted her. "Going to happen sooner than you think. I don't know why, Dee, but I just have this feeling something is going to happen very soon."

When the kids were tired of swimming, they all headed back up to the cabin. As Kale and Nate started pulling things out to make dinner, Devan helped the kids with their wet swimsuits. When the chaos was over, she decided to leave for a bit to clear her head and perhaps, write a little. She told Nate and Kale her plan to take out the boat as Veronica went off to take a bath. Justin and Jeane were nowhere to be seen.

As Devan walked out the door, she could hear someone following her. She turned around to see who it was. "Ugh, Jeane, what do you want?"

Jeane huffed. "God, Devan, you act like I make your skin crawl these days." *Well you do*, Devan thought to herself. "I just wanted to ride with you. I need a break from all that noise. Not to mention, I left my Gucci sunglasses on that island where we had the picnic.

"You mean your children?"

"Yes, *that* noise!"

"Fine, whatever. Untie the front and I'll get the back." They uncovered the boat and climbed in. Devan headed toward the island. When they arrived, Jeane took off searching for her sunglasses allowing Devan time to do some writing.

The sky began to darken every second they were out there.

"Jeane, I hope you found what you need because we need to leave now," she said as it thundered overhead.

"One more minute, Devan, I have to find them."

"What are you looking for that is so important?"

"My Gucci sunglasses."

It started raining. "Christ, Jeane, buy another a pair. We need to leave."

The rain was now coming down in sheets. Devan grabbed Jeane's arm, "We are leaving now!"

The girls jumped in the boat and Devan started the motor. Soon they were on their way back to the cabin. The water was getting choppy, and the boat was rocking back and forth with the momentum of the waves.

"Who the hell ever taught you to drive a boat?" Jeane hissed.

Devan slowed the motor so she could ride the waves instead of fighting them.

"You are going to make me sick," Jeane said, her face a light shade of green.

A huge bolt of lightning lit up the dark sky. "Shut up and sit down!" The waves knocked Jeane on her ass. Devan pulled into a cove.

"Seriously? You are beaching the boat? Drive back." Jeane demanded.

"Jeane would you rather sit here and wait out the storm, or be on the open water and get struck by lightning?"

Jeane sat there and sulked. "I need those sunglasses. They are expensive. Justin is right. You have no common sense."

"I don't have common sense? You are wanting to be in the middle of a lake in a lightning storm, yet I'm the one with no common sense? And please—like Justin knows anything about common sense."

"He's a genius when it comes to hooking a client. That's more than I can say for Kale," Jeane challenged.

Devan whipped her head around, water spraying right in Jeane's face. "Kale is by far a better person than Justin." Devan glared at her.

"I disagree. Besides you should be agreeing with what I am saying. After all Justin is your husband."

"Is he? He seems to enjoy spending more time with you rather than with me or even our kids." Devan fired back at her.

"That's work, Devan," Jeane said as though it were an adequate explanation.

"Would it make you feel better if I told you I believed you?"

"It's not what you think." Jeane was immediately defensive.

"I don't care what the fuck it is! All I know is his kids hardly see him. Your kids hardly see you. Neither of you enjoy them. You leave Kale and me to raise them on our own." Devan was losing her patience and quickly.

"You do a good job taking care of them," Jeane pointed out.

"Coming from you, I don't consider that a compliment." Devan said coldly.

"Let's just be honest with one another Dee. Neither of us is happy in our marriages. Your husband is never home and is consumed with work, and mine well, mine is—" Devan cut her off.

"Perfect! Yours is perfect! You can't even see it. You are so blinded by greed and whatever else—I don't even know!"

"Hardly! He is overly opinionated, too family conscious and he looks like a giant mountain man." She was right about the last thing. "I know he is part of your family and—"

"Yes, he is family, so you better shut your fucking mouth before you regret it." She grabbed Jeane's arm with one hand and made a fist with the other ready to take her down. Her eyes pierced right through Jeane. "You aren't worth it." Devan let go of Jeane's arm and dropped her fist.

"What did I do to you?" Jeane decided to press her luck. "First you blamed me for your parents moving and then something about ruining your life. Now you want to hit me for complaining about my own husband. I mean, I get that you are upset, and I can see how you would blame me, but this feels as though there is something else there." She could do it! She could tell her everything right here right now, yet what kind of damage would that cause Kale and those poor kids. She took a deep breath, sat down and placed her hands on the steering wheel and exhaled loudly.

"I'm sorry Jeane. My behavior is absolutely deplorable."

Jeane nodded, "It'll be okay. Justin warned me you were a hot head like Kale."

Devan scoffed. "Listen closely," she demanded. Devan stood up, walked out from behind the steering wheel, went over and bent down so she was face-to-face with Jeane. "I know you are not the honest person you claim to be. You are a sinister woman with secrets that no one knows." Jeane gulped. "Why don't you just leave Kale and the kids and make yourself happy. You don't want to be burdened with them. And if Kale is so horrible—"

"I don't hate them Devan," Jeane said.

"Well that's good to know, however, you don't exactly appreciate them either, do you? Be honest with yourself. Did you ever think that maybe doing what is best for your children would release you from that burden?"

"You make it sound like I'm a horrible mother," Jeane frowned.

"What's Sage's favorite color?"

"Pink of course."

"Wrong, it's green," Devan explained, as she knew she would have to. "Sage green to be exact."

"Oh yeah, because of her name. That makes sense." Jeane was starting to regret entering this conversation at all.

"What does Joey want to be when he grows up?"

"An architect, same as his dad," Jeane spoke confidently.

"Wrong again, he wants to be a marine biologist,"

"He's only thirteen, he doesn't even know what that is," Jeane said.

"Jeane, he's almost fifteen," Devan was slightly annoyed.

"Try me on Kai," Jeane challenged.

"Okay…" Devan began, "That's easy. Who is Kai's best friend at school?"

Jeane answered her triumphantly, "It's Joshua, the kid that just moved from Arizona!"

"Wrong, wrong again! He can't stand the kid from Arizona whose name is Brian. His best friend is—You don't deserve to know. Why are you really here Jeane?"

"I wanted my sunglasses!"

Devan rolled her eyes. "Why are you still with your family?"

"I care about them!"

"Bullshit! I think you stick around to make everyone miserable."

Jeane huffed but kept her mouth shut. Devan waited for a smartass comment, however Jeane didn't utter a single word. When the storm let up, they headed back to the cabin.

When they reached the dock, Justin was there to catch the boat and help tie it up. He told Jeane, "Your uncle called, we have to leave early for a meeting in Florida." Jeane hopped out of the boat as soon as she could and stalked toward the cabin.

After Justin tied the front of the boat and Devan tied the back, Devan got out and although Justin was right there, he didn't even offer to help her.

"You really should think about how you treat people," he said and trotted up the hill not giving her a chance to defend herself.

So, the witch texted her minion and got him to say they had to leave. Wow! Good riddance!

Chapter 29

Devan was almost ready for the wedding. She looked in the mirror and frowned. She put her hands to her hairline and tried pulling it back to make the lines on her forehead disappear. They only slightly went away. She peered down at the pile of make up on the counter and picked up her concealer. She opened it up and ran it under both of her eyes to cover her dark circles. As she blended it in, she wished she could go back to her twenties when her skin didn't show her age. She sighed and continued applying her make up. There was a knock on the door, "Monty you about ready?" She faced the mirror again and ran her hands down her sides. *Well, at least the dress is nice.*

She opened the door and Kale was still standing there. He stepped back and took a good long look at her. "You look amazing!"

"I appreciate the compliment, but you really should consider getting your eyes checked," she said, a trace of sadness in her voice.

"What does that mean?" Kale asked her, his eyebrows raised.

"I look old."

"Hardly," Kale exclaimed.

"Then you are blind," Devan retorted.

"No, you are—" Kale spoke as he stared in to her eyes. "I am looking at the most beautiful blue eyes I have ever seen, and they are looking back at me. I see lips that I want to kiss every second of every day. I see nothing but perfection when I look at you."

"Wow you *are* crazy," Devan gave a nervous chuckle. Justin never complimented her, and it was weird hearing it from someone when she felt so bad about herself all the time.

"You are right. I am crazy," Kale told her. "Crazy about you—always have been always will be."

As Devan, Veronica, Kale, and Nate were walking across the field, Devan remembered that she had left the book back at the cabin. She ran back, grabbed the package that contained the book and put it in her purse. Then she hurried to catch up to the others.

There were five rows of white chairs on the right and five rows on the left of an aisle of grass with rose petals sprinkled down center over a runner that led up to a beautifully decorated arbor. The chairs that were closest to the middle were accented with pale green bows. Nate was standing under the arbor. Will was confused when he showed up.

"What's going on?"

"You are about to get married," Nate told him. Will glanced around to see his family and friends.

"I'm getting married?" Will was in shock.

Nate nodded and put his hand on his shoulder. "Follow me, your bride will be here any minute." Nate escorted Will down to the alter. On the way he glimpsed at people and forced a smile and thanked them for being there, though he was still unsure what in the hell was going on. He looked at Nate and then out at the lake.

"So, I'm getting married and I have a bride?"

Nate pointed to the trees that Will had just come through. Alison was standing in a gorgeous white dress that was light and airy. The bottom was swinging in the breeze that was blowing in from the lake. Alison was being escorted by Billie who was wearing a pale green dress. Will took a deep breath and looked at Nate again, who smiled and gestured to the trees once more. Will turned his head and saw his future wife and his daughter coming towards him. They stopped in front of him.

"William McGrudle, will you marry me?" Alison asked.

"Is this a joke?" Will was still in shock.

Alison shook her head no.

"You got all these people together to come here so you could marry me?"

Alison nodded her head.

"Well, Christ, woman, a little warning would have been nice," Will said.

"It's a surprise wedding. I couldn't tell you," she explained.

"I'm surprised all right. So, I take it you expect me to go through with this after you have told me the past few years you don't wanna marry me? That you don't need a paper telling you who you can and can't love?"

"You told me when I was ready, and I'm ready now!" Alison was now slightly worried that maybe this wasn't such a good idea.

Will shook his head and wiped the sweat off his forehead again and looked her straight in the eyes. "So—what do I get?"

"You get me always and forever."

"Well correct me if I'm wrong, didn't I already have you?" he questioned.

"Yeah, but now it'll be on paper and it will be a lot harder to get rid of me," Alison said. "You finally get to call me your wife."

"Hmmm," Will sounded like he was trying to get his bearrings. "You takin' my last name?"

"If you'll let me," Alison replied softly.

"Okay. And I get to keep you, huh?"

"That's what I was thinking," she grinned.

"Ah, baby, that's all I have ever wanted. You know damn well I'll marry you," he beamed.

"Well, now that that's been decided. May I proceed?" Nate asked.

"You? You're gonna marry us?"

"Yes, if that's all right," Nate said.

"I didn't know you could do that."

"Yes, I have been ordained for quite some time, so that I could perform funeral services."

"Well, this wedding will go down in the books I tell you. Married by a mortician!" Will exclaimed.

Everyone laughed.

"Wait, so you all knew about this surprise wedding? And none of ya let it slip?"

All of the guests said 'yes'.

"Well, I'll be damned. Okay cousin, marry us then."

"Friends and family, we are gathered here today by something rare and beautiful—true love."

Veronica and Kale both squeezed Devan's hands they were holding. Devan knew that one day in the near future she and Kale would finally have their time. She rested her head on his arm and breathed in his scent. She was so glad that the two assholes had to leave. It made this moment perfect.

"I now pronounce you husband and wife. You may kiss your bride. Will didn't hesitate. He grabbed Alison around the waist, bent her over backwards and kissed her. Everyone applauded.

The marina was decorated for the occasion. It was amazing what they were able to accomplish in such a short time. The kids were already sitting at a table with a plateful of food when Devan and Kale found them. There was a nice array of different southern dishes and desserts. In the middle of the marina was a round table with a white three-tiered wedding cake.

As they were getting ready to cut the cake, Alison asked Devan to come up. Devan reached into her purse, took out the package she had put in there earlier and handed it to Alison. Alison then handed it to Will without explanation. He looked at it then said, "I'm sorry, honey, I didn't have time to get you a wedding gift." A roar of laughter came from the people who had crowded around them.

"Just open it," Alison urged. When Will opened the package, he saw a printed copy of the story that Devan and Alison had written together. He opened the book to the first page and read the dedication. Then he flipped a few pages ahead and read a couple of lines. Finally, he turned to Alison.

"This is our story." Will was trying not to let a tear escape that was in the corner of his eye. Alison nodded, "I had help from Devan and Veronica."

"I'd like to have y'alls attention." Will spoke loudly and the guests quieted down.

"I'd like to thank y'all for coming today and doing such a great job of not telling me anything." People laughed. "Seriously though, it means a lot to me and to my wife—so fun to say that—my wife. I also want to share a story with you." He took a sip from his glass and continued, "Several years ago I met this kid who wanted to impress his girlfriend. The second I saw them together I immediately thought of my long-lost love. Well, years later they came back and found a locket on one of the islands. Now this locket wasn't just some old rusty trinket, it was, in fact, the same locket my true love, Alison, had lost many years prior. It was a locket I had given her that had our pictures in it. When I opened it, I saw that my picture had faded to the point you could hardly see anything, but Alison's picture still showed her beauty. Fast forward a few years later, I get this call from the guy who had helped find the locket. He claimed he found my long-lost love. And today, we are here, surrounded by our family and friends, celebrating one of the happiest moments of our lives. All thanks to these two kids. Thank you, Devan and Kale. Words cannot express how grateful I am." Will picked up his glass and toasted. "Thanks to all of you for being here with us. Now let's celebrate!"

The wedding reception lasted well into the evening. They only had a few days of vacation left so Kale and Devan decided to leave about ten, apologizing for not staying until the end.

"Don't worry about it, man," Will said, Alison next to him. "We know you need to get these kids to bed," he glanced over at Cyrus, who was in the middle of a huge yawn.

"We have plans to take the boat out tomorrow in the afternoon," Devan said, "We'll stop by and say hi," she promised.

Alison had tears in her eyes again. "We cannot thank the two of you enough. You've made all our dreams come true!"

"Don't be silly, it was our pleasure!" Devan hugged them both.

"See you guys tomorrow!" Kale waved as he and Devan ushered the kids out the door and back to the cabin.

The next day Will took everyone out on a large pontoon with a hefty motor. They tubed, swam, and boated most of the day. On the way back they stopped in a hidden cove. The guys fished while the girls walked along the shoreline in search of lake treasures. Cyrus caught a five-pound blue channel catfish that he was very proud of. He couldn't wait to share the news with his father, who was of course not there to be a part of it.

After dinner Devan heard Cyrus calling her. "Mommy, can I call Daddy from the computer?" Cyrus begged carrying her lap top. She could see her laptop wobble in his arms. She quickly grabbed it and it set it down on the table gently.

"Cy, buddy, I told you, you have to ask before touching my stuff," Devan spoke gently.

"I'm sorry," Cyrus apologized. "Can I still call Daddy?"

Devan looked at her watch, "Let me text him first to make sure he's not in a meeting."

She texted Justin and he responded saying he just got to the hotel and was free to talk to Cyrus. She took the computer into the kitchen, set it on the counter, opened it and turned it on.

"Now, I have no idea how to get you started," she said to him. Joey came in and offered to help. "Hey Cy, I am an expert at Skype."

Devan smiled at Joey. He was so sweet. The adults were working on cleaning up the dinner mess while Cyrus was talking to his dad. When he was done, Callie sat down and talked to Justin as well. When Callie was finished Devan asked Justin how the meetings were going.

"Pretty good. Looks like we should be done by Tuesday. So, can you or Kale pick Jeane and me up at the airport on Wednesday evening?"

"Yeah, we should be back home by Sunday night," she said as she heard someone knocking on his door.

"Dee, I gotta go, that's dinner," Justin told her.

"All right," Devan said.

"I'll call you tomorrow," he promised.

When he stepped away from the screen, she got up and finished clearing the table.

Afterwards she went to the back deck with the other adults. Kale got up and walked back in to the cabin, saying that he left his phone in his room and needed to check his email. Ten seconds after he had he shut the door, he opened it asking Devan to come in.

She stepped through the open door and stopped dead in her tracks. She saw Justin's hotel room—the blankets and sheets were moving on the bed and they heard loud moaning. Devan's heart plummeted to her stomach. "I put it on mute. We can hear them, but they can't hear us," Kale told her.

Devan didn't say anything she just stood there watching. Then she heard it, that obnoxious giggle that she hated so badly. That sound that made her squirm inside and felt like nails on a chalkboard in her ears. Kale looked up at her to make sure she was okay. The expression on her face was disgust, but she still didn't say anything. The light flipped on in the room and it was obvious who it was. Kale jumped up and grabbed his phone.

"What are you doing?" Devan wanted to know.

"Just watch," he said. Kale texted Justin. Justin picked up his phone and rolled his eyes.

"Hey babe, Kale texted that he can't pick us up from the airport."

"Of course, he can't, he's about as worthless as they come. Oh well your stupid wife will do it if I ask her nicely." Justin's phone buzzed again.

"Um babe? Kale said he would appreciate it if you did not call him worthless," Justin looked up at Jeane, a questioning expression upon his face.

"Why in the hell did you tell him I said that?" Jeane asked, glaring at him.

His phone buzzed again. "He said you shouldn't call Devan stupid, and that we should turn around."

"What? Why?"

Justin had a terrified expression his face as he slowly pivoted. Jeane spun around, the scowl on her face transformed to a wide-eyed open mouth gawk.

Kale waved and hit the mute button so he could talk. "Hey, I think that maybe you should find another ride. We'll be at the lawyer's office." Jeane stared at the screen. As Kale slowly shut the lap top, he heard Justin freaking out.

"Oh my god, he's gonna kill me! He's fucking gonna kill me!"

Kale looked at Devan. This time her face was blank. "You okay?" Kale was sincere.

"I mean yeah—"

"You don't look okay—"

"I'm just in shock I guess," Devan wasn't sure what to say let alone what to feel.

"Oh, come on, you knew. We all have known deep down inside," Kale said, frowning at her.

"No, I'm not shocked about that,"

"Well then why are you shocked?"

"I thought it would be harder than this. They just fell right into our laps." Devan shrugged.

Veronica walked in the door, "And you have a witness."

"You have two witnesses." Nate added as he stepped behind her.

"The kids didn't see it, did they?"

"No, we had them go to the marina for ice cream," Nate said.

"What do we tell the kids?" Devan asked Kale.

"Let's enjoy the rest of this trip and we will handle the kids when we get home."

Devan wasn't sure what to do. Part of her wanted to take Kale in to the bedroom right then and there, yet part of her was pissed. She was pissed that she had wasted so much time and energy on Justin for so many years. She was still a bit worried that Jeane would try to do something to make life a living hell for Kale. Nevertheless, there was also this huge weight lifted off her chest. Soon her whole life would be ahead of her. Her dreams could finally start coming true. Justin wouldn't be around as much to drag her down. She would still have to deal with him because of the kids, but that would be it. She excused herself saying she needed some time to herself. On the way out the door she grabbed her phone. After about a ten-minute walk, she pulled her phone out and dialed a number.

"Antoinette? It's time."

Chapter 30

Justin and Jeane arrived at the lawyers' office unsure of what to expect. The administrative assistant led them to a room and had them sit down.

"He will be with you shortly," she told them as she backed out of the room through the door.

Justin was sweating profusely. Jeane handed him a pack of tissues from her purse. "I was planning on saving these for my fake cry, but the way you are melting screams GUILTY!"

"I'm sorry, I can't help it, I'm nervous, Jeane," Justin defended himself. She rolled her eyes as he blotted his face.

"Hello, my name is James Crenshaw," a good-looking man said as he walked into the office. "I'll be the one overseeing your case." He shook both Justin's and Jeane's hands, sat in his chair, then picked up two envelopes from his desk.

"I'm sorry my assistant just gave me your files." He flipped through the first file and said "Ms. Cadence, I see you are requesting a divorce from a Kale K. Iakona." He glanced up from the file. "K—ale Ia—kona from Hawaii?"

"I take it you know him?" Jeane inquired.

"I played football with him in high school." He picked up the second file and started sifting through it. The expression on his face went from a look of concentration to one of amusement. James' eyes darted back and forth between the two files, his smile growing bigger with each pass. Finally, he set the files down and laughed. "Ah this is too much."

"Excuse me, I don't see how this is amusing at all," Jeane stated, her voice full of annoyance.

"I'm sorry I just thought he married—never mind." James was doing some serious thinking as he reread Jeane's file and then Justin's, his head turning every few minutes. James' brow was furrowed with confusion though the same amusing grin was plastered upon his face. "Wow, okay," James said at last, trying to grasp what he had just read.

"You seem to be shocked. Why is that?" Jeane asked.

"How much time do you have?"

"As long as it takes," Jeane replied automatically.

James stood up and walked towards the door of his office. "Samantha, hold all my calls," He yelled out the door before he closed it and turned to look at the two people sitting in front of him. "Your husband stole my girlfriend in high school," James began to explain.

"Okay, no offense, but how is this relevant?" Jeane responded impatiently. "Maybe we should find another lawyer, Mr. Crenshaw. I don't think you'll be a good fit for us," She stood up.

"Oh no, you are going to want me on your case." He gestured for Jeane to sit back down.

"And why is that Mr. Crenshaw?"

"My girlfriend was Devan Montgomery. In fact, I heard she and Kale got married."

"They did—to us," Justin piped up.

"You," he pointed to Justin, "married Devan? She didn't marry Kale?"

"No dude, they have been family friends for years. They are practically siblings," Justin answered.

"Very interesting. Well, Mr. Jameson, I'm sorry to give you such bad news then. Your wife and Kale Iakona did not have a family relationship. They had something quite a bit deeper."

Jeane moved her eyes over to Justin. He was trying to put the pieces together.

"No, he's a good guy. No offense hon," he said to Jeane knowing that she thought Kale was not as good as he thought. "Kale would never do that to me, or to anyone."

"Wait, you two are together?" James was puzzled.

Jeane was embarrassed. "Kind of," she said quietly.

"Kinda? Really? Uh, we've been together for years, Jeane," Justin gave her a dirty look. He couldn't believe that she admitted it after accusing him of appearing *guilty* due to his perspiration.

She ignored him and continued. "We've been having an affair for years, and we just got caught red-handed," she said it as though it wasn't that big of a deal.

"Oh—so that makes things a little harder, you understand that, right?"

They both nodded.

"I'm sorry, are you sure there was nothing going on between them? If you saw them in high school—"

"Is this going to be too difficult for you Mr. Crenshaw?" Jeane asked.

"On the contrary, this will be quite exciting," James smirked.

After a long conversation, Justin and Jeane left. James gave them his card and held on to Jeane's hand a little too long. "Give me a call if you think of anything else."

In the car Justin, wouldn't drop the Kale and Devan thing. "I don't know if I like this guy—I don't believe him."

"You don't think it's possible?" Jeane's voice was full of doubt.

"No, I don't," Justin said stubbornly.

"I'm not so sure," Jeane sneered. "I never really thought about it before. He's way too overprotective of her."

"Uh, yeah, she's basically his little sister. He's always been that way with her."

"Justin shut up and look at the facts." The more Jeane thought about it, the more sense it was making to her, and she was getting frustrated with Justin's lack of understanding.

"What facts?" he grumbled.

"For starters, they are always defending one another to us."

"Yeah, they are like a family," Justin mused.

"They are always together,"

"Yes, Jeane, we tell them to help each other out while we are gone," Justin reminded her. "And we are always gone."

"How many times has he threatened you?" Jeane was determined to get Justin to see what the lawyer inferred.

"Can't say I didn't deserve it," he mumbled.

"Justin, stop being so stupid!"

❧❧❧

When Kale and Devan got back from their trip, he helped her unload her car and take things into her house.

"Hey, want me to take care of all those weeds tomorrow?" Kale asked her as they were walking.

"What weeds?" Devan took a suitcase out of his hands.

"The ones that are all over your front yard."

Devan glanced out her big picture window to see her front yard spotted in yellow. Cyrus and Kai were picking them. She hadn't noticed all the dandelions that had popped up.

"Nah, I don't mind them." The boys came in and each handed her a bouquet. She thanked them then put them in two cups full of water on her kitchen counter.

"I thought those things only popped up in the spring." Kale commented.

"Don't you guys have these in Hawaii as well? I never paid attention."

"Not like you do here. They are everywhere in Ohio."

"Yes, but they can bloom several times a year usually from May to October." *Why do I know that?*

"How's your little oak tree doing?" Kale looked on the counter and saw it next to the window.

"I'm not sure it is doing that well," Kale got a closer glimpse at the shriveling plant and recommended watering it more. "I think it just needs planted in the ground. I don't think it will last if we wait to take it to Hawaii."

"Maybe you should do that soon before it dies completely," Kale suggested. "Well, I'm gonna go home and unpack. Don't forget I'm picking you up at 9:45 tomorrow." He kissed her on the cheek and stepped out the door. She looked at the vase trying to figure out why she had this sudden interest in dandelions. *Devan get your head in the right place. You are meeting with the lawyer tomorrow.*

The next morning Kale picked up Devan. When they got to the lawyer's office, they saw Antoinette waiting for them in the lobby.

"Antoinette, what a surprise." Kale was shocked. He went over and kissed her on the cheek. Devan followed suit.

"You shouldn't be surprised, my dears, I always oversee my investments."

"You don't have to take this on, we can handle it," Kale told her.

"No, I am taking care of this. I'm going to make sure that my grandson does not get screwed over by that bitch," Antoinette said. "No offense Devan, but I'm not worried about Justin. He's going to be easy." Devan agreed. She knew exactly what Antoinette was saying.

"Ah Mrs. VonStross, how lovely to see you." A fairly tall man in his 30's with short dark hair, dark chocolate brown eyes, and wide, broad shoulders wearing a handsome dark blue suit shook her hand and kissed her on the cheek. He turned to face the other two.

"You must be Devan and Kale, it's a pleasure to meet you." He shook their hands. Devan thought he looked familiar, but she couldn't pin point where she had seen him before.

"My name is Brandon Swanson, I'll be handling your case," he smiled. "I apologize, my grandfather is out of town, however I promise to give you the same expertise you would have gotten from him."

"Brandon Swanson," Devan said out loud without meaning to.

"Yes," he said, knowingly.

"How do I know you?" Devan wondered.

"You may have heard my name a time or two in high school. I graduated two years after you did."

Devan checked him out. He could tell she was trying too hard. He decided to make it easier on her and said one word:

"Flagpole—"

"Oh my god, that was you?"

He affirmed that it was, apparently undisturbed that she remembered this about him.

"I am so sorry that happened to you," Devan began. She remembered who did it too and felt a swoop of sickness in the pit of her stomach.

"I'm over it now," Brandon professed. "And, no, I didn't go the psyche ward," he smiled at her.

"So, what happened to you?"

"My parents got a divorce, and I moved with my mom out of state," he informed her.

"Okay, you guys can catch up later. I have to be in Chicago at five for a meeting." Antoinette took charge.

"I'm sorry, follow me." Brandon instructed.

They followed him to a conference room where they sat and discussed what had happened prior.

"This really should not be that difficult. If you don't upset Jeane this could be done in about two to three months maybe even sooner." He then faced Devan, "As for you—I don't foresee any issues. However, I would suggest filing for alimony. You are entitled to it."

"I just want to be done," Devan assured him.

"Go home and really think about it," Antoinette added. Devan agreed to do that. They stood and Kale shook Brandon's hand. Devan grasped his hand, looked him in the eyes and said, "I'm sorry you were treated so poorly, but in spite of it you are a success."

"I like to think that," he chuckled.

September 2016

Kale drove by the Montgomery's old house and saw city trucks in the back, so he backed his car up and pulled in the driveway. He ran into the backyard and saw them cutting down a pine tree. The oak was still there. He breathed a sigh of relief. "Hey," he said as he walked up to one of the workers. The guy took his headphones off and looked up at Kale.

"Can I help you?" he asked politely.

"Yes, actually you can. This was my girlfriend's childhood home—" *Did I just say girlfriend?* He grinned to himself and continued. "See that huge oak? That was her favorite tree. I was wondering if I could have a part of it?"

The guy rubbed his jaw and grinned at Kale, "Sure thing," The worker glanced up at the massive tree. "What part did you want?"

Kale just looked at him and at the tree. He hadn't thought that far ahead. "Um…well, do you see where that rope is up there?" he pointed to the old tattered rope that was embedded in the lowest thick branch.

"Yup. How about I give you a few small branches? You can make a picture frame out of it, and then I'll cut off the part you showed me. Will that work?"

Kale nodded. The worker picked up a chainsaw and went to work. When he handed the pieces of wood to Kale he said, "She must be really special."

"She's the love of my life."

Kale shook his hand and started to leave. "Hey, tall dude," the guy called after him. Kale turned around to see him coming towards him with something in his hands. "I don't know if it will work or not, but you should take these acorns. Maybe she can grow an oak tree of her own."

Kale thanked him then asked, "When are they demolishing the house?"

The man asked Kale to follow him over to an informal desk made up of a piece of plywood balancing precariously on two uneven tool boxes. The worker held up two pieces of paper. Kale narrowed his brow as he checked out each one. The first one appeared to be a schedule. The second one was a sort of map of all the houses on the road.

"They are doing those two in a few weeks," the guy said as he pointed to the houses that were on the edge of the main road. "Looks like this one and the one across the street are scheduled after the holidays. Let me give you my number, and you can give me call if you want to bring her by. I have a buddy that does the house stuff who will be able to get you in." He dug in his pocket and handed Kale a business card.

"You're Mike?" Kale asked.

"Yup," he confirmed.

"I'm Kale," he stated as he extended his hand.

"Nice to meet you Kale. Maybe I'll hear from you after a while. Remember you have until January second to bring her back." Kale shook his hand and thanked him again.

When he got back in the truck, he saw he had missed a call from Jeane. He groaned as, he listened to the voicemail. She was requesting a lunch meeting in the next hour. He texted her back agreeing to meet her.

She was already waiting when he got to the restaurant. "Thank you for meeting me," Jeane began.

"Let's just get on with it, please," Kale said pulling out the chair and sitting down.

"Would you like to order something first?"

Why is she being nice? Kale thought. *What does she have up her sleeve?* "No, I want to know why I'm here," he said glaring at her.

"Relax Kale, you don't have to be so defensive," she snarked. "I just want to talk about what is going to happen with your future." She took a long sip of her red wine.

"Just take all the money Jeane, and let me have the kids, please," he pleaded.

"Kale, stop begging," she rolled her eyes. "Realistically speaking I won't be able to take care of the kids as well as you can. My offer is half of all the assets, you get full custody, but I get to see them *whenever* I want. You and the kids have to move to Hawaii, and—"she cleared her throat, "You have to stay on with the company for at least two years."

I thought I wouldn't have a job, and she's letting me have the kids and half of everything. Something doesn't feel right. Kale studied her face, searching for a hint; waiting for her to do something that would give him a clue as to what she was up to. "Is there anything else?" he finally asked.

"Yes, I want everything signed by tomorrow, so have your lawyer get you in right away. I want to file this so we can get it over and done." She grabbed her wine goblet and put it to her mouth to take another sip. Suddenly, instead of taking a drink she put it down and looked at Kale.

"Kale, have you seen Devan lately?"

"No," he replied a little too quickly, worried where this conversation was going.

"Will you be?" Jeane wondered.

"I don't know. Why do you ask?" Kale raised an eyebrow at her waiting for a smart-ass remark.

"I just wondered how she was with all of this," Jeane claimed, her sickening sweet voice was full of fake worry. "You guys have always had a *close* relationship, haven't you?" *I don't like where she is going with this. I knew it!* Kale tried to remain calm.

"Family bond of sorts," he responded.

"Mmmm, well she's probably going through a lot and will most likely need you to lean on. You should probably check on her. Especially since her family is not near." Jeane tried too hard to pretend to give a damn. Kale was well aware of her phony concern.

"Well, if that's it, then I need to go meet with my lawyer while he is in his office." Kale said as he stood up to take his leave. He wanted to get away from her as soon as he possibly could.

"That is all." Jeane turned her eyes away from Kale and took another sip of her wine.

❧❦ ❦❧

"I think she knows," Kale said to Brandon a short time later.

"What?"

"Jeane. I think she knows about Devan and me," he tried to explain. "I just have this terrible gut feeling like I've missed something in those papers and it's going to bite me in the ass."

"Kale, we've looked over everything with a fine-tooth comb," Brandon said. "Two things worry me—*you*, staying on with the company, and *her* getting to see the kids *whenever* she wants."

"I wouldn't worry too much about the kids, she's never had or made time for them anyway."

"Then go ahead and sign it. Become a free man!"

Kale signed it and handed it back to the lawyer.

"Kale, one last thing," he said. "I think it would be best if you and Devan only saw each other when other people are around until this is all done. If Jeane suspects anything before you go to court, she can throw all of this out and do whatever she can to make your life miserable. I assume she has a good lawyer. I don't want you to risk *anything*."

"Oh, I forgot to look. Who is her lawyer?" He picked up the folder and his eyes grew large.

"Oh shit! Of course," Kale closed his eyes. "This couldn't be that clean-cut."

"Something wrong?" Brandon asked. Kale's phone rang. He nodded at the lawyer but answered the phone. It was Devan.

"We have a huge problem! Do you know who Justin's lawyer is?" she said in a panicked voice.

"Let me guess—James the great?" Kale asked staring at the paper in his hands.

"How did you know?" Devan questioned him.

"I'm with Brandon now and just found out that's who Jeane is using too," Kale told her.

"Yeah, well you better talk to him and clarify everything. I was hoping this would be easy and straight forward!" Devan laughed nervously.

"Will do." Kale hung up the phone and took a deep breath.

"That was Devan. Justin is using the same lawyer," Kale sighed.

"It's not an issue, I am representing both of you," the lawyer said calmly.

"Well there's a slight conflict of interest. James Crenshaw used to date Devan in high school. I may or may not have threatened him several times that school year."

"I don't remember that," Brandon confessed. "I only remember all the abuse he put me through."

"I'm so sorry he got to you, too—Devan told me a little," Kale admitted. "Are you sure you want to do this?"

"Like I told Devan the other day, I'm over it. It might be a little awkward, but the only thing I'm worried about is what you are about to tell me." he looked closely at Kale, "What do I need to know?"

"I kind of stole Devan from him. Not exactly, yet that's what he believed." Kale sat down in the chair and added, "And then Devan and I were together pretty much the rest of our high school days. Everyone thought we were going to get married." Kale's eyes shifted down to the floor. "*I* thought we were going to get married."

He looked at Kale, wide-eyed and held out his hand. "Give me back those papers! I'm going to go over them a few more times, and have my partner check them as well—just to play it safe," he said. "And you need to remember what I said about Devan. I'll go over everything with her tomorrow. Keep it short when you see her."

"I really appreciate it. Thank you," Kale stood up, shook his hand, and got ready to leave.

"Is there anything else I need to know about?" Brandon asked. Kale stopped as memories of a certain storm rolled in to his mind, and how passion had taken ahold of him. *Should I or shouldn't I?* He didn't answer fast enough.

"Kale, I'm your lawyer. I need to know if there is anything that can hurt your case. We need to be prepared if she decides to turn this dissolution into a divorce."

Kale reluctantly sat back down in the chair.

Chapter 31

October 2016

Back in August, Nate had become Kale's running partner in the morning since Kale and Devan were trying to keep their distance from one another. Devan had requested Veronica to join her as well. While she wasn't one to run or jog, she agreed to walk with Devan to help keep her occupied. However, Devan had been so busy with the kids, the dissolution and many other things that she hadn't been able to see much of anyone over the past month or so.

"So, do you like Donald?" Veronica asked through a yawn one morning.

"Who's Donald?" Devan had no clue.

"Um...your lawyer," Veronica raised an eyebrow at her.

"Oh, no, it's Brandon."

"Brandon? I thought Antoinette set you up with Donald."

"How did I not tell you this? Brandon is Donald's grandson," Devan explained.

"And he's Swanny, the kid that was put on the flagpole."

"Swanny? Holy shit! That's awesome, now tell me more." Veronica said.

"Well, Justin hasn't contacted me at all. I have no idea what is up with him. I guess I didn't know what to expect, but I figured he'd contact me a few times. Oh well."

"Maybe he is really hurt," Veronica suggested.

"Him? Why the hell would he be hurt?" Devan fumed.

"Um...well," she started, "You know James didn't keep his mouth shut. And Justin's been under the impression that you and Kale have basically been cousins your whole life. He's always liked Kale."

"Yeah," Devan sneered. "He liked Kale better than his own wife."
"EX-wife!"

"Almost," Devan smiled.

"Well, I think you guys need to listen to Brandon and still avoid each other. I don't think Justin will be a problem, but Jeane *is* a problem. You and Kale have made it this long. It's not like you guys were doing anything anyway," she added. "So, it shouldn't be that big of a deal."

"Well..." Devan slowed her pace down.

Veronica stopped and captured Devan's arm making her come to a halt. "What did you do?"

Devan refused to look at her and gave a simplified answer of *stuff*.

"Stuff? What stuff and when?" Veronica asked.

"It's not important—" Devan tried to begin walking again.

"Shit too! You better tell me right now Devan Marie!!" Veronica demanded grabbing onto both of her arms. "I'm not going to let you go until you give me an exact detailed account of everything that happened!"

Devan knew that Veronica meant business. She looked her right in the eyes and sighed. "I will tell you in the privacy of my own home in my basement where the kids can't hear us. Hopefully they are still sleeping."

Veronica took off in a sprint to meet Devan at her house. She was anxious to get all the details. Devan ran after her. She was happy to see Veronica finally breaking a sweat. When they got to Devan's house, they checked to make sure the kids were asleep and then went straight to the basement where Devan started spilling all her secrets that she had kept hidden for the past few months. Veronica sat there and listened with her mouth open the whole time. Finally, Devan finished.

"Is that everything?" Veronica was disheartened. Devan nodded. "I cannot believe neither of you told me. I am disappointed, and happy, yet sad. It's a whirlwind of emotions over here." Veronica fanned herself. "You *know* you can trust me, *and* I'm your best friend!" she said offended. She was truly upset and hurt that Devan hadn't told her anything.

"I'm so sorry that I didn't tell you, Roni," she began. "It all happened so fast. My emotions were all over the place, and I didn't know what was going to happen." Devan took a deep breath. "Then we caught Justin and Jeane red-handed and I assumed it would be simple and easy, however nothing is ever easy when it comes to us." Devan was worried that she hurt her friend. "I really am sorry."

Veronica could see that Devan was sincere in her apology. "I'll forgive you on one condition,"

"What's that?" Devan asked.

"Next time, you have to tell me everything! And—the *moment* it happens," Veronica told her.

Devan laughed. "I promise!"

"Hopefully, you guys will get your *happily ever after* soon," Veronica winked. "When is your court date for the disillusion?"

"It's Friday," Devan said, as there was a fluttering in the pit of her stomach. She had no idea why she was apprehensive. Maybe it was because she was so close to getting what she had wanted her whole life—Kale. She voiced her feelings to Veronica.

"Nonsense, Devan," Veronica growled. "I think you're more worried about what Jeane might do to Kale!"

She has a point, Devan thought. *That woman is evil!*

⊷⊱ ⊰⊶

When Kale arrived at the municipal building on Friday, his lawyer, Brandon, and Devan were already there. He greeted them both with a handshake. It felt weird shaking Devan's hand, but it seemed more appropriate than hugging her like he wanted to do. Justin and Jeane approached them a few minutes later with their lawyer, James.

"James Crenshaw, attorney for Justin Jameson and Jeane Cadence. He extended his hand to Brandon.

"Brandon Swanson. I am representing Mr. Iakona and Mrs. Jameson."

Devan cringed at being called Mrs. Jameson. She couldn't wait to get rid of the name.

James strained his face like he was thinking hard. "Swanson, that sounds so familiar. I got suspended from school for three days from hanging a kid by that name on the flagpole. Good ol' Swanny." Devan's and Brandon's eyes met for a brief moment. James paused and eyeballed Brandon, "He couldn't possibly be related to you. He was tiny." He then nodded at Devan. "Mrs. Jameson, Mr. Iakona." Devan nodded back, unable to hide the look of disgust on her face from being called Mrs. Jameson again, which grew deeper after touching James's hand. She noticed he aged very well. She assumed he had Botox, the same as Jeane. His short brown hair was parted to the left. His skin had an unnatural golden glow. *They used the wrong color of spray tan on him*, Devan thought, but overall, he appeared professional and she didn't feel like she was near *James the Great*. It was nice to see that he had matured. *Maybe this won't be as uncomfortable as I imagined.* As James, Jeane, Kale and Brandon, walked into the court room, Devan and Justin sat down on opposite benches.

A few minutes had gone by and Justin finally spoke. "I'm sorry," he blurted out.

"A little late for that don't you think?" Devan replied.

"I mean, I'm sorry for..." he paused, "you're right."

Devan looked at him and saw what she guessed might be a tinge of remorse.

"Just know that I'm sorry for everything," he apologized.

"Okay, noted," was all Devan could muster. Justin didn't say anything else. He supposed it would be pointless, and he was right...Devan would never forgive him.

A little later the doors opened, and Jeane, Kale and both lawyers came out. The lawyers told Justin and Devan to come in and Kale and Jeane took a seat. "Would it be all right if I came by tomorrow afternoon while the kids are still in school and get the remainder of my belongings?" Jeane asked Kale.

He thought about it and glanced up at the ceiling then back at her. "Yeah, that's fine," Kale said. "Are you planning on seeing the kids before you go?"

"No, it might be best if I wait until you guys come out there for the holidays," she figured. "Have you decided when you are moving?"

Kale shook his head *no*. "I have to get the house ready to be put on the market, and truthfully, I want the kids to finish out the school year here."

"That makes sense, So, is Devan moving?"

"I honestly don't know…"

"Well, she should. Her family and your family are there, Justin will be there…*you* will be there," Jeane asserted.

Kale didn't like the tone in her voice. He shrugged his shoulders, "I guess that's not up to us, is it?" He was being honest as he and Devan hadn't discussed her moving yet. *I refuse to leave her behind!*

About a half hour later Devan, Justin and the lawyers came out. "Okay, let's go get the paperwork processed. Follow me," Brandon requested. Devan and Kale followed their lawyer, and Jeane and Justin followed theirs. When that was all taken care of, they headed out to the main entrance. Devan felt a presence behind her and hot breath on her neck.

"Wow after having two kids you still are pretty hot. Now that you will be single maybe we can pick up where we left off." It was James, and he was churning her stomach. She stood her ground and was as polite as possible.

"I respectfully decline," she said, remembering the last time she was alone with him. Devan shuttered at the thought…she could have died, and it would have been his fault between drugging her and crashing the car with her in it because he was drunk. She turned to walk away.

"Well, you really should reconsider," James voiced. "It's so hard to get back into the dating game especially with kids, and you have older ones too. Most guys don't like that." *And James the Great is back.* Devan rolled her eyes as she attempted to leave.

James grabbed her arm and pulled her towards him. Her lawyer had to keep a tight hold on Kale who was about to lose his cool. *How dare he touch her!* "Mr. Crenshaw please show my client respect," Brandon pressed while struggling to keep ahold of Kale.

James scoffed at Brandon and let go of Devan but peered intently into her eyes. "It's really a shame, you are so pretty." He touched a strand of her hair making her feel even more uncomfortable. Devan just stared at him, at a loss for words due to his behavior. "I know being a single mom is rough," James continued. "Then again maybe you already have someone waiting." He dropped her hair, turned and looked at Kale. "Have a good evening, Mr. Iakona," he said, and as he strutted past Devan, he smacked her ass. Kale shook the lawyer off and headed after James, eyes red and fists clenched.

Devan heard him coming and stepped in front of him "NO!" she screamed and wrapped her arms around his waist. He stopped. It had been weeks since he felt her arms holding him, and it felt so good. The sensation didn't last long. She was ripped away by Antoinette. "Not now," she voiced under her breath. "There are eyes everywhere." Devan reluctantly let go of Kale. Justin was shocked at his lawyer's actions. He still didn't fully believe James' story about Devan and Kale, especially after he saw James hit on Devan. He was thankful for his help, still something didn't sit well with him. As he stepped out the door, he saw James put his arm around Jeane as he whispered something in her ear. Justin looked back at Devan feeling like maybe he had made a mistake letting her get away. Perhaps, she wasn't as bad as he thought.

"Where in the hell did you come from?" Kale asked Antoinette completely distracted from James now.

"I told you, I always make sure my investments are taken care of," she said as she glared in the direction of Justin and Jeane before leading Devan and Kale out the door.

James, Justin, and Jeane were only twenty feet in front of them when James quit walking and pivoted around.

"Hey Kale, I never got a chance to ask…how are my sloppy seconds?"

"Mr. Crenshaw, you need to stop harassing my clients." Brandon was beginning to lose his patience. "It's very unprofessional."

James laughed. "You are right, guess the looney bin taught you some manners…Swanny!"

Kale took off and grabbed the panels on James' coat and lifted him off the ground.

"I don't know who the fuck you think you are…"

He was pulled off by Justin and Brandon. "Let go of him…Kale let him go…let go!" Brandon begged. Kale pulled James closer, his knuckles were stark white. "I regret ever saving your worthless life. I should have left you to burn in that car. You are lower than shit. You need to learn to treat people with respect," he spat.

"Come on Kale, it's not worth it, man," Justin said. "Hit me. I'm the one that deserves it." Justin put his hand on Kale's shoulder.

Kale shifted his infuriated eyes toward him, dropped James and focused on Justin. Devan thought Justin was going to piss in his pants right there in front of everyone.

"You are right," Kale calmed a bit. "He's not worth it." He raised his hand, and they all believed he was going to hit Justin. Instead he put his hand on his shoulder.

"I don't want to hit you," Kale exhaled.

"I'm sorry Kale. I'm really sorry." Justin's voice broke as he apologized. Devan was surprised; he sounded sincere.

Kale nodded, took his hand off Justin's shoulder and headed to his car.

"That was probably the smartest thing you have ever done Iakona!" James yelled after him. Kale turned around to see Justin grab ahold of James and get in his face.

"Leave him alone he's been through enough!" Justin shrieked. "You don't want to mess with him."

"You don't know what you are talking about," James bellowed. "Your head is so far up your ass…"

Justin lost it and hit James square in the jaw.

"I'm going to sue your ass," James threatened, rubbing his jaw.

Later that night Kale was home alone and was getting ready for bed. Everything that transpired that day was making his head spin. He was thankful that Veronica and Nate had the kids. He hadn't been sleeping well over the past week or so, unable to anticipate how the dissolution court day was going to play out. He needed an uninterrupted night's sleep. As he set his head down on the pillow, he wished Devan was lying right beside him. He knew eventually it would happen, and it was closer than it had ever been before. Kale pulled out the dream catcher that Nate had made him a few years ago. He rubbed the silky teal and black feathers between his fingers and placed it on the pillow next to him. He switched the light off and closed his eyes.

He followed her in to the grassy field. She stopped and wrapped her arms around him. "I love you," Devan exclaimed.

"I love you, too," Kale replied, automatically.

"I want to marry you, and finally be given the last name I was meant to have." She dropped her hands from him and picked up a matured dandelion.

Kale put his hand in his pocket and fiddled with the small black velvet box. Slowly he pulled it out and got down on one knee. "Devan Marie Montgomery will you marry me?" He opened the box and held it out to her. She looked down at the ring as tears streamed down her face.

He woke before she gave him an answer. He knew, though, without a doubt, it would be *yes*. Kale stretched and picked up his phone to see what time it was. A message popped up—it was Jeane reminding him that she would soon be over to retrieve her belongings.

Upon arrival, Jeane immediately began collecting her things. She also searched the house looking for any sign of Devan. She was extremely disappointed to find nothing.

"Do you need help loading anything?" Kale was trying to be nice.

"Yes, grab these two suitcases and those totes. I'm going to search the room again to make sure I have everything." The second he left the room, she searched through everything. Jeane went back to the bottom drawer of his nightstand and found a box. It was a tiny, black velvet box. "Hmmmm—" Before she had a chance to open it, Jeane could hear Kale coming up the stairs. She shoved it in her pocket just as he opened the door.

"Did you find anything else?" Kale asked.

"Yeah, I actually did. So that's it then. I'll see you guys around the holidays."

"I guess." Kale frowned.

"All right." She brushed past Kale, down the stairs, through the living room and out the door. Without hesitation, Jeane got into her car, pulled out of the driveway, and drove away.

Devan had been watching from her house, peeking out the window, waiting for Jeane to leave. The moment she saw Jeane's car drive by her house and down the road, Devan slammed the door behind her and ran down the street towards Kale's house. She was going to claim him as hers. She was going to kiss him all the way in to next week. Kale was walking towards her with a smile on his face.

"Is she really gone?" Devan was almost completely out of breath.

"Yes," he replied.

"She took all her stuff?" Devan panted

"Yes," he repeated.

"She's not coming back?"

"No, she's not," he answered.

"What time is it?" Devan asked suddenly taking a detour from her original plan of just attacking him.

Kale looked at his watch. "Almost noon."

"Are you hungry?"

"What do you think?" he laughed.

She should have known better than to ask that question. Kale was a bottomless pit. Why was she worried about food anyway? She wanted nothing more than to grab him and kiss him. And yet here, Devan was nervously dancing around it, like it was going to be her first kiss. She tried to push her thoughts out of her head. It would happen when it happened. Even though it had been so long since their lips had touched, she didn't make a move.

"Okay, let's go." She clutched his hand and attempted to pull him down the road towards his house.

"Wait," Kale chuckled making her stop.

"What?"

"Come here." In one swift move he swung her around and encompassed her. Kale looked down in to her bright eyes.

"We can go to lunch after,"

"After wha…" He slanted his lips on hers and didn't let her finish. She melted into his kiss. They stood there in the middle of the road, lost in each other's lips, holding on to one another.

Jeane drove a few miles down the road but had this sinking suspicion and something made her pull over. She turned the car back around and sped back towards Kale's house. As Jeane approached the house, she slowed the car, creeping down the road. She hit her brakes when she saw Kale and Devan in an embrace. She pulled out her phone and zoomed in. They weren't just hugging. They were kissing passionately.

"Like siblings my ass…take that Justin!" She snapped a few photos.

On the way to lunch, Devan watched the scenery out the window. A few minutes into the drive, she saw something and insisted that Kale pulled over.

"What's wrong?" Kale questioned with his voice full of concern.

"Just stop the truck," she pleaded. There it was…her "field of wishes." Everything finally made sense as the words Willow Cavendar spoke to her the day of Nate's and Veronica's wedding, echoed through her head.

When you see the field of green that is spotted with yellow, you'll know the time is near and your wait will soon be over. Devan remembered back to the Spring when she'd gotten a flat tire and Kale came to her rescue. The field had been lush and green with bright yellow dandelions everywhere.

When the howling north winds meet the warmth of the south winds, a long awaited, desire will arrive with the force of a beast. Devan and Kale were unloading boxes from his truck into the storage bin. The things flying around them when the wind picked up were not from a tree. They were dandelion seeds. A short time later all their inhibitions were lost in the storm where passion reigned, and promises were broken.

The truth will prevail right before the second full bloom. While at the lake in the summer Justin and Jeane had gotten caught in their full-fledged affair. When Kale and Devan came home a few days later, dandelions had popped up all over in her yard.

Things you have wanted will come to fruition as the last seedlings travel through the air just before the first frost appears on the ground. It was the fall and colder weather was on its way. Their dissolutions were finalized yesterday, and she and Kale could finally be together.

When the truck was still, she jumped out and ran out in to the field and shouted for Kale to follow her. As he ran to catch up to her he took in the green field and the white puffs that were peeking out from the long blades of grass and fallen leaves. It was *déjà vu*! When Kale finally caught up to Devan, she twirled to face him, put her arms around him and gazed up into his eyes.

"I love you!"

"I love you too!" Kale replied, relieved that he could express it freely.

"I'm serious. I want to marry you!" Devan admitted with as much passion as she could.

"Okay," he chuckled remembering the dream he recently had. All that was missing was the engagement ring.

"I want to be Mrs. Kale Iakona,"

"And you will be," Kale told her.

"I wish I could date you all over again and experience life the way we were meant to."

"Who says we can't?" Kale questioned.

Devan dropped her arms from him, picked up a dandelion and held it up. "Make a wish!"

Kale grinned down at her and shook his head *no*. "I don't need to make a wish."

"Why is that?" Devan raised her eyebrows, still holding out the dandelion.

"I finally have everything I have always wanted."

"Oh really?" She smiled and held out her free hand for him to take.

"I can finally have you," he spoke softly, taking her hand in his.

"I guess some dreams *do* come true," Devan told him.

You have no idea, he thought. "We have the rest of our lives to make all of our dreams and wishes come true!" Kale said then blew the seeds off the dandelion.

Devan beamed with the dandelion stem in one hand, Kale's hand in the other, as the white seeds floated in the air around them.

Justin was getting on the plane to go to Hawaii. Jeane was already seated, he was hoping for the window seat but someone was already there reading the newspaper. He sat down next to Jeane and kissed her on the cheek. "Hey sexy, how are you today?"

"I'm quite well. Are you ready for this move and to finally be rid of Devan? I'm sure glad that Kale is no longer my problem."

Justin scoffed, "You realize Devan is my kids' mother right?"

"I am aware of that,"

"I hate to tell you this but Kale and Devan will always be in our lives because of our children. We both lucked out that they are such good parents."

The newspaper rustled and Justin looked over. The person folded the newspaper and his face could be seen. He recognized the smirk instantly.

"What is he doing here?" he questioned Jeane.

"Uncle Alistar hired him. The company lawyer who was also his personal lawyer retired, so, I put in a good word for James."

"Looks like we will be working together," he smirked. "And no hard feelings about the other day, although I do expect an apology."

"I'm not apologizing, you are just lucky that it was me and not Kale."

"Yes, the wonderful Kale Iakona. I'm not afraid of him, like I'm not afraid of you. However, I do find it quite interesting that you are still thinking so highly of him considering…" James didn't finish his sentence.

"Considering what?"

Jeane opened her phone scrolled through it for a second and handed it to Justin. He looked at the picture longer than he should have then glanced at Jeane and James. He handed the phone back to Jeane and slumped down into his seat.

To be continued…

About the Author

Mindy Ford grew up in the suburbs of Summit County in Ohio where she started writing at a young age. Aloha Paradise is her first published book. She resides in Northwest Ohio where her imagination fuels her life.

Aloha Ohana

MINDY FORD

Aloha Ohana

Devan stepped out into the fresh air, took a deep breath and inhaled all the tropical scents. She heard the screen door open and saw Veronica coming through. "I can't believe you are awake this early," she told Veronica truly shocked that she had gotten out of bed. Devan already had her shoes on so she hopped down the steps and waited patiently for Veronica to put hers on.

Veronica carefully sat down on the step, slipped on her shoes and tied them tightly. Devan tilted her head and looked at her. There was something off about her. Veronica stood up and skipped down the stairs to meet Devan in the grass, and they headed to the beach to walk the shoreline.

Devan initiated small talk, while trying to figure out what was so different about her friend. She listened to Veronica talk about work, the funeral home, and just life in general when it hit her. "You're pregnant!"

Veronica stopped, "What?"

"You're pregnant, aren't you?" Devan watched as Veronica's pupils dilated and her cheeks turned red. "I knew it!"

"No one knows, not even Nate."

"When did you find out?"

"Three days ago. I've been dying to tell you, that's why I wanted to go for a walk. I couldn't keep it in anymore and…"

"I get it, I won't say a word to anyone."

Meanwhile back at the house, Kale was pacing the porch waiting for Devan's dad to wake up. He sat down on the hammock for a few seconds then he got up and paced some more. Finally, he heard someone stirring while he waited for the coffee to be done brewing. He had no idea when Devan and Veronica would be back, but he knew he didn't have much time. When Chris walked into the kitchen Kale handed him a cup.

"Good morning, Kale."

"Morning, Chris, you have a minute?"

"Sure son, let me get some cream and we can go sit down."

Kale went outside and scanned the neighborhood to see if Devan was anywhere near. Chris came out and sat down at the table. "What's up Kale?"

Kale sat there trying muster up the words, hoping that he could say everything that he needed to without any stumbling. *Kale stop being stupid!* He chastised himself.

"I have been thinking about asking Devan—"

"I was wondering how long it was going to take you. You know my answer is yes!" Chris cut him off.

"Well, it's not exactly—"

Kale was interrupted again, this time by Devan and Veronica.

"Hey guys," Devan said walking up the steps to the wraparound porch.

"Hey, there is coffee in the kitchen for you." Chris said. Devan smiled and touched Kale on the shoulder as she brushed past him.

"Get to it already," Chris whispered, winked at Kale then got up and went back in the house before Kale could utter another word.

That evening in the middle of dinner Kale stood up abruptly. *Well, I guess it's as good a time as ever. Everyone is here…* He looked around the room and saw everyone staring at him.

"Go on son," Chris urged.

Can't back down now. Deep breath Kale Kai…breathe. Kale turned to Devan, squatted down and grabbed her hands. "Devan Marie, would you…"

THE CAVENDAR SERIES—Book 1

THE
CAVENDAR
HOUSE
MINDY FORD

The Cavendar House

"You can't catch me Vinnie!" Veronica yelled as she ran down the sidewalk with her brother, Vinnie, in tow.

"Mom said at dusk we have to be home, and it's dusk."

She ignored her brother, like usual, and squeezed in between the wrought iron cemetery gates.

"Roni!"

"You'll have to find me!!" She shouted giggling to herself.

Vinnie shook his head. He hated when his sister went in there. It creeped him out to the point he would often have nightmares about it.

Veronica on the other hand, had loved this resting place for the dead as well as others ever since she'd been a small girl. This one was her favorite place. She would do cartwheels in between the grave sites, and there was never anyone to scold her. She would talk to the dead, hoping for an answer back, that she never got, but it didn't stop her one-sided conversations.

As she darted through the headstones, she would get a glimpse of where Vinnie was, making sure that he wasn't on her tail. He just stood at the gate waiting to see which place she would disappear to next.

"Come on Roni, we are going to get in so much trouble." Vinnie complained, his patience wearing thin.

Veronica giggled even more. She knew she wouldn't get into trouble because she was Daddy's Little Girl. "Come find me."

When she ducked down behind a large marker, she heard the gate creak open and another giggle escaped her lips. She heard the crunch of fallen leaves underneath Vinnie's feet, then turned her attention to the headstone she was using as a cover—

Archibold Bryant Cavendar
April 7, 1811-October 31, 1878

She peeked around the stone to see where Vinnie was. She didn't see him so she turned the other way and something caught her eye. The old abandoned house on the hill, that she never remembered anyone ever living in, had a faint light in the window on the side.

"Veronica," she heard someone whisper. She turned around expecting to see her brother, but no one was there.

"Veronica," she heard again a little louder. She looked behind her and in front of her this time. When she finally saw her brother, he was still all the way back by the gate.

"VERONICA!" The voice was loud right in her ear. She screamed or so she thought. She opened her mouth, but nothing came out. She saw movement out of the corner of her eye in the direction of the house. She turned her head slowly and saw a woman with long dark hair wearing white running to the house. She opened the door and when the door slammed behind her, the light in the window went out.

She woke up in a sweat. Reliving that nightmare for the past twenty-some years was something she didn't enjoy. She was convinced that it was the first time she had ever had a run-in with the supernatural…but it certainly wasn't the last.